Here's what readers are saying about
GYPSY NIGHTS—Lives on Tour,
Christine Fournier's first novel in her Gypsy series:

*To all of my theatre friends and lovers of the theatre,
I recommend you read* Gypsy Nights. *You'll enjoy life on
the road with a bunch of Gypsies. I know I did! Kudos!*
David Young

Just finished Gypsy Nights *and will need copies for other
show biz girlfriends, readers for the duration of the series.*
Jackie Steele

*This book offers an insider's view of life behind the show curtain
with vivid descriptions of locations throughout the country,
drawn from the author's first-hand knowledge during her
career and, very effective. I found the story wild and quite racy,
filled with exciting opening nights and unusual relationships.
The book is a true romantic novel. I look forward to more from
Ms. Fournier.* Victoria Madsen

*I liked Ms. Fournier's book and found her style of writing
enjoyable to read. You go girl!* Sandy Kenny

I enjoyed Gypsy Nights—Lives on Tour *a great deal. Hopes
and dreams of dancers as they audition and perform is deeply
felt by the writer and passed on to the reader. The intense and
complicated backstage relationships are shown in dramatic
highlight. Realistic details firmly set the story in time and place.*
Dennis Rystad

Go on the road with Ms. Fournier's Gypsy Nights! *A smart,
sassy, sexy ride. It would make one heck of a big screen show!*
Rob Strusinski

Romance, intrigue, adventure with a great gang of gypsies. Got so steamy at times, I had to wipe the sweat off my brow. A fun read! Joel Thom

I couldn't put this book down once I started! Gypsy Nights *is a wonderful combination of what life is like touring with a show and steamy love stories along the way. The author roped me in with the very real and relatable characters she created. I didn't want it to be over! I cannot wait for the next book in the series!* Morgan Kirvida

Gypsy Nights *is a delightful romp through the golden age of theater, the 60's. It captures the people and places and draws you in with its spellbinding plot. The entire book was joy to read and I could not wait to turn the next page. It's a book that only someone like Ms. Fournier, a former Broadway dancer could tell.* Christopher Teipner

Peek into the exciting lives of Broadway dancers on the road. Wow! Interesting, passionate, steamy. Zowee! Hot, hot, hot. Loved it! Joan LeSiege

From the beginning all that is promised in Gypsy Nights— *Lives on Tour, is fully realized. Mally and company really deliver! What a great start to a new series.* Mike Tracy

Gypsy Nights *is a rare opportunity to go behind the scenes into a world that few of us know. It is a glimpse of characters and creativity, intimate relationships of dancers, giving you a new appreciation of what goes into the process of putting together a show. Intrigues swirl around making that happen.* Suzanne Olson

GYPSY
CITY

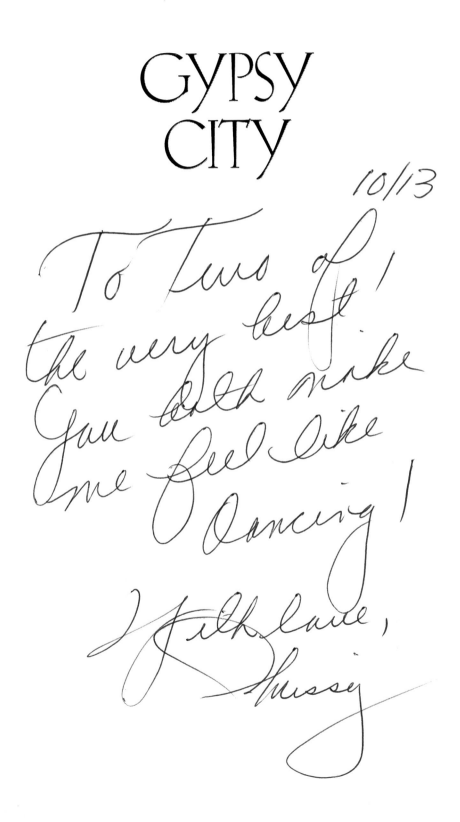

10/13

To Two of
the very best!
You both make
me feel like
Dancing!

With love,
Missy

By the same author:
Gypsy Nights

GYPSY CITY

A New Beginning

Christine Fournier

4 square books

First published in 2013

This paper edition published 2013 by 4 Square Books an imprint of Ebooks LLC.

Copyright © Christine Fournier, 2013

The moral right of the author has been asserted

ISBN 978-1-61766-231-7 (ebook)
ISBN 978-1-61766-230-0 (paper)

Printed in the United States of America through CreateSpace

Acknowledgment

Many years ago, a colleague in the industrial film business showed me an extensive collection of camels, statuary of every design, size, shape, and color lining a shelf in his office. Noting the impressive display, I asked, "Why camels?" He smiled patiently and replied, "A camel represents a horse by committee!"

As an author today, his sage comment many years ago reflects the process of storytelling. No one writes a book without help from many contributors. You might say a novel is a book by committee!

I would like to thank the following individuals, who assisted me preparing *Gypsy City*, the second of my four-novel series honoring Gypsies, dancers who go from show to show. You are all committee to my Camel! Bill Unumb, Copy Editor, for your humor, insight, and straight-from-the-cuff approach. Chris Fayers, Publisher, for your expertise, guidance, and integrity. John Lutz, Cover Artist, who captured my story with the stroke of his brush. Rachel Anderson, whose encouragement and experience provided direction. Sara Bartlett, Proof Reader, whose eye for literary details kept the story together. And my husband, Paul Fournier, whose belief, love and support makes it all happen.

Tribute

Of all the performers who have influenced me in my youth and my professional years, the late Gwen Verdon stands above all others as one who truly inspired. Her amazing charisma, honesty, humility, talent, and values, were qualities she emulated; sharing the stage with her in the original production of *Sweet Charity* was a gift I will carry with me always. Gwen, wherever you are, you're the absolute best!

Author's Note

For any aspiring musical theatre dancer, the ultimate goal is to dance on the Broadway stage. For me, being cast in the original Broadway production of *Sweet Charity*, directed and choreographed by the incomparable Bob Fosse and starring his muse, the brilliant Gwen Verdon, was a dream realized. To be part of something new, not yet proven, was not only exciting, it was a challenge, a privilege, and an experience I will never forget. The observations of and the lessons learned from that process are unforgettable. Working with such greats as playwright Neil Simon, composer Cy Coleman, lyricist Dorothy Fields, the inspiring Bob Fosse and Gwen Verdon, became part of my DNA, my creative voice in the work that has followed me the rest of my career. That part of my history gave me the impetus to write about the true hero of the theatre, the chorus dancer, the Gypsy. May you enjoy the dancer's journey with me.

Respectfully,
Christine Fournier
2013

Chapter 1

The Audition

"Hey, watch it, lady!" The yellow cab narrowly missed Mally Winthrop, as she hurried across the intersection of Broadway and 46th Street, the driver giving her the bird as he honked and sulked his way through morning rush hour.

A yellow haze hung over midtown, like a heavy comforter, unwanted at this time of year. The hot, thick air was annoying.

A line of women moved slowly toward the stage door on 46th Street. It was a relief to step out of the sun and into the shade of the theatre this September morning.

Entering the theatre backstage, Mally presented her Equity card and was promptly handed an audition form bearing the number 77. It was standard procedure to fill the card with the usual information, notably: age, height, weight, color of eyes and hair, and a brief listing of one's credits. Protocol demanded the impersonal but necessary form to be turned in to the management holding the audition. Mally smiled, believing any combination of '7' was lucky for her. 'We'll see,' she thought as she headed for the changing area in the basement.

Passing several women moving toward the stage area, she descended the stairs, finding a spot to squeeze into as she worked her way in the clump of animated chorines in the throes of undressing. Tension filled the air and murmurs from the hopeful gypsies punctuated the tight space, adding ambiance: a mixture of anticipation, dread and necessity.

Auditions were a necessary evil in a craft which demanded every ounce of one's being. There was also a need to feed, clothe and shelter one's self in order to remain in New York to study, work and grow in the highly competitive world of the New York theatre.

Mally was just one of hundreds of female dancers who would be auditioning for the new Owen Matthews show, *Centipede*, bound for Broadway the first of the year. The production, an all-dance review, would feature cream-of-the-crop dancers hand-picked for type, ability and experience. Those who could emulate Owen's demanding and unique style had the best chance of working in one of his ensembles.

Recently returning from a national tour of *Bravo Business,* one of Owen Matthews' biggest hits, Mally felt confident, fresh and ready for a new challenge and a more substantial credit; one of an original Broadway show. She was excited at the prospect of using her skill and challenged by the fact that there would be others vying for a spot in Owen's universe.

As she removed her street clothes, first kicking off her loafers and sliding out of her jeans, she noted a few pounds missing in recent weeks, as evidenced by the baggy fit of her pants. She took off her jacket and blouse, revealing a lavender blue leotard, chosen that morning because the color buoyed her confidence. It was by far the most flattering for her. Reaching in her dance bag, she pulled out her jazz shoes and finding a spot to sit, put them on.

"Hey lady, don't I know you?" Mally spotted Patricia Byrne coming toward her. Smiling, she stood and wrapped her arms around her pal. "God, I'm glad you're here."

"You know I wouldn't miss it." Pat and Mally had met at the Equity audition for the national tour of *Bravo Business*. Traveling together and being roommates for nine months, they had developed a deep friendship.

"How many women do you think are auditioning?"

"My guess is 200 at this call, and another 100 at the open call," recited Pat, who was no stranger to this nerve-wracking ritual.

"The numbers seemed to have doubled in a year. Oh well. You ready?"

"Ready, kiddo," said Pat, grabbing her dance bag and following Mally, as more women arrived. "Come easy, go hard, I always say," muttered Pat with a wry air.

The two hopefuls ascended the staircase, made their way to the wings and waited. The first groups were being taught some of Owen's most demanding steps. Looking through the throng, they spotted Jonas Martin, Owen's new assistant, demonstrating the combination they would have to perform to pass muster.

When their numbers were called, they took places in a group of twelve, nervously waiting before Jonas started shouting counts.

"I hate this part," whispered Pat, stretching in place, her heart thumping wildly in her chest. Mally leaned in, "Relax. You'll be absolutely sensational." From then on, it was a blur.

"Step cross touch front, step cross touch back. Kick ball-change, kick ball-change, step *relevé* turn and deep *plié* adding two outside *pirouettes*, then to the left and another kick ball-change, hold. Repeat to the other side, ladies," Jonas chanted, dancing the steps to perfection. Mally and Pat's group observed and followed, each finding her own niche, through her own body. There were four sets of eight as the combination became more complex, punctuated by an increase in the tempo. Then Jonas stopped the group.

"Pat, Mally, down here, please," shouted Jonas pointing to spots in the front line dividing center. "Other ladies, this is how the combination should look."

The pit pianist banged out the music following Jonas' "5, 6, 7, 8!" Again, counting out steps, Jonas led Pat and Mally as they ran the combination adding performance to the technical elements. At the conclusion, they moved back to their former positions and waited. Jonas ran the combination twice more and called a halt. Turning, he shouted out to the house "Anything to add, Owen?"

From the dark a commanding voice was heard. "Jonas, I'm coming up." Shifting from foot to foot, the women watched Owen Matthews, the best director and choreographer in New York, move down the aisle. Taking stairs two at a time, he crossed along the edge of the orchestra pit and strolled center. After consulting with Jonas, he turned to the group.

Slim and fit, in a dark shirt, tight jeans, and desert boots, he was every bit the icon of a young dancer's dream. His short, cropped hair, dimpled cheeks and mustache only accented his sensual allure. As he spoke, a stub of cigarette clung precariously at the corner of his mouth and around his neck a whistle, known to stop dancers on a dime.

"Ladies, Jonas knows my style inside and out. Pay attention and watch. I don't want to see mechanics. I want subtext, performance. Pull out all the emotion and energy you have and dance as though this is the last time you ever will. You are all giving me about 75 percent, and I want to see double that. Watch the style nuances. For instance, on the step cross touch, your shoulders should dip with the movement, your head held high, the feet very staccato, crisp, clean, punctuated. I don't want to see overcooked spaghetti. I want pointed toes. Exaggerate and accent it." He turned to Pat and winked.

"Miss Byrne, give me more. Jonas, run them again, and let's get going. We have a lot of dancers to see today."

Jonas ran the combination again, eliminating everyone except Mally and Pat, who were told to come back the next day at 10:00 am. Another group of women, waiting anxiously were next to be put through the grueling pace of Owen's demands and Jonas' instruction.

The audition continued to the late afternoon. Dancers came and left. Hearts were broken, confidence, too. The selection process was never easy or fair. Who knew what was in the mind of the power folks making decisions that might change one's life drastically, or remain status quo? Only Owen Matthews knew and he wasn't telling, at least not now.

Deep sighs, pulled muscles, sweaty tights and lost smiles punctuated the run-off of dancers as more and more were eliminated. Being good enough to dance on Broadway was a feat not meant for the faint of heart. Grit was the main ingredient needed to walk on a stage filled with hundreds of others. Talent, tenacity and thick skin were pluses in the audition process. Sweat, fear, loathing and hope were the by-products. In time, some would emerge triumphant, working for a director the caliber of Owen Matthews. Heaven help them!

Chapter 2

Flashbacks

Mally was primed, rested and ready. The women she would meet today were those narrowed down from a larger field of hopefuls from the previous day's audition; she would be competing with the crème de la crème of New York's dancers. Owen Matthews had an eye for talent and would pick only the best. Undaunted, she arose with the first annoying sound of her alarm.

Hurrying through the ritual of shower and make-up and under dressing dance clothes, she slipped into a favorite royal blue leotard. Adding jeans, a short-sleeved top, socks and tennis shoes, she was almost ready. Packing dance shoes and sheet music to her tote, she was on the way.

Walking to the subway took no time at all. She hurried down the stairs, placing a token in the turnstile as a train approached the station. With a screech and gust of wind, the silver snake came to a stop. Doors opened with a suck of air, expelling passengers as new ones entered with efficiency.

Mally boarded, found a seat and opened a copy of *Backstage*, the trade paper most-read by gypsies. She felt a pull as the train began to move, picking up speed as it entered the black abyss to the next station stop. Looking up from a page for a moment, she glanced around the car, spotting Kathy Olson and Marcy White holding on a pole a short distance down the aisle. The girls, former cast mates from the national tour of *Bravo Business*, saw her and waved as they headed her way. "Mal, how great to see you," said Kathy, hugging her enthusiastically. She had been Mally's former roommate.

"You look terrific! Being in love and engaged certainly agrees with you," added Marcy. "How is Griff, anyway?" "Griff's wonderful, couldn't be better. He's running auditions for Owen's new show."

"Well, that's a plus. We're on our way to finals," said Kathy, excitedly. "You are? Me, too! Pat will be there also."

"Now why doesn't that surprise me?" Kathy knew Pat's work from their previous association and knew she would be a shoo-in for the lead, given Owen's fierce regard for her talent and their relationship off stage.

"Well, I'm sure she'll be cast," Mally said with assurance. "There isn't a better female dancer in New York."

"Hey, here's our stop," said Marcy, moving toward the door, followed by the others. As the train stopped, doors opened, the girls moved quickly across the gap. Their conversation was lively as they walked down Broadway, bringing each other up to speed since the tour's closing.

"How's Sonja?" Kathy and Sonja had found each other on tour. Their budding friendship had turned into a committed relationship and both had blossomed. "Sonja is great! She's enrolling this fall at NYU. She wants to teach on the college level, preferably after she completes her degree."

"That's wonderful. Good for her! Please send my love," said Mally, spotting a line of women already at the stage door up the street. "Oh, oh, here we go!"

At the theatre, the group of top contenders had gathered. Attractive, fit women stood waiting to be called. Mally spotted Pat amongst the hopefuls and inched her way through the throng.

"Hi, Pat!" "God, I'm glad you're here, Mal. There sure are a lot of new faces! Oh, I see Kathy Olson and Marcy White. That's a plus," noted Pat, waving to them across the stage.

"Have you talked to Owen?" Mally knew that he was Pat's ticket to her future and she his muse on the coming show.

"He said he'd call after auditions. You know Owen. Always elusive until he's ready to move, on his time," said Pat.

Mally had been privy to Pat and Owen's affair from the beginning. Owen had made his move opening night in Norfolk, Virginia, seducing Pat, whom he greatly admired as a dancer and lusted for off stage.

He had won her completely on both counts. He was the flame to her moth. Their affair was intense through the entire tour.

Pat fell head over heels for her mentor. He, in turn, made it clear that, in order to be with him, she would have to accept the limits he placed on their relationship. He was based in New York and she was committed to a nine-month tour. At the time, Owen was still legally married though separated from Vera Daniels, his former wife and muse. Together they had shared many Broadway triumphs. He had made her a mega star and she helped make his reputation as the Great White Way's most acclaimed director and choreographer. His rampant and repeated infidelities and her alcoholism had driven them apart. Vera refused to give Owen a divorce, fiercely hanging on as punishment for his indiscretions. Her anger overrode reason.

When Owen showed up on the road, it was non-stop love making with Pat until he returned to New York. Pat would fall into a deep funk that only his calls or occasional visits would abate.

Without admitting his need for her, Owen sometimes went for weeks without calling. Then when he did turn up, the intensity of his unquenchable horniness and her emotional need would fan the flames of their mutual passion. Pat longed for his brief visits. He became her world.

Then the unimaginable happened! Owen began to need Pat, falling in love with her. Never had he invested emotionally in one woman. He finally convinced Vera to a Las Vegas divorce. Pat had won him and now she would have a spot in his new show. The audition was merely a formality. He already knew her abilities beyond the bedroom. He would make her a star.

On stage, Jonas Martin was demonstrating the audition steps from the previous day. He had added four more sections of eight counts. His attention to detail was inspiring. He knew Owen's style and would place demands on these finalists never experienced before at an audition.

Mally and Pat were called to the first group of four. Running through the steps felt good and eased the tension as they repeated exactly what was asked of them. When they were ready, the accompanist pounded out the introduction mingling with Jonas' "5, 6, 7, 8!"

Pat's dancing was inspired. Her limber body met the demands of the combination with ease as she twirled and leaped, kicked and stomped. She was easily the best in her group. Mally's bright personality showed through her technique as she danced Jonas' instruction to perfection. When finished, both were asked to wait.

Several more groups of young women repeated Owen's steps. Kathy and Marcy held up well as they out-danced the others in their group. When it was over, they were also asked to remain. Then, the inevitable!

Placing all who remained in a line-up, Jonas waited for Owen, who mounted the stage stairs with his usual fluidity. He was every bit the legend as he appeared to glide to center stage.

"Ladies, you are all excellent, but I only need eight. When I call your name please stay. The rest, thank you very much." Owen went through the dance cards, Jonas by his side. As numbers were announced, Mally spotted Griff in the corner of her eye. He was standing at the orchestra rail holding a clipboard going through papers with marked efficiency. The same efficiency that had attracted her the first time she laid eyes on him.

"Mally Winthrop, Patricia Byrne, Marcy White, Kathy Olson, Cynthia Charles, Fran Fairchild, Liz Gunther, and Nora Blake please stay." There was a shout of jubilation from the chosen few. The other women dejectedly walked away in search of their dance bags and other belongings scattered around the perimeter of the stage.

"Congratulations ladies and welcome to *Centipede!*" Walking the line, he shook hands with each of the glistening winners, noting the attractive ensemble he just put together. "This is Jonas Martin, my assistant. You will be working with him throughout the process and his word is mine."

Jonas smiled at the introduction. He had waited for this day a long time. He was no longer just another gypsy in a mass of contenders. He was an integral part of Owen's creative infrastructure, a position hard earned.

"Griff, please come forward and meet our ladies." Owen waited as Griff ascended the stairs to the stage, coming toward him as he walked the line of smiling young women. "Ladies, Griff Edwards is your production stage manager. There is no finer in the business. I leave you in the best hands." Owen turned and left the stage with Jonas at his heels.

"Ladies, you will be called in the next two weeks to sign your contracts at the offices of Kaplan and Maggli. Rehearsals will begin October 1st. Be prepared to sign a standard chorus contract with possible upgrades. The details will be discussed with you at the time of your signing. Thank you."

Mally watched Griff walk away. Her fiancé delighted her with his professional demeanor and dignity. She could hardly wait to get him alone. They were now sharing an apartment.

"When are the guys auditioning?" Kathy was excited as she hugged Mally, Marcy, and Pat.

"I think their callback is this afternoon at 2:00."

"Well, I'm sure glad this torture is over. I hate auditions," said Pat, noticeably relieved.

"Did you ever doubt you'd be cast?" Kathy knew that Pat was chosen months ago. "What do you mean by that?"

"Well, I think Owen knows your capabilities by now. I'm sure there was no question in his mind. That's all I meant," said Kathy, carefully steering away from the subject. She knew how touchy Pat could be regarding Owen.

"Hey, we should all celebrate," suggested Marcy. "How does Jack Dempsey's sound for lunch?" A group affirmative went up as the girls slipped on their street clothes over their dance wear and headed out. *Centipede* was to be a reality, their first Broadway credit, the adventure beginning.

Chapter 3

Cast of Characters

The men's audition had proved as grueling as the women's; only eight men from a field of about four hundred, the crème de la crème of dancers, were picked by Owen and Jonas.

Among the chosen was Joe Pinto, a Broadway veteran and favorite of Owen's. Joe had an edge, a grittiness that was sensuous and strong. He had replaced a dancer on tour after serving his time in the Broadway production of *Bravo Business* for two seasons. Once again, he had proved his ability to tackle Owen's demands with fierce intensity.

Jonas Martin would assist Owen in the process of putting the show together as well as star opposite Patricia Byrne. He was Owen's prototype dancer. His fluid technique and style couldn't be matched by anyone in the business. He looked forward to a long association with Owen's organization.

Phillipe Danier, Jonas' lover, brought sex appeal and masculinity to the ensemble. A former stripper, his technique was a surprise to some, but not to Jonas, who had seen him in Atlanta. It led to an audition with Owen and a position in the ensemble of *Bravo Business*.

Chad Chapman had earned his dancing chops on tour and was, by far, one of the most appealing performers Owen hired. Chad had youth, vigor and a boy-next-door quality that attracted both men and women. He was dependable and a fine technician.

Dick Landry and his wife and fellow gypsy, Dana, had toured in countless national companies winding up their touring career in *Bravo Business* for the past nine months. Their dream was to start a family, settle in New Jersey and give up the gypsy life. With Dana now pregnant and awaiting the birth of their first child, Dick would dance in the ensemble to pay the bills and serve as assistant stage manager under Griff Edwards.

Jim Sorenson and Jerry Thompson, veteran gypsies, rounded out the ensemble for the new show. They, too, had worked the last tour and would contribute their combined technique, experience, and maturity as performers.

Only Jeff Jenkins, hired as swing dancer, was new to the group. His credits included engagements at the Lido and Moulin Rouge in Paris, the Tropicana Hotel in Las Vegas and two years as a member of Alvin Ailey's company.

Owen was pleased with his choices. It had been a tough four days of auditioning and he was ready to relax and unwind with his favorite distraction, Pat Byrne. She was his muse, inspiration for his newest creative undertaking.

Their affair began in Norfolk, Virginia, during the opening week of the *Bravo Business* national tour, but the attraction began weeks before during the rehearsal process in New York. Pat, fascinated with her new mentor, had watched his every move in the studio, while he, first attracted by her brilliant dance technique, was drawn to her by his penchant for beautiful women and an insatiable libido.

With only sex on his mind, he had wooed Pat—always on his time and terms. Later, he had come to need her, an uncomfortable fit for independent Owen. He was masterful in his career and in bed, choosing the woman he desired for the moment, keeping them on a short leash.

Pat was different. Her incredible talent and potential kept him inspired and her beauty kept him wanting. And so, he kept returning to her. Now, she was the lead in his life and show. Vera Daniels, his estranged wife, reluctantly granted him a divorce. She had lost and Owen won. He was finally free of the strife and bitterness Vera had displayed for years. Owen's love affair with Pat was the catalyst.

Griff Edwards was ready for a break from the selection process. He was now production stage manager for Owen's organization and would handle the new show from beginning to end of run. He was pleased his work inspired Owen's confidence. He had commanded nine months of the *Bravo Business* tour and was ready to work in New York again. After many years on the road it would feel good to be home, with one very important addition, Mally Winthrop.

Mally attracted him the first time she signed her contract for *Bravo Business*. Her winsome, guileless manner, her fresh appealing looks were fixed in his mind. And so, he courted and won her. Their engagement had taken place on the road and, in a few weeks, they would be married in New York. They were sharing Griff's apartment in the city since the Boston run had ended prematurely. It was practical to set up housekeeping while preparing for a future together.

With the show cast, it was only a matter of weeks before the production would be in full swing. All involved looking forward to a new adventure on the Great White Way. The all-dance review would be a first for Broadway.

Owen had dreamed of a show without a libretto, composer, lyricist or principal actor/singers. Instead, this show would be a review of many styles of music, all utilized for the dancer and the dancer alone. Choreography would be the star with an all-dancer cast to facilitate his concept.

He would start with material, never before used in some of his past shows. There was always a trimming in the choreographic process; elements of staging that were dropped for the good of an overall concept. Several pieces shelved at the back of his mind would soon have their day.

Combining the music of many composers, several eras of musical theatre and talents of sixteen dancers, it was a difficult concept for producers and investors brokers to envision. They had all experienced their share of grandiose Broadway flops and were cautious with their money.

First, he would try to convince Vincent Lehrman to come on board. He and Vinny had a long history together, having shared a number of Broadway triumphs, including many with Vera Daniels, who was introduced to Owen by Lehrman himself. It was that initial meeting that had led to an unbeatable team, professional and personal.

Vinny Lehrman refused Owen's offer. He was tired, bent on retirement and looked forward to enjoying the fruits of his success. He preferred spending time at his mansion on Long Island and vacation at his properties in Bermuda and French Riviera.

Next, Owen approached the producing team of Joseph Kaplan and Leonard Maggli. They had always been competition for Lehrman, enjoying equal success with an impressive number of hits. However, of late, they were flagging. They needed something new, unusual, perhaps a name, or promising concept.

Through several backer auditions, Owen's dream child took hold, Kaplan and Maggli came on board as Producers, other investors as silent partners. Owen's *Centipede* was a go. Soon that germ of an idea, from somewhere in his opulently creative mind, would be a reality. The cast signed their contracts; creative meetings continued and rehearsal dates moved closer.

Chapter 4

Rehearsals

The 4th Floor of Dance Arts on 46th Street was alive with gypsies, all gathered to begin rehearsals for *Centipede.* And a handsome lot they were.

Several new faces appeared amongst the women dancers including veteran gypsy Cynthia Charles with three Broadway credits to her resume. Fran Fairchild, the personification of a musical theatre dancer, was seeking her first Broadway credit. Liz Gunther, fresh from ABT, had the strongest ballet technique and an elitist attitude. Nora Blake, new to New York but not to dance, had performed with companies in Copenhagen and London, was selected swing dancer. Mally, Pat, Kathy, and Marcy had proven their worth on tour and up to the demands of

Owen's work. They were now in good company with Owen's newest choices; he had a fine ensemble of women.

Jonas Martin, Phillipe Danier, Chad Chapman, Jim Sorenson, Jerry Thompson, Dick Landry and Joe Pinto had worked together on tour. Only Jeff Jenkins was new, his background and technique made him a great addition as a swing dancer, a necessary part, but not for everyone. He would cover seven, every number and position. It took special individuals to learn and replicate all choreography. Swings had to focus under pressure with little or no notice; they had their work cut out for them.

At 10:00 sharp, Griff Edwards announced the start of rehearsal. Many put out cigarettes; some took quick sips of water from the fountain, others left conversations dangling. Gathering in the large, mirrored studio, murmurs floated in the air dense with tension and anticipation.

"Ladies and gentlemen, welcome to your first day. We are pleased to have you join us. I am Griff Edwards, your production stage manager. Jonas Martin, Mr. Matthews' assistant, will also be a featured dancer," said Griff, gesturing toward Jonas. "Owen Matthews will be here soon. In the meantime Jonas will take you through a warm up. Questions anyone?" Jeff Jenkins put his hand up. "Yes, Jeff?"

"How long is the rehearsal period? I mean how long will we rehearse in New York?"

"Six weeks in New York and five out of town." Another hand shot up. "Cynthia?" "I was wondering in what cities the production tries out?" All eyes in the room were on the statuesque blonde in scanty trunks.

"Two weeks in Philadelphia, three in Detroit." Joe's hand went up. "Do we vote for an Equity chorus deputy now or later?"

"Good question. You will vote following lunch break today which is 1:00 to 2:00 pm"

"Thanks Griff," said Joe, shifting as he leaned against the radiator along the window.

"Okay, everyone, let's warm up." Jonas took his place at the front of the room, his back to the mirror. "Oh, by the way, this is Frank Dugan, your rehearsal pianist. Frank, this is our Centipede."

"Hi, everybody." Frank waved from behind the keyboard. The dancers scattered around the room, finding their own space to work. With a nod of his head, Frank began to play a Richard Rodgers piece. Jonas shouted out moves to prepare the dancers for the choreography to come.

The group moved in waves as they stretched and leaned into the warm-up. It felt good to be active, doing what one was trained for. In 15 minutes they were loose and ready, the air already heavy with perspiration.

A moment later, Owen Matthews walked in with his characteristic air of mystery. To some, he resembled a graceful, proud cat, while others—some detractors—described him as something of a peacock. He was profoundly charismatic and yet low key, intense and focused. His quest, nothing short of perfection; his genius well known.

All eyes watched the celebrated director move to the front of the room. Every mind was keenly aware of the privilege to work for him. Fear and excitement mixed as sixteen dancers prepared for the next six weeks.

"Good morning, all." A collective response went up amongst the gypsies. "Good morning!" Owen smiled as he walked through the attractive bunch.

"You are the elite, some of the finest dancers assembled for an unprecedented work." The air was thick with interest as each dancer stood riveted, all eyes on Owen.

"This show is strictly presentational, no book, no plot, just pure dancing. Some of you will be featured, but overall, this is an ensemble work. Everyone will work his or her ass off! No special privileges, no excuses, no slackers. I want to see each dancer give 150 to 200 percent. You will be tested, frustrated, pissed off. You might feel like quitting. But you'll be sensational when I'm through with you. Are there any questions, comments, or concerns? Speak now or forever hold your peace." There was silence, breathing, clearing of a throat, a nervous cough.

As Owen glanced around the room, his eyes fell on Pat, who was leaning against the back wall. A slight grin spread across his mouth. 'How perfect is this?' he thought, 'my best dancer and lover all in one.' He would take care of her later.

"Okay, Mr. Martin, you may begin." With a wave of his hand, Owen sauntered out of the studio, eyes following as he closed the door.

Jonas lined up his dancers, pairing those he felt complimented each other in height, body type and ability. Jeff Jenkins and Nora Blake, the two chosen swings, were paired and stood aside as the matching continued. Jonas saved the best for himself, Pat Byrne. She had been his partner on tour. He knew they were totally one when they danced together. It was Owen's plan to team them on this project. Paired, his two best wouldn't fail. They were brilliant and inspired performers.

Mally was paired with Chad Chapman again. They had been swings together on tour. Reliable, technically sound, with personalities that extended far beyond the orchestra section, Jonas knew they were great together.

Joe Pinto, the veteran gypsy, was paired with Cynthia Charles, who brought considerable Broadway credits to the duo, a good match for the experienced Joe.

Liz Gunther and Phillipe Danier were matched. Liz was striking, willow-like, ballet trained, with sophistication that complimented Phillipe's sensuality and incredible technique. The two were poster gypsies of the ideal dancer.

Jonas chose the remaining dance pairs selecting Dick Landry and Kathy Olson, Jerry Thompson and Marcy White, Jim Sorenson and Fran Fairchild. Looking over the group, he was pleased with his choices, excited to start work. Following lunch, the gypsies elected Joe Pinto as Equity Chorus Deputy and rehearsal resumed.

After another warm-up, the group was split, men on one side of the room, women on the other. Jonas began a series of fluid, adagio moves emphasized by slow motion, during which the men and women came together, with breathless, sensual stretches reaching out to their partners. Once contact was made, each couple began a variety of lifts and turns, ending in lunges until bodies were locked in suggestive, sensual poses, created to separate counts of eight. Frank provided musical support with Cole Porter's fitting and romantic *In The Still of The Night*.

The rest of the afternoon, heat consumed the dancers, a dense humidity rising and enveloping them as combinations were set and polished. Jonas and Pat worked together, fine-tuning the choreography, demonstrating what Owen created.

Through movements, dancers conveyed moments of sexual tension, couples turning on to each other, libidos letting loose, the symbol of lovemaking. In choreographic terms, there was no one more skilled than Owen at bringing sexuality to the stage, profoundly and utterly turning on an audience, defining physical attraction and sexual consumption.

Following rehearsal, the dancers repaired to the hallway to towel off, smoke, compare notes on their first *Centipede* encounter and get on with their evenings. It had been an exhilarating first day. The newcomers were bowled over by the intensity of rehearsal, while the veterans were satisfied, challenged and happy to be back at work.

Chapter 5

After Rehearsal

The daunting crush of rush hour in Times Square was annoying, especially following eight hours of ball-busting rehearsal. In spite of a consuming fatigue, Pat made her way through the throng, running along Broadway, spotting a cab as it slowed near the curb. Sprinting towards the yellow and black vehicle, she managed to get the attention of the driver just before another, an Ivy-League business type, pounced on the same. Smiling, she waved him off as she climbed in. The man frowned, but acknowledged the stunning redhead, who had edged him out of the ride. Tipping his hat, a flirtatious shrug followed. Pat barely noticed.

"West 66th Street between Columbus and the Park," she said breathlessly. Sinking into the seat, she settled back and thought about the past hours. She was in his show and she was his.

Owen. God, Owen. The very thought of him made her heart race with anticipation. Had it been almost a year since that opening night in Norfolk? The cast party where they tangoed in a hypnotic swoon of foreplay across the dance floor? The same evening, they made wild love the entire night. Her memories were vivid, wondrous.

As the blocks flew by, Pat mentally prepared for Owen. She was ready to indulge in wanton inexhaustible lovemaking. It had been weeks. Their down time was on hold while Owen auditioned dancers and planned the new show.

"That's the building, the one with the silver awning," Pat hastened, coming out of her pre-Owen trance.

"That'll be eight bucks even," the driver flipped up the meter. Pat obliged as she fished into her coin purse at the bottom of her coat pocket. "Here it is and a tip for you." The driver took the money without a glance.

"Good night, Miss." "Good night," she echoed, on her way out.

She looked at the building, feeling a familiar pull in her stomach. After all this time, she was still nervous when she approached Owen. The doorman smiled as she entered the lobby and walked toward the elevator. Inside, she set her dance bag on the floor and gave herself a quick once over. Running hands through her long mane, she applied a fresh coat of blusher to her lips. Attention to details made her feel beguiling and sexy.

At Owen's door she knocked softly. Suddenly, he was there, shirtless, hands on his hips. "Baby, come in," he beckoned, stepping aside to let her pass. She didn't get far. In moments, he was holding her, kissing her deeply as he ran his hands through her hair. His heat was making her dizzy, wet between her legs.

"Oh Owen, the choreography is brilliant. Jonas worked the Cole Porter adagio. It's thrilling. I mean it's incredible!"

"You're incredible, Baby. That's why you'll be a star when this show opens. Mark my words." He took her by the hand and led her down the hall into the den.

"Hungry? I stopped by the Carnegie on the way home. I could make you a sandwich. Corned beef? Ham?" "Not just yet, how about a drink first?" She sat on a stool as he went behind the bar.

"Great idea! I've chilled some champagne. A little celebrating is in order, don't you think?" Owen produced a bottle of Moet, popped the cork and filled two glasses. Handing her a glass, he lifted his.

"To you, Baby, my new star!" Pat nodded nervously and took a quick sip, the bubbles stinging as she swallowed. "Am I really your star?"

"Oh come on, Pat. We've discussed this before. One of the reasons I'm doing *Centipede* is because of you. You're the best dancer I've had in years. You'll blow the critics away. If I had the slightest doubt, you wouldn't be here now. So drop it, okay?"

"Okay. It's just that it's moving so fast! I never dreamed, a year ago, that this would happen when you cast me for the tour.

"That's show biz, Baby," Owen poured two more. Pat took it, then another, until she felt light, slightly high. Owen took her glass as he put his down.

"Hungry now?" "Yes, but not for corned beef," she giggled. The hint was taken. Owen lifted her into his arms and carried her to the bedroom. At the foot of his bed, he sat her down slowly and the ritual began.

Pat lifted her arms assisting as he slipped her blouse over her head. Removing her bra produced the breasts he adored. They were perky, ready and, he nibbled. Pat was aroused, anxious and slid down her skirt revealing sheer silk panties. Owen worked his way down until he was level with her mound. Kneeling, he peeled off her bikinis and applied his tongue. The familiar scent was sweet, intoxicating as he accelerated his moves, licking and sucking.

Pat sighed and caved in as Owen gently laid her on the bed and spread her legs. Slipping off his jeans, she saw his erection, throbbing. The same thrill, the same craving, time and time again. Owen was well-endowed, uncut and hard, ready to plunge into carnal bliss.

Moisture between her thighs slowly meandered down on the sheets, as Pat felt the warmth of his heat close by. Owen lowered himself and entered. Moving in and out, he pressed his pelvis more fervently with each move. Pat moaned her approval, her orgasm building. She tightened around him as he increased the tempo of his thrusts.

"Oh, give me all you've got," she wailed. The intensity of their passion was building as Pat let go. Owen stayed with her as their erotic choreography brought an exhilarating pressure, an excruciating peak, all-consuming release. They lay breathing quickly, their bodies and psyches truly spent.

"God, Baby, for crying out loud, you're the best," Owen sighed as he carefully rolled off of Pat. His cigarettes were on the nightstand, he shook one out and lit it for her. They shared; taking a drag was pure pleasure after sex.

Stay the night, Baby. Okay?" "Yes. I already told my parents I'd be flopping at Mally and Griff's." "Good girl. Just for that, I'll go easy on you," he laughed.

Sliding down next to Pat, Owen did what he did best, away from the stage. His mastery was making love and then some. What was a girl to do?

Downtown, west of Broadway in Chelsea, Mally hurried up the flight of stairs to Griff's apartment. When they became engaged toward the end of the tour, she had moved into his flat. Slipping her key into the lock and opening the door, a first whiff of something fabulous invaded her nose.

"Griff, you here?" She placed her jacket in the hall closet. Before she could move, she felt his strong arms around her. "Oh, my darling Griff," sighed Mally as she turned. From the moment she signed her *Bravo Business* contract last year, she was captivated by his professionalism and his respect. He, in turn, was wildly attracted to her wholesome personality and petite looks.

They kissed and hugged like two lovers, reconciling after years of separation. Arm in arm, they walked to the kitchen. "What smells so yummy?" Mally lifted the lid of the large pot and took a whiff.

"Guess! Your favorite! I made chili, the way you like it. It's been simmering since this morning. Want to taste?" Griff was all enthusiasm when cooking and pleasing Mally. Producing a ladle he added, "Be careful, it's hot!" Mally took a tentative bite after blowing on it.

"Oh, wow! Is this good! When do we eat?"

"Whenever you like. I know your appetite, especially after dancing," Mally reached into the cupboard for bowls, setting them on table mats. Digging into a nearby drawer, she found two tablespoons, placed them next to the bowls, adding napkins. "I don't suppose there's cornbread?"

Griff grinned as he opened the oven door. "Voila, my dear," he announced. Mally smelled the warm whoosh of something delightful, baking and beckoning.

Closing the oven door, Mally hugged Griff as tight as she could. "You think of everything, why didn't we meet years ago?" He stood six foot two, nearly a foot taller than she. Returning the squeeze, he enfolded her in his arms. "I love you, my sweet Mally." "And I love you, my darling Griff!"

Following the chili and cornbread, they enjoyed fresh fruit salad and set the dishes aside for later; it was time to relax, together. They found a comfortable spot, the sofa, in front of the fireplace. Kicking off her shoes and removing her cardigan, Mally snuggled tightly into Griff.

"How was your first day?" "The choreography is stunning. It really is. Jonas has already set one piece to Cole Porter. It's so romantic, so sensuous."

"I'm not surprised; his adagios are the best of the genre. I've never seen work equal to Owen's," remarked Griff. "He never ceases to impress me." "It was hard not to get turned on while we rehearsed. I mean, such line and suggestion," purred Mally.

"Oh? Want to show me?" It was a cue Mally responded to easily. Peeling out of her clothes she stood before him, seminude in her light bra and panties. The choreography began.

Mally hummed as she slowly slipped off her bra. Throwing it aside, she reached the waistband of her panties. Sliding them off, she tossed them to Griff. Moving the fabric across his lips, he savored faint traces of her scent. He was growing hard as she continued to move, teasing and tantalizing.

He could resist no longer and reached for her. The hard bulge at his fly made Mally smile. Slowly slipping off his pants and jockey shorts, she toyed with him, kissing and stroking.

"Oh make me come, my sweet Mally." Kneeling, she suckled and played, running her tongue up and down, applying more pressure as Griff moaned and begged for more. Mally was wet with excitement as she continued to ply him with her mouth, her breathing accelerating. He had taught her well.

"Sit on me, please," Griff lay back and quivered under her touch. Mally, sliding up and down brushed his chest with her breasts. "Faster please," was all she heard before the first burst of orgasm, coupled with his release. They held each other for a few minutes, their breathing syncopated, the feeling intense as ever. Supper was merely foreplay.

Chapter 6

The Powers That Be

The second day of rehearsal began with every gypsy in the ensemble feeling effects of the previous day. Groans rose from the talented troupe as they stretched and warmed their limbs and backs.

Jonas was sympathetic, having performed in several of Owen's previous hits. Though he had learned the material, his body resisted. "God, I'm getting old. Good thing I'm still frisky, sort of," he said with a giggle. A collective chorus of groans was returned.

Following the warm-up, Griff unexpectedly arrived accompanied by the producers, Joseph Kaplan and Leonard Maggli. Middle-aged, well-heeled and confident, they strode up to the front of the room and faced the cast. Griff made introductions.

"Ladies and Gentleman, may I present our producers, who are making *Centipede* possible. Gentleman, the Centipede," he added. Applause rang out as the gypsies took positions around the room.

"It's a pleasure to have you aboard," remarked Joseph Kaplan. "You will make this concept a reality. You are pioneers, bringing something new to Broadway. We are grateful to have you join us." Leonard Maggli continued.

"You should all be made aware that the presale is amazing. The box office staff has all they can do to handle calls, questions and requests for tickets. The ball is in your court, ladies and gentlemen. Have at it with our blessing. Any concerns address to Mr. Edwards. He is our direct liaison in all matters of the production. We're here for you. And thank you!"

The cast applauded as Kaplan and Maggli made their exit. Jonas called the group to their feet.

"No time to rest on your laurels. We will review the Porter piece and add another number today. Warmed up?" The group nodded. "Okay, let's begin!"

Frank was ready and the dancers took positions across the room from their partners. As the music began, Jonas met Pat center and worked the languid adagio with impeccable precision and nuance. They wound around each other, rising and falling, stretching and leaning, gliding and holding. Following, the other men raised their partners, allowing the lifts to unfold, as they moved slowly down their bodies, feigning consummation. Owen's choreography, depicting sexual interplay, was flawless. The dancers instinctively knew how to project his concept.

Nora and Jeff, the assigned swings of the show, ran the movements committing patterns to memory. Jeff was straight, loving the feel of Nora in his grasp. As they rubbed close, she leaned into his ear. "Hmm, sex without worry," she whispered.

The rehearsal continued until noon. Griff called lunch and the group retreated to the dressing rooms. Some smoked, craving nicotine. Others headed immediately to nearby eateries. Mally caught up to Pat at the elevator. "How's it going?" Pat tossed a look that said it all. Mally couldn't resist. "Ah, so how was Mr. Matthews last night?"

"Mal, he's amazing. He responds to my every need. The sex is hot." Mally deadpanned, "So I can expect to find a cinder where Patricia Byrne once stood?" Pat gave her a playful poke.

"I love being back in New York. Seeing Owen more often only makes me love him more. It's good Mal, really good."

"I'm happy for you, Pat. By the way, you look fabulous working with Jonas. What do you think of the choreography so far?"

"Are you serious? Owen's work is brilliant! The two walked up 46th Street to Howard Johnson's arm in arm.

Lunch over, the group reassembled to stretch and do the Porter piece once more. Jonas stepped out to watch, bidding Jeff to fill in. Following the review, Owen entered; sauntering across the floor and, as always, held all eyes in the room. Nerves were on alert; concentration at a peak.

"Okay kids, let's run it from the top. Let's see what you've got. Jonas, take your place center with Pat. Swings, step aside so I have an accurate picture. Thanks. Frank, let's begin. The dancers took their opening positions.

Lush music filled the studio as each couple began to move, reaching and stretching toward one another. The sensuous choreography looked splendid. As Owen keenly observed, he was pleased with Jonas' pairing. The adagio continued, bodies locked in embrace, heavy breathing, sweat and body fragrance taking on a life of its own.

Eager to observe his star, Owen stayed focused on Pat, watching her phenomenal body slide over Jonas. She was perfection, spellbinding, totally focused on her partner, giving her all to produce the effect Owen was looking for. The others matched their partners in ability, but it was how they looked together, that impressed him. Once again, he had made great casting choices. When the number finished, Owen did something uncharacteristic. He applauded. Through the sweat and heavy cadence of hyper breathing, the surprised dancers returned his applause.

"Good job, gang. Keep it up. It's going to get tougher." The group relaxed into a breather. "Take five," called Griff. The weary ones lay on the floor, while others dragged themselves to dance bags, digging out smokes. Some had to pee while others hit the coke machine. Satisfaction hung in the air as the gypsies took a well-earned break. In the meantime, Griff, Jonas, and Owen huddled.

"Great start to the week. Jonas, please begin teaching the tropical number. I want you to sort out the strongest dancers for the feature points of the mambo, samba, and rumba. Griff, have we set up fittings yet?"

"Yes, fittings will be the rest of the week during longer lunch breaks and after rehearsals, times will be posted and they'll have to eat quickly.

"Good. I'll catch up with you both later." With a wave of his hand, he left the room. Catching Pat's eye in the corridor, he kept his professional posture intact. "Nice work, Miss Byrne." "Thanks, Mr.

Matthews," Pat added. The façade worked for the newcomers. The *Bravo Business* gypsies knew better, having observed the intensity and complexity of their relationship for months on tour.

Following the break, Jonas assigned dancers the Latin styles he would utilize in the next number. The samba had to show fluid, formal movement. Phillipe was paired with Liz Gunther. His posture and line, coupled with her elegance and ballet technique made a great match. Mally and Chad were assigned the rumba, their precision and attention to Owen's style added to the look Jonas needed. Joe Pinto and Cynthia Charles would perform the mambo, their natural instinct for selling, would give the movements a tongue-in-cheek quality.

Three couples, three different Latin dance styles. The others were given chorus spots to back the six, a ricochet of choreography, interlacing all three styles of movement into a big finale finish. Everyone eagerly followed as Jonas laid out the patterns. Dick and Kathy learned the samba; Jerry and Marcy, the rumba; and Jim and Fran the mambo.

The rest of the afternoon flew by until 6:00 pm. The gypsies were done for the day, dismissed at last, tired bodies moving slowly. Phillipe changed and waited for Jonas, watching him through the door of the studio, sweaty and spent.

"Cheri, you look rung out," observed Phillipe, when at last Jonas emerged. "You're right, I'm wiped. I'm starting to feel all of my 35 years!"

Phillipe had replaced Gary Hanson, Jonas' partner of ten years, following an accident that forced Gary's retirement, during *Bravo Business'* engagement in Atlanta, Georgia. Phillipe auditioned for Owen and was hired immediately. He and Jonas fell into a liaison that grew into a committed partnership. They were soul mates now.

"I'm a whipped puppy, but a happy one. Owen's work is phenomenal. I can't get enough of it," admitted Jonas. Phillipe eyed him slyly.

"And you can't get enough of something else, Cheri. Come on, let's go home and I'll show you." Jonas smiled. He savored Phillipe's effect on him in bed. Tired as he was, he knew he would perk up once he was in the throes of their frequent torrid games.

"Go change, I'll meet you downstairs." Jonas had already perked up; he felt a shift in his dance belt, a good sign in spite of his fatigue. "I'm on my way," he shouted as he headed to change.

Phillipe entered the elevator and set his bag down, suddenly feeling the first wave of weariness. An arm reached in to stop the door. Joe Pinto entered and pressed the button for lobby.

"Well, well, you look tired. Getting a little too much at night?" Joe wanted to move in on Phillipe previously, when both had joined the tour at the same time. Phillipe's interest was strictly Jonas. He had no need to trick on him. He politely made an attempt to converse with Joe though it was obvious he was elsewhere.

"The work is challenging but satisfying," he said quietly. Joe smiled as he leaned in.

"I'm a challenge and satisfying also Phillipe. You ought to try a new flavor." Joe was rampantly horny most of the time and never apologized for his libido; having sex with as many as possible.

"Sorry, Joe, I'm off the market and you damn well know it," said Phillipe, an edge growing in his otherwise, soft voice. "I thought that was understood months ago."

"Well, shit, you can't blame a guy for trying; it's your loss, sweet pants." Phillipe ignored the comment as he exited past Joe.

A misty rain was falling on the busy midtown street, he pulled his collar up. The honking of irate drivers, mixed with the sounds of noisy pedestrians, all in a hurry, drew his attention. Vendors wrapping up their day, pushing empty carts down the street, blended with a view of eager customers in line at the box office across the street. The rhythm of Manhattan in motion was a unique distraction for the native Louisianan.

"Hey, handsome!" He heard Jonas. "Let's get out of here. Mess with me, Baby!"

"*Mais oui, Mon Cher. Allons ici!*" Jonas' breath suddenly caught short as he imagined the nuances Phillipe would apply. As if the past eight hours of rehearsal hadn't existed, he felt revitalized and ready to play. The thought hastened him to flag a nearby cab, Phillipe right behind. There would be little sleep tonight.

Chapter 7

The Process Unfolds

"What time is your fitting, Mal?" Today was the first costume fitting for *Centipede* at Nira Fontaine's studio, on 7th Avenue. Miss Fontaine, a designer of enormous repute, had earned kudos for her award-winning creations for ballet, opera, and film. Her costumes for Hollywood musicals were the best in the industry. She was demanding, intense and impossible to deal with if her expectations weren't met; her brilliance frequently a trying excuse for outrageous behavior. This was her first outing with Owen Matthews on the Great White Way.

"Mine's at 1:15, and hopefully, I'll be able to grab a sandwich," exclaimed Mally, as she pulled on her tights. Pat nodded, slipping out of her jeans. There would be a shortage of time to refuel today. "I'm called at 1:30. Do you want to share a cab over?" "Let's!"

At that moment, the firm voice of Griff Edwards came across. "Attention dancers. Please report to the main studio. Thank you!"

Jonas called the gypsies for their usual warm-up. A review followed, which the dancers worked through with diligence and enthusiasm. It was mid-week and two numbers had been taught and polished. The dancers were performing with aplomb.

Jonas was pleased with the ensemble. In addition to their dance technique, they were all strong actors.

Owen always stressed the subtext behind each piece. He believed in the emotional inner life of the performer as it applied to the material at hand. He wanted emotions, not merely mechanics. As a result, his work had strong impacts on audiences, show after show.

"Today, we'll be doing a jazz piece, heavily 40s in style, big-band type moves," announced Jonas. "Ladies, please change into your character shoes. Gentleman, your jazz shoes are fine." There was a general scurry as the women hurried to replace jazz shoes with heels. Returning to the floor, they watched Jonas as he described the choreography in detail.

"This piece is brassy, a stylish representation of movement circa World War II. Lots of jitterbug, lifts, precise ensemble combinations, strong features of duos, trios and foursomes. It will be a competition of sorts between the men and women, with a smash finish of everyone getting together. Let's begin!"

Jonas split the ensemble, placing the men upstage of the women. The men's moves were aggressive, masculine, like men returning from war. Each found a spot next to his partner. The women's moves were flirtatious and winsome. Jonas started with a big finish first, followed by individualized sections.

Pat was featured with Jonas, her counterpart, continuing their great partnership. Their adagio, brought applause from the others. It was hard to beat Owen's concept of a love duet. It had the drive, longing and sensuality he always insisted on.

A men's trio of Joe, Phillipe and Chad was tough to beat. Their masculinity, sensuality, and precision was reminiscent of the great Jerome Robbins' piece, *Fancy Free*, in which three sailors felt the freedom of being on leave in New York City after months at sea. The movements represented the pent-up, sexual longing and curiosity of men removed from women far too long.

The three females, Cynthia, Fran and Mally, held their own technically, producing frisky, sensuous movements of women longing for men. The choreography was precise, staccato and bouncy of women enjoying the game.

The men's moves were strong, forceful, irresistible. They feigned disinterest in the women, their ploy to win them over. Then, gliding into place, they took hold of their partners, now unable to resist their intention. Grouped together at last, the flirtation became an orgy of movement, men and women coming together after forced abstinence.

Sweat and hair pins flying, glistening bodies in soaked dance wear, the six dancers grasped, lifted, dipped and kissed, clinging to each other in a mass of spent forms. Entangled by their release, their representation conveyed sexual satisfaction. At the conclusion, the only sound was heavy breathing as the dancers sprawled on the floor, a tangle of satisfaction from their workout.

"Incredible, kids!" Jonas walked the room, smiling at each dancer. "You do Owen's work proud. He'll be in later to see what you've got." Griff announced lunch.

"Remember, those of you with fittings, get cab receipts and bring your lunch back here. The rest of you take an hour and a half. Others will be fitted following rehearsal today and again tomorrow at lunch. Check times on the call board. Thank you!" In spite of fatigue, Mally and Pat hurried in order to make their appointed fitting.

"Please stand over there and do the dance," insisted Nira Fontaine as she finished pinning Mally. "I must see the range of motion. Tell me if you feel any binding!"

Mally walked over to a small, upraised floor in the center of the designer's fitting room. She began a series of moves from the Cole Porter number, stretching as far as she could, incorporating her arms, legs and back, as she moved under the stretchy, one piece garment. 'Boy, this fabric is flexible,' she thought.

Nira had designed a unitard to meet the demands of Owen's concept and choreography. The garment left little to the imagination. Mally glimpsed the outline of her breasts and found her mound quite pronounced through the fabric, as she gazed into the full-length mirror. She felt a blush from her toes to her face, marking movements she would perform in this flesh-toned costume. "Is that all there is to this?"

"Of course, but we're adding a small skirt for modesty." explained Nira, with an exasperated huff. "Next!" Mally left the fitting, passing Pat, who stifling a giggle added, "Where's the rest of the costume?"

Mally disappeared into a curtained area and peeled out of the stretchy piece that hugged her form. Slipping into street clothes, she grabbed her bag and reached for a brush. Looking into the mirror, she smiled, noting how long her hair had grown since the tour. The color had been restored from the champagne beige she had worn on the road. The Lehrman organization had kept it up for the run of her contract and though she enjoyed being blonde, she was happy to return to her natural color. Mally looked at Pat, being pinned and tussled by Nira and her assistant and chuckled.

"My dear, you have such generous breasts and such a tiny waist! I'm envious!" Pat rolled her eyes. "Please stand over there and do the dance!" Pat complied, wishing the ordeal would end. 'That woman has some nerve making remarks about my tits,' she thought. Halfheartedly she marked through the movements she would have to do in the stretchy thing.

"That's all we need today. Kindly change and bring this back to me." Mally passed Pat on her way to the dressing area.

"I'll be waiting right here. We can get a sandwich at the deli downstairs and grab a cab back, okay?"

"I hope to shout," tossed Pat, as she disappeared behind the curtain. Mally glanced at her watch, realizing how little time they had before rehearsal. In seconds Pat was out and dressed. Handing her costume to Nira, she forced a smile and followed Mally.

"Thank you, ladies," said Nira, waving them off as she returned to business.

Costuming an all-dance show was not unusual for her, having designed for the ballet countless times. However, Owen Matthews was another story. He was reputed to be as difficult as she and she had no need for conflict. If anyone was to give ulcers, it would be her. Two enormous egos butting heads would be interesting.

Following a hasty stop for take-out, they grabbed a cab back to Dance Arts. Still lunchtime for some, the streets were packed with slow-moving vehicles, crosswalks thick with pedestrians clogging intersections, traffic grinding along, typical of New York.

"So what did you think of Nira's first design?" Pat had already begun chomping the corned beef on rye.

"A little on the suggestive side, but given the choreography, I don't wonder," smiled Pat. Mally noticed it was 2:15. Pulling up to the studio, the girls split the fare and headed to the elevator. Breathless, they arrived at the 4th Floor studio. The others were having last minute smokes, conversations, or stretching for the afternoon assault on limb and psyche. Mally wolfed down the last of her sandwich and washed it down with water. Pat put the remnants of hers in her bag for later. Dancing on a full stomach was impossible.

The sudden sound of Griff's voice across the hall hastened their change, street clothes came off, dance clothes pulled on. Pat slipped on her jazz shoes while Mally brushed her hair back into a ponytail. Hearts beating, a tummy twinge or two and the girls were back in business as they rushed to the big room. This was the big time now!

Chapter 8

Finishing Touches

"I've had it! This is just plain torture," Pat complained, as she peeled out of her leotard and tights, the sweaty fabric resisting. Forceful in her attempt to release the Lycra's grip from her aching body, the stubborn fabric finally let go. Collapsing in a chair, Mally looked on, weariness engulfing her as she slipped into her street clothes. Both relieved to have finished another day in the land of *Centipede.*

Hours earlier, Owen had arrived in a foul mood. During the course of rehearsal, he paced, yelled and complained at everyone within a glance.

Jonas took the barrage in stride. His past experience with Owen brought an understanding that his demand for perfection brought critical acclaim. The outbursts weren't personal, just a release of frustration until the choreography was perfect. Owen delivered the goods better than anyone on the Broadway scene. However, to some, it was easy to forget results when the painstaking journey to perfection bruised so intensely.

"You all look like shit! Unacceptable! Again!" Steaming, and bent, the ensemble continued the drudge, cringing at Owen's continuing, wrathful expletives, weary of his caustic mouth.

"What an asshole," Jeff Jenkins muttered under his breath. Stretching as far as his body would allow him, his leg muscles stubbornly resisted into a cramp. Jeff winced with each move. Physical discomfort he could take; emotional abuse was another story. "Genius is no excuse for a shit attitude," he huffed under his breath. In spite of the verbal barrage, he gritted his teeth, determined not to fold from Owen's crap. He would press on to make it right, no matter what.

Owen's regulars, those from his core of past shows, sallied on, caught up in the work, mesmerized by the force of Owen's persona and brilliance. Though they were in awe of him, the newcomers soon tired of his nasty approach as he drove them on and on. "Five minutes, please!" Griff announced the Equity-required break. The group split up, some sagging in the corners of the studio. A few grabbed smokes, while others made themselves available to the Coke machine and restrooms.

"He wasn't this tough last year," whispered Chad, glancing over at Phillipe. Both men had flopped on the hardwood floor near an open window, grateful to be prone. They gulped precious air from outside, as their chests rose and fell. Returning a sigh, Phillipe reached for a towel to mop sweat from the back of his neck, his wavy dark hair in a sticky tangle as it met the terry fabric. Glistening and spent, they agreed it was tougher working on an original show, with all the changes that occurred daily.

"I don't understand why I'm so bushed," remarked Nora, the swing dancer. "I've worked this hard for others."

"I'll bet the others weren't Owen Matthews," tossed Pat. "That's true. He's a first! Intimidating as hell, but God, so sexy," she murmured, eyes cast on his pelvis.

Arching an eyebrow, Pat caught the remark, quickly sizing up the newcomer. When it came to Owen, other women were threats and not acceptable on her radar. They shook Pat's confidence. From the very beginning of their affair, she struggled to let go of the insecurity she felt with Owen. He was elusive and his fidelity always questionable. No, she'd have to keep a watchful eye on him and Nora.

The dancers were called back, slumping as they took their positions for the finale. Once again, Jonas gave the countdown and the ensemble sprang into action. Sweat flying, feet skimming the floor's surface, they exploded into a mass of whirling entities, precise, unwavering and determined to please Owen. A whistle blew. Everyone came to a dead halt.

"Well, this is more like it! Owen leaned against the mirror carefully scrutinizing his ensemble, a small grin turning up the corners of his mouth. As he gazed around the assemblage, his eyes fell on Pat. The sweat glistening on her body only emphasized her obvious attributes in brief attire. He couldn't wait to make love, his hands exploring, his mouth tasting, his body writhing in a burst of erotic synchronicity with hers and at the end, the splendor of release.

"Jonas, enough for today," he ordered. "You can keep this bunch, but keep driving them," he chuckled, as he strolled toward the door, the ever-present cigarette dangling from his lips. As he passed Pat, he gave a little wink, indicating "later." The day was won. The group was whipped, and the studio emptied.

"Come here, I want to hold you, Baby." Pat slid into Owen's waiting arms, the door closing behind her. Dropping her dance bag and coat, she settled to his body, feeling his warmth. Nuzzling, he playfully kissed her eyelids as his hands explored her breasts. She was wet with want as her arms encircled his waist.

"Baby, you were incredible today," he whispered. "Come on, let me show you my appreciation," he whispered, leading her gently to the bedroom. Pat's heart beat faster as she anticipated what was to come. Owen loved the power he had over her in the studio and in bed. "Don't worry, Baby, you're going to get it," his whisper hoarse over his growing arousal. Agony and ecstasy was an apt description for that day.

Chapter 9

On To Philly

It was Sunday morning. "That was a fast six weeks." Mally noted, standing in front of their brownstone on Manhattan's lower west side. The morning sun etched a warm trail on her face. Her stomach rumbled slightly, reminding her that she hadn't taken time for breakfast.

"Darling, let's get a move on. The company call is close," cautioned Griff, while loading bags into a waiting cab. Within minutes they were between Broadway and 8th, at the Royal Theatre, one of Broadway's most revered showplaces. This grand lady of theatres had been home to the production for the final week of rehearsals.

A large bus stood ready at the curb 'Centipede' on the side window. Mally boarded, placing her bag in the overhead, other's following suit like a parade of ants. Griff was on the street taking a head count. Fred Martin, the new company manager, would join them in the City of Brotherly Love. All eagerly anticipated Philadelphia, the first stop of the show's out-of-town tryouts.

"May I interest you in hot tea and Danish?" Pat approached Mally with her usual burst of energy, carrying a white paper bag from the deli next door.

"Pat, you're a life saver! Griff and I didn't have time for breakfast! You know how motion sick I get on an empty stomach. Remember those Smoky Mountain switchbacks? Anyway, living with Griff, food becomes secondary," she confessed, giggling as they hugged. Griff called "All aboard." They selected seats, sat quickly and dug in the deli bag. Steaming coffee, tea and pastries were waiting.

"God, what would I do without java?" Pat sipped with enthusiasm as she watched the fragrant vapor rise, moisturizing her face. "It's saved me more than once on these morning hops."

Mally thought of the first few weeks of the *Bravo Business* tour when their friendship was new, becoming close quickly. Both were in the blush of excitement over their first big Equity job. How wonderful it had all been! They were experienced now. Each found a partner. Each had fallen in love during those early months.

Pat was the first, falling the hardest almost immediately. When Owen took her to his bed that opening night in Norfolk, she was wildly attracted by his obvious brilliance and glamour, the need for sex, becoming insatiable when they made love. It wasn't long before she was hooked by his irresistible attention and cunning, in and out of the bedroom.

Mally was attracted to Griff more gradually. His Sir Galahad demeanor, his respect and attention to her was compelling until, at last, he declared his love following their first intimacy.

Finishing the last bite of pastry, Pat crumpled the wrapping paper, loosening flakes of dried icing that fell into her lap. Licking her forefinger, she fastidiously picked up each tiny morsel, depositing them on her tongue, enjoying the last taste. She was never one to waste icing, even crumbs.

The gypsies settled in for the ride to Philly, as the bus rolled slowly away, a rousing cheer from the passengers drowned out the noisy diesel. Owen and Griff had a last minute meeting with Kaplan and Maggli and not on board; they would take a train to Philly later. Jonas was traveling with the cast and, although Owen's assistant, he still considered himself a dancer from the ranks. Happy to be sitting next to his partner, Phillipe, he rode along observing his old pals and the new members of the company.

They were an interesting mix. He could count on Owen's seasoned choices. He had nine months to observe and work with them on their previous tour. The newcomers showed promise, and he felt instinctively that Owen had made the best selection. He especially liked the swings, Nora and Jeff. They had the toughest job covering all the dance positions in the numbers.

Nora had a built-in sensuality that burst into tireless energy and enthusiasm. She was a brunette, with short, wavy hair, a tiny physique and a beautiful smile that held the straight men in the company rapt. And, she was a flirt. Jeff Jenkins, the male swing, could attest to that.

At times when he was partnering her, it was evident that she liked the contact as close as possible, the feel of his hands sliding over her. Egging him on at every opportunity, her whispers in his ear could distract, not to mention harden a certain part of his anatomy.

Jeff was attractive. He was medium height, stocky, but fine-tuned, cut well throughout. His dimples, short-cropped hair and great ass didn't go unnoticed by several in the company, both men and women. Since he was partnered with Nora, time and time again, she was the exclusive benefactor of such appeal. It was rumored that they were sleeping together, but in fact, Jeff was in an exclusive relationship with his girlfriend, planning to get married as soon as the show returned to New York. Nora, on the other hand, was open for business.

The bus moved through Manhattan to the Lincoln Tunnel and south. Soon they would hit the New Jersey Turnpike. It was a picture perfect day to travel and the gypsies were enjoying the temporary reprieve from constant rehearsing.

The company was scheduled to perform at the Monarch Theatre in downtown Philadelphia. Known as the theatre host of tryouts and tours, the Monarch was close to hotels and restaurants in the heart of the city. The house and backstage area mimicked most Broadway theatres in size and design, making them convenient to adapt to.

As was the custom for companies on tour, management posted hotel sheets, with several choices for the cast. Longer runs could be accommodated with apartment hotels but, for a two-week engagement, most hotels offered a special rate to performers, crew and orchestra.

Mally would room with Griff while Pat decided to go it alone the first two weeks. She fully expected Owen to be near enough to insist she share his bed whenever the spirit moved.

The bus cruised along the New Jersey Turnpike, passing Secaucus, infamous for the aroma of refineries "Oh God," wailed Chad. "If the world has an asshole, this is it!"

There was laughter from some and groans from others. Soon the countryside was free of population, turning into lush landscapes of woods and fields.

Having stopped for lunch along the way, it was midafternoon when the bus rolled into the city. All along Lombard Street, the company observed

the beginning of rush hour, commuters and cars jamming the intersections. Philly's finest were visible as they conducted vehicles through stop
light changes. In a few minutes, they were in front of the hotel.

"God, I love this town," declared Jonas as he pulled his bag from
the overhead. Phillipe had yet to play Philly and was looking forward
to a new experience. Since they had become lovers on the previous
tour, Jonas was a guide of sorts, showing Phillipe around in various
cities, repeats from previous tours. As they fell more deeply in love,
they enjoyed sharing new adventures, delighting in each other and the
venues unfolding week after week.

"Get me to the hotel already," sighed Pat. Her need for down time
was apparent when she wasn't putting out in the dance studio. When
performing, she tended to give her all to the point of exhaustion.
Whatever was left was Owen's. He was her constant preoccupation and
had always been since their first time.

"You want to grab a sandwich?" Mally was starting to feel her
blood sugar drop and food was the only way to quell the intense sig-
nals from her stomach.

"You bet! Let's check in first," Pat suggested. She was also ready for
nourishment. With a night off before the first tech, she was planned
to spoil herself with good food, a luxury bath and hopefully, a call
from Owen.

She always waited. Owen was selfish to the point of insufferable.
His tendency was to live fully, madly and on his time and terms. Ever
elusive, demanding and intense, he could turn Pat into putty, malleable and ready with just a phone call or a glance in her direction. He
was uncompromising and rigid. Pat willingly followed his edict for she
was smart enough to know the rewards were worth it!

Hadn't he given her the best choreography, the top spot on stage,
the billing, potential rave reviews to come? Best of all, he was hers,
period. And she made sure that everyone knew it. Yet, she constantly
worried someone would take her place. Perhaps another ambitious
chorine, a better dancer than herself, would catch Owen's wandering
eye. After all, his reputation had been built by his ability to find a new
talent, bed her and create the next Broadway sensation. But, Patricia
Byrne wasn't about to let go, be upstaged or cast aside to make room
for another. She would be watching, carefully.

Owen's core of regulars, his female dancers, knew better than to make waves. They were no problem, as they had observed Owen and Pat's relationship in full bloom on the previous tour. No one posed a threat from the chorus ranks. They understood the dynamics of the duo. However, the newcomers would bear Pat's undivided attention.

Pat had scarcely checked in when the call came. "Baby, I have a meeting in an hour with Griff and Jonas, some details to work out. Dinner, later?" She trembled. "What time?"

"Don't know yet. I'll phone you," he said, a slight irritation in his voice. "Take some time to rest. You'll need it, Baby!"

"Yes, Owen. I'll be here." Pat placed the receiver back on the cradle and flopped on the bed. Sleep came quickly.

Joe Pinto headed for the hotel bar. A drink, maybe several, sounded good, dinner could wait. More butch than gay in appearance, Viceroys were his brand and his scotch, always neat. Tonight, he was horny, ready to get laid and thought he might get lucky at the bar. Lighting a cigarette as he sat, he took a deep drag and ordered a double on the rocks. He paused to consider the scenery while he waited for liquid relief. Several men were in the lounge with women. As he continued taking inventory, he suddenly stopped, noticing a lone figure seated a few tables away.

There was familiarity about the guy, but what? He'd had more than his share of tricks along the way, so many guys he couldn't remember a single one. Hell, there was no end to the carnal high he would relish, the willing partners he'd consume. When done, he'd cast them aside, moving on to the next and next.

A wave of excitement crept over his skin; he had to check this guy out. After snuffing his cigarette, he worked his way across the room. "Have we met before?" Joe was primed for pleasure. The guy turned.

"Oh my God, Joe!" It was Jordan Hendrix, a conquest from the previous tour during the Des Moines run, Joe's hometown. "What the hell?" Jordan stood, all six foot three of him. He was stunning and alone.

"What are you doing in Philly?" "Please join me." Jordan said. Joe pulled up a chair; he did not need a second invitation. The waiter noticed the added guest and a round of drinks, ordered.

"I'm taking a course here, my new company is paying. I'll be here a couple of weeks. And you?" This was a more relaxed Jordan, confident, low-key and definitely attractive—even more so.

"We're here trying out a pre-Broadway show at the Monarch. I'm staying here," he said slyly, giving Jordan an entrée.

"This is unbelievable! Imagine running into you here, now." The drinks arrived. Joe took the scotch in hand and sipped, gratefully. Jordan stirred his Martini eyeing Joe with interest.

"I'm out." Joe stopped suddenly, the scotch burning the back of his throat. He cast a surprised look at Jordan, a grin forming. "Oh?" Joe could hardly contain himself, a twinge behind his fly.

"Yes, I came out to my wife a few months ago. She and the children stayed, I left the marriage, my job and Des Moines." He put his drink down and looked longingly at Joe. "I couldn't live a lie anymore. After you left, I was miserable. It wasn't just about you, you know. I had to free myself from the bondage of fear, my conditioning and honor my needs."

"Wow. This is something. So what happens next?" He drew a little closer. Jordan smiled and took his hand. "I never expected to run into you again. I have been with a few men since leaving Diane, but it hasn't been the same. You spoiled me."

Joe took the cue and paid the tab. "Coming?" Jordan followed closely out of the bar.

The phone was jangling as Pat stirred to its annoying sound. She reached for the receiver and propped herself up on an elbow.

"Baby, I've finished with the meeting. Some orchestrations have been altered and I am horny as hell!" Pat let out a slow breath as her fog lifted. Owen continued, "How about some dinner? Then we can get down to business!" Pat rose and struggled with her robe and one free hand.

"Yes, I'd love some Owen. I can be ready in 45 minutes." "Meet you in the lobby by the concierge desk. We'll go to Bookbinder's; they serve the best seafood in town.

"Wonderful. See you then." Pat's hands shook as she put the receiver back. She never got over the excitement of a night with Owen. First a hot shower, her latest lingerie and one of her slinkiest outfits.

Her amazing body always drew attention from onlookers, but he was the only one she would please tonight.

Stepping into the warm cascade, her body felt the luxury of slippery hands. Pausing at her mound, she caressed herself briefly; the real deal was on the way, soon.

Owen had a few minutes to relax before meeting Pat, a smoke break would be just right. Some days, slow deep drags of nicotine were almost as satisfying as a good roll in the sack. As he pondered what was to come later, the phone rang. He took another drag, letting it ring before picking up.

"Hello, Owen." For a moment he froze, recognizing the breathy, sexy tone of the caller. "Vera? What the fuck?" His tone impersonal, irritated. "Now Darling, that's hardly a greeting! How many months has it been?" Owen put down his smoke and carefully formed his words.

"Long enough, I guess." He could scarcely put his mind around what was happening. Hadn't he and Vera divorced on a ragged, impassable note? He hadn't heard her voice or thought of her in months. It was over. After years of psychological abuse, torment and intolerable exchanges between them, the end was definite; at least that's what he thought.

"Why the call?" He was fishing now, trying to find an out. "Well, Joe and I are here in Philly, and I wanted to say hello, to see how you are. That's all!" "Who the hell is Joe?" Owen was having difficulty being even remotely cordial. "Darling, come on! Joseph Kaplan is one of the major producers of your show! I thought you knew." "Hardly! I don't get intimately sociable with the money people save to get what I need for financing. I haven't read his diary," he intoned sarcastically.

"Well, FYI, we're engaged to be married. We were introduced shortly after our divorce. He's a dream and he's crazy about me. He invited me to see the opening of your show. I couldn't resist." "And?" Owen was growing impatient with each passing minute. "And I thought we could meet for a drink, share old times," Vera purred.

"No thanks, Vera. I'm here to work, to get this show up. I don't see any advantage or reason in our getting together."

"Well, I'm not here to get you up," she murmured, suggestively.

"Well, what a relief! Listen, Vera, we're done. We've been done for years. What part of this don't you understand?"

"I just thought one friendly drink. That's all," said Vera, defensive now. "It's better if we don't see each other, Vera. I'm doing this show. I'm heavily involved and I think we should let it go at that."

"Are you still with that Byrne bitch? I thought you might have thrown her away by now. Your proclivity for female company tends to demand variety!" "Go to hell, Vera. I'm through talking. I hope you and Kaplan have a nice life," he said caustically, hanging up.

A bit of scotch would help his mood but, 'there's no time for that now,' he reasoned. A quick bathroom stop to freshen up, Pat would be waiting.

Chapter 10

The Philly Experience

Monday morning was here, set up was underway; clean up rehearsals posted for tomorrow at 10:00 and 2:00. There would undoubtedly be changes here and there, knowing Owen's desire for perfection and adjustments when working in a new space. Not all out-of-town venues were duplicates of Broadway houses. Philadelphia was an exception; a few of their legit houses matched the Great White Way.

Mally woke with excitement. Rolling over to peer at the clock, she realized Griff had left for the theatre early to meet and greet his local crew. These jobbers were booked ahead whenever a new or touring show came to town.

Many of the techies had worked with Griff before and were familiar with his type operation. He was always organized and well prepared. Setting up shows for him was considered one of their easier gigs. Everyone appreciated the opportunity to be part of his team.

Tuesday's company call was set for 10:00. Jonas was ready to work, full of his usual ebullient energy. In contrast to others, being out of town and in a new show delighted him. He was a touring animal at heart since his gypsy days began. Phillipe was with him and felt the excitement build as they approached the stage door.

"Cheri, slow down! You'll incinerate my feet trying to keep up with you." "Phillipe, I can't help it. Who knows where this show will take us? It's Owen's finest work to date and, believe me when I say this; I think the show will be a big hit!"

"All right, Cheri, I believe you. You know better than I how all this works!" Jonas smiled as he reached over and gave Phillipe's derriere a generous pat. "I know how you work and believe me, you're the inspiration." Phillipe returned the gesture.

The stage was crowded with dancers. Bodies stretched and groaned. "Everyone, please come center stage for a brief meeting!" Jonas was surrounded as the company approached.

"We are going to run the show as soon as Griff and crew are set. With minimal scenery, it shouldn't be too long. So we'll have time to sort and clean anything ragged. You've had three days off, so warm up now and be ready to go," he suggested.

A fine lot of dancers, the best of New York, all present and accounted for. During six weeks of heavy duty training, no one had quit! They were ready now! Ready to show off the creative concept of sensuous dance in a new format, hopefully a winner for all involved.

Nora asked, "Will Owen be rehearsing us?" "Owen is in meetings this morning. In his absence, he asked me to clean numbers and clear up any stage glitches." A hand shot up. "Yes, Cynthia?" "Are the costumes ready?"

"Not yet. We'll be running without right now," replied Dick. Though he was still dancing in the show, he filled in for Griff when needed. "Okay, places for the top of the show!" "Just the opening and final numbers this morning, we'll break for lunch and be back by 1:30."

They were out of the huddle and in positions in a minute. Jimmy Desmond was at the keyboard, in the pit and ready. He played through the overture, the company moving to the music, stretching from positions in the wings. Racing hearts, pulses and thoughts immersed each dancer. Suddenly, the curtain rose, a mass of swirling bodies, now an amoebic whole, colorful, dazzling to behold, burst forth.

The magic had begun. The stage tableau began to move. First one, then two, then several dancers began to glide, twirl and fill the space as they repeated all they had learned. Each was true to his vision; each step fused into one, conceptually. The choreography was sultry, sensuous, playful, witty and comical. Bodies were steamed, taut and wet and in-the-face raw. The gypsies would soon take the audience's breath away.

When the last steps stopped, the blackout done, the company joined hands in a bow. Dancers, who were featured in a number, took solo bows; then, en masse, a final bow.

"Everyone, come to the house." The voice was Griff's, commanding and strong from the back of the theatre. The cast came down the stairs and slowly filled the first rows of seats. Some were in towels; others had already thrown on sweatshirts and jeans over their dance clothes.

"Good run-through, people. Jonas, did you see any problems?" "We had some tight spacing here and there, people trying to get used to the numbers."

"Yes. People, the numbers have been placed along the edge of the pit, beginning with "0" at center. Please use them to reference your position. If you have questions about what number to work on in a given piece, check with Jonas. The numbers will keep the spacing accurate and your safety is critical, so be aware of them at all times."

"Are the numbers standard? In ballet we never went by numbers. We found spots throughout the house," remarked Liz Gunther, former ballerina.

"Theatre choreography always follows numbers," said Griff. "It's the final addition to keep you all in place. No guess work here. You're excused. Half hour call is 1:30. Please be back and ready for more at 2:00. See you then." The spent and sweaty dancers were hungry.

Mally caught up with Pat and gave her a hug. "This feels like déjà vu. Remember back in Norfolk? Remember that first week in the show? It's starting to feel strangely familiar, like history repeating."

"Yes, except you and I are no longer the new ones. We've got some history with this process, and I have Owen. You have Griff! What could be better, kiddo?" "Nothing, absolutely nothing," said Mally, grinning from ear to ear. "Come on, let's grab a bite."

Vera Daniels resented Owen's rude response to her phone call. After all, hadn't she been responsible for his success? 'The nerve of that SOB,' she thought as she prepared herself for her fiancé, the show's producer. Joe would show her some appreciation, adoration and caring she had come to expect. In her favorite negligee, she glanced at her reflection in the full length mirror. Smiling, she ran her hands down her torso and over her pelvis. Her touch bringing chills as she remembered how easily Owen could turn her on, how often they had made love with fury and intensity that brought them to bliss and satisfaction.

She missed their sex life. Owen was the best, even after they split and lived separately. Sitting at the dressing table, she brushed her long hair, admiring the sheen, as she heard the door open.

"Oh, Baby Doll?" The familiar voice, tinged with just enough Bronx, spoke of a man who knew his way around and never let Vera forget how indispensable he was.

"Wow, Baby Doll, you look fantastic. Come here, come to Daddy, now." The request was his usual, making her feel wanted and sexy. His command was a guaranteed turn on.

Slowly rising from the chair, she walked deliberately, teasing him with every step. When Vera was within reach, Joe wasted no time and sprang into action. His hands groped at her satin covering. Kissing her hard on the mouth, he rubbed and gently pinched her nipples, now peaked and ready for tasting.

"I'm going to take you just the way you like it," he whispered, his voice hoarse with anticipation. Vera took a deep breath and waited. In an instant, he had her on the bed, pinning her down, tasting all of her. She moaned and pulled him closer, legs wider. He mounted her with a fury that took her breath. Sliding in and out, without wasting a moment, he succumbed to release in seconds. Breathing heavy as he held her down, kissing and groping more. Then, without word or ceremony, he rolled off, his labored breathing causing her concern.

"Joe, are you all right?" Moments later, Kaplan managed, "Yes, Baby Doll. That was intense!" Vera lay there, fighting her disappointment. She wanted satisfaction of her own and he never gave her enough time. This was his usual way of having intimacy. Choking back tears, she remembered Owen taking his time with her, making sure she was satisfied, his prowess and her pleasure always a sure thing.

Vera sat up and covered herself with the robe as she headed for the bathroom. Once behind the closed door, she sat on the commode and buried her face in her hands. The sobs came instantly, wrenching her chest. Vera grabbed a towel and pressed it to her face, trying to hide her frustration. In the interim, Joe sprawled on the bed and began making calls. The hotel operator connected him to the backstage line. Dick Landry picked up.

"Monarch backstage. This is Landry." "Griff Edwards, please. This is Joe Kaplan. I'll hold." Seconds flew by.

"Griff Edwards." "Griff, Joe Kaplan. Say how did the tech go this morning?"

"Joe, we only had a few minute spatial problems. Tech is in place for the 2:00 pm run."

"Good. I thought I'd stop in for a look-see this afternoon. See you then. Say, I'll be bringing Ms. Daniels with me. Thanks, Griff."

He turned to see Vera. "Baby Doll, you're too much. Come to Daddy." Vera obliged.

Reaching out, Joe took her face in his hands, kissing her tenderly. Gently, he ran his hands through her hair, his eyes locked on hers. Pulling her closer he sighed, as his pulse quickened.

"Baby Doll, marry me. I mean this week, here in Philly. Let's make it official." Vera's face grew serious and after planning her words carefully, she spoke.

"Joe, I need time. I thought it was all settled. I thought we would get married next spring, on my birthday. Please give me more time." His voice became softer as he kissed her gently.

"All right, Baby Doll, whatever you say. I'm yours." "Thanks Joe."

After the tech, Phillipe and Jonas had time to slip away to their hotel. Jonas sighed as he put his dance bag down.

"Cheri, are you not happy with rehearsal?" Jonas turned and reached out to Phillipe, who sat on the bed removing his shoes. Spent and happy, he hugged his partner close.

"The company was terrific this morning. Everyone is working full out, paying attention to all the nuances Owen set. I couldn't be happier!"

"You look spent, Cheri. Anything I can do?" Jonas slowly lay down on his stomach. "A massage would feel fabulous!" "I have just the thing, Cheri," he said, reaching in his bag. He set a bottle of baby oil on the nightstand. Jonas sighed, anticipating Phillipe's adept hands, as they went to work.

Spreading enough oil to lubricate his fingers, he moved slowly, easing down the taut body lying there. Jonas' buttocks tightened at his touch. Gently, Phillipe applied just enough pressure, working deep into his thigh and calf muscles. Jonas begged for more.

"Oh, Babe, yes," he hissed as Phillipe's moves grew more intense. He began to raise his ass until he had to roll over. His large erection waited. Phillipe took the cue, applying his hands up and down, the strokes increasing until the rush of ecstasy and release. As Jonas' climax subsided, reaching for Phillipe, he kissed him deeply.

"That's just the best! Oh Babe, I love you so much!" Phillipe smiled as he gently touched Jonas' face. "I love you too, Cheri." A glance at the clock showed it was an hour before check-in time.

Chapter 11

A Tech Affair

Wednesday was a special day; this morning a couple numbers needed a bit more clean-up and a tech run with lights and cues should do it. Home stretch was around the corner.

It was half hour call and the gypsies filed in. Set up was complete and the air charged with excitement, the same excitement each performer shared. It was time for a full run, a chance to display those hard-earned wares. Each dancer had sweated, sworn, given up mentally and physically during moments of rehearsal – and yet had returned for more Owen. He paced, he insisted, his cruel remarks cutting deep, but in the end, he got his way. He was a taskmaster, a bastard, a genius. He was admired, loved, despised, depending on how the rehearsal went.

As the clock ticked closer to 2:00, Joe Kaplan accompanied Vera Daniels into the theatre amid shouts of tech commands, orchestra tuning and the dull underscoring of muffled conversations from the creators out front.

"Owen, how are you?" Kaplan had spotted the director in a confab with Griff half way up the house. "Hello, Joe. Good to see you." Then he noticed his ex taking up the rear. "Vera."

"Owen." The air was frosty at best. Joe, sensing the tension, pointed to a nearby seat on the aisle for Vera. "Baby Doll, you'll be comfortable there." He continued pleasantries with both men until Griff, sensing the inevitable 15-minute call, excused himself.

"So do we have a winner here, Owen?" Kaplan's track record was one of the best in New York.

"We're ready for an audience," mused Owen, who could take or leave producers in general.

"This cast is the best I've worked with. I think the choreography worthy of them." He glanced over at Vera briefly, but he had made his point, judging from her scowl in his direction. Vera had once occupied the space of perfection in his work. Rubbing it in felt like a backhand to her ego.

"Well, I'm looking forward to what you've got. I'm sure it will be worth the investment."

"We'll see, Joe. We'll see. Now, if you'll excuse me, I have to get backstage."

Vera watched her former husband walk through the house and up the stage stairs. The curtain swallowed him as he disappeared around the edge of the proscenium arch.

"Baby Doll, you seem distracted." Joe sat down next to Vera and reached around her shoulders, giving her a gentle pat. "You're not still hung up on the director, are you?" "No Joe," she lied. "It's been over forever." But in her heart, she loved him, struggling continually to let go.

"Five minutes," Griff announced through the backstage squawk box. In the dressing rooms, a wave of anticipation mixed with nerves ran through the gypsies as they prepared for a full out run. Last minute stretching, getting familiar with costumes, putting final touches on make-up and hair intensified the pre-show drama.

Pat twisted her hair into a French twist. Her long mane had been trimmed eight inches prior to leaving New York. For *Centipede's* wild dancing her hair had to be worry-free. She was more concerned with Nora, who seemed obsessed with Owen.

"Mal, how does my hair look?" Pat placed the final pin and turned to her pal. "I like the style! Is it going to hold through the torture?" Pat shrugged but smiled at her pal's reference. Today's run would test them all with the addition of costumes, lights and orchestra.

"One can hope, Sweetie. One can hope!" Grabbing a pair of tights, she extended her right leg, allowing the fabric to embrace her toes. As she guided the fabric up her leg, she carefully inched the material until it was taut.

Mally's hair was in a ponytail, anchored into submission by a considerable amount of Aqua Net. She wasn't partial to the fragrance, but it did serve to hold her hair presentable during the rigors of performing.

"Please report to the Green Room, Company." Griff's words cut through the air. The cast hustled to the actor's lounge backstage. Sixteen dancers, all psyched to begin what they considered the ultimate challenge and honor—to carry out the master's wishes. All were eager to please. Entering the throng, Owen was calm. Looking over every dancer as he spoke, all eyes were on him.

"We have our first complete tech ahead of us this afternoon, ladies and gentlemen. Naturally, I expect everyone to be in top form, aware of positioning, each other and totally immersed in the subtext of the choreography, as full out as you can dance it. Remember the music and movement are all that matter. Break a leg!" As he walked out, Griff took over.

"Are there any questions or concerns? If so, now is the only time you have before the run. Cynthia?"

"If we have trouble with a costume during the run, who should we see?" There were a few nods from others.

"Any concerns should be reported to me, I will pass on your notes to Nira Fontaine and crew, who are here today. Incidentally, Mr. Kaplan is out front this afternoon and Mr. Maggli will be here opening night. Neither has seen the work in rehearsal, their first impressions will be this afternoon and Friday evening. Make it good, please! Places!"

In the house, Nira Fontaine sat tenth row center, notebook in hand and able to observe the entire stage. Eagerly, she waited to see how the lighting would show off her costumes. Nira was well known for her brilliant movie and opera designs, but this was a first with Matthews. She was confident he would love the pains she took to make his dancers look sensational. Though she had met the gypsies at informal fittings and requested a sampling of the most demanding movements; she had yet to see the show. This tech performance would also be the first for her assistants, Andre and Tallulah.

Sandy Irvin was musical director and conductor for this venture. He had conducted *Bravo Business*, both on Broadway and national tours. On his music stand was not a typical score, not an original musical, but rather a compilation of many composers' works. He looked forward to the change of pace as he stepped to the podium. His base musicians from New York, sat ready for the downbeat. Philly jobbers made up the rest of the orchestra, their eyes waiting for their cue.

And, then it all began. Curtain rising, a spot engulfed Sandy as house lights dimmed and stage lights slowly added color. A wash of blue blanketed the stage, dancers posed in tableau, a freeze frame of total stillness. Gradually, the light brightened as a crash of brass took off. The freezes came to life on the dancers. Percussive movements sending them reeling into form and rhythm. All sixteen, glided, turned and leapt! *Centipede* was alive!

From the darkness, Vera watched, eyes welling. Owen's genius, so apparent, sharpened her regret. Matthews and Daniels on the Great White Way! – Once upon a time, but no longer, days of fame and wonderment now gone forever. He had made her, she had been his star, and now, one of the greatest collaborations in Broadway history, was a faint memory, forgotten by most. Continually stabbing her with regret, she was in a trench of loss.

Owen watched his incredible troupe, his mind recording every detail, every nuance, the timing and the flow of his choreography. And, he watched Pat. She stirred him into psychic fever, her incredible body drawing him, intensifying his longing for her. His hunch was right. She would be a star, his star. Broadway was about to be set on its ass. He would make it happen. He would see to it.

Centipede was a wild ride throughout the afternoon, culminating in the unexpected. As the dancers began the second act opening number, the men, sailor's on shore leave, flirted, attracted and succumbed to their women. Wantonly lifting their partners in sensual contact, the adagio was full of sexual longing and satisfaction. As the number reached its peak, the choreographed slides down the men's bodies worked well for the women, but not the skin tight body stockings underneath their skirts. Fabrics strained and split, running in long irregular gashes down each female dancer until there appeared to be large shreds of diaphanous cloth hanging from each.

A sudden whistle blew, stopping all action, the orchestra screeching to silence. The house lights came on and Owen was down the aisle in a fury. Griff stepped out from his cue desk to assess the situation. The women, noticeably shaking, examined the mess that had been their costumes moments before. The men shifted as they waited for the inevitable eruption.

The consensus amongst the cast was—while Nira's reputation for quality work in movies was deserved, she knew little about costuming for theatre dance. The designs had to withstand the range of dancer's motions 8 shows a week, 52 weeks a year. When the gypsies were fitted at Nira's studio, her superior air and her Hollywood behavior were viewed with skepticism and humor by some. Requesting each dancer perform a bit of choreography for each costume on a 4 x 4 floor was an amusing request but impossible to execute. How could one dance full out?

Owen climbed to the stage, walking toward his troupe, grouped in riveted attention. Reaching for Pat, he walked her downstage. Taking a piece of her costume in hand, he ran his fingers the length of the fabric, scrutinizing every inch of it, now hanging in shreds.

"What the fuck is this, a Woolworth's special? Get Nira Fontaine up here now!" Nira and her assistants stood slowly, coming down the aisle with collective dignity, as they approached the director. Tallulah carried the master sketchbook and Andre helped Nira up the stairs. Her face was passive as she stood in front of a fuming Owen. Carefully she put her cheaters on and nodded to Tallulah to hand over the sketches. "Mr. Matthews, you and your team approved these sketches. You signed off on them weeks ago. As you can see, the shore leave number is exactly as it was designed, no more no less," she remarked, with a superior tone to frame her defense.

"Miss Fontaine, this is a dance show, pure and simple! This fabric is not up to the wear and tear of my choreography. I don't give a fuck how beautiful it looks when it catches the light or your movie credits. I'm interested in functional and practical dance wear. Ever hear of Lycra? I need the women's costumes replaced by this time tomorrow! I don't care how you and your lackeys correct this atrocity. I don't give a fuck how many movies you've designed or how many Oscars you have. This is legitimate theatre, so fix the problem!" He turned to Griff as he worked to calm down.

"Griff, give the company ten minutes for the girls to change back to rehearsal clothes and we'll begin the second act again."

"Mr. Matthews," hissed Nira, barely holding it together, "Is that all?" Owen turned back to her and moved in close, standing nose to nose. "For now, Miss Fontaine, for now," he said with a compelling tone.

He turned leaving Nira standing center stage with nothing but air and ire. Andre, visibly shaken by Owen's verbal assault on his boss, stood motionless. Tallulah, the more jaded of the two, muttered quietly, "What a dick that director is." Nira overheard and approached, "Darling, they're all dicks in New York. Haven't you noticed?" The three disappeared into the house.

"All right cast, you have ten minutes, ten minutes to act two," announced Griff. When he finished, he followed Owen into the house, accompanied by Jonas. In mid house, he pulled them into a huddle.

"Jonas, keep a tight watch on the rest of the evening and how the kids work in those costumes, okay?" Griff, make a note that those replacement costumes for the women must be in at least an hour before tomorrow afternoon's tech. I don't want the women dancing around on stage with their tits and asses hanging out!" Griff nodded and headed back to his desk.

Back in the dressing room, the women quickly changed to rehearsal clothes. Conversations were muffled and the mood was laced with tension, remembering the recent scene.

"Wow, I sure wouldn't want to get on Owen's bad side," remarked Nora, as she added a fresh coat of lipstick. Looking into the mirror, she couldn't help but notice Pat's stare, cold and disapproving. In minutes, the sound of Griff's voice rang through the room, "Places for act two!"

Later, the evening rehearsal passed quickly, the gypsies working their magic for Owen. There had been no missteps, no lack of focus or energy, but a swift explosion of genius generated by dozens of feet, perfect bodies gyrating, sliding, lifting, all packaged by a brilliant concept, a fusion of creative wantonness and fierce execution.

Backstage, spirits were high as dancers disrobed, showered and planned a post-performance celebration. They made it through the acid test, the complete tech run-through, in spite of splitting costumes, a caustic scene and a slight delay of act two. It was now time to let loose: to drink, smoke, gossip, or possibly get laid—an attractive thought.

Several cast members found a local watering hole near the theater, popular after hours and frequented by touring companies. Mally, Pat, Phillipe, Joe, and Chad took a table, while Kathy, Marcy, Fran, and Nora grabbed a second nearby. As they settled in, drinks were the first order of business, followed by food. It was time to refuel.

Griff, Owen, Jonas, and Dick wandered in and to a quiet area near the back to confer. Jonas waved at Phillipe as he walked by. Now that he was on the management side as well as lead dancer, he had to be part of staff meetings, pre and post-show. It was a new role, one he relished and worked hard for.

As the group chatted and drank, there was a sudden presence in the bar. Joseph Kaplan entered, a statuesque redhead on his arm. The woman, in her mid-forties, was stunning. Each move and gesture belied one of star power, a mega force. As they passed, Joe Pinto nudged Pat.

"Note the ex-Lady Matthews. Man, she's still put together in spite of the mileage. I worked in a couple of hits with her. Even the fag boys would have taken a piece of that!"

As his eyes stay glued to Vera, he didn't see Pat get up and head for the restroom. Mally noticed and followed. As she entered she found Pat on her knees, throwing up her drink, gagging and sobbing. "Pat, what is it? What's the matter?" Groaning, Pat stood slowly as Mally steadied her. Helping her to a sink, she ran the cold tap and Pat rinsed.

"Pat, there's a chair over there. Please sit down and tell me what's going on!" Once settled, a barrage of sobs started again.

"Oh, Mal, Vera Daniels is here! She came in with the producer! I'm so afraid!" "Pat, for God's sake, she can't hurt you. She doesn't even know you!" "What if she finds out I'm the one with Owen?" "What difference does that make now? She and Owen are over, divorced."

"Mal, you are so naïve! Owen has told me how vindictive and controlling she is. I bet she'd do anything to get him back! If she's with the producer, she could find a way to have me fired. I wouldn't put it past her!"

"No one's going to fire you, Pat. You've got to let this go. Owen loves you! He's built this show around you. Be reasonable or it will eat you alive." "Oh Mal, I'm so tired of worrying. You're right. I know he loves me."

"Good! Let's go back to our friends. You need something to eat. You didn't eat before the show, remember? I'll bet you're starved. Come on!" Mally grabbed Pat's hand and led her back into the throng.

As they passed Vera and Joe deep in conversation, Pat couldn't help notice how gorgeous she was. After years of alcohol abuse, Owen's constant infidelity and her mindless sleeping around, Vera was simply luminous in spite of it all.

Returning to the table, the group conversation was in high gear. Pat still edgy and distracted didn't want beer and her burger wasn't doing it. She was ravenous for Owen. Her insecurities were rising. She needed him to hold, love and praise her.

Across the room the production team was still busily engaged in a confab of exhilaration and deep concentration. Owen was giving notes and holding court as Griff, Jonas, and Dick focused on the business of *Centipede.*

Time ticked by and the group gradually dispersed. Sated with food and drink, it was time to find a pillow. There was still much ahead of the gypsies before the press opening Friday night. Only two more run-throughs and this molded, rehearsed critter, *Centipede,* would face public scrutiny. Philadelphia audiences were some of the most sophisticated outside of New York. There was a lot riding on this show. Soon they would feel its impact.

As the bar cleared out, Jonas excused himself and went to his room. He was anxious to hear what Phillipe would say about Nira Fontaine's fiasco. Owen and Griff said goodnight and headed their separate ways. Dick phoned home to check on Dana, she was almost due and he felt comfort hearing her soft, southern voice. Mally walked Pat to the lobby, giving her a reassuring hug before they parted.

"Pat, when you start to worry, remember how much Owen loves you. You're the star of his show, the reason he wanted to do *Centipede* in the first place. Try and get some sleep, okay?" Pat nodded as she stepped in the elevator, weary and ready to forget Vera Daniels.

Mally checked for messages before heading to her room; passing the lounge she saw Vera Daniels alone at the bar. She was speaking in a loud voice to no one in particular, the bartender doing his best to accommodate her. Mally wondered how a woman like Vera Daniels could lose her edge, become washed up, a victim of her own making. What price did one have to pay for stardom? Apparently, Vera had paid dearly. She was finished, with only a past to remind her how far she had fallen.

Chapter 12

Old Ties

The production team was pleased with the previous night's first full run. From Griff's perspective, the Philadelphia jobbers handled their assignments well alongside the New York crew without a stumble. All technical aspects of the show were in place including Sandy's orchestrations and the Philly musicians who played to perfection. *Centipede* was ready to roll.

The setting for *Centipede* was minimalist; no cumbersome set, hanging pieces or units on tracks to break the flow of the show's two-hour running time.

The concept and execution was exactly as Owen planned it, the creative staff carried out every minute detail. The full cyclorama upstage and a variety of light changes were all that was necessary to feature the only star—The Choreography. His baby was about to take its first steps.

Owen returned to his suite, weary and ready for alcohol and sleep. A night with Pat would have to wait as exhaustion and reason took over, crippling his sexual need temporarily. Now was the time to replenish mind and body. Friday, the press would show up. *Centipede* was all that mattered.

Dropping his jacket and briefcase on a settee, he walked to the bar and poured himself a drink. He had barely settled when the phone rang. 'Who in hell would have the balls to call this late?' Reaching for his lighter he lit a much-needed smoke. Taking a deep drag, he picked up the receiver.

"Matthews." Only silence. "Hello?" There was only a heartbeat of time passing, then a sigh cutting into him. "Owen, it's me," whispered Vera, her voice obviously thickened with booze. Owen held his breath.

"What do you want?" The edge was obvious as he took another drag. "I want to talk to you. Please, Owen." She sounded vulnerable. "Go on Vera, I'm listening." Another moment passed. "The show is brilliant, your best work to date, you bastard," she slurred. "Owen, why did we end this? I still love you. I would do anything for you, anything!" Vera sobbed uncontrollably. "Vera, stop! Just stop! I thought it was understood that we're finished. Don't you get it?" "No! I still love you. I want you!"

Owen's voice rose in anger, as he snuffed out his cigarette. "What the hell? Why do you persist? You're with the producer! I'm in love with someone else! Vera, it's finished! Oh, yeah, that's it! You're drunk and horny! Kaplan isn't enough for you!" "You asshole, Owen, face it, you needed me. Without me, you wouldn't be anywhere!"

"Vera, it's over, kaput. Have a nice life and don't call me again." Vera unleashed a tirade of venom, shouting, "I hope you flop, you son of a bitch!" An abrupt click was all she got.

Dropping the phone, Vera staggered to the bar. Her hand shook as she poured another Jack Daniels. Slipping into a chair, she emptied the glass, leaned back and closed her eyes.

Reaching down and opening her negligee, she began the frequent ritual, bringing herself pleasure imagining it was Owen, with his ribald ingenuity. "Oh God, Owen," she groaned until at last her orgasm erupted. As she peaked, the door opened.

Quickly she sat up, repairing herself as she wiped tears away. Kaplan's arrival meant one thing; he would expect her full attention and sex.

On another floor Mally anticipated Griff's return. Aching muscles and exhaustion held her defiantly as she filled the tub for a bubble bath. Sore from the tech dress, she slipped her tired legs and touchy feet into the billowy foam, allowing the warmth to caress her body. She began to doze, only aware of the pure pleasure she felt as she soaked. Moments later the sound of the bathroom door brought her back.

"Darling, you look so comfy in there!" Griff's voice was soothing, with only a tinge of fatigue. He knelt, reaching over the tub caressing and kissing her gently, bringing a sigh. The moment was sweet.

Griff took her hands, helping her out of the bubbly brew. When she was upright, he took a towel and began drying her gently, as if wiping down a rare piece of sculpture. Griff enjoyed watching Mally's growing arousal as he moved down her body. Guiding his hands was pure pleasure as she allowed him access. With a sweeping motion, she was in his powerful arms.

Carrying her to the bedroom, he placed her gently on the bed. As she lay in anticipation, he removed his clothes and joined her. Fatigue gave way to sheer delight as they made love. It was the release both needed after the long rehearsal day. Wrapped in each other's arms they fell into a deep sleep. Tomorrow was coming soon.

In just two days, *Centipede* would be viewed by the Philadelphia public and press. It had been a grueling but artistically satisfying six weeks of preparation. No amount of guessing or predicting could alleviate the pressure the cast, crew and management felt. Friday would be upon them soon enough.

Chapter 13

Philly Opening

The previous days were now a blur as *Centipede* prepped for the press. Friday night, the opening only minutes away.

Backstage, a hot bed of activity was underway on every level. Griff and his crew did one last check of lighting and sound, all was well and ready. Dressers were on hand ready to assist the gypsies with quick changes through the show. Dressing rooms were buzzing with excitement, gossip and final touches to make-up and hair. In the basement, outside the orchestra pit, Sandy and his musicians were having a last minute smoke and ready to move on Griff's cue.

Out front the first night crowd was a mass of energy and anticipation, waiting for an Owen Matthews production. Hype preceded *Centipede's* arrival and was tumultuous, a frequently featured topic on radio, TV and newspapers; Owen's newest show was a mystery. Imagine the concept of an all-dance review for Broadway! Philly audiences were savvy, demanding the best. They expected it from Owen Matthews, the fair-haired former hoofer and had never been disappointed.

Joe and Vera chatted with well-wishers, as champagne was offered. Vera looked ravishing next to Kaplan, who was always recognized and respected. He was now the money man of Broadway, the heir apparent to his predecessor, the incomparable Vinny Lehrman, who produced numerous Broadway hits in his day. Now retired, Lehrman had been approached by Owen but, declined, claiming it was time to retire. Joseph Kaplan accepted the project, believing it a sure-fire winner.

"Hey, Joe, we almost didn't make it," shouted Leonard Maggli, Kaplan's partner, as he hurriedly worked his way through the crowd. "Damn, the air traffic out of La Guardia was nuts, backed up for over an hour!" Calming down, he saw his favorite diva, brilliantly coiffed, her ample cleavage displayed enticingly. Maggli quickly diverted his eyes to Vera's face as she caught him staring.

"Good evening, Vera. It's a pleasure to see you," soothed Maggli, his oily platitudes in high gear. "You're as entrancing as ever!" Vera leaned toward Maggli and gave him a careful peck on the cheek. Leonard could be a bother, his syrupy rhetoric lacking guile and mystique. However, he was Joe's colleague and required respect, even if feigned.

Standing at Maggli's side was an attractive fellow in his mid-thirties, observing all the action around him with interest.

"Joe, I believe you know my new assistant, Gary Hanson." Gary extended a handshake, his gaze not missing the luminous woman at the producer's side. She was stunning, well-heeled—a little worn, but still impressive. And there was the slight presence of booze, with a trace of fragrance that had grown stale. The lady was clearly enjoying attention and trying desperately to keep up. Her eyes revealed a woman attempting to ride on past glories.

"Gary Hanson, may I present Vera Daniels." Gary took her hand, raising it to his lips, a perfectly timed ritual of respect. He was no outsider when it came to the Who's Who of show biz. Vera Daniels! Who in the theatre hadn't heard of her? Vera, once the toast of New York, washed up and no longer among the pantheon of greats. Gary had been in the chorus of two of her biggest hits, hits she had shared with her then mentor and husband, Owen, and she, his indispensable muse.

A former gypsy, Gary had been a consistent performer, well-liked by management. Through no fault of his own, he was critically injured by a hit and run driver, during the Atlanta run of *Bravo Business*. The severity of his injuries forcing him to remain behind as the company continued on. After months of physical therapy, he returned to New York living with his aunt until ready to work again. Dancing was out for good, he had to look for other show business possibilities. A friend mentioned an opening, Producer, Leonard Maggli was seeking an assistant. The interview was positive. Maggli hired him on the spot.

Jonas and Gary had been lovers and partners for ten years. Gary's forced retirement changed everything, including their relationship. Jonas moved on, falling in love with Phillipe Danier, whom he now considered his soul mate. Gary was left, forgotten. There had been no contact with Jonas for months. Gary, seeing the futility of the situation, just let go. During their years together, Jonas always remarked how Gary was able to take life as it unfolded, unlike himself.

And now, Hanson was in Philadelphia with his new boss, Maggli, to witness the birth of Owen's new show. As lobby lights blinked encouraging the crowd to enter the house, Joe led Vera to the VIP section, followed by Leonard and Gary.

Backstage, Griff's order of, "Places, please," rang out. The familiar call to action brought the gypsies to their feet. As they moved to the stage; the electricity was palpable.

"Here we go," shouted Jonas, ready to take on the Philly crowd. "Let's nail it," added Chad, followed by several shouts of "yeah," as the other men descended the stairs.

"It's finally happening," oozed Nora, hurrying along. Cynthia, Fran and Liz followed, chatting in bubbly unison. "Save it for the stage, bitch," hissed Pat. The remark was not missed.

"Pat!" Smoothing a stray strand of hair, Pat continued. "Mal, I can't stand that swing girl. She's a born bitch, a prick tease! She wants to fuck Owen!" Mally knew Pat could make a mountain out of an ant hill. She'd lived with Pat's constant insecurity for over a year.

"Pat, forget her, please! After tonight you'll be a star! Don't sweat Nora. It's beneath you. Okay?" "Mal, as usual, you're the voice of reason. Thanks!" The girls hugged and took their positions. Meanwhile, Sandy's musicians walked to the pit, Sandy held back, milking his arrival.

A hush fell over the enthusiastic house as the lights began to dim. "Five, four, three, two, one, Sandy, go!" Griff's cue brought Sandy out and up to his place at the podium. A blast of applause greeted him as he stepped forward, bringing a Cheshire cat smile to his face as he bowed smartly. Holding the moment, he turned, raised his baton and brought the first notes of music to life on the downbeat.

Curtain rising as stage lights came up on a rainbow panorama of delicate colors. For all to see, the dancers appeared like a Rodin sculpture. Perfection!

As the music filled the stage, one by one, the gypsies moved, dominating the space, unraveling into syncopation of animation. The show was off and running to wild applause and cheers from all over the house.

Centipede was born! The dancers moving full out—undulating, kicking, lifting and swaying. Accompanied by the strains of Cole Porter, the group seemed possessed with one purpose, to bring magic.

Pat and Jonas were on fire performing their duet at the end of act one. Before they had finished their final lift the audience was on their feet. In the blackout, they scurried off stage. The 20 minute intermission gave the gypsies' time to dry, change and hydrate.

"Did you get a load of that reaction?" Jonas was all bubbles and hugs as he entered the changing area. The male chorus stripped down to dance belts, sweaty and spent from the workout. Jonas found an isolated corner. He peeled out of his costume with great difficulty, the fabric clinging. Phillipe noticed and moved over to join him.

"Cheri, let me assist," Reaching for a towel he began to dry Jonas. The action was a turn on, as much as Jonas fought it. He could feel a hard-on as it began to stand at attention. Phillipe leaned in with a conspiratorial whisper, "Let's continue this later, Cheri!" "Oh, yes," Jonas purred, anticipating hot sex after the show. Phillipe turned him on like no other.

The second act entr'acte began; gypsies took their places for the "Sailors in Port" number. The girls looked saucy in their short skirts and fitted low-cut tops, while the men looked crisp in their tidy sailor whites. Pat and Jonas took position center waiting for their musical cue. The other couples stood off stage, ready to come on for their features.

With a burst of brass from the pit, the number began as wild applause once again issued forth. The first half of the show had served as a great warm-up. The second act was on fire: fun and sexy, the men lifting their girls in an erotic swirl, suggestive and frisky with their physical contact, each movement blatant in its subtext: men long at sea, horny with want and women wanting to be taken; the time limit on shore leave intensifying the moments. As the number wound down, sailors saying goodbyes, girls waving them off, the audience didn't wait for the finish. En masse, on their feet, they cheered and yelled. Pandemonium was in high gear.

The producers were on their feet as well. Vera remained seated, tears meandering down her face, her make-up in clumps. Several cocktails during intermission had exacerbated her longing for Owen, to be once again part of his life and success. But the cold, hard truth was she was forgettable, a vague memory. The thought lay bitter within her.

When the applause died, lights came up on the next number. Following each, the audience showed appreciation. There was no stopping *Centipede,* potentially the biggest thing to hit the boards in years. Broadway was weeks away, but it would surely succeed if this audience was any indication.

At the back of the house, Owen counted every section, every movement, every moment. He was pleased. Nothing was missed. Not surprising was his pleasure watching Pat. She alone personified perfection dancing his work, every minute detail of his style. He would have to wait to express his appreciation. First, the party, praise from producers, the press and afterglow that his cast richly deserved.

The audience was on its feet before the first curtain; applause continuing through a dozen calls. When the curtain finally descended, the gypsies broke into a cacophony of yelling and screaming. Mass hysteria took over. Only Griff could quell the totally spent, sweaty, chorus shouting their pleasure, embracing their comrades.

"Company, please return to your change areas and hang up your costumes. We'll meet you at the Broad Street Hilton, 2nd Floor, Freedom Ballroom. It's time to celebrate!"

Mally and Pat hugged as they moved toward the stairs. After weeks of preparation, it was time to let loose, to celebrate. In spite of the heavy physical, emotional and mental output, there was always enough energy to party and party they would!

Griff was pleased as he called his crew together for the post-show. His careful selection of technicians, experience and his personality had made the difference.

"Great first full run with an audience, guys! Thanks so much." He continued, a smile spreading on his face, "It's time to relax, enjoy some brew, good food and compliments. See you all at the Hilton."

In the lobby, Vera had all she could do to stay upright. As she grasped Joe's elbow, she held on with all the strength she still had. "Baby Doll, are you all right?" Kaplan's passion for Vera belied his own denial. With or without booze fueling her moods, he was mad for her. He had become her enabler and protector. "Do you want me to take you back to our hotel?"

"Damn you, Joe," Vera snapped, pulling away. "I'm not missing the party, so save it!" "Baby Doll, you're tight, out of it!" With a shove, Vera pushed him. "Screw you! I'm going, so call me a cab, now!" Even in the bag, Vera held the strings. Withholding sex was her most potent lever and she knew it. "You want some later, Joe? Call me a fucking cab!"

Kaplan sighed, took Vera's hand and led her to the curb. This evening's success was critical for the Kaplan and Maggli organization. Vera's drunkenness could produce a taint over the otherwise celebratory nature of the evening. Kaplan steeled himself for a mine field of unpredictable behavior. The critics, company, staff and team of *Centipede* awaited him, as did invited dignitaries. Hailing a cab, he helped Vera in and closed the door. As the cab pulled away, he thought of better times.

Chapter 14

The Party

The lights of Philadelphia blinked all around as they rode to the Hilton. Oblivious to the City of Brotherly Love, Vera was anesthetized by complimentary champagne at the theatre and several Jack Daniels at their hotel.

How she detested the small talk, fawning, and shallow chit chat at openings. Feigning interest was a game, the booze her cover. After all, she was a Broadway legend. People revered her, were in awe of her. She had to keep her image going, though in truth, she had little confidence to spare.

Joe glanced over at the silent, stone-faced woman at his side. Memories of her came flooding back. He had fallen hard—was it just six months ago? She was a stunner! He'd never met a woman so beautifully paved, or one he wanted as much. What man in his right mind wouldn't?

He was deeply in love. Vera's beauty, still in evidence, her body and rampant libido needs matched his. Wining, dining and bedding her brought him immense satisfaction and fed his ego. Their coupling was fueled by cash and convenience. They lived in a constant state of excess, consuming each other day and night.

The cab was at the Hilton and Joe paid the driver. Taking Vera's arm he led her into the hotel, she was weaving through the lobby trying to gain equilibrium with each step. At the elevator, Kaplan pressed a button and waited for the door to close. He turned to her with ardor of a love-sick boy.

"Baby Doll, are you going to stay mad? Please, let's enjoy! The show is a sure winner, and you're more beautiful than ever." Vera smiled through her haze and reached for his fly, sliding down the zipper and giving his hardening cock a deliberate squeeze. Kaplan let out a sigh, savoring her hand. As the door slid open, he zipped his pants, steadying her for a party in full swing.

The Hilton ballroom was alive with activity. The press mingled with VIPs, cast and crew, management and first nighters, all keen to be part of the celebration. *Centipede* had brought down the house. The innovative, never-before-seen concept was soon heading to Broadway and would undoubtedly be an enormous hit. For the Kaplan-Maggli organization, that meant profit. For Owen, it meant, "I told you so!" He had never flagged in his belief that his idea would sweep the theatre world, in spite of the initial resistance to his proposals. If tonight's response was any indication, he was home free.

On the dance floor, several of the gypsies gyrated and spun to the percussive beat. The musicians played their hearts out, enjoying the obvious pleasure of those on the floor. Jonas danced with Nora, while

Phillipe partnered Cynthia. Other cast members, including Joe, Jim, Fran and Liz all danced free form, competing to see who would garner the most attention.

Chad was in the glow of romance as his girl accompanied him to the party. Mary Jane Douglas was close to becoming his fiancée, just as soon as she finished her degree in Psychology from Wayne State University in Detroit. She had flown in to spend precious time with him. They were saving money to eventually live in New York. Mary Jane would try to find a clinical job in her field.

The ballroom was packed as celebrants enjoyed the open bar, buffet and incredible eye candy. Performers were stunning—attractive, fit and young. They were the public's fantasy. Who was with whom? Which dancers were gay? Were they great in bed?

Maggli walked proudly through the throng of well-wishers, with Gary close behind. It was obvious Kaplan-Maggli had produced a hit! As they approached a table of gypsies, Gary stopped short noticing a familiar figure, Jonas, holding court. Jonas noticed Gary immediately. "Gary you look great," he said cheerfully. Reaching out, he took Gary in his arms and gave him a bear hug. Gary stood, arms limp at his side, not knowing how to react. It had been over a year since the accident and though his injuries had healed, his psyche was still tender. The memory of Jonas' rampant infidelity throughout their partnership lingered. In contrast, Gary had always remained faithful.

"Jonas, the show looks great." Jonas smiled, his pride showing, "Come over. I want to introduce you!" Gary followed, reluctantly.

"You know Phillipe, of course." Phillipe stood, extending his hand to Gary, who took it briefly. "And this is Cynthia and Nora, two great additions to the show." Gary smiled, slightly. Jonas continued, noting the awkward moment.

"Gary was a gypsy, a terrific dancer." "Oh," said Nora, giving a little wave. "Nice to meet you," she added with little sincerity.

"Well, I better get going," said Gary, looking around for Maggli. "Good to see you, Jonas," he said, glancing at Phillipe, who nodded. "Good luck with the show. It's going to be a big hit."

"Thanks, Hon. Take care of yourself." Gary hurried off, the emotional pain still there.

Owen visited with reporters and critics alike. Secretly, he detested the intrusion, the meaningless conversations, the adoration and fawning. He would prefer a one-on-one with Pat, the thought of making love to her hastened his desire. Already he was charting the evening ahead in his suite: Pat naked in his arms, a champagne buzz and sex, lots of it.

Across the room Mally, Griff, and Dick huddled around a large carafe of wine. Dana was too far along to travel, the baby's arrival only weeks away. Dick, now Assistant Stage Manager, enjoyed his new job; he doubled in the ensemble, but was looking forward to working in management fulltime.

"Mally darling, you look exquisite," said Griff, his obvious pride spilling over. Mally was stunning in her new dress, her radiance like a bright marquee.

"Oh, Griff, I thought *Bravo Business* was thrilling, but this? Unbelievable!" Mally took his hand and kissed him gently. Griff sighed, pulling her close. He wished they could leave immediately, but knowing an early exit was considered rude. No, he would bide his time. Making love to Mally later was worth the wait.

Pat wandered the crowd looking for Owen. Leaving the dance floor, she stepped to the terrace and heard a heated argument. A large hedge of shrubbery blocked her view. Straining for details one of the voices was familiar - Owen!

"I told you earlier to back off," he snarled. Pat wondered, 'Who was he talking to? Nora Blake?' She'd been obvious for weeks. Moving closer while staying hidden, she heard the woman begging, slurring words, completely out of control.

"Fuck me, Owen, come on! Face it, you want to," she howled. A fierce scuffle ensued as sounds cut through the air. "Off me, bitch!" he yelled. Then a slap so violent it crackled. Pat had heard enough. Rushing around the hedge, she stopped short. A woman was on the ground, her mouth bleeding profusely. 'Oh God, it's Vera!' Owen stood, shaking with rage.

Realizing they were no longer alone, he turned. "Pat! Shit, what are you doing here?" His adrenalin was in overdrive. "Get the fuck out of here, now!" His sudden fury frightened her as she ran to the elevator and pushed a button for the lobby and grabbed a cab out front.

Back on the terrace, Owen pulled Vera up roughly. She stumbled, shouting caustically, "You bastard, you'll be sorry. I'll fix you, you son of a bitch!"

"Oh? How, Vera? Confessing to your boyfriend you want to fuck me for old time's sake?"

"This isn't over, Owen!" "Yes it is," he snapped. "Now get out of my sight!"

For a moment, he took a hard look at her. How could he have wasted his talent on Vera, relentlessly in pursuit of her success? He had loved her like no other. And now, she was drunk, washed up.

"Good bye Vera." Hurrying back to the party, he searched for Pat, steering his way through the crowd. Suddenly a large woman with a shark-like leer came at him with a mic in hand.

"Mr. Matthews, you've got a hit on your hands," the ample reporter exclaimed. "Do you have any comments, Mr. Matthews?" "None, lady," he tossed, going in the opposite direction.

"Well, that was rude, I must say," she remarked to her cameraman.

Joe was concerned. 'Where is she?' Vera had disappeared during the festivities and, knowing she was inebriated when they arrived, worried she might be out of control somewhere. He began to search the halls.

Meanwhile, Vera had stumbled into a nearby restroom, relieved to be alone. Steadying herself at the sink, she turned on the cold tap and rinsed off the caked blood. It was difficult, painful; her face had begun to swell. She must hide the damage so Joe would never know. 'I'll create a story, after all I'm an actress, one of the best.'

After removing the evidence as best she could, additional general repair was in order. She gently combed her hair, wincing as she hooked a tangle. Face powder was next to cover and camouflage the bruise. Fresh lipstick was last as she took an approving look. 'Ah, my décolletage,' she thought, repositioning her ample breasts. She couldn't disappoint him.

The air was cool as Pat let herself in. Sobbing she replayed what she had witnessed at the Hilton. She'd never seen Owen so angry, so out of control. In the thirteen months together, there were moments of doubt, misunderstandings and jealousy, but never anything hateful or cruel. 'Could that happen to me if Owen moves on?' She shuddered at the thought.

Suddenly, loud banging on the door. "Pat, are you there? Please, Baby, open up!" Owen's voice brought chills running through her entire being. Peering through the viewer, one look brought Owen close up, a drawn look of concern etched on his face. Pat melted as she removed the chain and opened the door.

There was a rush as Owen swept into the room, reached for Pat and pulled her close. His manner was gentle now, the antithesis of his recent behavior as he whispered, "Baby, I'm so sorry you had to see that. Vera was crazed and drunk again."

His mouth found hers as he began caressing her face. Pat caved under his touch, his once again.

Chapter 15

The Reviews

Light found its way into the room. Jonas stirred, painfully squinting as he opened his crusty eyes. With the first sign of morning, he welcomed the sun's warmth against his face. The morning brought awareness of too much partying the previous night.

Phillipe's arms enfolded him. Spooning, they had fallen asleep quickly. Jonas loved the feel of Phillipe. His taut body was a delight, his smell intoxicating every sense. Not wishing to disturb, Jonas gently inched his way off the bed. Last night's torrid sex was all over him and he had to pee. Moving toward the bathroom, he welcomed a chance to stretch and relieve his bladder.

They had returned late from a triumphant evening, somewhat tipsy and horny as hell. The long awaited opening, subsequent party and praise was heady and exciting, but the crush of the crowd created a need to return to their hotel. In spite of fatigue, they engaged in randy sex for hours. Now, a hot shower was just the thing to sooth tired muscles. As he turned on the spray, the door opened and Phillipe stood smiling at him.

He was stunning, perfectly proportioned, head to toes, long legs and irresistible tight buns. The dark curly ringlets of hair that hung at the nape of his neck, and the patch at his genitals stirred Jonas. He was totally turned on as Phillipe joined him under the warm spray. Standing close, he reached for the soap and lathered Jonas, playing with his shaft. "Oh Babe, yes!" cried Jonas, unable to hold back. As Jonas peaked, Phillipe's mouth covered his, through the explosion. He held tightly to Phillipe, his release complete.

"Oh Babe, you're the absolute best," he murmured kissing Phillipe. "Oh? Show me, Cheri," he whispered, fully erect, waiting for the same. Through the ensuing moments Jonas held firm, reveling in the pleasure he brought. When he finished, he turned off the water and grabbed a towel. "Nice towel rack," he giggled, hanging it on Phillipe's still attentive anatomy.

"We better get ready. I'm starved and there's not a lot of time before we report," said Jonas, it was 10:45. "What time is the call, Cheri?" "It's at noon. We have two runs today."

15 minutes later, groomed and dressed, they went to the corner diner for the daily breakfast special. They featured 3 egg omelets for $2.99 and today's was their favorite, ham and cheese. "Black coffees and two specials with toast, please," said Jonas. They fueled up for another full day of *Centipede*.

On the way to the theatre Phillipe asked, "Do you think there will be any more changes next week? I've been told that shows continue to be fine-tuned." "Possibly and, most likely since the show's still new," replied Jonas.

Griff was awake when the phone rang. He had been up for a short time having showered and shaved. Mally was still sleeping, as he picked up.

"Griff, Owen." The voice on the other end was tinged with enthusiasm. "It looks like we've got ourselves a hit! *The Philadelphia Inquirer* has given us a rave, as well as several TV news stations!" "That's great,

Owen." "Yeah, well it won't be this easy in Detroit, as you well know. They're always laying for an Owen Matthews show in car town!"

"It's hard to say until we test the waters. Who knows? Maybe this concept will disarm them." "I knew there was a reason I hired you, Griff. You always see the positive side. Well pal, time will tell, right?"

"You set the call for noon. What is your plan today?" Owen was always one step ahead of everyone, including Griff. "We'll give them a pep talk; share the reviews and a short clean-up."

"OK, see you then, thanks for the good word! You make my job easy." Mally was stirring slightly as he glanced over. Checking the clock, it was time to wake her, time to get to the theatre. In a few hours, the matinee would be in full swing. He had a preset to do before long and a rumble in his stomach reminded him that breakfast was needed soon.

'First things first, Griffen,' he thought as he bent over the bed. Leaning down, he kissed her tenderly. She looked so inviting, so sensuous lying there. He pulled back the sheet, her naked body taking his breath away. Startled by the chill, she opened her eyes.

"What time is it?" They had returned only a few hours before, exhausted from the revelry of opening night. Tired, they had a quick nightcap and slipped into bed, no loveys tonight. In minutes, they were both asleep, wrapped in each other's arms.

"Time to get up, my darling. How was your sleep?" Mally smiled, stretching as she reached for him. "Come here," she whispered. It was temptation at its best, irresistible at any hour. Sitting on the edge of the bed, she guided his hand to her mound. Griff playfully touched and teased. It didn't take very long as she let go, erupting in ripples. 'Self-made orgasms were never like this,' she thought, recalling the first time her young fingers explored and found pleasure. A warm shower followed as Griff ordered breakfast for them.

Twelve floors up, the mood was different. Joe Kaplan had found Vera wandering the Hilton the previous evening. The revelers were few and had passed him commenting on his success. At the moment his sulk was obvious, compliments forgotten.

'How dare she cause me worry?' He was all too aware that she was totally wasted. How many had seen her in that condition? He was worried about his image and hers. On the way back to the hotel, he struggled to keep her upright while flagging down a cab on Broad Street. With sheer determination and much difficulty he got her to their suite and put her to bed.

Hours later, fresh sunlight peeking through the drapes, Joe woke and looked at the disheveled wave of red hair on the pillow; he heard soft moans and noticed movement. Vera appeared from under a wad of bedclothes, intensely hung over. He wasn't happy or horny. 'God, the fucking I'm getting isn't worth the fucking I'm getting,' he mused. Slowly making it upright, Vera fought the morning, sunlight and a splitting headache.

"Joe, I need a shot with a beer chaser! Please Joe." Like a robot, he went to the bar, his only recourse to enable, to appease, to prove his love. In spite of his disgust, he was hopeful she loved him. He was mad for Vera, convincing himself that booze was her lifeline, her means of existing.

Jack Daniels, was her preferred morning and evening anesthetic; he studied the glass of amber fluid, still mystified that this could bandage pain and regret, at least temporarily. Next, a cold beer in another glass.

Downing her friend 'Jack' quickly, the beer chaser followed close behind. She was detached, numbed, in a zone, nightgown loose, straps off her shoulders. Inching her way back on the bed, she mumbled, "Fuck me, Joe? You still want to, don't you?" She raised her arms over her head, "Come on, damn it, hurry up!"

Reluctantly, he pulled the satin nightgown off noticing new bruises, a raised and purple area below her right eye and mottled skin on her cheek. "What the hell?" Tossing the nightgown aside, he looked closer. "Baby Doll, what the fuck happened?"

She was caught! How would she explain last night's skirmish with Owen? In spite of her condition, she navigated a story Joe would buy. After all, she had pulled it off before. "Oh Joe, I didn't want to tell you, this being opening week and all." Kaplan sat down, staring at her with the scrutiny of a prosecuting attorney.

"Owen Matthews did this! I ran into him last night. Joe, honey, he tried to rape me. I fought and fought and he hit me. My screams scared him off! It was horrible, horrible!" Vera began to cry, falling into a pillow, trying to make it good. Kaplan slowly stood, shaking.

"I don't believe this," he bellowed. "I don't fucking believe this!" Grabbing a cigarette, he lit and paced back and forth. Vera propped up further and watched his ire rising to such a feverish pitch he might have a coronary. She was enjoying this, enjoying his upset. 'Blaming Owen was brilliant! He'd be sorry.'

Stumping out his smoke, he sat on the bed, his eyes never leaving her. "You're telling me after all this time, Matthews wants to fuck you on his opening night?" Vera nodded, "Yes, Joe. He wanted to."

"Bull shit, I don't believe it! It's a fucking lie!" Suddenly Vera realized, 'I've gone too far.'

"Joe, why would I lie? He's never accepted our divorce. He's never stopped wanting me."

"Nonsense, you've convinced yourself of that. I happen to know he's got it bad for one of the girls in the show. He's been through with you for some time!" The remark stung.

"How dare you to talk to me like that, Joe?" Kaplan grabbed her wrists, forcing her down, his face beet red. "Never bring his name up again, do you understand?" Vera squirmed trying to wrench herself free, but Kaplan held firm. Sobs filled the room as he finally released her. "Come on, time to check out and go back to New York. The show's a hit, we're all done here."

Chapter 16

The Wrap-up

The first weekend of *Centipede* ended, bringing raves from the public. Pure dance shows were unknown to theatre fans. As each performance ended, it was clear his latest form of musical theatre captivated audiences in Philadelphia. The short run was sold out. Owen's brainchild was a new sensation.

The cast and production team prepared for the last two shows. It was Saturday and following the matinee and evening performances, excitement was building. Detroit was next. How would audiences there react? Sunday was dark, a day off for union performers. *Centipede* would take a break. Crews would pack up, load out, and move the show to the next venue, the Fisher Theatre.

The weather had turned cold, a sign that winter was just around the corner. The company would spend Thanksgiving in Michigan and Christmas in New York. A week of previews would usher in the Broadway opening mid-January.

Although cast call was 1:00, some gypsies arrived early and gathered in the house; only two shows to go, then they'd be off to motor city. Some chatted; others sat staring at the empty stage. A few dozed finding a short nap beneficial, for the long day ahead. Only an occasional sound from a crew member broke through the quiet house.

Mally and Pat were enjoying warm beverages as they watched the company file in. Jonas and Phillipe joined them. "Two shows to go, my sweets," crooned Jonas, looking forward to moving on. The Fisher is a great theatre complex, but Detroit is so-so." "We've never played Detroit," stated Pat. It was not a stop for *Bravo Business*. What's it like?" "It's a blue collar town with a careworn inner city," he said with a knowing smile.

Joe, Jerry, and Jim, sauntered in. Sitting together they gossiped, drank coffee and enjoyed the eye candy provided by Chad and Jeff, both straight and highly unlikely tricks.

"Boy, Chad's a honey," whispered Jim, who was always cruising. "I'd like to lap that up."

"Hell, I wanted to nail him last year, but no go," added Jerry, with regret. Joe listened, a knowing smile forming.

"Have you run out of sissies, Jer?" Glaring, Jerry snapped, "You're a cheeky bitch! Get stuffed!" Joe loved to get a rise out of him. "Quiet, you'll scare the straight boys, you trashy queen!"

"Who's a trashy queen, Joe? You can't keep it in your pants," snorted Jerry, feeling triumphant. "Pipe down, you Mary," whispered Jim, growing irritated. For a moment there was silence.

Joe whispered in Jerry's ear. "Maybe Jeffrey boy will take some of mine since there's so little of yours!" No time for a comeback, Jerry pulled away just as the production team arrived. Owen and Griff took the stairs to the stage.

"Company, please move in closer and sit in the first two rows, house left, please," said Griff. The gypsies moved and waited for the meeting to start. "I think we're all here," said Griff, finishing a head count. When he had their attention he began.

"We have two shows today. At the end of the performance this evening, please turn in your wardrobe to the dressers. Before you leave, make sure you have collected all your personal belongings. Anything left will be tossed. Be sure to have your trunks out in the hall by 2:00 a.m. Take hand luggage with you with enough clothes and toiletries for travel and one day off. The chosen hotels are on the callboard. Be sure you check where you will be staying. Be in front of our hotel at 6:45 a.m. Buses will take you to the airport. You are booked on Northwest Airlines flight #336, leaving at 9:00. Don't miss it! Questions anyone? A hand popped up. "Yes, Nora?"

"How far is the Fisher Theatre complex from our hotels?"

"The Fisher is within a half mile. I believe most of you are at the Davenport which is right across the boulevard. It's a pretty convenient set-up. However, the downtown area isn't safe and a cab ride away. We don't recommend you go into the inner city unless in groups. Please carry the phone number of the theatre, which I will post for your convenience."

"Will there be additional rehearsals, before the opening next Friday?" Jeff, being new to the process, wanted details. Owen replied, "We will continue to tighten the show. There will be no previews before opening, but we will clean, tighten and make changes if necessary. At this point, I believe the show is solid and ready. However, I expect all of you to maintain the integrity of the work, stay fresh, focused and committed."

Nora nudged Cynthia, glancing at Owen, as she whispered, "I'm focused all right, on him!" Pat heard the remark. Cupping her hand as she seethed, "The bitch is trouble, Mal! I can feel it."

"Oh for heaven's sake Pat, stop it!" Pat's insecurity was wearing thin.

"If there are no further questions, you are excused," said Griff. "Half hour, please!" As the company filed up the steps to the stage and dressing rooms, Nora bided her time until everyone had left. She approached Owen as she reached the stage.

"Owen, could I have a word with you?" He looked at the attractive brunette. "Yes, Nora. What can I do for you?" Nora stepped closer, within range to feel his breath on her face.

"I was wondering if there would be a chance to become a regular in New York?" Owen smiled. She hadn't gone unnoticed in rehearsal, imagining her sexually. At the moment, he was flattered by her interest, but kept his business tone.

"You're an exceptional dancer, and I admire your dedication. I'll keep you in mind," he said, stepping aside. "Thank you Owen. You won't regret it."

"Good show, Nora." As she walked away, he went to the stage door for a smoke. The two shows went quickly. Spirits were high as the company prepared for travel.

Griff and crew dismantled the stage décor—lights, units, sound board, rigging and scrim. Costumes and shoes were carefully packed. Undergarments would be laundered in Detroit, costumes dry cleaned and repaired if necessary. Nira and her crew had returned to New York, having completed the costume renovations. Roxanne Gray, a colleague of Griff's for years, was now in charge of wardrobe. Sandy and his core musicians packed for the trip. The locals had been great to work with.

There was no time tonight for carnal distractions, or drinks. Packing, sleeping and waking in time for the morning call was foremost in their minds. Detroit would be home to *Centipede* for the next three weeks.

Chapter 17

Motor City

Morning came quickly, a rude awakening for Pat. The alarm blasted at 5:30, sending her into a struggle of jarred nerves and numbness. She was still in a fog as she sat to pee. Relieving her bladder was the first order of business as she reflected on last night's performance.

Centipede was a dancer's dream, but at this hour, it was hard to justify the workout, judging how sore and wasted she felt. As she stood and flushed, she caught a glimpse in the mirror. What a shock! Usually her approval began with application of face paint and generous applause. Travel days were impossible.

'You'll need serious repair, Irish.' Turning on the shower, she waited for the right temperature and stepped into the spray. The heat and wetness on her skin was refreshing, helping her wake up; she sighed and reached for the shampoo. 'Thank God I trimmed eight inches off this mop for the show,' she thought with a smile.

Running her hands down her body she thought of Owen. 'Had it been only a few days since they made love?' She was horny again, the lack of sex annoying. Closing her eyes, she imagined his hands on her. Her fingers would have to suffice today, her body shaking as she peaked, grateful for the release, rinse and relaxation. After drying off, she glanced at her watch, realizing the call was in 45 minutes! 'What will Detroit be like?' She'd know soon, as she hurried to dress.

The gypsies waited patiently in the cold, clustering together for warmth, sipping coffee. This early call was a killer, many complaining of soreness and exhaustion. The consensus was always "no pain, no gain" mantra, but at this hour and in this condition, the travel day ahead would be a welcome relief.

Through the darkness, headlights shone, as an airport bus pulled up. With a loud whoosh, the door opened, allowing still sleepy and weary gypsies to take seats for the 25-minute ride.

Pat, Mally, Jonas and Phillipe stuffed their dance bags into the overhead rack and settled in. Pat had grabbed coffee. Mally was delighted to find tea at the hotel kiosk. Jonas had his customary Coke in hand, while Phillipe carried a small thermos filled with ice water, his preferred drink.

The bus filled, Fred Martin, the company manager, took a final head count, all were there. In seconds, the door closed and the trip began. The buildings of downtown sped by as quiet descended over the group. Before long, the airport was in view. Fred stood as the bus came to a stop.

"Attention, company! Please go into the terminal and wait near the door until everyone is present and accounted for. I will distribute tickets at that time. Thank you." When they were assembled, Fred spoke. "Listen carefully; go to Northwest Airlines, Gate 5. Your flight number is 336. Please remain in the gate area until we are called to board. Thank you."

Within the hour, the flight to Detroit was in the air. The company quieted as the new Boeing 727 lifted into the sky over Pennsylvania and turned to its northwest route. Show people were traditionally nervous, always superstitious and relieved to arrive, to dance another day.

Most of the company dozed during the 2½ hour flight. Mally loved flying and had taken a window seat to view the country from aloft, enjoying the colorful and varied patches below.

Pat, on the other hand, dreaded flying. From her first time to Norfolk last year and all times since, she was nervous, with sweaty hands and hyper thoughts, grateful for every landing.

Detroit Metro Airport was alive with activity as the gypsies deplaned and grouped around Fred. "Follow me; our bus to town is this way," indicating the double doors ahead. The bus was at curbside and the group climbed aboard. Tomorrow was time to replenish, relax, write home and catch up with off-stage activities.

Chapter 18

Routine and Rest

Griff and his crew arrived later Sunday, checked in and went directly to the Fisher Theatre to get familiar with backstage. *Centipede* trucks pulled in late Monday morning, delayed a few hours by a sudden snow storm on the Ohio Turnpike. Griff's drivers were some of the best, but even for veterans, bad weather could produce delay and a time crunch for set up.

The sleepers were awakened by a jarring phone. Griff, groggy with fatigue, reached for the receiver. "This is Edwards," he said, as he glanced at his watch.

"Griff, this is Ed Franklin. We're in!" "Good God, Ed. You okay? I got your message late last night. How bad was it?"

"We held up in Sandusky for a few hours. Visibility was nil, so no way in hell did we chance it! All's well." "Great! Get some shut eye and a hot shower. We'll see you at three." Thanks, boss, see you later."

Griff glanced at Mally. 'Even asleep, you're an angel,' he thought, thrilled to be hers. Had it only been a year?

Slipping out of bed, he padded to the door and found complimentary copies of *The Detroit News* and *Free Press*. In his carry-on bag at the foot of the bed, he found instant coffee, travel mug, and an immersion coil heater. The brew was not the greatest, but it would do for now.

Minutes later, water boiling, his morning brew was ready. A Chicago boy at heart, he drank it black, sipping carefully. In moments, he felt his senses awaken as he began to read the news of the day.

Two ads for *Centipede* caught his eye. He noted the details, wondering how Detroit audiences and critics would respond to Owen's newest invention. The town was traditionally tough on his shows. After overwhelming and favorable response in Philadelphia, hopefully, Detroit audiences might follow suit.

After scanning the papers, he set them aside and headed to the bathroom to tinkle and shower. 'I'll give my darling a few extra minutes of sleep,' he thought stepping into the tub. Setting the water to the right temperature the spill gently enveloped him while he lathered, it felt good. Out of the corner of his eye he noticed the shower curtain moving; and, there in all her glory and birthday suit, was Mally, admiring the view.

"Let me do that," she said, stepping into the tub and embracing him. Taking over the soap she did his back first, then lower. He sighed at her touch and gentle strokes responding with growing parts. She continued caressing his shaft, enjoying her handiwork. "Turn around," she said softly. Without hesitation, he was completely hers.

She kneeled, rinsed off the suds and took him in her mouth, moving back and forth, fondling his buttocks; his moans getting louder and longer. "Oh, Mally, yes, yes, harder, more," he urged. Tonguing and licking him was fun! Feeling his climax close, he steadied himself bracing on her shoulders until he let go, each ripple bigger than the last. When he was able to speak, he took her face in his hands, kissing her gently. "I love you so much, my angel."

"Come with me, darling man, you're not done yet." Taking his hand, she guided him out of the tub and wrapped a fluffy towel around his waist. Motioning him to sit on the toilet lid, she reached for another towel. Griff took it, drying her gently, as he moved down her body. It was obvious she was now aroused. Her fragrance was enticing, her mound within inches. Dropping the towel, he gently plied her open, caressing and fingering as he tasted. Mally began to writhe with each thrust, his finger moving faster then slower, pausing to caress and tongue the nub of pleasure, her orgasm pressure was building. "More Griff, more," she begged, gripping the towel bar behind him. Suddenly, her body exploded into ripples of pure pleasure as he held her firmly. "Oh my love, your taste is ambrosia!" When calmed, he released her gently and glanced at his watch.

"I have to meet the crew at noon, we better order breakfast!" "I'm starved also, I'll eat anything!" A smile passed between them as they began dressing.

Griff ordered their favorites: eggs over easy, sausage and a side of pancakes for himself and a cheese omelet, toast, and tea for her. Time was moving fast, the *Centipede* dry tech was at 4:00. All technical elements of the production would be in place, the show running cue-to-cue without performers.

Today's activity included unloading and setting up. So far, there were no obvious problems. The Fisher, a time-honored venue, was one of the best on the circuit.

Owen's day included conference calls to the power boys, Kaplan and Maggli and a handful of investors. Next, he would sit next to Griff, noting details during the dry run. The evening was reserved for Pat. He would insist on sharing a quiet dinner with her in his suite followed by a night of erotic fun. He had purposely held back, stifling his rampant libido. She was a distraction and there was too much at stake to loosen his hold on *Centipede*. He had to admit he was feeling a lack of her and definitely wanted his needs met. After all, they were dark tonight, and he, horny as hell.

Jonas was primed. His position on Owen's team would soon allow him to hang up his dancing shoes. He had no illusions. As a professional dancer, his career would be short-lived. Like any professional athlete, age would take its toll and, eventually, he would have to find other work; hopefully something more rewarding and long lasting. Owen had opened a door. Likewise, Phillipe, a brilliant dancer with stunning looks and savvy, would eventually have to look for other creative avenues. One option might be in the fashion world where he could work as a model. His drive, sophistication and sense of style would serve him well. For now, he was content to work for Owen and be with his soul mate.

Pat was restless. She missed Owen. Seeing him day after day during rehearsals and the impersonal way he acted toward her on company time was frustrating. Knowing his interest in her would always take second to his artistic process galled her, adding insecurity and doubt. Only deep sleep or being held in his arms could lift her moods. No, Pat wanted assurances that their bond was unbreakable, solid against ambitious chorines, an ex-wife's persistence and demands of the business. Reaching for the phone, she dialed Griff's suite. An ebullient voice greeted her.

"Hello?" "Mal, it's me! What are you doing today?"

"Oh Pat, I was hoping you'd call! Griff's already at the Fisher. I have the whole day to myself! What sounds good?" Pat was quick to respond. "How about going shopping and later to a movie?"

Mally's voice grew serious, "Pat, remember we were told it isn't very safe in this city if we don't know our way around. But, we could ask the concierge's advice." "Good idea! What's your time frame?" "How about 30 minutes in the lobby? Okay with you?" "Perfect! See you soon," replied Pat. A day with her best friend would be a great distraction from her insecurity. Every moment off stage was waiting to get back on for his pleasure and praise.

Chapter 19

Back to Work

Tuesday's call was noon. A rested ensemble grouped in the first two rows perusing the Fisher's auditorium, which was larger than many Broadway theatres. When roll was taken, Griff spoke.

"Company, welcome to Detroit. As you can see, this theatre is well-appointed. The Fisher Building adjoining us has many shops, good restaurants and a popular piano bar. Outside, Grand Boulevard is constantly busy, so use caution when crossing to and from the hotel. Find your dressing rooms and choose your spots. Check out the backstage and note the changing areas. You'll be working with local wardrobe support serving as your dressers, the same as in Philadelphia. Take a moment to introduce yourselves.

"The wardrobe has been sorted, marked and placed in the changing areas on the lower level under the stage. Check where your costumes have been hung and your shoes placed. Please walk the route to stage right and left. Also, remember to keep your voices down near the pit." As Griff concluded, Owen arrived. "Do you have anything to add?"

"Gang, we have four days to the opening. I'll be taking notes and cleaning rough spots in the choreography. You've had two days off, so don't be lax! The show must be as clean and sharp as the last performance in Philly." Griff added, "Owen, do you want to say anything about the Detroit press?"

"Well, to be honest, it's a tough room. Detroit is surprisingly hip and short on praise! We are dealing with a new concept here and *Centipede* may or may not be well accepted by the public or media."

Nora leaned in to Jonas whispering, "I've heard they lay for Owen every time he comes here." Jonas shrugged.

"Is there a question, Nora?" Blushing, she responded quickly. "No, Owen! I just think it's unfair for people to criticize such an amazing work," she gushed. She was considered a brown nose. "Oh, for Christ's sake," mumbled Pat, rolling her eyes. "Be careful, Pat! Just let it go," whispered Mally.

"Is there anything else to add? It's time to work. Take a half hour to change, hydrate and stretch." "We'll start at the top," added Griff.

The days were long as the gypsies anticipated Friday's official opening. On Thursday afternoon, the tech dress was going smoothly. The second act number was moving full out when Jerry Thompson's jazz shoe caught an edge during a triple spin. Stumbling to the stage floor, his screams stopped the show. Griff brought the stage lights down and work lights up immediately. Rushing to Jerry's side, it was obvious he was severely injured. Others clustered around as he writhed in pain.

"Goddamn, this hurts," he wailed. "Get him to the green room," Owen bellowed. Chad, Jonas, and Phillipe carried Jerry to the actor's lounge, placing him on the couch.

"Griff, call Dr. Kennedy, the house doc! Get some ice too, damn it," he ordered. During his dance career he had seen many injuries. He had a bad feeling about this one.

"On the way, Griff," Dick called, as he ran to the lobby.

"Where's Jeff? Get Jeff, we must continue the run," Griff added. I'm right here, Griff," said Jeff, joining the shaken group.

"Griff, is Dr. Kennedy on site?" Like a concerned father, Owen knelt at Jerry's side trying to calm him.

"Jerry, the doctor has been called. Try not to move." Beads of sweat covered Jerry's forehead, his body shaking in pain.

"This is a mother fucker," he cried as Griff returned. "Kennedy's on the way. He's in the building. His nurse was able to contact him."

"Where's the goddamn ice?" "Here, Owen!" Dick returned with an ice bucket, plastic bag and two bar towels.

"Put the ice in the bag, wrap a towel around it. Jerry, lie still. We're going to make you comfortable until the doc gets here." There was a sudden commotion as Dr. Kennedy arrived.

"Company, please go to your dressing rooms until we call you back," said Griff. "Jonas, please start running Jenkins through the numbers.

Dick, close the door." There were murmurs as the gypsies filed out.

"Get his pants off so I can examine him," said Kennedy. "Young man, please lie still so we can take care of you."

Jerry squirmed and moaned as Owen and Griff held him. "Easy, Jerry, try to lift your butt," Owen said, calmly.

Once the pants were off, Kennedy examined his knee probing and moving it slowly.

"I can't take much more of this," cried Jerry. Kennedy frowned.

"He has torn his Meniscus and needs surgery as soon as possible. We'll get him to Detroit General. Mr. Edwards, please call the number on this card for an ambulance." Jerry moaned again.

"I have something for pain in my kit," he said, pointing to his bag. Griff gave it to him. Kennedy took out a needle and small vial. In seconds, the needle was in Jerry's arm and his whimpering subsided. Minutes later paramedics were on hand, placed him on a stretcher and were on their way. Griff turned to Owen.

"We'll have to go with Jenkins. Jonas is rehearsing him now." "Good! Damn, this should not have happened to Jerry. He's been with me for years," said Owen, regret in his voice. "He'll not be able to work for a while; his knee is shot, perhaps his career as well. Who can we bring in?"

"Let me check the chorus roster of Kaplan and Maggli, someone available as soon as possible. In the meantime Jeff, will be on duty. Owen, should I call the cast back tonight for a full run?"

"We have no choice. Set the call for 6:30 and we'll run at 7:30. No costumes or make-up needed. Let's get the details worked out. I'll start with notes for the sailor number and continue."

"OK, I'll keep you posted about a replacement," said Griff, reassuringly. He'd contact Kaplan and report the details regarding Jerry.

"You're on top of it as always. Thanks, Griff." Owen left the green room and back to his hotel. Though Owen showed little to no empathy during rehearsals, he considered the loss of one of his own upsetting. As a dancer, he had seen how serious injury could sideline a career. Jerry had served him well on several shows. He was reliable, consistent and technically viable. But a hard fact remained. Jerry had aged and the ending of his career was predictable and realistic. Unfortunately it happened sooner than later.

In his backstage office Griff pondered the course ahead. There were many good dancers but who was the right fit and on such short notice? Pulling his file, he began scanning names. 'The guy needs to be an excellent technician, attractive and a damn quick study,' he thought. A familiar name jumped out. Tim Bartel. He was young, handsome and a veteran of at least two Broadway shows and a national tour, according to his resume. He had been in the original Broadway cast of *Bravo Business* for a year, 'so he's familiar to Owen.' Noting a Manhattan number, Griff dialed. "Hello, Tim Bartel?" "This is. Who's calling?"

"Tim, this is Griff Edwards from Owen Matthews' Productions. Is this a good time?" "Yes, it's fine. What's going on?"

"Kaplan and Maggli are producing a new Matthews' show opening early January. We need a replacement for one of our male dancers who's been injured and unable to continue. Are you available?"

"You're kidding! My unemployment insurance runs out next week!" "Well then?" "Hell yes! Do I need to audition?" "We know your credentials, Tim. You can cut this in short order. How soon can you get to Detroit?" "I'll have to tell my roommate. His girl wants to move in. She's been pressuring him, so, this is perfect!"

"Good. I will arrange your flight from New York and all other details. We'd like you here by tomorrow evening. Our swing will take over until you learn the show." "Who was injured? Anyone I know?" "Jerry Thompson. He's been one of Owen's regulars for years." "Jerry? You're kidding! He teaches jazz at Dance Arts on occasion. Hell of a teacher!" "I'll call back in a few hours with your flight information. Pack for three weeks, and save your receipts. We'll see you soon." "Thanks, Mr. Edwards. I look forward to it."

That evening the rehearsal passed without a snag. Jeff handled Jerry's spot as though he'd performed it for weeks. The proficiency of a swing was critical to any production and Jeff had it.

The press opening, tomorrow night, would be the ultimate test for Owen. He was relieved knowing they were ready in spite of the unexpected setback. Jerry's replacement was now on the way, Jenkins was set and, the show would go on.

Chapter 20

The New Guy

Tim Bartel was single, straight and a womanizer. He was also an outstanding dancer and performer, having garnered considerable praise and notice in his short career.

Born and raised on Long Island, he was the only son among five daughters born to Jack and Ellie Bartel, both former nightclub performers. The Bartels were known for their repartee and soft shoe style and featured on lounge stages of Las Vegas in their day. After retiring from show business, Jack and Ellie opened a neighborhood grocery store with success and settled down to raise their kids. They were determined to keep their children from a life on the wicked stage.

However, little Tim had the bug. From the time he was old enough to execute a basic time step, he wanted to dance. When he wasn't attending school, he was in the basement of the Bartel's modest home, performing in front of a large mirror, mimicking what he had seen in the movies and TV. Gene Kelly was his favorite. He responded to the acrobatic, graceful, masculine style that Kelly demonstrated in his films. He wanted to be just like him.

When he was twelve, he begged for lessons. His request met with skepticism, but clearly his parents saw his gift. After much soul-searching, they gave in, enrolling him in a nearby dance school headed by Andy Simmons, also a former Vegas headliner. Andy took the young man on, teaching him the basics including ballet and tap. From the very beginning, it was clear that Tim had both talent and a drive to succeed. When Andy had taught Tim everything he could, it was time for his young protégé to study in the big city. He arranged an audition at the School of Performing Arts. Tim passed muster and would begin in the fall.

That summer, as a special birthday present, his parents decided to enroll Tim in a two-week camp in the Catskills. It would be his last opportunity for a while to participate in outdoor activities including hiking, swimming, and crafts.

In addition to dance, he had also discovered girls. He noticed them in grade school and admired them from a safe distance. By age thirteen, his curiosity had grown so intense, he thought he would burst. They were mysterious and masturbation was old news. He wanted to experience the real thing.

It happened at summer camp. Her name was Monica and she was stacked! He could tell she liked him, too! She was an older woman of sixteen, a teen counselor and lifeguard. Judging by her flirting and body language, she also seemed experienced in more mature activities. What she could see in his bathing suit was worth pursuing.

It was the last night of camp and "lights out" had been called. Tim waited until everyone in his cabin had settled down. When the other boys were asleep, he eased his way out of the bottom bunk, took a flashlight from under his pillow and tiptoed to the door.

The moon was full and hung in the sky like a magical light, leading him to Monica. She had her own room, which gave her advantage of secrecy. She was waiting on the porch in the darkness as he approached. His flashlight beam caught her standing in the shadows.

"Come on, let's go down there, Tim," she said, pointing to an old barn down the path. "It's not safe in the cabin. Someone might interrupt."

The night was warm and sultry as she led him through the tall grass, her fragrance intoxicating. Tim could see her nipples through the thin camisole, her shorts high enough to outline her mound as the moon etched them in light.

The door creaked as they entered the building. Moving carefully along a wall, she found an old oil lantern; she had been here before and was ready with a match. Lighting it, she carried it to a corner tack room and put it on the floor. It smelled a bit, but the flickering light was just right.

"Oh, thank you Monica, thank you!" Tears meandered down his face as he held her, his heart beating more slowly now. He was no longer a virgin! She had seen to it!

"We better get back, Tim. Sometimes the leaders do a head count and we don't want you caught with your pants down," she giggled. They dressed, put out the lantern and she took Tim's hand. "Come on, sweet boy, time to go." They walked to the cabins as quietly as possible, the silence occasionally broken by one or the other stepping on fallen branches. At her door, he stopped and pulled her close.

"Can I see you again, Monica? Please! I need to, I want to!" She frowned and shook her head.

"Sorry, sweet boy. This was a one-shot time. I go back to Connecticut the day after tomorrow and you have to go home. My boyfriend would be very jealous if he knew what we did!"

"I need you, Monica. I need more, please!" He was shaking, tears spilled down his face. Hugging him tightly she stroked his back.

"Oh Sweetie, shush. You'll find a girl back home to fuck. I promise! This is just the first of many fucks for you. You're good. You really are!" Tim relaxed, laying his head against her shoulder.

"I'll never forget you, never!" Gently, Monica released him and smiled. "Goodbye, sweet boy. Have a good life!" She turned abruptly and entered her cabin.

A wave of sadness enveloped Tim as he walked away slowly. Tomorrow he would return to his family. And next week, he would start his dance journey. How bad could that be?

Tim was on his way, a flight had been arranged out of La Guardia. Seated in the rear of the aircraft, he noticed a stunning woman at the window across the aisle. Her curly red hair fell to her shoulders and a few freckles splashed across her face. She was just his type in tight-fitting pants and sweater. As he continued to stare, she glanced, returning a smile that seemed inviting.

'God, I'd fuck her in a heartbeat,' he thought. In seconds, he was up and crossing the aisle. Sitting down, he fastened his seat belt and turned toward her, using his best come-on.

"Hi, I'm Tim and you are?" Tossing her hair, she looked over with apparent interest. His breath caught as she scrutinized him, a sensual energy invading him, causing a slight disturbance in his Jockeys.

"I'm Ginger." 'Hard part's over,' he thought, his eyes never leaving her.

"Are you getting off in Detroit?" "Yes, I'm a teacher at Wayne State. I've been on sabbatical in London for the past year." "No kidding? That's interesting," he replied, feigning interest. He had to have this one.

"I'm on my way to Detroit to join a production, I'm a professional dancer." "You are? That's exciting. How long will you be in town?" It was looking promising, obvious mutual interest was forming. Tim was hopeful. "Three weeks. We're at the Fisher Theatre. I'll phone once I'm placed in the show. I might be able to get you a seat."

Ginger smiled as she reached for her purse, pen, pad, wrote her phone number for him. "I'm free on Tuesdays and Thursdays. It's a short cab ride from the Fisher." 'This is unreal,' Tim thought, taking the paper, as an announcement was made.

"Ladies and Gentleman, we are beginning our descent into the Detroit area. Please make sure your seats are upright and tray tables back and in a locked position for landing. We will be arriving at Detroit Metro in twenty minutes. Thank you!" They landed right on time.

"Well, Ginger, nice talking to you," said Tim, using his best tone of nonchalance. A look of disappointment crossed her face.

He loved it! "Will you be calling?" 'Clearly, she's bagged and ready for me,' he thought smugly.

"If there's time, yes," he replied with a business tone. "I'm in rehearsal next week and then I'll see." 'Bartel, you're masterful. She's practically begging for a fuck.' What a life!

Chapter 21

An Old Foe

Griff was doing paperwork when his backstage phone rang. The familiar voice of Ralph, the doorman, came through.

"Mr. Edwards, there's a young gentleman here who says he's to report to you. The name is Bartel, Tim Bartel." "Thanks, Ralph, send him back." A wave of relief came over Griff as he put down the phone and walked to the file, pulling a standard chorus contract. There was a knock.

"Come in, Tim." The door opened, a grinning Tim Bartel was there. "Welcome to Detroit, Tim."

"Thanks, Mr. Edwards," he responded, shaking Griff's hand. "Please call me Griff," he said, offering a chair. Tim loosened his brown suede jacket. "How was the trip?"

"It was fine. Good weather, no delays," he said, placing his jacket on the back of the chair.

"Tim, here's your standard chorus contract. You know the drill. Three weeks here at the Fisher, one week off between Christmas and New Year's and two preview weeks in New York, followed by the official opening January 15th at the Royal. You're registered across the street at the Lexington Apartments. It's a decent rate and you'll have access to a kitchen. Most of the cast and crew are staying there."

"When do I start rehearsals? I want to get to it as soon as possible."

"We're dark on Sunday, as you know, so you'll begin Monday and go in the following week. I'd like you to observe the shows tomorrow and familiarize with the work. Jeff Jenkins, our swing, is covering the spot you'll take. I think you'll find the staging exciting and challenging to replicate. Do you have any questions?"

"No, I don't think so, not at the moment anyway." "Be back here at 7:45 so I can introduce you to the cast." "Thanks, Griff. You've been very helpful." "Where's your luggage?" "Oh, the doorman is holding my bags. I packed for three weeks, like you suggested." "Good. I like a man who takes suggestions," said Griff with a smile. "Sign three copies of your contract and return two to me tonight. Keep one for yourself." "Thanks, I will." "Take some time to relax while you can. You have a heavy rehearsal schedule." Tim picked up his jacket and left. 'Getting here is half the job; the rest is a snap,' he thought. Ralph was waiting with his luggage.

Backstage, activity was in full throttle. The dressing rooms alive with pre-show jitters, muffled conversations, make-up and hair prep. Though 7:30 was half hour call, many of the company arrived earlier for extra time to prepare. Most gypsies did barre exercises to strengthen and stretch. Warm-ups were critical. Griff's call was minutes away. The girls chatted as they applied eyeliner and false lashes. There had been a lot of gossip since Jerry's accident.

Nora chimed her way in, "I wonder who will replace Jerry? Has anyone heard?" Mally and Pat exchanged looks. "He'll have to be a fast study and have great technique to pick up this choreography," remarked Cynthia. "Maybe he's good looking and straight," chirped Nora, always hopeful. The others laughed.

"Are you horny?" Liz loved to mock Nora, the perfect foil. "That's nervy, Liz. I don't ask you about your sex life," returned Nora with an edge. She was a target in the dressing room, fairly earned by her big mouth. Nora chalked it up to envy. In her mind, she considered herself one of the most attractive women and the best dancer. "That woman is insufferable," muttered Pat. "Relax, we have a show to do," coaxed Mally. Pat rolled her eyes and continued combing her hair. Twisting it into a chignon, she weighted it with bobby pins and applied Aqua Net.

Griff's voice came through. "Half hour, half hour please. Please report to the green room at 7:50 for a short meeting. Thanks!"

The cast gathered in the actors' lounge. There was a wave of excitement as sounds from the house indicated a sellout. Who could guess Detroit's reaction to *Centipede*?

Griff and Owen worked their way through the group, followed by a new face. Heads turned and whispers floated, 'Who's the guy?' Griff took over.

"Ladies and Gentleman, we are fortunate to have a solid replacement for Jerry. Please welcome Tim Bartel!" There was enthusiastic clapping. Pat stood pale and motionless. Mally noticed, whispering, "Pat, what is it?" She was greeted with silence.

"Tim will watch shows this weekend and begin Monday. Jonas will teach Jerry's show. The company placement call is Friday at 10:00 am." "Tonight is critical, so we need your 200 percent. Detroit is a tough town, so dazzle them," Owen added. With resounding applause, the company dispersed as Griff called, "Places!"

Pat lingered, tears welling up. Paralyzed, she remained frozen. Mally, concerned, reached and hugged her close. "Pat, what is it? Tell me, please!" "It's a long, shitty story. I'll fill you in later," Pat replied, trembling. "Right now, I have to pull it together to get through the show!" Walking to the wings, they passed Nora and Cynthia engaged in animated whispers.

"God, he's gorgeous, perfect for *Centipede*! Did you notice the tight jeans? Oh, man!" Cynthia threw her a look of disgust. "Down girl, the man just arrived. He might be a shit heel in a perfect body." "Well, I like the bad ones," said Nora matter-of-factly. Cynthia turned away, clearly fed up. "The overture's starting. Let's go!" The girls took opening positions as the lights came up. Tim Bartel was shown to the back of the house.

The overture erupted with the sound of brass and *Centipede* was off and running. Bright stage lights revealed dancers, frozen in tableau, a perfect sculpture. Then, slowly, dancer after dancer began to move a swirling mass of perfection. The immediate applause was music to Owen's ears. As the performance continued, each number received loud approval from the crowd. Clearly, it seemed the production had met Detroit's challenge, always critical of Owen's work.

From his position, Tim scanned the group, noting each dancer's technique and style. One woman, a redhead, was the best of the lot. Her body was perfection, her talent eclipsing all others. 'Damn, she looks familiar,' he thought. Noting her long legs, her Irish looks and her charismatic performance, Tim reached back in memory trying to make a connection.

'I know her,' he mused, 'but how?' He couldn't take his eyes off of her. The other female dancers were superfluous at this point. At intermission, he bumped into Owen, who had stepped outside for a needed smoke.

"I'm Tim," he said, extending his hand to the director. "What incredible work!" "Glad you like it, kid. I remember you. *Bravo Business*, the original company, right?" "Yes sir. I left after six months to do a gig at the *Folies Bergère* in Paris."

"Is that what happened to you? Well, if this is a hit, I hope you'll stay on. You're a dynamic dancer, if memory serves. This show requires the best." "Thanks, Owen, glad to be here." Owen smiled knowingly. "I wonder if you'll say that the end of next week? This show will wipe you out, kid! See you Monday."

Later, following standing ovations and many group bows, the cast would gather at the Fisher's best watering hole to further the celebration. Drinks were on management and the mood was heady.

In the dressing room, spirits were high as the gypsies changed. Pat, distraught as she was, didn't want to miss the party. Owen would be preoccupied with the press, giving interviews and receiving congratulations. She approached Mally, who was redoing her make-up and hair.

"Mal, will you go to the party with me? It's Owen's big night, so I'll be solo. I don't want to be alone." By now, the dressing room had emptied.

"Pat, what happened? Why were you so unglued before the show? Tell me," she insisted. Tears welled, spilling down Pat's cheeks. "Oh Mal, it's horrible! Jerry's replacement was my first lover. It happened in high school. God, did I fall hard! He pretended to love me while all along he just wanted sex. When he got bored, he dumped me!" Pat's sobs were intense, her shoulders rising and falling. "He used and humiliated me. It's taken me years to get over it."

"It seems you're still not over it, Pat. No wonder you're so insecure about Owen. You think he'll dump you too. Am I right?" Pat shook her head, "Is it that obvious?" "Yes, it is. Oh Sweetie, I'm so sorry!"

"I'll never trust another man again because of that bastard! Oh Mal, what am I going to do? He's joined the show!" "You're going to ignore him, that's what," insisted Mally. "That's easier said than done!" She reached for Kleenex and dabbed her eyes. "I don't really have a choice, do I?" "No, frankly you don't. So come on, fix that gorgeous face of yours and let's go have some fun." "Oh Mal, what would I do without you? You're like a soothing balm when I'm on fire."

The cast party was in full swing when the girls arrived. Griff, Jonas and Phillipe were in a large booth. Dick Landry, Griff's shadow, was absent, having excused himself from the festivities to phone Dana.

At the other end of the room, Owen was awash in TV lights, inundated by gushing reporters, all clamoring for an exclusive. It was mayhem, as the girls pushed their way through the crowd. The hubbub was deafening.

"Girls, you look fabulous," shouted Jonas waving. "Come join us." Griff stood and helped Mally into the booth. Jonas reached for Pat and pulled her to his lap. He kissed her cheek, enthusiastically. "You look very sexy Miss Byrne! If I weren't a fairy I'd have my way with you!" *Mon Cher*, get in line," Phillipe added, winking.

Pat acknowledged their compliments, smiling weakly, her eyes darting. Distracted, she made no effort to join the conversation. Jonas signaled a passing server, who stopped at their table. Never one to overlook an attractive guy, he smiled, giving him the once over. "We'd like another round, please."

"What would you like? Champagne is on the house." "Order whatever you'd like. It's on me," Griff enthused. "Mally, what are you having?" "I'll have Chablis." Griff turned to Pat, "What would you like?" There was no response. Jonas gave Pat a playful nudge. "Hey Irish, what are you having?" Again, no response. "Pat!"

Suddenly Pat was with them. "Oh, sorry, I'll have a glass of the house red." Jonas leaned over and whispered, "Are you okay?" Pat forced a smile, patting his face. "I'm fine, just tired. It's been a long day." By now, the waiter, growing antsy, looked at Griff. "Sir, what are you having?"

"I'll have an extra dry martini with a twist." "Gin or vodka, sir?" "I'll have Tanqueray, thanks." Jonas and Phillipe continued to admire the view. The waiter was nicely built, showing an abundant package. "What can I get for you?" Phillipe noticed and playfully gave Jonas a poke.

"He'll have a beer, whatever you have on tap. And I would like Courvoisier on the rocks, please." "Thanks, I'll be back shortly." "I should have asked him for a bar towel to wipe your chin, Cheri," Phillipe teased. "Well, he is hung, Babe. You must admit!" Phillipe shrugged and turned his attention back on Griff, Mally, and Pat.

"The show felt good tonight, my friends. Griff, how did it look?" "It was excellent. You were all right on the mark. I'm sure Jeff appreciated the support. He did a hell of a job!" Jonas grew serious. "Is there any word on Jerry? He should have been here." "He had surgery this morning. Dr. Kennedy called and said it went well." "How long will he be out of commission?"

"Kennedy said a couple of months. He'll have to go to rehab here for a few weeks before he can travel," remarked Griff.

"Has Ray Jordan been notified? He's Jerry's partner." "Yes. Ray will be coming here to take Jerry home. Do you know him, Jonas?" "Yes. Ray's definitely one of the good guys. They've been together fifteen years." Mally was listening with interest. "Is Ray in the business, Jonas?"

"No! Of all things, he's a bar owner! Do you know Sweet Surrender? It's a cozy little place on 55th and 9th. Ray's owned it for years. It's one of the classier gay bars in the city."

"Very interesting," remarked Griff, as their round arrived. Griff took the check and paid with cash. Jonas assisted, handing out the drinks, adding a wink.

"This calls for a smart toast," said Jonas. They all raised their glasses, except Pat. "Ah, Pat, come on! Let's toast," insisted Jonas. Reluctantly picking up her glass, she went through the motions. Jonas took over. "Here's to the *Centipede*!" They all cheered.

Much later, a jarring phone awakened Pat. Fighting her way from deep sleep, she reached for the receiver and struggled to pick up. The familiar voice brought her around.

"Baby, how are you?" The sound of Owen's voice was comforting. "Oh, Owen, how did it go?"

"You could knock me over with a feather. We've won favor in car town," he enthused. His tone changed. "I didn't see you, Baby. Where were you?" "I sat with Griff and Mally all night. I knew you'd be involved." "Well, I'm free now and ready to be involved with you." Pat's stomach tightened. "Grab a cab and come to the Hilton, Baby. I'll be waiting. Suite 2500." There was a click.

Pat put the phone down. Her mind was racing as she tried to wake up. She was cumbersome as she dressed, throwing on jeans, a peasant blouse, and sneakers. Reaching for her bag, she took out a brush and ran it through her hair. A touch of lipstick would have to do. 'Oh, God, I better grab my diaphragm,' she thought, imagining Owen all over her. He would be insatiable. It had been a while and sleepy as she was, she, too, was hungry for sex.

Walking toward the elevators, she suddenly realized she was going in the wrong direction. Backtracking, she rounded a corner and heard lustful sounds. Quickly she ducked into a nearby ice machine alcove. Peering around the edge she saw them, locked together! Thank God, they hadn't seen her! As she focused more intently she saw what she would never imagine in a public hallway.

'Oh my God, it's Nora Blake,' she realized. Nora's legs were wrapped around a guy, her dress shoved up to her chest, her panties on the carpet. The guy was turning Nora, positioning her against the wall. Then a shock, Tim Bartel! Bile rose in her throat as she tried to stay concealed.

Slipping out unnoticed, she ran to the stairwell and began her descent. Nausea was building as she made it to the lobby. Running past the concierge, she reached the ladies room, entered the nearest stall and vomited. When the heaving slowed down, she wiped her mouth with toilet paper. Finally, the retching stopped and she leaned against the stall divider. Taking a deep breath, she noticed how foul her mouth tasted; she wiped her face again.

The past had come back in an instant. She remembered the day Tim told her he was through. The shock and despair! How she ran into the girl's room at school and threw up. How she suffered the humiliation of overhearing a nameless girl discussing what a good fuck Tim had given her! Detail after detail coming at her while she, wasted and weak was unable to move from the bathroom floor. She shivered remembering each detail, so permanent in her psyche.

When she was able to move, she pulled herself up and opened the door. Walking to the sink, she turned on the water and caught her image. 'I'm a mess,' she thought running her hands in the cold spill and rinsing her mouth. 'Owen must never know,' she told herself. 'And, I'm late!' Quickly she brushed her hair and freshened lipstick. Taking a moment to assess, she sighed at her less-than-perfect appearance.

Leaving the ladies room, she crossed the lobby and through the revolving door. Spotting a Yellow, she signaled the driver. She hastily got in and took another deep breath. 'I can't be this distraught,' she thought, over and over to herself. Requesting the Hilton, she leaned back and planned her strategy. Tonight, she'd have to do her best acting, Tony Award-worthy at the very least!

Chapter 22

Predictable Pans

It was well past 1:00 am when Pat arrived at Owen's hotel. She was edgy trying to forget Tim and Nora humping in the hall. Trying to pull herself together, she knocked. In seconds, Owen stood, barefoot, shirtless, in tight jeans, his package enticing.

"Baby, you're late. I was worried." His concern was obvious. I couldn't get a cab right away," she lied. "I'm so sorry!" "It's okay, Baby. Come in and get comfortable. I was about to order room service."

Pat walked to the sitting room and removed her coat. Working off her sneakers, she settled on the sofa. A fire was crackling and candles flickered here and there. Beautifully upholstered furniture and plush drapes added the right touch. Cushy pillows had been invitingly placed in front of the fire. Owen was masterful, setting the perfect romantic scene. Pat's eyes took it all in, anticipating the night ahead. Slowly Owen leaned down and gave her a long, deep kiss.

"What would you like to eat, Baby? They have a tasty after-midnight-menu." "Whatever you're having," she murmured weakly.

"Good, 'cause I can't have my baby starving," he insisted. "Come on, I'll order and you eat. You'll need all your energy for what I have planned." Pat felt the familiar tightening in her gut, as she settled in. She was more than ready.

The door buzzed. What a short night! Pat sighed and rolled over as Owen sat up, trying to navigate through drowsiness. Easing out of bed, he slipped on his jeans and went to the door. In the gap below, he spotted and retrieved the Detroit morning papers. He moved into the sitting room and turned on a lamp. Opening the *Detroit News* first, he paged through it to the first review of *Centipede*. As he scanned the words, he felt a wave of shock as he read:

> *Celebrated director-choreographer Owen Matthews has brought a different kind of critter to Motor City this season, Centipede. Oh rue the day! Apparently the director, at least for the time being, has quit his last composer, lyricist and librettist, concocting instead a tasty dish, an offering complicated in execution, but lacking honesty and substance.*
>
> *Structured as a musical dance review, as opposed to a full-scale musical, Matthews has cast an ensemble of Broadway's best dancers, a handsome troupe of performers, handpicked to please, titillate and impress, but without depth or purpose. This showy offering would better serve a cabaret somewhere Off-Broadway, rather than The Great White Way.*
>
> *During the two-hour running, dancers are put through number after numbers, pacing like racehorses determined to win, do or die, but impossible to achieve with stakes this high. Matthews' brand, typically rehearsed to perfection, set the bar far beyond his charges' ability to understand his intention.*
>
> *Patricia Byrne and Jonas Martin, featured dancers are impressive and set the pace as leaders of the pack. The ensemble ably translate Matthews' concept into a technically impressive whole, but more often than not, flaunting erotic, sexual movements, masking any true depth of emotional authenticity. Instead Mr. Matthews favors swagger, the "look at us" kind of attitude that comes across monotonously time and time again.*

*Perhaps the director needs to take another hard look, rethink
and revamp, in order to take back to New York, a show that is
heartfelt and meaningful. In other words, Mr. Matthews, please
bring back a good, old fashioned musical."*

Owen set the paper down. Reaching for a cigarette, his hands
shook as he dialed the phone. The hotel operator answered. "I'd like
Griffen Edwards' suite, please." The voice responded, "One moment,
please." Owen heard the voice of comfort pick up. "Griff Edwards."

"This is Owen, Griff. Have you seen the shit review in today's
Detroit News?" One could cut the air with a knife, as Griff cleared his
throat, choosing his words carefully. "Yes, I've read both! *The Free Press*
was less kind than *The Detroit News* for my money. "

"What do you mean, less kind?" Owen's voice had an edge. "How
do you figure the *Free Press* was less kind? The *Detroit News* guy just
shoved his complete contempt right up my ass," he said, his voice shaking, volume rising.

"You know they gun for you here, Owen. It's a tradition," said
Griff, trying to add humor to the moment. "Why are you surprised?
Don't forget this burg is one big factory from end to end. No culture
lost here, face it!" "Well, those two-faced fuckers, those I allowed an
interview last night, were either kissing my butt, or secretly plotting
my demise." "Forget them, Owen. We have a show to run here temporarily and then we can get the hell out of Dodge!"

"Comforting thought! Well, have a good day off, Griff. Hell, you've
earned it," Owen said affirmatively. "Monday's another day. And just
two more weeks in this dump of a town. I guess I can deal," he said,
facetiously. "Right now, I'm going back to bed!" Hanging up, he walked
to the bar and poured a shot of scotch. He needed reinforcement,
breakfast could wait. Bruising was never an option for his artistic sen-
sibility. Thank God for Pat! She'd be his distraction for the time being.

Chapter 23

Grin and Bear It

It was Monday; Jonas woke early, showered, shaved and left Phillipe to sleep in. He decided to grab breakfast in the coffee shop and scan the morning news. He noted the disdain shown to *Centipede* by the local press. In spite of the reviews, he was feeling optimistic and ready to put a newcomer in the show.

Choosing a stool at the counter, he ordered coffee, cutting it with cream and sugar to start. Today was his first rehearsal with Tim Bartel and he was psyched knowing the replacement's reputation as a solid technician and charismatic performer. Tim had worked for the Kaplan-Maggli group before, as well as producer Vinnie Lehrman, having been in the original production of *Bravo Business*, another Owen Matthews mega hit.

"Can I help you?" A heavy-set waitress stood with pad and pen at the ready, her face greasy and red with an upsweep hairdo that was starting to straggle. "Yes, please. I'll have two eggs over easy, bacon crispy, home fries and white toast, easy on the butter." "You got it! May I warm your coffee?" Jonas nodded and returned to his notes.

'Let's see, Jerry is downstage left of center on number one for the opening freeze. He partners Fran during the first number,' he noted. He was meticulous and a stickler for detail, a skill learned from his boss. Director-choreographers relied on assistants to remount staging accurately. As he sipped his coffee, he felt a tap on his shoulder. Turning he saw the new guy.

"Good morning, Jonas. We haven't met formally," said Tim Bartel, extending his hand. "Hi, join me," said Jonas, placing his bag on the floor. Jonas began, "So how do you like the show?" "It's different, innovative. The staging is challenging, but that's always better," he remarked.

The waitress returned with Jonas' order and slapped down the check. She glanced at Tim. "Are you ordering?" It was clear that she had opened early that morning and had developed an early edge.

"Well, hi, beautiful!" He winked adding, "I'll have coffee black and a short stack. Thanks," he said puckering a kiss in her direction. The tired server perked up, taking a closer look. 'If I were 15 years younger and 60 pounds lighter, I'd nab this one,' she thought as she scribbled the order on her pad. "You got it, sweetie. Be just a minute," she chortled, trotting off, clearly re-energized. Jonas watched with amusement. "Say, seems you're a force with the ladies!" "I dig women. Can't live without them. They're usually mine for the taking," Tim quipped, clearly sure of himself.

"Well, the girls in the company will be all over you! We fags are definitely into flesh of the other," he said with a chuckle. Tim shrugged.

"Who and how you fuck is your business," he said dryly. Jonas finished breakfast and paid the check, he had a job to do. 'This guy is fucking direct,' he mused. "See you at the theatre, 10:00 sharp, okay?" "I'll be there. Thanks!"

The waitress returned with Tim's order, putting it down like it was Waterford Crystal. She smiled broadly as she refilled his cup. "Can I get you anything else, sweetie?" Her voice oozed like squeeze bottle honey. Leaning towards him, her sizeable breasts brushed the straw holder.

"I can't think of another thing, beautiful," he pandered. "If you were any sweeter, I'd have you instead of this Maple syrup." The woman blushed and drew back. "Here's your check," she stammered, hurrying away. Tim enjoyed pancakes and wielding charm. 'Tim, you're a bad boy,' he thought, clearly amused.

At 10:00, Jonas was ready for work, stretching and trying to rejuvenate tired muscles. 'Shit, a day off and I'm wiped,' he complained to no one.

"I'm here," said a voice off stage. Jonas saw Tim emerge from the shadows into the spill of work light. He was dressed in dance pants and clearly, well hung. Tim's obvious asset could be a distraction if he let it. A tank top revealed well-toned arms that Jonas could only imagine around him. He wore jazz shoes and a towel draped around his neck.

"You warmed up?" "Yeah, hot to trot. Lay it on me," he said confidently. Jonas introduced Tim to rehearsal pianist, Sam Conway, a local. He sat drinking coffee and reading the *Free Press.*

"The show runs two hours. Owen favors jazz and soft shoe, but has a passion for ballet-trained dancers, so if you have that, so much the better." "I can keep up with the best of them," said Tim. 'This guy's not short on confidence,' Jonas mused. "Okay then, let's go!" Sam took a last sip of coffee and folded the paper.

For two hours, they worked tirelessly. Jonas demonstrated, explaining subtext and placement for each number. At noon, they took a break. At 1:00, they were back at it, Tim catching on quickly to each step, nuance, never flagging. The day flew. Tim learned four numbers, while Jonas sagged. 'This guy has enough confidence for the whole company,' he thought. Though he found Tim's bravado grating, he admired his skill. At 5:00 Jonas called it quits for the day. "See you at 10:00 tomorrow." "Thanks for your help, Jonas," said Tim, who was spent but sincere. The sun was low in the sky as they left the stage door, the first gulp of fresh air invading their senses. Jonas was ready for a nap before *Centipede* tonight.

The iffy reviews hadn't discouraged the gypsies, as they began a new week. The dressing rooms were alive with activity, the group eager to show their stuff. Pat was subdued. She glanced at Nora in the mirror, recalling the blatant scene she'd witnessed. 'What a whore, I wonder if anyone else knows?' Mally noticed and whispered, "Hey, are you all right?" Pat smirked as she put her lipstick brush down. "I've got the goods on Miss Blake and I hope she's too sore to pee for a month," she said, snickering. Mally frowned, whispering, "What are you talking about?" "I'll fill you in later. For now, I'm enjoying this!"

Mally returned to her face, which was far from ready. False lashes to apply, eyeliner to add and rouge to highlight her cheeks, she enjoyed the ritual. Her hair had grown long in a year and she loved pulling it back in a ponytail! So much hair! She had always worn it pixie in high school, then a bob in college. Her medium brown hair contrasted to the shade she wore for *Bravo Business.*

Vinny Lehrman had chosen Mally and another to become blondes for the show. Management agreed to maintain their color for the run of contract, restoring their natural hair at tour's end. Often mistaken for a blonde, Mally enjoyed the ruse. She smiled, recalling the hair caper. So much had happened from *Bravo Business* to *Centipede*. The Minnesota college girl had acquired the confidence of a seasoned gypsy. Griff's voice cut through. "Cast, green room please. Thanks."

"Better get a move on, Mal," Pat said, slipping on her robe for the walk to the change area. Nora's imposing voice topped everyone's. "God, she never stops," muttered Pat. "She certainly has a lot of balls for a nothing," added Cynthia.

"Why do you dislike her so much, Pat?" Pat slowed, putting them at the rear of the pack. "Because, Cyn, she's a loud, opportunistic whore." Mally countered, "Well, say what you really feel." Pat had developed an edge, unlike the girl she first met.

"Oh come on Mal, you know as well as I that she would give her right tit to have Owen. She's so damn obvious it's pathetic!" "May I remind you that Owen is in love with Patricia Byrne. How much proof do you need? The man created *Centipede* around you."

"Company, let me have your attention." The group quieted, waiting for an announcement.

"A week from this Thursday is Thanksgiving. We'll do a matinee, but no evening performance. The owners of the Fisher have cordially invited us to a catered dinner after the show. This includes tech management, crew, volunteer ushers and box office staff. Naturally, you are all welcome. Please wear appropriate attire. Yes, Nora?"

"So we won't have a show to do following dinner? Does that mean we have the rest of the night off?" "Yes," Griff replied. Pat shifted from one foot to the other, impatiently. "Can you believe that bimbo thinks we could dance after eating?" Jonas caught the remark and nudged Pat. "Take it easy, Tiger!"

The group dispersed taking their pre-show positions. Sounds of a full house filtered through the show drop. "I guess critics can be full of shit," remarked Chad. Joe Pinto caught up. "Hey, Chad, haven't seen your girl around. Did you break up or what?" Frowning, Chad hastened, "None of your business, Joe." "Well, if you're in the market, I'd be willing to fill you up," he said wickedly. Griff's "Places, please" provided a comfortable out. Chad hurried to his preset spot upstage center.

Taking position, his mind reeled. It was true, his fiancée, Mary Jane Douglas, had just ended their relationship. Leaving Michigan for life in Manhattan was unthinkable in spite of her love for Chad. No, he belonged in show biz and she, psychology. After graduation, she would seek a clinical position in Detroit and finish her Ph.D. at Wayne State University.

The sellout continued, audiences showing their appreciation night after night. Owen was elated and frankly surprised. He'd never been favored in Detroit, a fact that left him defensive and prickly. His gamble had taken hold! Wonder of wonders! In spite of the critics and media, this public loved the show! Happily, a good sign that *Centipede* would triumph in New York.

Chapter 24

The New Addition

At 1:00 Friday, the gypsies gathered for the replacement call. They warmed up with anticipation knowing any addition or change to a show created excitement. Jerry's replacement created curiosity and gossip. Was he gay or straight? The subject was always of interest to both the men and women.

Pat knew all she needed. She purposely sat as far back in the group as she could. 'God, what if he recognizes me?' Thankful she wasn't chosen Jerry's partner, she'd be stuck with Tim's hands all over her. The thought made her nauseous. Joe zeroed in on the new guy immediately. It was hard to miss the generous package. 'He'd be a slice of heaven to play with,' he fantasized.

"Company, let's begin!" Jonas and Owen took the stage as Griff counted heads. Sam was ready at the keys. Owen began. "Gang, we have a long afternoon ahead of us, so stay focused and we'll get through this in short order. I want to start at the top of the show and take Mr. Bartel through each number. Keep in mind that Jeff will cover Jonas, freeing him to observe and take notes. No need to dance full until I say so. Sam, I would like the music a little under tempo to start."

"Anything else, Griff?" "We'll only be using work lights today and we may be stopping at times. Your patience is appreciated." A hand went up. "Yes, Nora?" "Owen, do you want me to sit this out, since I'm not covering anyone at the moment?" "Griff, where would you like Miss Blake?" 'Send the bitch to Antarctica,' Pat mused. "Nora, please sit in the house this afternoon. Now, if there's nothing further, let's get started! Places." Immediately, the gypsies were on their feet.

Tim took his position for the opening freeze. His partner, Fran Fairchild, was delighted. As they posed she whispered, "Welcome! It's great to have you!" Tim looked through her, indifferently. 'Cut the small talk, bitch. You're not my type,' he thought disdainfully.

Each number unfolded seamlessly as the company worked through *Centipede*. No missteps, no disruptions. Tim Bartel was spot on, his technique flawless, his performing inspired. "This guy is good," said Chad to the others.

"Take five," announced Griff. The group broke into individual cliques. Pat went into the house to distance herself. Leaning back, she closed her eyes attempting to shut out the world. Suddenly, it was hard to miss the exchange behind her. Pat took a deep breath.

"Can we get together later?" The voice was Nora's. "Sure, what's your room number?" 'Oh God, Tim,' thought Pat, uneasily. "It's 520," said Nora, eagerly. "I'll meet you after the show about 11:00." "Okay. Stop by the bar first and buy us beer," he ordered. Booze always loosened things up. 'If she comes on like the other night,' he thought, 'I'll be fucking my brains out!' "Places for the second act," yelled Griff. Pat waited for Tim to return to the stage.

The second act unfolded with ease. Tim was inspired as he danced Jerry's spot. Out in the house, Owen watched with pleasure. Turning to Jonas he whispered, "This guy has intensity like mine back in the day!" Jonas agreed.

"He'll go far if he can temper that ego!" Owen looked surprised. "What do you mean? What am I missing here?" "He's a prick," Jonas countered. "As long as he delivers, he can be a world class prick! I'm not running a social club," he tossed. Jonas had said enough and returned to his notes.

Later, the gypsies dispersed. It was time for a break before the evening show. The rehearsal was an ideal warm-up. Pat went out the stage door. She was upset and starved. Spotting her pal, she caught up. "Mal, you want to grab a bite? I need food!" "Sure, Griff is working straight through to the call."

"There's a cozy little bistro next door to our hotel. Should we give it a try?" "Let's go! We can clean up later." The girls hurried across the street dodging cars. It was late afternoon, the sun was setting and fresh air was a welcome change.

The show came down at 10:15. Nora was the first to leave the dressing room. Breathless with excitement, "See you girls tomorrow," she shouted, heading down the stairs, two at a time. She had to clean up before Tim arrived.

Stopping at the lobby bar, she ordered four beers to go and gave the barman a generous tip. Crossing Grand Boulevard, she entered the hotel at a clip, rushed to the elevator and pressed #5. The door closed slowly. "This thing moves like a turtle," she said with annoyance. The elevator finally stopped at her floor.

Nora moved down the hall, fumbling for a key. Kicking off her shoes as she entered, she put the beer in the tiny fridge. Undressing quickly, she reached for a washcloth, wet and soaped it foamy, washing all the important areas. 'Now where is my deodorant?' She was impatient, excited. Next, a dab of her favorite perfume here and there, clean panties and robe. It was a bit worn but would do for the amount of time she'd be in it. Brushing her teeth followed by a swish of mouthwash completed her hygiene. Suddenly, a knock. "Just a sec," she shouted. Before opening the door, she paused for one last check in the mirror and then peered through the peephole. As nonchalant as she could, she opened the door. Tim walked in, moving past her like she was a post.

"Hi, you," she chirped, ignoring the slight. "What have you got to drink around here?" He tossed his jacket on a chair. "I got us a couple of beers. Pabst Blue Ribbon, okay?" "I prefer Molson, but sometimes, beer is beer, I guess that'll do. Where is it?" Nora went to the fridge, opened two beers and handed one to Tim. "Do you want a glass?"

"Sure." She fetched glasses and poured for him. Doing the same for herself she took a swig and pointed to a small couch across the room. "Let's sit over there." Tim grabbed her hand and pulled her toward it. He was more aggressive than she expected. When seated, she attempted small talk.

"I thought rehearsal went well today. How do you feel?" Tim took a generous swig and grinned.

"It's a piece of cake! The work is challenging but suits me fine."

"I'm glad you're here," she said, a little coy now. Tim put down his bottle and took hers. "Let's knock off the small talk and get down to business! Come on!" He stood and pulled her to him. Backing her toward the bed, he slipped her robe off and ran his hands down her torso and below. Nora loved his approach! He had no interest in romance, just balling. Heaven!

Without hesitation, he had her on the bed, sliding off her panties, his hands all over her mound. Nora moaned her want, pulling him down to her, begging him to finger and suck. By now she was frenzied. Tim purposely held off until he had her attention. He stood, teasing as he inched his briefs to the floor. "So you want this, bitch?" He was fully hard as he stroked himself, taunting her. "Yes, oh yes," Nora chanted. Tim was larger than average, the way she liked it. Slowly he lowered himself and entered, pumping with such force, she screamed in surprise.

"Take it, bitch! Come on, take it", he demanded, relishing his dominance. 'This one's wet beyond belief,' he thought. "You're a horny little thing, aren't you, bitch?" Nora moaned as she felt her orgasm quickly building. "More Tim, more," she hissed. Grabbing her wrists, he forcefully held her as he continued to slide in and out. Nora had reached the breaking point, finally letting go in waves that nearly knocked him off. Seconds later his climax followed like an eruption. "You horny little bitch", he hollered rocking and twisting; the aftershocks slowly subsiding.

Nora lay still, totally euphoric. Tim eased his way off and stretched. The air was fragrant, their bodies soaked. As Nora sat up, she felt a delicious ache between her legs, his wetness all over her. "You want another beer?" She nodded. Tim sauntered to the fridge with an obvious air of satisfaction, like a Cheetah having outrun its prey.

Nora plumped two pillows behind her. She felt fabulous. 'He's easily the best fuck ever. I must be doing something right,' she thought. Tim returned with her beer. The first swallow of cold liquid felt like gold! He studied Nora from the chair where he now sat.

"Man, can you fuck! Have you always been this good?" She smiled broadly, feeling like she'd taken first prize.

"I loved sex at 15! My first was an older man, who fucked me for over a year. Then he split," she said, matter-of-factly. "Mine was an older woman of 16! I was 13. It was a one-time deal, but intense! Want to go again?" "Sure, why not?"

Without missing a beat, they finished their beers and back on the bed. It didn't matter that she had a matinee in a few hours. She was the chosen one and she was insatiable!

The weekend passed as the gypsies performed three shows. Tim watched each performance taking mental notes for his debut the coming week. He felt great! The choreography fit him perfectly and so did the Blake bitch! Life was sweet!

Chapter 25

A New Week

Monday night and Tim was psyched! He was ready to perform as he walked to the green room. The cast was waiting as Owen arrived.

"Company, as you are aware, Mr. Bartel joins us tonight. I expect you to keep your spacing and placement accurate to the letter. Give it all you've got!" Griff followed.

"We're sold out for the rest of the run. Good news in spite of so-so reviews. Please keep the same energy and accuracy that you had back in Philadelphia. Remember, this is Thanksgiving week and, on Thursday, we'll do a matinee performance only. A Thanksgiving Dinner will follow at the Collier Restaurant, here in the complex. Please plan on arriving promptly at 6:00. Now, places, please!"

Fran stood next to Tim. Flattening her back, she did a few gentle bounces to loosen up. Glancing up, she noticed his eyes on her. Was it her warm-up that caught his eye or her ass? She wasn't sure. Rumor had it he was humping Nora. This came as no surprise to her considering what a blabber mouth Nora was. Fran contracted her torso and gently rounded her spine, slowly rolling her back to an upright position. Tim was watching and threw an obvious wink, causing her to down shift her eyes, in an effort to ignore him. 'What an arrogant jerk this guy is,' she thought.

As the overture began, stage lights rose, spilling pastel hues of color over the gypsies. The large show drop rose slowly revealing a tableau of tangled motionless bodies. Clad in form-fitting, flesh-toned, body suits, the dancers looked totally nude, save for swatches of colorful scarves modestly placed here and there.

The group began moving like a giant amoeba, reaching languidly, contracting and posing again. As each couple broke free of the group, the audience burst into wild applause.

Tim took Fran firmly by the waist, lifting her high above his head. Turning her to begin her descent down his body, he was careful to place his hands where he would be able to control the lift. She was feather light and easy to maneuver. As they completed the move, others did the same in repeated fashion, a few measures of music in between. Their execution was flawless as the number continued. Sustained movement in adagio was far more challenging because of the control required. Quick steps required energy and tempo. All through the show, there were variations of both from number to number.

During the sailor number at the top of the second act, Tim watched closely as a trio with Jonas, Phillipe and Chad danced brilliantly. Their partners, Pat, Mally, and Cynthia flirted, as the men swaggered toward them. Owen's choreography had whimsy and charm but included bold sensuality as well.

Pat and Jonas worked their way down stage right near the proscenium arch. Tim, standing beyond the sight line couldn't help but notice. They worked perfectly together! Jonas was a masterful partner. As their bodies intertwined, it was difficult to look away. His technique was brilliant and she was breathtaking to watch. He imagined himself getting into that body! Together, Jonas and Pat were flawless, tender and sensual.

Suddenly, it hit him! 'Goddamn, that's the girl I fucked from Performing Arts Academy five years ago!' He couldn't believe it! No, he must be mistaken. That other girl was a needy, clingy, anorexic mouse! This girl was a wet dream waiting to happen! He continued trying to piece it together. 'Christ, what is her name?' As he ruminated, the number came to an end, thundering applause ringing out, as the lights went to a blackout.

By show's end, the audience was on its feet, applause rocking off the walls of the house. Curtain call after call continued. The gypsies graciously smiled through the audience's accolades. What a contrast to the critical response of the previous week.

Spirits were high as the company went to the changing areas and make-up rooms to clean up. The men acknowledged Tim with a group cheer. He had fit right into the show without a hitch. Joe and Jim watched from a distance, admiring the view. Tim removed his dance belt, exchanging it for a pair of briefs. 'Man, what equipment,' Joe thought, perking up. He was the first to approach.

"Hey, Tim, care to join us for some liquid refreshment? Chad, Jim and Jeff are coming." Jonas held back, pleased with Tim's performance, but not anxious to socialize. His first impression was still the same. Talent be damned, the guy was a super prick. Joe noticed how quiet Jonas was, as did Phillipe.

"Jonas, are you and Phillipe joining?" Sensing reluctance on Jonas' part, Phillipe spoke up.

"I'm kind of tired and fighting a cold. Jonas, what do you think?" Jonas played along.

"Yeah, I'm feeling kind of on the edge. There's a bug going around, so I think we'll pass." Joe shrugged, slipping on his jeans. Tim and the others finishing dressing and headed out.

When they were alone, Phillipe put his arms around Jonas and pulled him close. Something was off. He could sense it. "Cheri, what is it?" Jonas let out a sigh, relishing Phillipe's hug and concern.

"I don't know. I can't put my finger on it, but this Tim Bartel spells trouble." "Cheri, what is it about him that bothers you so much?" "He's a super prick, an egomaniac and I don't trust him. For example, ever since he joined the company, Pat has been so distracted. She's indifferent, moody and not fully focused on her work. It's just not like her."

"You're not overreacting are you, Cheri?" Jonas pulled away, shaking his head and took a seat. "Phillipe, I know Pat. Usually whatever is distressing her off stage, doesn't have the slightest effect on her performance. She's spot on! It's who she is. It's her wiring." "Might it have something to do with Owen? Is there any conflict? Has she mentioned anything?"

"I know when Owen has caused an upset. I spent our last tour getting used to their relationship issues. Pat never keeps a thing from me. No, this has something to do with Bartel. I feel it in my gut." "Maybe she's confided in Mal, being as close as they are." Jonas brightened. "That's it! I'll talk to Mal. If anyone knows what's causing this it's her."

Jonas stood and walked over to the coat rack. Slipping on his coat and scarf, he glanced at Phillipe. "Come on, Babe, let's get out of here.

I'm beat!" Phillipe followed, grabbing his jacket and gloves as they left the room.

The guys were into their third round when Nora wandered to the table. She was obviously tipsy, her motor mouth in overdrive as she bypassed the others and headed for Tim. Looking up from his beer, he could see a potential problem.

"Hi, Timmy, whatcha doing?" She was on a roll as she proceeded to wrap her arms around him and pull in close. Her words were a slur, but her intention was obvious as she whispered in his ear, "Want to fuck?" If Tim was embarrassed, he didn't let on. Removing her arms, he turned, smiled and said nonchalantly, "Nora, you're drunk. Why don't you go to bed?" Nora came back for more, this time more obvious. "Good idea! Come on, fuck me!"

Chad and Jeff, obviously uncomfortable, excused themselves and headed for the bar. Only Joe and Jim remained, quietly sipping their drinks. Tim stood and pulled out some bills. "Here guys, I'll leave this for my share. I think I'll see Miss Blake to the hotel." Joe stopped him.

"Tim, keep your money. This is our treat." Jim threw Joe a look that said, 'It's fuck time, the lucky girl!' "Thanks for the evening. See you at call. Come on, Nora." Without another word he pulled her out of the bar and to Grand Boulevard. The wind was blowing hard as they crossed the empty street. The fresh air helped clear Tim's head. They hurried into the hotel and elevator.

Once on the 5th Floor, Nora found her room key and handed it to Tim. He was silent as he unlocked the door. Nora entered first, weaving and giggling. Throwing her coat on the floor, she reached for Tim's and pulled at one of the sleeves, removing it, then the other.

Tim crossed the room and sat down. Gesturing for her, she eagerly crossed to him. Now standing directly in front of him, she stood breathless, waiting for his next move. He began removing her clothes, slipping off her sweater first, then her jeans. Nora kicked off her flats eager to cooperate. She wanted it and the sooner the better! When she was nude, he led her to the bed. Nora's growing excitement distracted her. Tim was still fully clothed.

"Lie down face down," he ordered. Nora sighed doing what she was told. She couldn't wait to begin. "Wait here. I'll be right back," he insisted. Nora turned her head, trying to steal a look. The quiet engulfed her, the bedspread feeling soft beneath her face.

Tim grabbed her with a force that almost knocked the wind out of her. She felt her arms pulled behind her, wrists being tied. A scarf followed, stuffed in her mouth, his hot breath in her ear whispering, "So you want a fuck, bitch? Well, get a load of this!" That was the last thing she heard as she felt the hardness of his shaft drive into her rectum, searing pain stabbing as he pumped and pumped, sodomizing her. Nora tried to scream but it was no use! Tim had thought of everything. When he had taken the tie from her bathrobe, he saw a scarf on the dresser, just the thing to keep her quiet while he gave her what she deserved.

Next, he rolled her on her back, viciously spreading her legs as he proceeded to penetrate vaginally. Nora wriggled and twisted, trying to force him off, but it was no use. He was in charge, delivering the goods the way he had planned it back at the bar. 'No horny, little nothing bitch was going to embarrass him! He'd fix her so she'd never bother him again,' he gloated.

All through the ensuing rape, he said nothing but smiled broadly at his control, his power. When he felt his climax about to erupt, he lifted off, ripped the gag from her mouth, forcefully holding her face as he came. Again and again, Nora gagged trying to spit him away but to no avail. Tim had total control. Then he slowly rolled to the side and stood by the bed, taking no notice of her.

He was still fully clothed. Tucking himself in, he zipped his fly and turned to her. Nora lay prone, unable to move. Tears streaked her cheeks as she sobbed. Tim stared long and hard at her until she grew quieter, with only an occasional sob cutting the air.

"Now you listen to me. If you ever tell anyone about this, you'll be in a lot worse shape than you are right now. Don't ever come near me again, drunk or sober! I'm done with you." Without another word, Tim reached down and rolled Nora on her stomach, loosening her hands. Throwing the tie at her he picked up his jacket and walked to the door. After hanging the "do not disturb" sign on the outside knob he returned to the bed, getting nose to nose with Nora. Remember what I said, bitch!" Then he was gone.

Nora lay still for what seemed like an eternity. She was cold, sober and weak. Slowly she tried to stand, but fell back on the bed sobbing.

Her anus throbbed, as she lay there, terrified and alone. When she could manage, she slowly sat up and tried to think what to do. A red spot on the bed coverlet had spread, she was bleeding. She was too weak to stand, so she crawled toward the bathroom. Using the toilet seat to push herself up she reached a washcloth and turned on the tap, mixing hot and cold in the bowl. Soaking the cloth, she slowly wiped away the caked blood.

'How could he do this to me? What did I do wrong?' Those and many questions would go unanswered. For now, she had to try and sleep. 'Maybe when I wake up this will have been a nightmare,' she thought shuddering. The truth was only too clear. Tim Bartel was a predator, who had played her and raped her! Sleep would be her only ally, if only she could. Tomorrow, she'd have to decide what to do.

Chapter 26

Thanksgiving

The week's performances were moving quickly. Based on audience response night after night, the prediction was *Centipede* would take New York by storm. Who would have guessed Detroit would accept Owen's concept? The show had drawn mixed reviews opening weekend, predictably insulting, but the proof of success came from the public. They bought tickets, spread the word and could make or break a show if it didn't deliver.

Nora kept a low profile since the night of the assault, isolating herself from the company. No one questioned her absence from the cast. She was under contract to check in at half hour only, available in the event injury or illness. Jeff had done so after Jerry's injury. Swing dancers functioned only temporarily. They were not considered part of the cast performing eight shows a week. Once Nora checked in, she was free to leave as long as she was available at a given phone number. She had changed her living arrangement and relieved not to cover at the moment.

The thought of running into Tim Bartel terrified her, the memory of the rape deep in her psyche. The only person informed of her hotel change was Griff. He thought it odd until Nora advised her allergies were triggered by mold in the hotel carpeting. He made note in her file and the matter was closed.

Pat was distracted, moody, lonely and vulnerable. Owen hadn't called and her state of mind hadn't improved with Tim in the show. Avoiding him was foremost in her mind. Mally and Griff were planning their wedding following *Centipede's* Broadway opening. Jonas and Phillipe had actually developed colds, staying in as much as possible until show time.

Following the Wednesday night show, Jonas was heading out of the theatre, Mally just ahead of him. "Mal, I need to speak to you," he said, gravely. "Jonas, for heaven's sake, what is it?" He pointed to a small bar across the street.

"This will only take a few minutes. I'll buy you a drink," he said, with an urgency that compelled her to accept. Holding hands they ran across Grand Boulevard, the sharp wind cutting across their faces. They entered the bar, finding warmth and quiet. Grabbing a booth near a crackling fire, Jonas went to the bar and ordered a beer and a house white. Returning, he sat down and handed her a glass. There was silence at first as they sipped and relaxed.

"This feels like a night in a Norfolk bar last year. Remember?" Mally smiled, remembering how Jonas and she developed a firm friendship over Pat.

"Here we go again!" Jonas smiled wearily, taking her hand. "Mal, I need your help. I'm worried about our girl, again! She's hasn't been herself over the past week. I know something is wrong, but I can't figure it out." Mally listened, trying to recall anything unusual. "Gosh, Jonas, I have no idea. She hasn't seen a lot of Owen since we arrived, but she understands the pressure he's under, so that can't be it." "Has she said anything out of the ordinary or behaved differently?" "There is something I recall about the night Tim Bartel was introduced. I remember we were waiting in the green room and when he walked in, there was a lightning change in her!" Jonas was ready to hear more. "Later, when I questioned her, she got very upset, telling me about her past history with him. He was her first lover back in high school. She was in love and he betrayed and humiliated her deeply. It must have been horrendous, because it obviously still bothers her!"

"Shit! I knew it! I knew there was something about that guy! This explains a lot, Mal. My girl has been distracted and moody. I knew something wasn't right about that son of a bitch!" "What can we do, Jonas? He's in the show now." "We'll have to protect her by keeping close watch. I can't tell Owen. That would spell disaster!" "Anyway, that's my guess, Jonas. I hope it helps."

"Miss Mal, you've helped more than you know. Come on, I'll see you to the hotel. Let's keep this to ourselves. No sense in getting the situation stirred up any more than it already is, okay?"

"I love you so much, Jonas. Thanks for always being here for us!"

Jonas paid the check and they reentered the cold. Snow flurries were whirling as an icy wind dominated the night air. It was definitely Thanksgiving week, with winter around the corner.

An unpredicted snowstorm hit the Detroit area early Thanksgiving Day. By midday, snow plows were out in force, Grand Boulevard being one of the first cleared. The matinee would go as scheduled, it was a sold out show.

The company arrived before half hour, dressed for winter. They had been advised by Griff to pack for all weather conditions. Most of the gypsies had taken his advice and were sporting winter coats, scarves, hats, and gloves. A few brave souls were still dressed in fall attire, with only light jackets.

As 2:00 drew near, the girls were in the final stages of prepping make-up and hair. Some warmed up outside the area designated for quick changes. Others preferred the wings, psyching themselves. Matinee performances were more challenging for those recently awake and the usually subdued audiences. It was tempting to mark, to save energy for an evening show. However, marking—dancing with half the energy output—was scorned by most dancers and certainly not tolerated by management.

At the first chords of the overture, Jonas took his place in the group pose, top of the act. He glanced over at Tim, feeling disgust rising in his chest. However, as much as he disliked the guy, his job was to dance the lead and assist Owen, carrying out his every wish. What he wished most was that Bartel would get lost. He'd sooner send him to the ends of the earth than tolerate him indefinitely. Owen was unaware that his lover and star dancer had an unhappy past with the guy. It wasn't Jonas' intention to report such information. However, he felt responsible for Pat's welfare and would be monitoring the guy just in case.

The matinee ended at 5:15. The gypsies looked forward to Thanksgiving dinner. Most returned to their hotels to shower, change and dress in the spirit of the holiday.

Jeff hadn't seen Nora around the theatre in nearly a week and had become concerned. After the show, he hurried back to his hotel to check on her. Calling the front desk, he was informed that she had checked out, without a forwarding address. He phoned Griff. "Edwards."

"Griff, this is Jenkins, I'm looking for Nora. She apparently checked out of our hotel. Do you know how to reach her?" "Yes, Jeff. Nora is now at the Benton Arms Apartments, two blocks south of the Fisher. She moved for health reasons."

"Do you know if she's coming to the dinner tonight? I haven't seen her this week." "Nora is aware of time and location. She'll most likely be there."

"Thanks, Griff. I appreciate the heads up." Jeff put down the phone, far from appeased. Re-dialing the hotel operator, he requested information.

"Could you give me the number for the Benton Arms Apartments?" The voice responded, "Just one minute, sir. Please hold." The pause seemed to go on forever. Holding the receiver he removed his socks with a free hand. As he continued to wait, he managed to wriggle out of his jeans with difficulty, tugging a leg at a time. The operator returned.

"Thank you for holding. The number is 398-5800." Jeff breathed a sigh of relief as he depressed the receiver button and redialed. "Benton Arms, how may I help you?" "Miss Nora Blake, please."

"One moment, I'll connect," said the operator. Several rings passed when Jeff heard a small voice. "Hello?"

"Nora? This is Jeff. Are you okay? I haven't seen you all week," he said, concern in his voice.

"How did you find me?" Nora sounded distant.

"I called Griff. He said you had moved! What's going on?" "Nothing, Jeff. I'm dealing with allergies, so I had to change hotels," she lied. A long pause followed.

"My allergies have been horrible, it's been a relief not to dance," she lied again. "I've just needed time away."

"Want to be my date for dinner? It should be great, turkey with all the fixings," he enthused. "I'll come and pick you up." "I don't think so," she said, fighting back tears. "I think I'll stay in, okay?" Jeff wasn't buying it, but he acquiesced. "Well, okay, if you're sure Nora." "Yes, I'm sure, have a good time." Jeff hung up, sensing something wasn't right. Disappointed, he showered and dressed for the Collier.

Dinner was in full swing as the gypsies enjoyed cocktails and hors d'oeuvres, waiting for the main event. Fred Collier, owner and chef, announced with enthusiasm, "Ladies and Gentleman, dinner is served!" Everyone sat at their preferred tables. Mally and Griff's group included Jonas, Phillipe, Pat and Chad. Owen was seated with the owners of the Fisher. Dick Landry was late but expected, as he called to check on Dana.

Tim sat with Cynthia, Liz, Kathy and Marcy. Fran remained aloof, joining Joe and Jim at their table. Jeff arrived and they waved him over to an extra seat. Nora, curiously absent, caused some to speculate. Pat whispered to Chad "Where is loud mouth this evening?" Chad shrugged digging into the Caesar salad. Griff and Mally sat quietly enjoying the delicious cuisine. Jonas and Phillipe ate heartily, as the food brought back appetites lost during recent colds.

Across the room Tim held court like a Lion in charge of his pride. He was getting attention he felt he deserved, the new guy, a fabulous dancer and a stud at that. Cynthia, Liz, and Marcy held onto every word.

Kathy remained unimpressed. She had known men like this when dating before she came out. He was typical of so many guys in the business; giant egos driven to conquer women and stepping on anyone to get ahead. He was boring. Tuning him out was a snap, she was going to enjoy dinner and phone her partner later. Sonja was back at college working on a master's degree in education. They missed each other more than ever.

As the evening continued, many excused themselves and headed elsewhere. Pat stayed with Chad, he was good company and like a kid brother. She was the youngest and only sister of three strapping Irishmen and enjoyed male energy. With the exception of Mal, her closest pal, she preferred being with male friends, not dates.

Continuing to impress his table companions, Tim was looking for action. Who could he nail? He was in a festive mood and horny as hell. Kathy was on the butch side and Marcy was a flake. Cynthia had the longest legs, the kind that would feel intense wrapped around him. She might like to get laid as there was no talk of a boyfriend. Or maybe Liz, who threw out a holier-than-thou-attitude, but might be fun to unleash in bed.

Another round of drinks was ordered. As the chatter continued, Tim became more insufferable. Kathy excused herself and left. Marcy decided to join her. Liz was clearly bored with this lothario and said goodnight, pausing to thank Fred Collier for the wonderful evening.

Only Cynthia remained, still caught up in Tim's jazzy chat. As they drank, he moved closer, taking the seat next to her. She was clearly attracted. He wasn't her usual type, but he was a hunk and she might like a change.

"So, is there a boyfriend back in New York?" Tim was nothing short of direct. He placed his arm on the back of her chair. "Not any- more," she said easily. I broke up with my boyfriend of five years before rehearsals started. Jack wanted to settle and I wanted more." Tim brightened. 'Maybe this babe is horny! So much the better,' he thought, planning his next move.

Brushing his fingertips across the back of her neck, he sensed she was enjoying it. Leaning closer, he whispered in her ear. "I would like to get to know you better. You're a beautiful woman," he soothed, con- tinuing. "Most women don't have your intelligence and certainly not your dance talent." Cynthia was caving in, the compliments coming at her making her vulnerable. 'This babe is as good as mine,' he thought as he sensed her growing desire. "I want to make love to you, Cynthia." She nodded weakly absorbed in him, ready to let him take her.

Signaling a passing waiter, Tim paid the bar tab. He stood and offered his hand. "Come on, I know a good place to show you how fabulous you are!" Cynthia rose from her chair, euphoric and curious. 'He likes me. He wants me,' she thought breathlessly. Together they stopped at the check room for their winter gear. As they walked the concourse, Tim slipped his arm around her waist, pulling her closer. "You need to get laid properly, babe. You can count on me."

The snow had returned, falling continuously. It was still early enough to enjoy the remaining hours, working off dinner. Tim had a plan, having every intention of carrying it out. And he did!

Chapter 27

One More Week

Thanksgiving was over, *Centipede's* last week in Detroit was about to begin. Cold temperatures and sleet made trudging to the Fisher unpleasant. The thoroughfare seemed wider by aggressive, prevailing winds. Fighting to stay upright was not the kind of workout the gypsies enjoyed. The cold tightened muscles, making the pre-show warm-up harder to complete. Vaporizers were added to the dressing rooms, leg warmers in evidence, immersion rods at hand for instant hot beverages. Winter was early and here to stay.

With another week to go, Pat was more than ready to return to the Bronx and her family! Owen's endless preoccupation with the show, the public's approval, the constant tightening, adding, or changing of choreography left fallow periods without him. It wasn't enough to be his muse, having been given the star turn in *Centipede*. She needed reassurance their relationship was solid.

Then there was Tim Bartel! How she loathed him! After all, he threw her away like garbage years before. She seldom dated after that heartbreaking experience, preferring the company of gay men instead. They were safe and understanding.

Blaine Courtman was an exception and had been a convenient distraction during separations from Owen the previous year. Blaine had wealth, privilege and loved sex, which he offered generously. He was mad about Pat, hoping to marry her. His biggest mistake was assuming she felt the same. In her eyes, he couldn't compare with Owen. He was a mere ripple in Owen's wake.

As she prepared for the final eight shows, she saw an end to the empty nights on the road, a chance to catch-up with her parents and brothers. Her family was her refuge and would provide the stability and the attention she craved.

Mally and Griff looked forward to their return to Manhattan and settling into life together. Their wedding would follow the Broadway opening. It would be a small, intimate ceremony, a reception at Sardi's for colleagues and a honeymoon night at the Waldorf. The *Bravo Business* cast had pooled their resources for the couple to spend a night at the elegant hotel. The gift was given at closing night in Boston.

Mally would ask her mother and stepdad to give her away. Frank was the only father she had ever known and Paula had raised her as a single parent, making them incredibly close. They were the perfect choice! Griff asked Dick Landry to be his best man. Mally chose Pat to serve as her maid of honor. Now, in just a few weeks, they would be wed.

On Wednesday, Fran Fairchild called in sick with stomach flu, leaving her weak, dehydrated, unable to perform. Nora had slipped in at half hour and was informed by Griff that she would be going on.

'Oh God, that means I have to work with Tim, she thought, filled with fear. Her hand shook as she signed in. In her mind, she clearly remembered the night of the assault. What could she do? She couldn't conveniently feign illness! As the only swing girl, she was duty bound to go on. Pausing near the stairwell, her mind flooded with grim thoughts. Suddenly she overheard voices at the call board, first Cynthia's, then Tim's!

"Hey, catch you later, okay?" Tim's voice sent a chill through Nora. "Okay! I'll meet you at the bar." Nora heard low murmurs then, silence. Quickly she bolted up the stairs. No need to encounter the enemy any sooner than she absolutely had to. It would be a rough night.

At the 15 minute call, Jonas' voice broke through the backstage hubbub. "Nora and Tim please report to the green room." Nora stood, slightly shaky and headed downstairs. It was impossible to miss Tim as she walked into the actor's lounge. He was there and ready.

"Okay kids, with Fran out, let's talk through the opening number," said Jonas, a slight urgency in his manner. "Let's go over here," he suggested, pointing to the upstage area. Tim appeared nonchalant as he followed Jonas. Nora's heart was beating wildly as she followed close behind.

"Since you've never worked this number together, I want to be sure you're on the same page. Tim, Nora is much smaller than Fran, so keep in mind there is less to lift, which might affect your timing. Let's see it." Without a moment's pause, Tim had Nora skyward, turning her in his powerful hands. As she slid down his body, she might as well have been a duffel bag, for all his interest. When they completed the lift, he looked right through her, showing no emotion whatsoever.

"That works fine, kids. Okay, you know the rest, so have at it!" Tim shrugged and walked away. 'He didn't say a word,' Nora thought, relaxing a little. As the overture began, she took her place in the group. It was if they had never met, much less had sex!

The number unfolded seamlessly as if Nora had done it dozens of times. Tim was only focused on the choreography. When the number finished, the blackout came fast. Nora groped her way off stage, relieved that it was over. The opening was the only number she had to work directly with him. It was painfully clear that Tim considered her a non-person.

Fran Fairchild returned the following evening, much to Nora's relief. She was off the hook for now! She reported in, saw that everyone was present and took off. As she passed through the stage door, she ran into Jeff as he arrived.

"Hey, stranger, how are you?" Nora smiled obligingly as she continued to walk away. "Hey, wait up! I'll just be a second," said Jeff, stopping at the call board. Everyone had signed in, so he was a free man for the evening. Catching up to Nora, he fell in step with her. "I missed you at Thanksgiving." Nora relaxed a little.

"I was under the weather. My allergies have been rough," she said, convincingly. "Yeah, that's what Griff told me. I had no idea you'd changed hotels. Are you all right now?"

"Yes, I'm okay. I just want to get back to New York. I'm not crazy about being on the road." "Can I buy you a beer?" Nora paused for a moment, considering. 'Jeff's okay,' she reasoned.

"Sure, that sounds nice, how about that little pub across the street?" "Let's go!" Jeff took her hand as they crossed Grand Boulevard. There was a light drizzle starting as they entered the bar. Finding two empty stools, they sat, loosening their coats. Jeff ordered two beers on tap. Then he turned to Nora.

"You know, I've been a little concerned this past week. You don't seem yourself." "Oh, why is that?" Jeff studied Nora for a moment, taking her hand. "I can't put my finger on it. I remember your enthusiasm about being in the show, doing Owen's work back in New York."

"It's that obvious?" Tears filled her eyes as she reached for a napkin. Jeff was surprised and curious. "Nora, for crying out loud, what is it?" Suddenly, the floodgates opened and Nora began to sob. Reaching for Jeff, she leaned against his shoulder as waves of emotion erupted.

"Oh Jeff, I don't know what to do! Something awful happened, something I can't share with anyone!" By now, Jeff was upset. "You can tell me! Come on now. What's so bad?" Nora tried to collect herself.

"I've been hiding for a reason. I'm afraid! Something happened last week!" Jeff stood and took her hand. "Let's find a more private place to talk." Without hesitation, they picked up their beers and located an unoccupied booth in the corner. Jeff settled next to Nora, putting his arm around her shoulder.

"Okay, tell me what's going on," he asked.

"I met a guy last week, a stranger. We were both attracted to each other, so we got it on. Things were okay at first, until he got rough. He raped me! There was nothing I could do. He threatened me and left." Jeff listened to every word, trying to keep calm, as Nora began to cry again.

"Why didn't you report this? "What could I report? He told me his name was Jack, that's all. But before he left, he threatened me if I ever told anyone." "Jesus, this is terrible."

"Now you understand why I haven't been around. And you must never tell anyone about this, especially management."

"God, Nora. I'm so sorry this happened. I wish you'd come to me!" "And do what, Jeff? The guy's vanished, off the radar. The only thing I can do is try to forget it," she said sadly.

"Well, we're getting out of here Sunday. Is there anything I can do in the meantime?" "Please, Jeff, just be my friend. I need one, okay?" Silently, they left the bar. Jeff walked Nora back to her hotel, seeing her to her room. Sadly, there was nothing more to say. They simply hugged. Jeff waited until she fastened the door chain. Then he left, shaken to the core.

Saturday night at half hour, Griff announced a short meeting for 7:50 in the green room. When everyone was accounted for, Griff began announcements.

"Company, as you know, tonight is our final night in Detroit. Please note the following before you leave the theatre. Make sure all your costumes and shoes are turned in. Check around your area for personal belongings. All of your luggage must be secured and marked with your New York address for pickup at 2:00 am. The call is 7:30 in the morning. Be downstairs at your hotel ready to board the airport bus. The flight to La Guardia is scheduled to depart Detroit Metro at 10:00. When you arrive at the airport, you will be met and given a ticket. Look for Northwest Flight 320. Are there any questions?" Liz raised her hand. "Yes, Liz?"

"How long is the flight to New York and will we have transportation to the city?"

"The flight is 2½ hours. Once in the terminal go to the Carey Transportation area just outside the building and look for a bus marked *Centipede,* it will take you to midtown and the Royal Theatre. From then on, you're on your own. Any other questions?" Griff spotted a hand at the back of the group. "Yes, Jeff?"

"When and where do we report next?" There would be little time for a break considering previews would begin at the end of next week.

"We will meet Tuesday at 1:00 at the Royal, *Centipede's* new home. You'll receive all the information next week. We will be in previews for three weeks, with a week off between Christmas and New Year's. The opening has been moved up to the first week in January. Now, if there are no further questions, places, please!"

As the overture began, there was tangible excitement. After weeks of rehearsal in New York, two weeks in Philadelphia and three in Detroit, it was time to go home! Home to the bright lights of Broadway and, hopefully, to a long running hit!

Chapter 28

Home in Manhattan

The plane dipped approaching La Guardia. On board, the gypsies were anticipating arrival in their city of dreams. After all, this was the place to make it happen, Broadway!

For some, five weeks on the road was too long. Choosing to work a national tour was one thing, out-of-town tryouts quite another. Tours were carbon copies of an original Broadway show, remounted and complete, ready to go. An unknown work in production was still morphing and being tested by audience response. Decisions that would alter already learned and rehearsed choreography were possible. Frequent changes, some challenging and interesting at times could also be frustrating and tedious. It was also a cautionary experience, like thin ice underfoot. How great it would be to start previews soon!

The landing and taxiing to the terminal was smooth, the return to terra firma reassuring. Most performing artists were nervous fliers, somewhat superstitious, preferring solid ground under their feet. When the stewardess announced, "Welcome to New York," general applause broke out. Stair ramps wheeled up, doors opened, the gypsies were on the move again, a short one. At the Transportation Door, a Carey bus marked *Centipede* was waiting, Manhattan next.

Griff, base crew and orchestra were scheduled to fly to La Guardia later that day. Production staff never traveled with the company following a load-out. The transit trucks had to be loaded under Griff's careful scrutiny and all other loose ends accounted for. Once equipment was underway, keys were turned back to the Fisher management and hotel bills paid.

On route, Griff pictured Mally at the door, welcoming him with delicious hugs and kisses. He couldn't wait to enfold her, make love to her and share their first home cooked meal in weeks. He loved their nest, their life and was looking forward to making it official: Mr. and Mrs. Griffen Edwards!

He would insist she keep her maiden name, Winthrop, for the stage. Most show business women kept their legal and professional names separate. Autonomy was important when a couple had careers in the same business.

He would never stand in her way. Mally was 15 years his junior, a fact he thought about often. She was on the brink of a successful career and his firmly established. Would she want children? Would he be too old watching them grow up? Would he be able to provide for his family once he was past his prime? These and many questions crossed his mind frequently, but the love they shared topped the concerns.

Owen preferred traveling alone, without the distraction of production associates and issues. It gave him time to relax, to enjoy his favorite scotch and read the *New York Times*, Sunday edition. He looked forward to being home, off Central Park West in the 60s.

He loved that space! It was his private domain, his sanctuary from the world. His only visitor was Pat, when he invited her. Returning to the city would create less opportunity to be with her intimately. She would be living with her parents. He surmised the Byrnes still thought of their girl an innocent homebody, dug in. No, they would have to be cagey, getting together between shows on matinee days, or creating an excuse that Pat was staying with friends. For now, this arrangement would have to work. Owen wasn't keen on cohabitation.

Jonas and Phillipe were thrilled to be home. They had taken a flat together in the west '60s off of Central Park West, an area popular with show people. The proximity to work was convenient and preferred. The selection of bars, bodegas, convenience stores and restaurants appealed to those who liked the new Lincoln Center area.

There had been little time for settling in, following the closing of the *Bravo Business* tour, before auditions were posted for *Centipede*. The boys decided to wait until they were both gainfully employed and economically sound to begin plans for their domicile. Jonas had a good friend, Mark Corson, an actor and carpenter, who free-lanced between jobs. He was a design genius, creating space out of very little.

Their railroad flat had potential, places for built-ins, additional closets and cubicles. They would add a new kitchen, as Phillipe was fond of cooking and modernize the bathroom, removing the vintage tile, tub and aging fixtures. Once the show had opened favorably, the redo would begin!

Jeff had become protective of Nora since the night she confided in him. When they arrived and were deposited at the Royal, Jeff insisted on sharing a cab. Nora had rented a room off West End Avenue in the 80s and coincidentally, Jeff was sharing quarters with two guys attending Columbia University a few blocks east near Central Park. Nora agreed to check in with Jeff when he dropped her off. She was still shaken and feeling uneasy about things in general.

"Here are my numbers," he said reassuringly writing them down. One is my service number, you can get a message to me day and night," he insisted. "Thank you, Jeff. I don't know what I would have done without you," she said, no trace of intimacy in her voice. Jeff was in a relationship and was likely faithful. Besides, the thought of having sex with anyone after the assault was nauseating. If chorus girls could double as nuns today, she was a ready candidate!

Jeff left her at the door. He waved as he started walking east. Nora watched until he was out of sight and opened the door. 'I wish I could rewind the tape and start over,' she thought.

It was 4:30 when Pat's cab pulled up to The Blarney. Paying the fare, she grabbed her bags and closed the door. The sight of the family bar filled her with delight. She hadn't called ahead wanting to surprise them.

Late afternoon was left at the door as she walked into the familiar place. The warmth of a crackling fire was welcoming and soothing, the room already decorated for Christmas.

Claiming a stool at the end of the bar, she placed her bags on the floor. Her dad was nowhere in sight, but her twin, Patrick, was at the helm pouring shots. One glance in her direction and he bounded over, navigating around the counter. He picked her up with such force she felt her breath leaving her.

"Lord Almighty, look who is back," he yelled, causing a few customers to stare. He was clearly delighted to see her. Tears filled her eyes as she accepted his embrace. He pulled back to a look, scrutinizing her from head to foot.

"My God, you're beautiful. Does Ma know you're here? Pop's on an errand at the moment!" "I wanted to surprise all of you! We just got in this afternoon from Detroit. The show's back!"

"Saints preserve us. This is great news! When is opening? Would you like a brew? Have you lost some weight?" Question after question tumbled out, causing her to laugh. "Slow down, brother. Give me a chance to catch my breath," she giggled. "I'll take Guinness," she ordered, crowing with delight. Patrick took off around the bar, shouting over his shoulder, "Done, little sister!"

Pat picked up her things and moved to a table. She wanted to take it all in, every detail of her father's pub. From her seat she had full view of the front door. She relaxed as Patrick brought her a glassful. He had a glass as well and raised it, "To you, beautiful sister," he said and then took a large swallow. Leaning back, he took a solid look at his twin across the table.

So how are you, Sis? You look a little skinny and a wee bit tired! Pat remained nonchalant, expressionless. "Well, truth be told, out-of-town tryouts are a grind. I won't miss those weeks!" Patrick watched her with interest. Then he smiled.

"You know, Tom O'Brian keeps asking about you. Now that you're back, he'll ask you out."

"For crying out loud, Patrick, I have absolutely no interest in dating him or anyone else for that matter!" Surprised by her adamant response, he withdrew a bit. "Hey Sis, calm down. No one is proposing marriage. I meant a simple date," he said, trying to cool the air between them. "Look, I'll decide whom and when to date! Are we clear?"

"Well, you certainly haven't lost your Irish wherever you just come from!" He stood, took his glass, and turned away. "I have to work. The brew is on the house. Welcome back," he tossed, without feeling. 'Welcome back indeed,' thought Pat. 'Nothing around here ever changes.' She shifted, trying to decide what to do next. Suddenly, the door opened and Alan and Maureen appeared. Pat stood hoping they'd glance her way.

Patrick was one step ahead, waving at them. "Look what the wind blew in," he shouted. Alan turned and stopped short. Maureen bumped him from behind and came around to his side.

"Patricia!" Alan rushed toward his only daughter and caught her up in his arms. Maureen followed. "Saints preserve us, darling girl, you're home," she cried. The three huddled, tears flowing, laughter and questions. "In heaven's name, when did you get in? We had no idea it was today. You never called," said Maureen, almost scolding in tone. "I wanted to surprise you. Obviously, I did," grinned Pat, as she held them close.

"Well, this calls for a brew," insisted Alan. Waving at Patrick, he ordered three Guinness on tap. Maureen protested, "We never drink in the daytime, Alan, for heaven's sake!" "This is not just any day, Patricia's home," he declared happily. Then, whistling, he announced to the few customers, "This one's on the Blarney. Order up!" There was non-stop merriment as the Byrnes celebrated. Later, older brothers Mickey and Sean arrived home to continue the celebration.

It was late when Pat entered her old bedroom. The walls seemed to close in as she fell on the bed fully clothed. Time was meaningless. Confusion swirled about her as she lay there, reliving the past eleven weeks. So much had happened. Images moved through her mind as she pictured herself dancing down center stage, Jonas deftly partnering her. She could see Mal, deliciously in love, keeping her company, never leaving her side in times of insecurity and doubt. The image of Tim

Bartel, gloating in his own self-importance caught her by surprise! The thought of him left her shaken and angry. He was like a sliver in her foot, an infectious, festering, foreign body.

Her thoughts then turned to Owen! He was ingenious, intense, intriguing, the only one who could fill her body and soul. She was his and they were back in New York! Arriving home was a relief, but for Pat, so much more. She had hope and perhaps hope would lead to a commitment from him. If hope came with a guarantee, she was home safe!

Chapter 29

New Developments

The phone woke Griff. "Damn it," he grumbled, reaching but dropping it over the side of the night stand. Mally stirred and rolled over, oblivious to the fumble on the other side of the bed. Without his cheater glasses, the dark room made it difficult to see in spite of daylight peeking under the window shade. Moving his hand along the floor, he traced the carpet until he felt the receiver, claiming it with annoyance.

"Edwards," the irritation in his voice obvious. The sound of Joe Kaplan's secretary, Marion Dupree, brought him to full attention as she whined her greeting.

"Mr. Edwards, sorry to disturb, but I have Mr. Kaplan on the line. Please hold." Griff sighed, followed by a deep breath. The tightness in his back and shoulders were sore reminders of the pack up and load out the day before. 'Had it only been yesterday?' His thought was interrupted by Kaplan's Brooklyn-tinged voice.

"Good Morning Griff, Kaplan here. How was the wrap-up in Detroit?" Griff wasn't used to Kaplan making a social call. There was something on his mind.

"Fine, Joe. We had the usual cooperation of the Fisher, nothing out of the ordinary in the strike and the weather held." "Good deal. Say, we have an unexpected development for *Centipede*. It may affect the scheduled move-in tomorrow."

Griff sat breathless, waiting for the proverbial ax to fall. In that empty space between hearing and processing, he found his cheaters, reached for the lamp switch and opened a drawer, grabbing a pad and pen. Sitting on the edge of the bed, he went into management mode, completely unruffled and fully awake. "What's the development, Joe? Let's have it!"

"Well, first of all, the calendar for *Centipede* has been slightly altered. Mr. Matthews has already been notified. We will start official previews on the 18th of December for three weeks. We're dark Christmas and return to previews with no break on New Year's. Presale indicates we're sold out. The official opening is slated for January 15th," he continued, rattling off details.

"So, what's your directive regarding this change?" Griff was always prepared to improvise, one of many facets in his job. Mentally, he was already charting the production's course.

"Well, you will detain the move-in for a week. The Royal is undergoing some interior upgrading and not ready for us to occupy until December 11th, a firm date."

"Is there storage space available for our equipment until then? We need to insure and protect our tech element until ready." As Griff wrote down details quickly, his cheaters kept sliding down his nose. 'This is why they pay me the big bucks,' he thought, a smile crossing his face.

"Stop in tomorrow and we'll finalize our course," Kaplan added. Griff interrupted. "The cast will have to be notified, as well as our musicians, tech staff and all jobbers," he insisted. "You're always on top of it, Griff. How do you do it?" "That's why you pay me the big bucks, Joe," Griff said with amusement.

Then another detail occurred to him. "You will have to arrange a rehearsal space for the cast. This delay will be murder on our performers. They've been working steady, tirelessly for the past eleven weeks on *Centipede* and they are expecting to rehearse and perform this coming week!" He was adamant. Kaplan paused, thinking.

"We will rent the large studio in Dance Arts for your rehearsal needs. Our office will reserve it strictly for the time prior to the move into the Royal. How does that work for you, Griff?"

"It should be fine. I will call the company into a meeting tomorrow. Say your offices at 1:00?"

"No problem. I will have Marion reserve the conference room. May I throw in a catered lunch as well?" "You're all class, Joe. Thanks so much. I will take care of notifying the cast of the meeting time and location tomorrow. I'll also inform Owen. See you then." "Thanks, Griff. We're lucky to have you." The conversation ended.

Griff removed his glasses, dropped the pad and pen and switched off the lamp. He leaned back against the headboard and closed his eyes, temporarily shutting out Kaplan's news. Mally stirred, rolled on her side and reached for him. "Darling, what was that all about?"

Griff opened his arms and enfolded her body into his. Her skin was warm, tender and soft. Soon his mouth found hers and he kissed her deeply, his tongue tracing hers. Mally sighed and pressed closer. She was an innocent when they met, a virgin so sweet, so curious, gentle. Together, they created ways to satisfy each other, coming from deep love and respect. Gently, they made love, falling into a sleepy trance when they had finished. Mally reached for the covers, noting Griff was already asleep. She kissed him softly and dozed off.

It was close to 1:00 at the Kaplan-Maggli office. Marion was on duty at the front desk, greeting the gypsies as they filed in and directing them to the conference room.

Griff, Owen, and Jonas were immersed in conversation. On one side of the room two carts filled with sandwiches, sides, desserts and an array of beverages were waiting. The producers had thought of everything. As the room filled, Griff welcomed the cast. He began his usual head count, cross checking the cast list. Gazing down the room, he noted quizzical looks and questioning eyes of the gypsies. His call late yesterday had been surprising to some, while the more seasoned took the news in stride. When the conference room was full, Griff waited for the group to quiet down.

"Company, thank you for coming today. Before we get started, I would like to introduce our producers, Joseph Kaplan and Leonard

Maggli." The room burst into applause, the two men walked to the front of the room. Kaplan spoke first.

"It's great to see you all here. Griff tells me that you are to be commended for completing eleven weeks of commitment and challenging work. Mr. Maggli and I are pleased with audience feedback and five successful weeks out-of-town." The gypsies burst into applause. Kaplan quieted the group, raising his hand. "Lenny, anything to add?" Maggli stepped forward.

"Joe is quite right! You're an amazing cast and *Centipede* will set records! Presale of previews indicates an early sell-out, with a trajectory of at least a two-year run. The Royal Box office staff is trying to keep up with phones ringing off the hook," he said, boastfully. "Keep it up, folks!" "Before we begin to give you our update, please take a few minutes to enjoy lunch," said Joe, gesturing to the carts.

"They always feed the condemned before the ax falls," mumbled Joe. The comment wasn't lost on Jim. "Don't project, Mary! Did you bring your crystal ball?" Joe rolled his eyes and headed to the food. Following lunch, Owen's voice dominated. "All right, settle down, let's get back to business!" Owen's voice was always compelling on or off stage.

"You've been called, because we have a change to deal with this week. The Royal is delaying our occupancy until December 11th, when renovations are completed. This doesn't buy any of us a vacation. If anything, we'll all push harder to make this happen. We've rented the large studio at Dance Arts, 4th Floor. It's imperative that every one of you work to your maximum. We must keep the show viable at all costs when we meet the public on December 18th! We start Thursday at 10:00, so be ready to go! Do you have anything else, Griff?"

"You have a bonus day off. I suggest you use the time to get settled. We will expect you at Dance Arts, 10:00 sharp on Thursday morning! Are there any questions?" Tim's hand went up. "Yes, Tim?"

"Will we be making choreographic changes? I just went into the show as is and would like a heads up." Owen glanced directly at Tim, shooting him a look of disdain that cut through the air.

"Well, Mr. Bartel, the show is frozen as far as I'm concerned. Perhaps you remember the process from your brief stint in the original *Bravo Business*!" Tim held his gaze as Owen continued.

"We'll be maintaining set choreography and making any spatial adjustments necessary. You do what you were hired to do, Mr. Bartel and I'll do what needs doing! Clear?" Tim's face showed no hint of Owen's sarcasm. Jonas and Mally exchanged glances. Pat looked away, irritated by Tim's interruption. Jonas whispered to Phillipe, "That prick will get his one of these days!" Phillipe gave Jonas a gentle nudge whispering, "*Cheri, ce n'est rien!*"

The meeting broke up at 3:00 pm, the room cleared, save for Owen, Jonas and Griff, who continued charting *Centipede's* course for the next two weeks.

Nora was nauseous. Food didn't sit well the past few days. She slipped away to the women's room to discard her lunch. Leaning over the commode, she heard two women enter. Attempting to control her gag reflex, she reached for toilet paper to cover her mouth. She began breathing deeply through her nose. The exchange taking place caught her attention. Tim's name came up repeatedly.

"Is Tim still doing you?" A soft chuckle was heard with more questions and comments. Nora leaned against the stall, straining for details. "God, he's good! He scared me at first when we started fucking. He's dominating! He gets aroused the more you beg! He's tried some stuff on me that's downright weird, stuff I've never tried before. Boy, did he get me going. He's fabulous!"

"Are you going to continue to fuck now that we're back?" Nora listened intently. 'My God, it's Cynthia! And Fran! She's getting off just hearing details.' Cynthia continued, "I certainly hope so! I still have a ways to go!" Fran laughed adding, "What a bad girl you are, naughty, naughty!" The two left laughing.

Nora sank down, her throat choked with tears. She'd been used and thrown away. And now, she was sick, nauseous every morning. Pulling herself up, it was time to go home, take a nap and forget about Bartel. The scar on her psyche was more intruding than her empty, touchy gut.

Chapter 30

The Unexpected

Thursday was here and the Dance Arts studio was filling quickly. Rehearsal would begin in 15 minutes. Energy filled the air, as the *Centipede* ensemble arrived for 10:00 am call. Changing to dance wear as quickly as they could, when dressed, they warmed up in Studio A. A few smokers were lagging and dragging, sipping Cokes in the corridor, their version of breakfast. It was a relief for many that the Tuesday meeting brought news of a delay, not a closing of the show. It was not uncommon for new productions to close out of town during tryouts. This was not the case for *Centipede*. There was an ease in the atmosphere as they gathered.

Griff joined Jonas at the front of the room. Frank Dugan, the rehearsal accompanist, ready at the keyboard, taking the last drag from his cigarette. He watched as the dancers stretched, he admired these hard working kids. His daughter, Corey, had become a soloist with Merce Cunningham's company. He understood what it took to achieve success: dedication, drive, hard work and bold face luck! Timing was critical, to be ready when opportunity knocked and Corey's timing was golden. He couldn't be a prouder dad.

"People, continue stretching while Griff talks," said Jonas, raising his voice over the chatter. Those still in the hall hurriedly put out cigarettes and took sips of water before joining the group.

"Good Morning! I hope all of you had a productive time off. I have a couple of announcements before Owen arrives. We are on Equity time, as always, so take your five-minute breaks when called. Lunch will be one hour, resuming rehearsal at 2:00. You will be excused at

6:00. We will meet tomorrow at the same time, etc." As Griff finished his remarks, Owen sauntered in, moving cat-like toward the mirror at the front of the room. He stood admiring the company as he listened to Griff. When announcements were done, Owen took over.

"Okay, people, we're here to work. You've had a couple of days off to get soft! We have to move forward now to bring this baby in. Work hard; keep the staging tight, clean and true to the concept. Don't lose the subtext you've worked for in each number. There's no time to be lax. *Centipede* has a ways to go before we hit Broadway. Sloughing off will not be tolerated!" He called Jonas forward.

"I want you to sit this one out and take notes for me. Jeff will cover your spot." Jeff hadn't planned on this, but was happy for the chance to fill in and get the workout. Jonas would judge what shape the gypsies were in after a four-day break.

"If there's nothing more, I leave you in good hands," he said, patting Jonas on the shoulder. "Start at the top and work them full out." Turning to leave, he caught Pat's eye across the room and smiled. "See you later," he tossed, strolling out the door.

Frank began playing. The gypsies, groaning into moves, worked to loosen the tightness inactivity had brought. As the warm-up continued, they slowly unlocked, their bodies facile. The company was back in business! After ten minutes, Jonas called for attention.

"Okay, gang, we have to get through two hours of choreography, so let's start with the opening and work through. Nora, come observe from here. Jeff, you got all the placements?"

"I believe so, Jonas. I had to cover while you put Bartel in the show, remember?" Jonas remembered all right! 'Shit, what a scramble replacing Jerry,' he mused. "Yes, you were really on top of it, thanks again."

Chad's hand went up. "Yes Chad, what is it?" "Have you heard how Jerry is doing?"

"Yes, as a matter of fact, I spoke with Ray Jordan, Jerry's partner, last night. Jerry's doing well and the doctor decided to release him. Ray is flying to Detroit this weekend to bring him home." A cheer went up. "Okay, back to work. There's a lot to do today."

The rehearsal began. It was good to be home on familiar ground! As the music filled the studio, elation came through with a magnificent force! The room buzzed as dancers dipped, lifted and whirled, approaching the perfection that Owen envisioned. It was a great first day back!

Pat was physically spent but emotionally charged after receiving Owen's message. "Baby, come to my place later, I miss you!" She rushed through the change from sweaty leotard and tights to jeans and loose fitting top. Slipping on flats, she took a quick look in the dressing room mirror, deciding a touch-up was in order. Grabbing the big-pronged brush she was never without she worked through her damp hair, wincing as she encountered a few surprise knots.

"Ouch! Shit," she muttered as she tried to control the thick waves. 'I had eight inches cut off and it's still a pain in the ass to brush!' Yet, she continued to wear it long, the color and texture were features she was proud of. 'Now a touch of lipstick and powder and that'll have to do,' she thought, anticipating Owen's scrutiny. Stuffing soggy rehearsal clothes and make-up pouch into her dance bag she headed for the elevator.

Pressing the main floor button, she waited, impatiently. As the door began to close, a pair of hands reaching in, the doors re-opened. Tim Bartel stepped inside! 'Oh my God, it's him,' she thought, cold reality flooding over her.

"Hi, Honey," he said, casually. Pat felt a knot forming in her stomach, as her heart began to race. Looking down at her feet, she avoided direct contact, though she felt his eyes all over her. She was trapped!

"Whoa, cat got your tongue?" He moved closer. "I finally figured out who you are," he said with a nonchalant tone. Pat felt panicked, the confines of the space adding to her anxiety. The walls were closing in as she looked everywhere except at him. Tim grinned as he backed her in a corner.

"Yeah, I fucked you plenty. You were an easy squeeze back then. Man, I'll bet you're plenty broken in by now, right?" Suddenly, Pat's anger flashed, her Irish rising. She took a bold step toward him, getting right in his face, her eyes blazing.

"You're an asshole, Bartel! I know as much as I care to, you piece of shit! If you ever come near me again, I'll report you to management!" Tim stepped back, surprised by Pat's outburst. She was on a roll, without fear, without hesitation. His natural bravado slipped slightly, as he stood gaping. "Are we clear, scumbag?"

As the elevator door opened, Pat stormed out and headed to the front door. Jonas and Phillipe were standing outside chatting, as they waited for the sudden downpour to stop. Pat came out of the building with a force that nearly knocked them down. Jonas reached out, breaking her stride. "Hey, slow down, Sweetie! What's going on?" Pat glanced behind her, nodding in Tim's direction and adding, "Why don't you ask him?" Jonas caught on immediately, blocking Tim as he tried to pass. "Okay, Bartel, what's going on?" Tim paused, a sly smirk on his face.

"I recognized Miss Byrne from high school. I was just being friendly," he said, regaining his cool. "Oh, is that right? Well, it doesn't look like she wants to be friendly! Isn't that right?"

Tim stood his ground. "Look, she overreacted. She's an uptight bitch, in case you hadn't noticed," he said firmly. Jonas took a step toward Tim, grabbing him by his lapels. Phillipe moved in ready to separate them.

"Be careful, Bartel," warned Jonas. "You're walking a fine line, so just stay the hell away. You got it?" Tim proceeded to shrug Jonas off. "Loud and clear," he said, arrogance oozing out of him. Jonas stepped aside, allowing him to exit. He stepped into the rain and disappeared down the street. Jonas took a big breath and turned to Phillipe.

"That guy is trouble. He'll probably try to screw every girl in the cast!" Phillipe listened, aware of Jonas' concern. "Cheri, they're all adults, capable of saying 'no' to *Monsieur 'Le Bête.'*

"*Le Bête*? Translation please, Babe." Phillipe smiled knowingly as he gave Jonas' ass a slap. "It means 'The Beast' in French, Cheri."

Jonas chuckled. "Oh Babe, let's go home and let our beasts come out," he whispered. The rain letting up as they hailed a cab to home, to play.

Tim Bartel was pissed off. He despised being rebuked by anyone, especially the Byrne bitch and her fairy consort. As he walked up 8th Avenue, he felt his temper slowly ebbing, but not his libido. Spotting a phone booth, he took out his phone book and scanned for Cynthia's number. Quickly dialing he waited. On the third ring, Cynthia's voice came through. "Hello?"

"It's me, Tim," he said casually. How are you after today, tired or horny?" He heard a giggle.

"Well, what do you think?" "I could use a fuck! Interested?" There was a pause, followed by a breathy sigh. "Yes, come over now," she said, her anticipation palpable. "See you soon. We'll shower together. I want you clean and fresh," he ordered. "Yes." There was a click.

Cynthia had come to enjoy Tim's domination and his demands. He got her going more than any other man she'd been with. She loved his body, his strength, his size, which was considerable and his quirky sexual techniques. It would be a physical night. She could count on it.

Chapter 31

Previews and Shocks

December 11th arrived soon enough, following a week of exhausting rehearsals to tighten and improve *Centipede.*

The Royal's interior was brand new with beautifully appointed seating, carpeting, drapes and a mammoth show curtain. Shades of royal blue, burgundy and gold complimented the lavish décor. Aisle runners were done in hues and patterns that complimented the color scheme.

The outer lobby was spectacular: French Empire style furniture, potted palms and flowering plants adding to the lavish atmosphere. Additional bars would be set up at the ends of the lobby for preview shows. The box office would accommodate more lines of ticket buyers. The Royal management added to their staff of ushers, concession clerks, bartenders and box office. And, two stage door men would rotate shifts during the eight-show week. They were ready on all levels.

The building had fallen on hard times over decades. Because of its historical significance on The Great White Way, a core of new owners agreed to rehab it. A contract was drawn by vote of the board and refurbishment underway. The Royal Theatre would be a 'Showplace,' again. The location was perfect!

Standing at the intersection of Shubert Alley and 45th Street, just west of Broadway, it was within steps of Sardi's, the time-honored restaurant of celebrities, the well-heeled and those wanting to see or be seen. A much-anticipated attraction like *Centipede* was bound to increase profitability for Messrs. Kaplan and Maggli and their investors. Potentially, an Owen Matthews show could run for years, delivering huge profits for many.

Griff found the stage and backstage area updated and was pleased with the easy move-in. His Broadway crew was among the best in the business. The technical aspects for *Centipede* were less complex than other shows he'd worked, making the set-up quick and relatively smooth.

At 1:00, Griff, Owen and Jonas waited for the company to assemble. Griff took roll as they settled. After conferring briefly, Griff spoke.

"Company, welcome to your new home at the Royal. Please note the physical set-up and location of quick change areas and access staircases to stage right and left. Acquaint yourselves with the backstage elevator. It runs from basement to the 5th Floor. It's original and has been overhauled, but it still moves slowly. Get used to timing yourselves when you use it. You may find the stairs more convenient and expedient. The number of passengers at one time is limited to four." Joe rolled his eyes, anticipating the worst. "Shit, imagine being trapped inside that baby when it breaks down," he muttered under his breath. His buddy Jim caught the remark, giving him a playful poke. "Trapped is being interviewed by a case worker when filing for unemployment," he offered. Joe grinned, "You made your point, Mary!" Griff continued his announcements.

"We will run the show, top to finale, this afternoon. We've already worked cue-to-cue, so this run is for your benefit. We'll skip costumes and make-up. Questions or concerns anyone?"

Jeff's hand popped up. "Will I be covering Jonas today?"

"No, Jonas will do the full show. You and Nora are welcome to sit out front and observe." Jeff threw a warm smile in Nora's direction.

She barely noticed. Owen spoke next. "Company, you have full advantage working on this stage now. Make any adjustments necessary to get used to the new floor. Watch your sight lines and be aware of your spacing on numbers at the stage edge. We will run the show with full lights and Frank on piano from the pit. We'll have the full *Centipede* orchestra, first preview, December 18th. Please work full out! Griff, let's begin."

The gypsies took their positions in the first formation at the top of the show. As Frank finished the overture, the massive curtain rose slowly in perfect sync with the lights. With music rising from the pit, the human sculpture down center stage sprang to life. Number after number sped by, the choreography tight, well-placed and clean.

The rehearsal wrapped at 6:00 pm and gypsies dispersed to their favorite hangouts at restaurants and bars in the theatre district. Some went home, exhausted. The fresh air felt good after the confines of the theatre. A light snow had begun. As Jeff walked up 8th Avenue, he noticed Nora a short distance ahead. Catching up to her, he fell in step as they walked.

"Hey kid, want to grab a bite?" There was no response as Nora continued, to the corner of 8th Avenue and 50th Street. She stopped and turned to face him squarely. Jeff was suddenly concerned as he noticed tears.

"Nora, what's wrong? Tell me!" Stepping toward him, she threw her arms around his neck with such force he almost lost footing. "Hey, what's going on?" He pulled away and took a good look at her. "Come on, we're going in here," he said, pointing to a small café. "Let me take your dance bag," he insisted. Offering his free hand, he led her to a cozy place. A sign at the hostess station read, "Please seat yourself."

Jeff chose a table for two in the corner by the kitchen door. Helping Nora off with her coat and muffler, he slipped out of his jacket and hung both on the coat rack nearby. "I'm so hungry I could eat my shoes," he laughed, trying to cheer her. "What would you like to drink? They should have a house red or white. Or maybe you'd prefer beer?" Nora shook her head.

"I'm not feeling well enough to drink alcohol, but I'll take a ginger ale, please." Jeff waved to the waiter across the room. He headed their way. "Yes? What are you two having?" "We'd like a ginger ale for the lady and I'll take whatever you have on tap." "I'll have that for you in a second. Would you like menus?" Jeff nodded. Nora remained silent.

"Okay, Toots, what in hell is going on with you?" Nora buried her face in her hands and sobbed. Scrambled words came tumbling out as Jeff strained to understand her outburst. "Oh Jeff, I don't know what to do, where to turn! I missed my period and I've never missed my period. I'm over a week late!"

Jeff reached for her hands, bringing them down to the table. He held them gently and tried to smile. "Have you seen a doctor?" "Yes, I went to see a doctor on 86th and Central Park West. He's a stranger," she said flatly. "Well?" "I'm pregnant," she wailed. Jeff leaned in, trying to quiet her. "Are you sure, Nora? You're not just imagining things?"

"I'm nauseous every morning. I can't sleep and I cry at the drop of a hat!" Jeff got up and moved his chair closer. Sitting next to her, he wrapped his arms around her tiny frame. "Oh, Baby, don't cry," he said gently. Nora's sobs turned to whimpers as she clung to him. "I'm so afraid and so alone!" Jeff listened, processing this new development. "Do you know whose it is?" Nora pulled back and looked directly at him. Her eyes flared. "Yes! It's that guy I told you about, Jack. He's the only one I've had sex with in months! I was drunk at the time and forgot to use my diaphragm!" "Jesus, Nora. What are you going to do?" Nora noticed the waiter approaching. He placed the drinks in front of them.

"Do you want to order now?" Nora shook her head. "I'm not hungry Jeff, but you go ahead," she said wearily. The waiter turned to Jeff, pen poised. "I'll have a cheeseburger medium with fried onions, a large order of fries, extra ketchup!" "You got it," the waiter said. Jeff turned to Nora and grinned. "I'm kind of hungry. Will my eating upset you?"

"Of course not, please!" The quiet between them became unsettling, as Jeff sipped his beer. Nora took a few sips of her ginger ale, stopped, moving the glass away. The tears began again.

"I have to get rid of it. I don't want this baby!" Jeff took another sip, finishing his drink. Reaching for his bag, he pulled out a pencil and pad. Scribbling something, he handed her the paper.

"This is the number of a close friend of mine, Darla Fredericks. She knows someone who can help." "Who does she know, for crying out loud?" Nora's voice was rising, panic obvious.

"Someone who can end this pregnancy," Jeff whispered.

"Are you serious?" Jeff nodded carefully. "Yeah, she knows an abortionist on the Lower East Side. When she got knocked up by a lover, she had no choice. She was married and her husband couldn't produce sperm. It would have been a dead giveaway. She didn't want to fuck up the marriage, so she got rid of it. You know it's illegal, right?" Nora nodded sadly. "How much is this going to cost?" "It depends. The going rate is anywhere from $300-500. It's risky, so they charge a lot." "Jeff, I don't have that kind of money," Nora said, trembling. "Yeah, well I do. I was saving it for a rainy day. Looks like it's pouring," he said with a half-smile. "Oh, Jeff, I can't let you do that! What would your girlfriend say?"

"Well, I haven't mentioned this, but Faye and I broke up before we left for Philly. She isn't in the business. My constant contact with the women I work with made her insanely jealous. She was always accusing me of having affairs. I couldn't handle her insecurity, so we ended it."

"Did you love her?" Jeff looked at the waiter approaching. "Here you are, sir. Can I get you anything else?"

"Yes, another beer and the check, thanks." Jeff lifted the bun, adding the extra pickles on the side and more ketchup. "They never give you enough pickles," he claimed, taking his first big bite. "Are you sure you don't want some?" Nora made a face, a small smile beginning. "No. Actually, I think that would do me in about now." Jeff continued wolfing down the burger, pausing in between bites to sip on his beer.

"Did you love your girlfriend?" "Yes, I loved her very much. I wanted to marry Faye, but I couldn't take the jealousy anymore." "I'm sorry, Jeff. I really am." Jeff looked at her for a second, put down his sandwich and took her hand.

"I want to help, Nora. Please let me! I'll see you through this. Give Darla a call. She'll refer you." "Will you go with me?" Jeff took Nora in his arms, holding her gently. "Of course I will. You'll have to set it up for our day off. No one must know."

"Oh Jeff, thank you," she cried. They pulled apart as the waiter returned with the bill. Jeff opened his wallet, producing cash to pay the check. Rising, he retrieved their coats and helped Nora on with hers before putting on his jacket. "Are you ready?"

"I guess I will have to be, won't I?" Arm in arm they left the café and walked up 8th Avenue. Snow was falling faster, now piling up on curbs and in gutters. Jeff let out a whistle as a yellow cab slowed up at the light. Getting in, he pulled her next to him. "Come on, I'll take you home."

As they sped off, Jeff's lips found Nora's. He was gentle, sweet and so kind. Nora couldn't believe this was happening. 'I've been with a savage and now a saint,' she thought, cuddling closer. The journey to this point had been lonely, but the ride uptown was anything but. Thank heaven for Jeff Jenkins!

Chapter 32

Resolution

Not knowing what to expect, Nora was terrified phoning Darla Fredericks. On the third ring, a female voice picked up.

"Hello?" "Darla Fredericks?" There was a momentary pause. "Yes. Are you Nora?" "Yes. How did you know?" "Our mutual friend called and said I'd be hearing from you." Nora let out a sigh. "May I have the information? I have to take care of this fast," said Nora, anxiously. "Yes. I understand. Jeff's a good friend." "Is it painful? Will I be able to go to work?"

"It depends. Judith Hathaway is a retired surgical nurse. She knows what she's doing. She won't mess you up if she can help it. She can be reached at Murray Hill 6-3926. When you call, tell her Darla referred you." "I don't know how to repay you, Darla." "Just be careful and make sure Jeff is close by." She sat, unable to grasp her predicament.

Dialing the phone again, Nora waited breathlessly. A strong voice answered. "Yes?" "Miss Hathaway?" "This is. Who's calling?" Nora shook as she responded carefully. "Darla told me to call. I need help." There was a pause and the voice softened. "I can help. How far along?

Timing is critical." "I'd say about three weeks. A doctor has confirmed the pregnancy." "I see. The price is $400, payable before the procedure. Do we understand each other?" Judith's voice had a slight edge.

"Yes, I understand. Are you available Sunday, December 17th?" Judith paused to consider the date. "Sunday's unusual. But yes, come promptly at 10:00. The procedure will take approximately ten minutes. The address is 419 East 8th Street, Apt. 4C. Tell no one and come alone." "Thank you, Miss Hathaway. I'll be there." Nora hung up feeling more alone than ever before.

Rehearsals at the Royal progressed, the show finally needing an audience. The Kaplan-Maggli firm arranged several interviews for print and TV. Advance publicity was everywhere. Billboards in Times Square, subway stations and major thoroughfares to and from the city heralded the arrival of *Centipede.*

Front page ads ran in the trades: *Show Business, Backstage,* and *Variety.* Several promos looped continuously on local radio stations. A lengthy article with photographs would be in the Sunday *New York Times* prior to the January opening.

The main attraction was Owen. Three networks clamored for him for their late night talk shows. This meant a potential ratings boost for the lucky hosts, always battling for the number one spot. He was considered the most brilliant and controversial director-choreographer on Broadway for the past two decades.

Monday of preview week, Griff posted a notice. A feature writer from the *New York Times* would be coming Thursday, December 14th at 1:00 for interviews, group and individual photos. It was mandatory for all cast members to be there with hair and make-up done, fully costumed. Owen would be interviewed elsewhere at a time of his choosing.

The fuss over Owen was getting to Pat. There she sat in the Bronx, desperately wanting to be more visible. It wasn't enough to dance eight performances of *Centipede* a week. Late night lovemaking was infrequent and she needed much more! How she wished to be his partner 24/7! She longed for them to be acknowledged as a couple at press parties, romantic dinners, concerts, or strolling through Central Park on

Sundays. How fabulous it would be to stop for brunch at The Russian Tea Room together or attend the annual Tony Awards on his arm! She wanted it all!

It had been a week since they had made love. Pat ruminated as she lay on her bed, feeling the need for physical release. Her libido was in overdrive as she got up and crossed to the door, locking it. Returning to her bed, she stretched out across the comforter, and closed her eyes. Imagining Owen was easy as she created the scenario.

She is nude, Owen in briefs, large equipment obvious through the cotton. He kneels before her sliding her panties to her ankles. His hands on her abdomen, his fingertips delicately brush her mound, playfully twisting her pubic hair. Touching further, he gains entrance to her most private self. Moving his finger in and out, he probes and plays bringing her nipples to full attention. Pat is wet with wanting, her pelvis moving side to side, pressure building until she explodes with ripples of pleasure.

The vision vanishes and she is alone, perspiration coating her body, her hand moist. As her breathing relaxes, Maureen's voice is heard outside her door, announcing dinner. And, as always, her eyes fill with tears, tears of longing. 'Oh Owen, please need me. I can't live without you.'

Time accelerated toward the first preview, Monday, December 18th. Tech runs with the cast and the final tech dress on Saturday had the gypsies of *Centipede* ready. The choreography had been fine-tuned and rehearsed to a new level of excellence. It was time for the New York public to view Owen's latest.

The company was in the midst of pre-show prep: hair and make-up, costumes and last minute stretching. Enthusiasm was high with soft conversations throughout the dressing rooms. Jonas and Phillipe listened to the gossip amongst the gay boys. Joe and Jim spoke of their recent conquests after the grind of rehearsals. Chad remained quiet, taking little notice. Occasionally, he talked to Dick Landry about Dana's pregnancy. She was due the end of the month. Chad admired Dick's ambition for a career in management.

Tim Bartel was at the far end of the room. He was the lone wolf of the company and had little interest in the boys, their exploits, or gaining approval. He considered himself the best dancer and was one of the few straight men in the cast. He liked Chad's ability and youth, found Jeff a reliable and accurate swing, but had no opinion of Phillipe one way or the other except the obvious. 'Just another pretty faggot,' he thought derisively. Since the scolding at Dance Arts, he kept his distance from Jonas. He was uncomfortable knowing Jonas and Pat were close.

Musing over the company women, he took inventory. He had discarded Nora, a cheap, horny nothing. Cynthia was able to please him, but he was growing tired of her. Kathy was a fucking lesbian, Marcy a flake and the others downright snotty. Mally was not on his radar. He never messed with another man's woman. He had no need for used goods. No, he'd seek a new assortment elsewhere.

The final tech dress was complete. The show was ready for the first audience the day after tomorrow. Everyone was ready to show off *Centipede.* They couldn't miss!

Owen needed some downtime to relax before the big push. He was horny and Pat would satisfy his rampant libido. They had spent little time together the last weeks. This weekend, before previews, was a perfect opportunity to have her totally. Stopping at the stage door, he waited. Suddenly, he spotted the flowing red hair and exquisite body moving toward him. As she approached, he reached out. Pat could see the longing in his eyes.

"Baby, how are you?" "I'm okay, I guess. I miss you, but I'm sure you know that," she said with an edge. Looking around, he checked for personnel, the coast was clear. Taking a step closer, he took her face in his hands, caressing her gently. Leaning down, he kissed, pressing into her mouth with fervor. Pat sighed under his touch. She was already wet, as he explored her with his tongue.

"Let's go to my place. We have some serious catching up to do," he said softly. Without another word, he took her by the hand, walked out of the theatre and hailed a cab. Sliding in the back seat, he took her in his arms and kissed her again. "I've missed you, Baby. I'm going to show you how much," he whispered. The cab pulled from the curb. Owen was always insatiable and she the happy recipient! The wait was over!

Chapter 33

Consequences

The wind was biting and the day bitterly cold as Nora and Jeff made their way to Judith Hathaway's apartment. Their plan was simple. Jeff would remain outside during the procedure and take Nora to his place to recover. They must use caution. Judith's warning of 'come alone,' meant exactly that. The procedure would be scrubbed if they were found out.

Jeff's reassuring hug brought tears. Wiping them, Nora climbed the stairs leading to the entrance of a vintage brownstone. Finding "Hathaway" on the bank of names and numbers, she pressed a button. Seconds passed and she heard that familiar strong voice through the speaker on the mailboxes. "Yes?"

"Miss Hathaway? This is Nora Blake." A short pause and a buzzer sounded. The door clicked open as Nora pushed her way into the inside hall. Looking ahead, she saw a staircase leading to all floors in the building. Taking a deep breath, she began the climb. With each step, she became more frightened. What she was submitting to was against the law. And yet, there was no other choice for her. She reached Judith's apartment and knocked softly.

The door opened. A small, sinewy man stood dressed in an overcoat, hat over his eyebrows, a cigarette hanging on his lip. He gestured for her to enter and quickly checked the hallway before closing and sliding the bolt. "Where's the $400?" Nora took out her wallet and counted. His manner was all business, never giving her direct eye contact. As he re-counted, the smoke from his cigarette curled around her head. Finishing, he pointed to a small sofa in the corner, "Sit down. I'll tell her you're here."

Nora felt shaky. The apartment was tidy but sterile looking, lacking any warmth. The windows had dark shades, closing off the outside. The sinewy man disappeared into another room, Nora heard whispers. Suddenly, a heavy-set woman appeared wearing medical clothing. Her hair, in an upsweep, was held by a net. She was plain and wore an expression of indifference.

"Miss Blake, come here." Judith looked her over as though she was a piece of meat. Time stood still. "How much do you weigh?" "105 pounds," Nora said, her hands shaking. "Well, follow me in here," she said, stepping aside. The room was chilly, adding to her apprehension. "Get undressed and lie down on the table," she said, automatically. "You can hang your things over that chair. I want everything off from the waist down." 'What a cold fish,' Nora thought. Nonetheless, she did as she was told.

Removing her coat, scarf, shoes, and socks, Nora's slacks and panties followed. Placing them in a pile on the chair, she moved slowly to the procedure table. It was hard to miss the stirrups and the plastic covering on the floor. A row of surgical instruments was lined up on a side table.

"Now get settled. I'll be back in a minute," she said, her tone compelling. Nora lay down on the table trembling. The room seemed to close in on her. Tears meandered down her cheeks, into her ears. Judith returned shortly with Canadian Club and a glass. Putting the glass on the table, she opened the whiskey and poured a double shot. "Here, drink this. It'll relax you." Nora leaned on her elbow, taking the glass. Swallowing the contents quickly, she gagged, it burned. For a few moments, Judith stood with her back to Nora, who smelled anesthetic in the air.

"Miss Hathaway, what are those tools?" She pointed to the instruments as Judith turned. 'No goddamn customer in memory has asked me this,' she thought, irritated with the inquiry. "Well, if you must know these will end the pregnancy. Here is endo-specula, this, an MVA, and this, a uterine curette," she recited. "The lesson is over, Miss Blake!" Nora felt a knot in her stomach, her face growing tense. Judith approached.

"All right, put your feet in the stirrups. I will drape you. I'm going to coat your vagina with iodine. You will feel the specula as I open you up," she said matter-of-factly. Nora scooted down until she could reach the stirrups with her feet. The metal was cold. Judith, now masked, wore surgical gloves. Methodically, she inserted the specula. Nora winced, closing her eyes. The whiskey was beginning to numb her senses slightly as she prayed for it to be over fast. Without hesitation, Judith continued.

Nora screamed as she felt the sharp object enter and twist. Pain rushed through her brain causing her to squirm. "Lie still," Judith ordered, "and shut up!" Nora was dizzy with each stabbing sensation from Judith's MVA. Then she blacked out. When she opened her eyes, she was clammy all over. The pain was excruciating, throbbing, her insides protesting. She noticed Judith standing next to the table, observing her like some lab animal.

"Miss Blake, you lost some blood, so I want you to stay put for a few minutes. When you are able to get off the table, get dressed and leave. Tell no one about this." Nora was shocked at Judith's callousness. She had just cut into her body! Slowly, she found her voice through the fog of pain. "What should I do now?"

"Well, don't bathe for 24 hours. Sponge baths are all right. And rest! You don't want to hemorrhage! Take Tylenol for pain every four to six hours if needed. No aspirin!" After wiping up she placed the instruments in a sterilizer and slipped off her gloves. "I will be using the room in an hour, so please change and go," she snapped, dismissing her. Nora heard the door shut.

Warm tears resurfaced as Nora lay there. Anger, humiliation and pain rose up in a swirl of emotion as she felt the first contraction of her abdomen. "Oh God, please help me," she whimpered.

Minutes passed before she could push herself to a sit. Slipping her feet out of the stirrups, she dangled her legs over the side and stood on the cold floor. She felt a jar in her pelvis, causing her to wince. On the plastic covering beneath the table were splotches of blood, reminders of the horror she just endured.

Nora reached for her clothing. Each move was painful, she felt like she was tearing inside. A warm trickle between her legs caused her to gasp as she slipped on her panties. Looking down she noticed dark red spots, more traces of Judith's handiwork. Getting dressed was a challenge.

Slowly, socks and slacks next and, finally, her shoes went on easily. Reaching for her coat, scarf, and purse, she opened the door and slipped out. The sinewy man was down the hall, smoking, he glanced and immediately looked away.

The staircase was like crossing a minefield. Holding the banister tightly and with slow aching steps, she descended to the lobby. Stepping out the door, she gulped the fresh winter air and looked frantically for Jeff. He was there, across the street, huddling in a doorway. She waved as she held herself upright against the door jam. Jeff caught the signal immediately and rushed to her. The shock on his face said it all.

"God, Nora! Are you all right? Can you walk to the corner? I'll find us a cab!" "Help me, Jeff. I'm falling apart," she sobbed. He wasted no time, scooping her up in his arms. She was light, almost weightless. Nora clung to him burying her face in his shoulder, muffling the sobs. Reaching the corner, a cab was halfway up the block; he waved, adding a loud whistle. The yellow pulled up. Jeff lowered her gently, opened the door carefully guiding her in.

"Driver, please take us to 225 West 106th," he said. Nora began to doze off, leaning against his chest. The driver headed across town to the West Side Highway. Jeff never took his eyes from her. Nora's breathing was deep, coma-like. 'This whole thing is crazy,' he thought, as street after street flew by. Turning off the highway, the cab found Broadway, turned left and drove north. Jeff contemplated the situation. 'I'll take care of her and keep her safe from guys like that bastard Jack,' he thought. She was delicate and beautiful, this tiny slip of a woman in his arms. He felt his heart open, tears welling up. Jeff Jenkins knew he was falling in love, again.

Later that evening, he dozed in a chair as Nora slept in his bed. His roommates were away for the weekend, making it convenient to bring her there. He wouldn't risk leaving her alone. He remembered the humiliation and pain in her eyes.

It was a rough night. Between waking fitfully and falling back into deep sleep, Nora was trying unconsciously to distance herself from her terrible ordeal. Sleep was the kindest remedy. The emotional pain would take longer than her body to bounce back. She was fit, strong and young. And now, she wasn't strapped with a baby! Thank God!

"Jeff, where are you?" He rose quickly and came to her. "Could I have some water?" Her voice was barely audible, the strain of intense emotion tightening it. "I'll be right back," he hastened. Disappearing for a minute, he returned with water, handed her the glass, carefully guiding her hand. She took two or three sips, groaned, and handed it back, closing her eyes. "Can I get you anything else? Are you hungry? Do you need to use the bathroom?" Nora shook her head. "Just sleep, Jeff. Please let me sleep." "I'm going to the other room for a while. Sleep as long as you can. I'll take you home tomorrow, okay?" She was already asleep.

Jeff thought about the first official preview. How would she handle checking in? God forbid, if one of the gals was out tomorrow night! 'Don't project, Jeff. It'll be fine,' he thought, reassuring himself. Turning on TV for distraction, he mused, 'Tomorrow has to be a lot better than this past day from hell.' The unknown held surprises, hopefully happy ones.

Chapter 34

Preview Time

After three months of intense preparation, it was reckoning time. There was little doubt that *Centipede* would soon be the talk of the town.

Excitement built as the newly refurbished Royal house filled with eager patrons, all wishing to be among the first to see the newest Matthews' show. In a half hour, it would begin, bringing performers and audience together.

Hours before, Jeff had taken Nora home. She had slept off and on most of the previous day and night at his place. Monday was the beginning of preview week and getting back on track was essential to keeping her job.

She had occasional throbbing and the wrenching pain had eased overnight. A long sleep had been healing and Jeff's caring for her had been a miracle. Who else could she trust? Who else would have been so protective? He had encouraged her to eat and helped her bathe. Nora was feeling better physically, but emotionally, she was wiped out. Coping would be a tough test.

Cast members could be very catty and unkind. She never felt accepted by the women. And the men? Well! One had turned out to be the enemy. A chill ran up her spine. No one should suffer as she had at his hands. How she wished she had the balls to report him! Griff would fire Tim's ass! Or maybe the guys would beat the crap out of him first! The thought brought a slight smile.

"Thank God, they're all in," she whispered to Jeff, as she looked over the female cast list. Jeff checked the men's list as well. Smiling, he gave Nora's shoulder a pat when he realized neither of them would be going on. Now they could slip away once the show had started. Only if an injury occurred during performance would either of them have to cover. As they considered this, the stage door opened, and Owen entered. "Good evening, you two. Everybody in?" "Yep! All are here," said Jeff.

"Well in that case, why don't you stake a spot in the back of the house? I want you to see the show with an audience. It's been a while and it wouldn't hurt to review," he insisted. Nora's heart sank as she glanced at Jeff, who was stumped. He wanted to take her home to rest and recover. Owen noticed Nora's pale complexion. "Are you all right, Nora?"

Jeff spoke up, navigating carefully. "Owen, Nora's got a bit of stomach flu. I was relieved she doesn't have to cover tonight. I'm off, too. I was hoping to see her home. She needs to shake this thing." Owen studied the two carefully.

"I don't want this bug around, so get the hell out of here!" Then he softened. "Take care of yourselves and call Griff tomorrow to check in. I'll let him know you're taking off tonight." "Thanks so much, Owen," murmured Nora, taking Jeff's hand. Owen couldn't help but smile.

"Jeff, please take good care of this lady. She's the best swing I've ever had." He turned and headed backstage. Jeff put his arm around Nora, giving her a squeeze. "Hon, that's fabulous praise coming from him!" Nora grinned for the first time in weeks.

It was almost show time! Griff called the cast to the green room for a short meeting. They gathered expectantly like racehorses at the starting gate. What a fine group! The women, slim and stunning in their body suits, hair tied back, Broadway eyes! The men firm, solid, their bodies accented by the fabric of their costumes. They were determined, ready, and unstoppable!

"Company, this is our first official preview," Griff began. "The pre-publicity on this has been widespread and the public is primed. Our show is new, never before imagined on a Broadway stage. Expectations are high out front and we're sold out for the next two weeks. What happens now will greatly affect our official opening and run. So give it all you've got. Thank you!"

It was Owen's turn. "This is why you've taken my verbal bludgeoning, worked your asses off to achieve *Centipede!* You deserve the highest praise for your dedication and commitment. From here out, it's going to be cake, ladies and gentlemen! Let's bring in a winner!" Owen glanced at Pat, smiling warmly. "Places, please," shouted Griff. The group moved to the stage ready to dazzle.

Pat was the last to leave the green room. As she moved toward stage right, she felt a hand reach for her, pulling her into the shadows. Startled, she gasped as warm lips pressed her mouth, arms circling her waist. "Owen!" "Baby, I'm so proud of you! After tonight, Patricia Byrne will be a known in this town!"

Pat looked around carefully. Reaching for his face she kissed him gently. "Oh Owen, I love you!" Owen pulled closer, nuzzling her neck. "Baby, I'd fuck you right here, but you've a show to do," he whispered. "Catch you later and that's a promise." He slipped behind a backdrop leaving Pat predictably wet. Hearing the overture, she moved quickly to join Jonas for the first number.

"Break a leg, Irish," he said, grinning. Pat gave him a quick hug as they took their opening pose. The curtain began to rise.

Two hours of *Centipede* flew by. The audience didn't wait for the company bow. They were on their feet en masse, applauding and screaming as the finale ended. On stage, the gypsies stood, bathing in the overwhelming approval. Sweat-soaked bodies, chests heaving, they waited for the adrenaline rush to calm. How good it felt!

When the last bow was taken, the cast waited for the immense show curtain to descend. As the audience slowly exited the house, the company hugged, yelled and hurried off stage to change. Time to celebrate! Owen was ecstatic as he went to Griff's desk. Griff was still in tech mode as he wrapped up crew details for the night.

"Mr. Edwards, we've done it again," said Owen extending his hand. "It's a sure winner, Owen."

"Please make an announcement right away. Tell the company to meet at Barrymore's for a drink on me as soon as they're ready!" "They'll appreciate it," remarked Griff, picking up his microphone. Owen winked.

"Hell, I'd give them an extra week's pay if I were Kaplan," he said with uncharacteristic enthusiasm. "See you at Barrymore's. Don't be late, Mr. Edwards!" Griff called the cast.

"Attention! Please join Mr. Matthews at Barrymore's for a company toast. Drinks are on him!"

Upstairs, the girls in various stages of undress kibitzed and cleaned up. Mally and Pat chatted as they toweled off, while others redid make-up and straggling hair. Only Cynthia sat stone-faced and brooding. Fran caught her grimace in the mirror and moved closer.

"Hey Cyn, what's going on? You've been kind of moody." Cynthia was removing her make-up with cold cream, wiping off the excess with tissue. "Bartel's avoiding me. I don't get it. I thought he dug our fucking!" "Maybe he has a girlfriend stashed somewhere."

"Are you kidding? That guy isn't about commitment. He's one of the bad boys, Fran!" "Why don't you come right out and ask him, Cyn?" Cynthia was aghast. "Fran, you can't be serious! I won't stoop to that. Anyway, it's his loss," she muttered, not quite believing it.

"Let's go to Barrymore's. I'll bet there are other fish to fry," urged Fran. Cynthia finished taking her make-up off and walked to the sink. She ran her hands under the warm water, rinsing her face. "Give me five minutes and I'll be ready to go."

Fran sat waiting. She couldn't stop thinking about Tim Bartel's penchant for using women. Contemptible! Her good friend Cynthia was now a castoff, which pissed her off. She, too, had experienced similar men and understood the humiliation of being thought used goods. 'That creep needs to be put in his place,' she told herself. 'It's just a matter of time before I get him good!'

Mally had changed into jeans and was pulling on a sweater when she heard Jonas' voice in the hall. Looking through the neck hole, she saw his happy smile, his enthusiasm filling the room. "Hey Ladies, you heard the man! Hoof it over to Barrymore's as soon as possible! See you there!" He dashed away in seconds.

Pat was noticeably quiet, deliberately taking her time to get ready. Loosening her chignon, she let her hair down and began to brush out the snarls with great effort. Mally watched, noticing her mood change. "Are you coming to Barrymore's? Owen will expect you."

Pat sighed and put down her hairbrush. "Mal, I'm so frustrated. He never lets on about us. I'm always single in group situations. I feel unimportant to him," she whispered. "Pat, for crying out loud, how long has this been going on? You once told me that Owen set the rules in your relationship. You aren't allowed to make demands on him."

"Yes, but that was in the beginning. I honestly thought he'd change after his divorce." "Well, he hasn't. You definitely have competition." Pat looked shocked. "God, do you know something I don't?" "Patricia Byrne, the competition is his other lover, the work. You know that! Now come on. Let's go to Barrymore's." Resigned, Pat stood, slipped on her boots and grabbed her coat.

"Mal, you're my voice of reason and I love you!" "I love you too, silly girl! Now let's go," she urged. Dressed in their winter gear, they left the dressing room and headed downstairs. Heavy snow was falling as they exited the theatre.

The company had gathered and the mood was high. The bar was crowded with gypsies ordering drinks at Owen's invitation. At a large table in the main room, he sat holding court. Several cast members stood by, the conversation lively as they recounted the evening. Griff arrived and found the girls standing at the bar, waiting to order.

"I'm looking for a date," said Griff, nuzzling Mally, playfully. They kissed. Pat glanced around the room. Her eyes found Owen, who was clearly enjoying the attention and fawning.

Griff's voice brought her attention. "What are you lovely ladies having?" "I'll have a Bacardi on the rocks," said Pat. "Your usual,

Chablis?" "Yes, please." Griff signaled the barman, who worked his way down the line. "Hi! We'll have a Bacardi on the rocks, a glass of Chablis and make mine a Tanqueray martini, with a twist."

"Coming shortly, sir," he said, moving quickly. Mally and Griff cuddled watching the fun.

Their drinks arrived; Griff passed them around and raised his glass. "To the two finest ladies in town," he crowed, taking a first sip. Catching Owen's wave across the room, he smiled. "The masterful Matthews beckons, come on!" The trio joined the happy throng.

Owen was helped to the table top. Raising his glass, he observed his brilliant corps as they smiled at him adoringly. "You people do me proud. Your effort has raised the bar on Broadway." His gaze found Pat. Then a surprise! "I'd like to propose a toast to all of you." They raised their glasses, taking a sip as he continued. "I want to make a special toast to the beautiful and brilliant, Miss Patricia Byrne!" Everyone turned to Pat, who stood, shocked!

"Here, here!" yelled Jonas.

With glasses raised, the group cheered and drank. Owen took a sip and eased down off the table. Careful not to spill his scotch, he worked his way to Pat's side. "Baby, you're the best!" Without missing a beat, he took her in his arms and kissed her full on the mouth! The crowd whistled and shouted as Pat went limp. Through the noise and revelry, he brushed her ear with his lips. "Come on, I know a better way to celebrate." Without another word, he chugged his drink, took hers and placed their glasses on a nearby table.

"Are you ready, Baby?" Pat nodded as if in a trance. Working his way through the crowd pulling Pat along, he spotted Griff and waved. Then they were out the door. Ready for a private party, he hailed a cab. Slipping into the backseat with his muse, he pulled her close as they drove away. Tonguing and touching her was just the beginning as they sped uptown.

Fran couldn't leave well enough alone. She noticed Tim slip out a side door. 'He's probably grabbing a smoke,' she thought. Pulling her coat collar up, she stepped out into the alley. The snow was still falling heavily. Tim stood a few feet away, under an awning.

"Got a light?" Tim looked over and shrugged, producing a lighter. Fran took a cigarette from her bag, lit it and handed it back. "Thanks."

Inhaling, she let the smoke out slowly, her lips relishing the exhale. Tim watched her impassively, his eyes never changing expression.

"Some show tonight, huh?" After a few seconds, he moved closer. "Yeah, it felt right." Fran took a breath, her heart accelerating as she planned her course. Taking another drag, she turned to face him, letting out the smoke, watching it curl around his face.

"You're an amazing dancer, Tim. I can't stop watching you." Tim's eyes flickered slightly, a sly smile on his face. "I'm even more amazing when I fuck!" A flush rose on Fran's face in spite of the cold. "Really, I hadn't heard that," she said matter-of-factly. Tim didn't miss a beat as he took her chin in hand, running his tongue over her mouth. Dropping her cigarette in the snow, she allowed him access, trying to keep her wits about her. "You want to find out?"

He pushed her against the building, leaving little choice. His hands deftly felt for the opening of her coat. Fran gasped as his hands found her breasts. Moving down her torso, he stopped. Expertly he reached the zipper on her jeans and slid it down. She was warm and wet, his hands feeling the dampness. Fran moaned her approval in spite of herself. Panting for more, her libido was winning over reason. Before she could take a needed breath, he plunged his tongue deep into the back of her throat, while his hands groped and pulled down her jeans. Her panties slid down easily.

Time, place and cold were superfluous as he braced her against the building. Fran did nothing to stop him, caught up by the intensity of his persistence. No time to protest or change her mind as the first thrust entered with abandon. 'Damn, he's large,' she thought, trying to fight her growing orgasm. She was hanging on by a thread as Tim continued thrust after thrust. He was now in complete control, pumping until she let go, her orgasm possessing every inch of her.

Knees weak, barely able to stand, she felt Tim's climax explode like a bomb in the night air. Moments passed as his adrenalin slowed, his carnal cunning complete. He pulled out abruptly. There was no gentle lingering, no soft words of appreciation, only a quick slam and bam! Bartel got off. She felt cheap.

Fran stood for a moment staring at him. Without a word, she reached down and pulled up her panties, her jeans following, wet with snow. She had to think fast. 'How can I get this son-of-a bitch?'

Glancing over, she noticed a waiter staring incredulously. Quickly he ducked inside. Her embarrassment was brief. The disgust lingered.

'What now? This creep needs to be put down, but how?' Tim smirked as he repaired himself. He was still slightly erect, as he tucked in. Moving toward her, he placed his hands against the wall so she couldn't move. He gloated as he ran his finger around her face, ending in her mouth.

"How was that? You were good and wet, a great slide into home base," he chuckled. Fran's stomach turned, but she readied herself to finish it. Pushing him away she stepped from the wall.

"Nice fuck, Tim, but I've had better." Utter surprise registered on his face. "You may be king fuck to some, but you're really just a shallow prick!"

He couldn't believe it! This skinny bitch was berating him after he spent his energy balling her! Reeling back, he brought his fist up, ready to strike. "I'll fix you, you fucking cow!" Fran stood her ground, her heart beating out of control. Trying to remember the Judo pointers she learned six months before, she readied herself.

Tim moved in for the kill, howling obscenities. Suddenly, he was pulled back by two pairs of hands, grabbing from behind. His arms were pinned behind his back as he was overpowered. He was forcibly turned around by someone strong. Griff! And that fag dick, Jonas Martin!

"Miss Fairchild, please leave now," Griff ordered, his eyes never leaving Tim's. Fran made a quick exit down the alley, disappearing on the street.

"Now then, Mr. Bartel, just what in the hell do you think you're doing?" Tim squirmed trying to free himself, but he could not. Instead, pissed as he was, he feigned civility. "We were having a little fun. That's all," he explained. Griff glanced at Jonas and back at Tim, releasing him. "It didn't look like the lady was having a little fun, Mr. Bartel." "Yeah, she enjoyed it," he said, smugly. Jonas sighed, his disgust obvious.

Griff continued. "So here's what I think. You're never to approach Miss Fairchild again while in our employ. If I hear of any threats to her or any other woman in this company, I'll come down hard. You'll be fired and brought up on charges with Equity. Understood?" For a moment, there was only silence as Tim formed his words carefully.

"It's nobody's business when two consenting adults are having some fun." "Yours is a warped sense of fun, Mr. Bartel. The lady was about to defend herself! It is now my business. I'm warning you just this once. I suggest you take me seriously. Now take a hike." Griff and Jonas watched Tim go until he disappeared at the end of the alley.

"That guy is major trouble, Griff. I knew it from the minute he arrived." "Not to worry, Jonas. He's going to behave, or he's canned. End of story." The snow continued as they walked back to the bar, joining the remaining throng.

Chapter 35

Moving Right Along

Previews continued to sellout crowds. Audiences were bowled over by this new form of entertainment. The presale for the Broadway opening was phenomenal! Already the first month was sold out with ticket sales booming. Scalpers, already at work, charged the highest prices to those willing to pay top dollar to see the newest, most controversial offering from Owen Matthews!

The company had settled back into the comforts of home base. Rehearsals were few, as Owen saw improvement night after night. Jeff had gone in for Jonas on matinee days, so he could take notes. Finding little to tighten and clean, the gypsies had more time for personal matters.

Nora was back checking in, watching the show and spending every spare minute off stage with Jeff. They were growing close. Jeff's deep affection for Nora was slowly helping her trust again. Her experience with Tim Bartel had left her psyche in tatters, but Jeff's kindness and respect was healing.

In the Bronx, the Byrnes were preparing for the Christmas rush. The pub was decorated with green strands of fir looped across the room, red poinsettias placed here and there; creating a warmth and holiday flavor that was irresistible. White candles in red and green holders were placed at tables and booths, adding ambiance of the coming Yule. Most favorite of all, the giant Christmas tree brought in from New Jersey, standing proudly at the back of the room. It had become a tradition to acquire a real tree from a farm across the Hudson. The Byrne boys made it a special ritual cutting it down and bringing it home every year. Pat would be home this year, and the family was looking forward to celebrating with her. They would all trim the giant fir together.

With the holiday approaching, the entire city was decorated from top to bottom. Retail was at its yearly peak, the stores along 5th Avenue were filled with shoppers. The weather was cold, with more snow than Manhattan and the boroughs had seen in years. But the weather hadn't deterred residents and tourists alike from enjoying the special world of Manhattan at holiday time.

Central Park's ice rink was constantly full of enthusiastic skaters and onlookers of all ages. Rockefeller Center's traditional mammoth tree standing high in the plaza brought crowds of enthusiasts and skaters as well. Radio City Music Hall's annual Christmas show was attended by record crowds and the Broadway theatres turned patrons away in droves. Daily ticket sales were at an all-time high. All this commercial activity was encouraging to the Kaplan-Maggli organization, anticipating a healthy run and big dollars ahead for *Centipede*.

The cast was given Christmas and the 26th off. They would return on the 27th to continue previews. The prospect of a hit was exciting for all concerned.

Since the night at Barrymore's, Owen and Pat were together frequently. On Wednesday between matinee and evening performances and on Saturday the same, they would share a meal and Owen's bed. He insisted she stay overnight on the weekend. Alan and Maureen Bryne had no idea that their only daughter was sleeping with anyone, nor would they have approved. Pat's little secret was being kept by Griff and Mally, who provided a much-needed alibi. As far as the Byrnes knew, Pat stayed midtown for convenience sake, sparing her the commute on matinee days.

Griff went along, because he guarded with discretion Owen and Pat's affair on tour. He protected them during the Jackie Eldridge-Vera Daniels mess, providing the necessary course of action to fire Jackie, who nearly created a war between Owen and Vera, with Pat the collateral damage. He was fiercely loyal to Owen and a gentleman of discretion in all matters.

Mally had a different view of their arrangement, hoping that, by Pat spending more time with Owen, her expectations would be more realistic. From Mally's perspective, Owen was clearly not a nester nor had any intention of making a permanent commitment. Pat's insecurity was largely based on not knowing what their future held. He was and always had been elusive, independent and non-committal in matters of the heart. For now, Pat would take what was offered—the occasional overnight, time spent between shows, with insistent libidos driving their intense love making.

With the opening January 15th, Griff and Mally would follow with plans for their wedding. The date was set for Sunday, February 14th, Valentine's Day. Since Broadway was dark on Sundays, it was a perfect time to include their colleagues.

They wanted to keep it simple, with Mally's parents flying in to give her away. Griff picked Dick Landry for best man and she chose Pat her maid of honor. They were thinking of a simple, traditional service by a justice of the peace with a reception at Sardi's. They liked the idea since neither practiced a formal religion. Their wedding night would be in the honeymoon suite at the Waldorf.

In keeping with the holiday spirit, Jonas and Phillipe decided to have an open house, inviting members of the cast as well as other friends in the business. Christmas Eve seemed a good time to entertain. Many gypsies were without their families or traditions after moving to New York from all parts of the country, leaving families and friends behind. Having a place to gather with show biz friends seemed the right thing to host. Jonas understood this better than anyone.

Pat wanted to spend the holiday with Owen, not knowing whether he celebrated the season. She was obligated to her family, a tradition that must be kept. As they sat in his kitchen eating breakfast, she broached the subject.

"What are your plans for Christmas?" Owen set down his coffee cup. He looked pensive. It was hard to read his thoughts.

"Baby, I don't celebrate. The holidays have been lost on me for years. My parents died long ago and my sibs are scattered all over the country."

"Funny, I've never heard you talk about your family, come to think of it," she said, her curiosity growing. "Not much to tell. I split when I was young and the only place I've considered home is New York."

"I wish you could drop by sometime over the break. I've got a big, outgoing Irish family! My mom asks about the show all the time. I think they would be thrilled to meet you!"

"Gee Baby, I don't know. That's a lot to bite off," said Owen, reluctance in his voice.

"I'm not very sociable with outsiders," he admitted. "Well, couldn't you give it a try?" There was an edge to Pat's voice. "They're simple folk without snooty airs."

"I'll think about it, okay? Don't push me, Baby. It's never a good idea," he replied. Pat's heart sank. 'It's so little to ask,' she thought pensively. Getting up from the table, she cleared the dishes, cups and place-mats. The quiet between them was wide as the sea. Finally Owen broke the silence.

"Come here, Baby," he said, pulling her onto his lap. "I told you when we first got together not to make demands on me. Remember? I love you, but I'm not ready to do the family thing." Reaching for her chin, he kissed her softly. "Isn't this enough?"

Without another word, he took her by the hand, leading to the bedroom. Lost in carnal oblivion, they consumed each other the rest of the day.

Griff put a notice on the call-board at Jonas' request. The invitation was simple:

Attention All! Jonas Martin and Phillipe Danier hereby invite you to share their holiday spirit on Christmas Eve, 7 to 10. Come as you are and enjoy food and drink to celebrate the Yule! Address: 49 West 68th Street-Apt. 3C. Regrets only!

This was to be their first official gathering as a couple. They looked forward to the cast attending. Among guests invited was Jerry Thompson, newly recovered from his knee surgery, accompanied by his partner. Gary Hanson, Jonas' ex, whose number was found in the New York White Pages, was notified. They asked Dick Landry to come with his wife, Dana, who was due soon. Kathy Olson would bring her partner, Sonja Berger and the New York crew was encouraged to stop by.

As Christmas Eve grew closer, Jonas and Phillipe enjoyed planning the menu, shopping, and decorating their apartment. They found a beautiful Fraser fir on 11th Avenue, brought in from New Jersey. It stood in the front window, sparkling with blue lights and silver and gold ornaments. Phillipe's penchant for design had turned the tree into a splendid vision. They were filled with joy as their first holiday together at home approached.

Chapter 36

Christmas in New York

A feathery blanket of fresh snow was falling gently on the city as folks arrived at Jonas and Phillipe's cozy apartment in the west 60's. It was a perfect night to gather and enjoy the Yule. With two days off, the cast was ready for holiday camaraderie and relaxation.

The apartment was beautifully decorated, starting with the welcoming tree, a preview of cheer for those entering the building. Arriving on the 3rd Floor, it was hard to miss the fragrance of Wassail through the open door: apples, allspice, cinnamon, cloves, nutmeg and ginger. Bayberry candles placed here and there added a winter feeling and the gas fireplace was warm and inviting.

Mally, Griff, and Pat arrived first, toting gifts. Jonas hugged them and took coats. Carrying them to the bedroom, he deposited them on what would become an enormous pile. Pat put gifts under the tree just as Jonas returned. He caught Griff and Mally kissing under the mistletoe. "Hung just for you two lovebirds," he chuckled.

Pat made her way to the kitchen in search of Phillipe, who was busying himself with food prep. An ingenious cook, he had a knack for combining common ingredients to create unique flavors. As he saw Pat, he stopped dicing and hugged her warmly. "You look gorgeous, Cherie." Pat smiled and kissed his cheek.

Noticing a tray of hors d'oeuvres, she helped herself. "This looks scrumptious! What is it?" Phillipe kept prepping as he chatted. "That small morsel is a specialty of mine: goat cheese with cranberry and orange chutney. You like?" Pat rolled her eyes. "I think I'll die happy," she said grabbing another.

The doorbell rang. Jonas admitted the new arrivals and went out to the landing. Peering over the railing, he didn't recognize the very pregnant woman at first. Dick came into view, holding Dana's arm. Jonas couldn't believe it! "Dana! Oh my Dana!" he shouted happily. She returned her gorgeous smile and kept climbing with great effort.

Arriving on the landing, Jonas opened his arms, trying with difficulty to hug her. How different she looked from their closing night in Boston! She was only weeks along then and now, she was about to pop! Dick followed, beaming with pride. "Nice job, Daddy! Watch your step, Dana."

As they entered the apartment, the expectant couple was hard to miss. A rush of hugs from those already assembled ensued. "How are you?" "Do you know the baby's sex?" "When are you due?" Questions fired right and left brought giggles from Dana as Dick took her coat. Mally was the first to pat Dana's belly, considerable in size from her former dancer's body. "You're just glowing! Are you feeling okay?"

Dana waddled into the room, claiming the first comfortable chair she saw. Dick helped her settle. "I'm fat and overdue! If the baby isn't here by Monday, our doctor has promised to induce."

"Oh my God, Dana!" Pat shouted as she entered the room. Phillipe followed close behind. More hugs and kisses were swapped. The group settled around the soon-to-be-parents, hanging on every word.

"What a surprise, Cherie! Dick never let on you were coming," said Phillipe, smiling. We wanted to surprise you. Dana felt up to it and we both needed distraction! This waiting is torture," confessed Dick, helping her back into the chair.

The bell rang again, bringing Jonas to his feet. Buzzing the door, he entered the corridor and looked down the stairs. Several cast members chattered as they climbed bearing gifts. Liz, Fran, and Cynthia arrived first, dressed to the nines. Following close behind were Joe and Jim, assisting another surprise guest, Jerry Thompson! All entered the apartment chattering happily.

A massive shout exploded as everyone hurried to the door to welcome Jerry, who was balancing on crutches. Jonas took coats and purses and disappeared down the hall. Joe and Jim followed, removing their jackets, after helping Jerry with his. Jerry headed to the sofa, parking his crutches nearby. He looked rested and relaxed and eager to catch up with his fellow gypsies.

The doorbell rang again and again as more guests arrived. Jonas continued to play host, welcoming arrivals and taking coats. Wassail was available as well as red and white wine, beer, and soft drinks. Phillipe tended to the table, bringing trays of food out to guests. Pat elected to assist him as she was dateless, Owen's whereabouts unknown. Chad brought a date, a pretty blonde with a bright blue eyes and charming smile. Introduced as Cindy Swanson, she appeared shy and slightly intimidated by the outgoing people milling around.

The bell sounded again. This time, Griff took over, buzzing guests in. Nora and Jeff entered, hand in hand. Their arrival together didn't go unnoticed as the girls exchanged looks. Jeff helped Nora off with her coat and disappeared down the hall. Nora waved to Jonas, who came up and gave her a hug. "You're looking lovely tonight, Miss Nora. How are you feeling?" "Never better," she said, looking around. Soon Jeff was back, taking her hand as they looked for something to drink.

"Well, feature that. True love has found Miss Blake," Cynthia snickered. "Oh come on, Cyn. She's okay," said Fran. Cynthia rolled her eyes. "I can't stand her big mouth, always yapping for all to hear!"

"Well, maybe Jeff's won the big mouth's heart," Fran suggested. "Yeah, with his big you know what," giggled Cynthia. "Cyn, what a potty mouth," scolded Fran with mock indignation. "Did you acquire that from B?"

"Who's B?" "Well, who do you think? Bartel, the supreme dick-head of all time," whispered Fran. "For crying out loud, Fran, please don't bring him up again. I just hope he isn't coming tonight!" "Are you kidding? That scumbag won't waste his time here," said Fran. The doorbell sounded again, interrupting their conversation.

Jonas opened the door after pressing the buzzer. Looking down the stairs, he spotted Kathy and Sonja, heading up the stairs. Tickled to see Sonja, he rushed forward, throwing his arms around her. "Baby Doll, I've missed you! How's your new life at NYU?" Sonja clung to Jonas, tears welling. "I've missed you all so much. Kathy mentioned the party and I had to come." Kathy held an enormous poinsettia, handing it graciously to Jonas and kissing him on the cheek. "Hi Boss!"

The girls entered and removed their coats. All the former *Bravo Business* gypsies clustered around, happy to see their old pal. Sonja had blossomed in six months, looking beautiful and confident. It was easy to see how returning to college had been the right choice. Spotting the Landrys, they greeted them enthusiastically.

The bell continued to ring. Many others stopped in, some unknown to the *Centipede* gang.

Marcy White called, begging off with an unwelcome cold.

The big surprise of the evening was Gary Hanson, Jonas' for-mer partner. He had called earlier in the day to wish them a Merry Christmas. Jonas suggested he stop by for a drink and a reunion with the *Bravo Business* family. He arrived, accompanied by a stunning man. Jonas was surprised that Gary had a date and such a good look-ing one at that. He welcomed them both.

"Jonas, I'd like you to meet my partner, Steve Jackson. Steve, this is Jonas Martin." Steve extended his hand. "It's a pleasure to meet you, Jonas. Gary has told me a lot about you." Gary looked around the apart-ment. Spotting familiar and dear people, he waved enthusiastically.

"Where's Phillipe?" Jonas gestured toward the kitchen. "My hus-band, the chef, is otherwise occupied. He should be out shortly. Let me take your coats. Please enjoy drinks and a table of yummy food."

From across the room, Joe, and Jim checked Steve out. He was gorgeous—tall, slim, with dark hair and eyes. "How did Hanson man-age this?" Jim leaned in and gave Joe a nudge. "He deserves some TLC.

Jonas dumped him hard! Don't you remember?" "I don't. I arrived after the accident."

"Oh, that's right. Well, long story short, Jonas tricked on Gary with Phillipe. Then Gary was severely injured by a hit and run and left behind in Atlanta to recuperate. Phillipe replaced Gary. Poor guy, talk about adding insult to critical injury. They were together ten years."

As the night wore on, the partygoers chatted, ate, and drank happily in the spirit of Christmas. Tim Bartel was not among them. Not surprisingly, nobody seemed to care.

Griff and Dick were deep in conversation when Dana suddenly appeared from the bathroom, distraught. She was shaking and doubled over. Dick looked up and guessed immediately.

"Dana, what's happening?" "Dick, honey, my water just broke. I think I'm in labor!" She gasped, doubling over. The party came to a grinding halt as guests gathered around.

"Let's get a cab. We've got to call Edelstein and have him meet us at St. Vincent's," said Dick taking charge. Jonas ran into the bedroom and frantically searched for their coats under the pile. Retrieving them from the heap, Dick helped Dana into hers and grabbing his, reached into his pocket, producing a business card. "Where's Griff?" "Here, Dick. What do you need?" "Griff, this is Dr. Sam Edelstein, Dana's ob-gyn," he said, handing over the card. Please call and leave a message that the Landrys are en route to St. Vincent's. I'm certain Dana's in labor." A loud gasp erupted from Dana as she doubled over. "Dick, please, we have to go, now!"

"Will one of you guys help?" Phillipe ran for his jacket and joined the Landrys as they started down to the lobby. Outside the building, they carefully navigated the snow covered stairs, Dick keeping a tight rein on Dana. There was no cab in sight. Phillipe squinted through the falling snow. "I'm going to the corner," he hastened. "We'll have better luck on Central Park West," he shouted and took off in a sprint. The Landrys followed, Dana barely able to keep up. The contractions were increasing in strength and frequency.

"Oh Dick, they're coming faster. I can't have our baby on the street", she wailed. Finally catching up, they could see a cab, door open, driver leaning toward them. Dick helped Dana in and slid in next to her. "Thanks a million, Phillipe! We'll keep you posted," he shouted as he pulled the door shut. The cab pulled away, the piling snow crunching under the tires. "St. Vincent's please, driver. My wife's in labor!"

Phillipe watched until they were out of sight. Turning, he walked slowly back to the apartment, breathing in the fresh air. He felt a mixture of joy and sadness as he let himself in. 'Waiting for a baby to arrive in our lives will never happen,' he thought pensively.

Christmas day arrived with a flurry of activity at the Blarney. The Byrnes prepared to serve a complete dinner with all the trimmings to their regular customers. They had started the tradition when Alan and Maureen first married, following the acquisition of the pub.

Several tables were placed together to accommodate guests. Serving family-style, the offerings included traditional Irish stew, corned beef and cabbage, cream of turnip soup, colcannon, soda bread and preacher pie, all with as much Guinness as one cared to drink!

Maureen and her boys had worked for days planning the menu, shopping and setting the scene. Alan cleaned while his sons arranged the table set-up. There was always a large crowd of relatives, friends and neighbors. The dinner was planned for 5:00, just before sundown.

With *Centipede* occupying most of her time, Owen the rest, Pat was absent for most of the preparation She felt guilty knowing that, as a Byrne, she was expected to help and was doing little. Pat had moved on. Emotionally, she'd left home for good, though she still slept in her old bed. It was all a show to please, something she worked at. No, being home was difficult. How she longed for the day she would move out!

The party at Jonas and Phillipe's had gone on past midnight. As the guests cleared out, Pat was concerned about getting to the Bronx. It was late and she didn't want to travel by train at that hour. She wasn't flush enough to take a cab. The boys lived two blocks from the new Lincoln Center in the west 60s. Owen lived nearby, but she didn't dare show up uninvited.

Griff suggested she crash in their extra bedroom, returning home in the morning. For now she was grateful to be with such good friends. She found the room cozy and the furnishings comfortable. A full-size bathroom was down the hall. The bed had been turned down and the soft lamp light from the night stand cast a warm glow over the room. Fresh towels and a new bar of soap sat on the dresser.

Pat stripped to her panties and got into bed exhausted. Lonely and out of sorts, she missed Owen more than ever. Where was he tonight? Was he alone? How did he spend Christmas Eve? Was he at a bar or with professional friends? He had no family, no roots. He couldn't be bothered showing up at the party. Thoughts weighed heavy on her as she fell into a deep sleep. Morning arrived with a gentle knock. She heard a familiar voice as the door opened slightly.

"Pat, it's time to get up! We've got fresh coffee brewing and Griff is making his fabulous omelet," Mally announced, her enthusiasm never waning. On tour, Pat was always amazed by her friend's morning pep and energy. 'Must be a Minnesota thing,' she mused. Pulling herself together, she eased her way out of bed and looked in the mirror.

"God Irish, you're a mess," she said to her reflection. Smeared eye make-up and bed hair did nothing for her mood. Reaching into her bag, she dragged out a small bottle of baby oil, took some toilet tissue and wiped her eyes clean. She ran warm water, lathered the soap and washed the make-up residue off. Her faithful hairbrush was definitely needed as she retrieved it from her bottomless bag. After considerable effort and a few expletives, her hair was manageable. Pulling it back in a ponytail, she returned to the room, slipped into her dress and to the kitchen.

Griff was humming as he prepped ingredients for his creation. Pat smelled a mix of onions, green peppers, and mushrooms, sautéing in a large skillet. Heaven! She was starved! Mally was setting the table, adding cutlery, colorful napkins and plates. The topper was a lovely vase of Christmas holly and tea roses.

When the toast popped up, she grabbed tongs, put them on a plate and buttered them well. Having come from dairy land area, margarine was a 'no-no.' There was a new jar of crunchy peanut butter in the cupboard and a crock of Apricot jam purchased at Lund's, an upscale grocery chain in the Twin Cities. Paula had shipped it from Minnesota, along with her regular monthly package of homemade goodies. She loved to keep her only child mindful of her Midwest roots.

"Pat, would you like some coffee? Or I can make you tea if you prefer." Pat smiled at her best pal. "Coffee's great, thanks." "Have a seat. The main attraction is ready," said Griff grinning. Cooking was his passion, second only to Mally.

Carefully he removed the omelet from the pan and placed it onto a large platter. Carrying it to the table, he set it on a trivet and sat down. Mally took Pat's plate and handed it to Griff, who cut into the eggs. Scooping up a generous piece, he put it on her plate and passed it back. Next, he portioned their servings. "Have some toast, ladies. The bread is homemade, Granny Eunice Edwards' recipe. She used to grow her own flax," he said proudly.

"Where did you find this guy, Mal? He's a dream," said Pat, winking at Griff. Mally had to giggle, remembering how quickly she fell in love with him. "He enchanted my bosom and stole me away," she said blowing Griff a kiss. The phone rang.

"Wouldn't you know it? Just when we've got our mouths in gear, Ma Bell interrupts," he said, reaching the phone. The girls began eating, occasionally glancing at Griff. He smiled broadly as he finished the call. "Dick and Dana are parents," he announced.

"Oh, wow! Details! I want details," insisted Pat. "Do they have a boy or girl?" Baby Michael Richard Landry was born at 12:04, weighing eight pounds, nine ounces. Both mom and son are doing splendidly," he announced in his best reporter fashion. "A Christmas child is wonderful," Mally enthused.

"Remember during our Omaha run, when Dana could only handle tea and toast? She was too nauseous to even consider a steak," Pat recalled, smiling. "They were both over the moon when they found out they were pregnant," Mally added.

"This calls for a toast! Ladies, raise your orange juice." The girls obliged, giggling. "To Dana, Dick, and baby Michael, a long and happy life!" "Here, here," agreed Pat, chugging her juice. When breakfast was over, she eyed the clock and decided it was time to go home. "Can I wash or dry the dishes before I leave?" "No, it's fine," said Griff. "I imagine your family will be looking for you."

"Thank you both for the stay-over. I really appreciate you two so much," she said, hugging them. Grabbing her coat and scarf, she slipped them on and picked up her dance bag. They walked her to the door. Pat felt her eyes welling up as she departed hastily, tossing "Merry

Christmas" over her shoulder. She wasn't gone five minutes when the phone rang. Griff picked up. He was surprised to hear Owen's voice.

"Merry Christmas, Griff! I hope I'm not disturbing on the holiday." "You're not disturbing at all, Owen. Merry Christmas! What can I do for you?" I was unable to stop by the party last night. I'm wondering if you have Pat's home address?" "I do, but you're more likely to see her if you stop by the family pub, the Blarney. The Byrnes host a traditional Christmas feast for all their customers. It's quite the gathering, I'm told. The feast starts at 5:00."

"Where's the bar located?" "It's hard to miss. It's on the corner of 3rd Avenue and 149th Street. You can take the Lexington Avenue Express. Get on at 59th Street. It'll take you directly there. Or you could take a cab. Trains run less frequently today."

"Griff, you're a winner, as always! Thanks so much." "If you haven't heard yet, Dick Landry became a poppa last night. Dana gave birth to a boy, Michael Richard. I thought you'd like to know." "That's just great! Thanks for the update. You and your lady have a great Christmas, all right?" "Thanks, Owen. Good luck in the Bronx," he added playfully. They hung up.

What started as a refusal to meet Pat's people had morphed into a change of heart. Owen was curious and lonely. He had spent far too many Christmases waiting for last call. He would numb his senses with enough scotch and eager women were only too willing to have sex for just a night. The satisfaction was temporary, briefly calming his rampant libido. When the sex was over, he felt empty, used up.

Who were Pat's people? How did they manage to stay close? Would he be welcomed? There was only one way to find out. Looking at his watch, he would kill time until he hopped a train.

Chapter 37

Surprises

The Blarney was filled to capacity as the Byrnes hosted their annual holiday bash. Tables full of regulars dined eagerly as Maureen, Pat and her brothers served tray after tray of traditional Irish dishes. Alan stood captain of the bar, pouring steins of Guinness for toasts to families from the neighborhood. Alan was the first to share pride in his ancestry, regaling those nearby with stories of Ireland and of his emigration to the U.S. as a boy.

Many Irish immigrants had settled in the Bronx generations ago. Alan and his brothers had come to live with relatives as new arrivals fresh from Kilcullen. Their parents had stayed back, working their small parcel of farmland. They were dirt poor but wanted their sons to have the opportunity to live a more prosperous life in America.

The four Byrne brothers had succeeded. Alan's brother, Patrick, built a construction company from scratch. Michael became an attorney, specializing in labor law and Shawn, chief of police. Alan, the most engaging of the four, sought the hospitality business, building the Blarney into the best pub in the Bronx.

As dinner continued, Alan spotted a newcomer walking in the door. The gentleman had a graceful bearing, slight of build, with an air of sophistication. A cigarette dangled from his lips, he was dressed in black. "Good evening, sir, welcome," Alan said, indicating an empty stool in front of him. Owen sat, loosened his coat and snuffed out his cigarette in a nearby ashtray.

"What's your pleasure Sir? Drinks are on the house today," he announced with pleasure.

"Would you happen to have Glenfiddich? Alan grinned at the stranger. "How would you like that, Sir?" "On the rocks, neat," said Owen, glancing around the room. Alan poured the scotch over ice, handing it to him. Owen took a sip and reached into his pocket, pulling out another cigarette. Before he could get his lighter, Alan held out a lighted match. "Thanks. I appreciate it." Owen took a drag and continued looking over the crowd.

"You're new here, aren't you? I've never seen you in the Blarney." "That's right, my first time in the Bronx!" "Saints bless us! You're not serious?" Owen nodded and took another drag. "I heard I should check out the finest pub in the five boroughs." Alan grinned. "Well, whoever told you was dead right," he boasted.

"Tell me, you must know everyone around here. Are you familiar with Patricia Byrne?" Alan's face suddenly turned to a frown. He leaned forward on the bar. Nose to nose with Owen, his demeanor went from rapid fire friendly to suspicious. "I do indeed. Who wants to know?" His manner was edgy. "I'm a friend who wants to wish her a Merry Christmas," said Owen.

"Well then, do you see a redhead over there?" Owen noticed Pat clearing dishes. "I'll see if she can take a minute." Alan whistled at a strapping young man who immediately came over.

"Patrick, tell Patricia she has a visitor. This gentleman appears to know her."

"Certainly, Pop! Be right back!" Owen watched the fellow go to Pat and briefly converse. He quickly turned, determined to surprise. He didn't have to wait long, Pat approached. "Yes, Dad, what is it? Something you need?" Alan looked from Pat to Owen, then back again.

"No Patricia, this gentleman needs something," he said, indicating Owen. He turned, his arms outstretched. "Merry Christmas, Baby!" Pat's squeal bounced across the room. "Owen!" Jumping into his arms, she kissed him fully on the mouth. The commotion drew immediate attention as heads turned, conversation halted and folks stopped eating. More surprised than his daughter, Alan stood stoic, not able to move or speak.

"What a surprise! How did you find me?" Owen gently let Pat down and cupped his hands around her face. Looking deep into her eyes, he kissed her gently. "It's actually Griff's fault. He told me how to find the Bronx," he said with a chuckle. "Owen, I've missed you," murmured Pat as she stroked his face. Alan, feeling a bit awkward, cleared his throat. "Patricia, will you kindly introduce us?"

"Dad, I would like you to meet Owen Matthews. Owen, this is my father, Alan Byrne!" Both men looked at each other, a few silent seconds passing between them. Owen took the initiative, extending his hand. Alan returned the handshake, laughing heartily.

"Glory be, St. Patrick himself!" Owen looked puzzled. Pat caught on immediately. "Dad's heard so much about you, first with *Bravo Business* and now *Centipede*. For the first time, he can put a face to the name!" Maureen peeked out the kitchen door to see what was going on and noticed the lithe man in black, totally attentive to her daughter. Pat's brothers glanced in his direction.

"Boys, come and meet Owen Matthews, the director of Pat's show," said Alan warmly. Patrick extended his hand first, followed by Mickey and Sean. Maureen joined in, giving Owen a hug. Pulling back she eyed him carefully. "My, you're surely a handsome lad," she said without restraint.

"This is certainly an honor, Mr. Matthews! Please join us for supper," she insisted. "Patrick, bring a plate for Mr. Matthews. "Please call me Owen, Mrs. Byrne. Mr. Matthews is far too formal," he soothed. His manner caused Maureen to blush, captivated entirely.

"Patricia, take a break and join Owen. You haven't eaten all day, my girl!" "Ma, stop!" Owen reached over, giving Pat a playful nudge. "Listen to your mother, Baby!" Alan and the boys laughed, knowing Pat's contrary nature.

More food and drink were offered as people arrived. Those leaving stopped to thank the Byrnes for their hospitality. When the last customers finally departed, tables were cleared with only the Byrnes and Owen remaining. Pat was glowing as she saw the rapport building between Alan and Owen.

Her brothers excused themselves to help Maureen with the clean-up. She had gone to the kitchen to begin what would take hours—washing dishes, pans, and utensils. Cleaning the kitchen was a major undertaking. However, there was little left to store as guests had finished the lot of it.

It was late when Owen made his exit. He said goodnight to the family, hugging Maureen and thanking Alan and the boys. Mickey insisted on driving him to Manhattan. "Tough to get a train," he explained. "Besides, I'm wide awake and there's less traffic."

"Well, thanks! I appreciate this," said Owen, clearly touched. They exited the Blarney and walked around the corner to the rear of the building. A large truck was parked at the end of the alley. "Mick, can I ride along, please?" Prolonging time with Owen was what she wished for most.

"Now Sis, Pop thinks you should stay and help Ma. I think so, too. I'll be over here, Owen," he said, walking away. Discipline was essential to the family. The Byrnes had taught their children the importance of hard work before pleasure. When Mickey's back was turned, Pat embraced Owen, holding on for dear life.

"Hey Baby, come on. I have to go. It's late." He bent down, taking her chin and kissed her deeply. Pat sighed. "I'll miss you," she said, holding back tears. "I'll see you the day after tomorrow, okay? Enjoy your time off." Pat waved as he walked away. A conflict was building within. She felt herself pulling away from the safety and comfort of family, preferring the uncertainty of being with a man she couldn't live without.

It was December 27th. The cast would resume previews tonight, leading up to the official opening. It was close. The green room filled with excited gypsies, waiting on Griff and Owen a few minutes before curtain. Those who had attended Jonas and Phillipe's soiree busied themselves thanking their hosts. At five minutes to curtain, Griff entered the room, followed by Owen and Dick. The group quieted.

"Company, we welcome you back! We trust your holiday was pleasant. I have just a couple of announcements," he said, noticing Dick raising his hand. "Yes, Dick?"

"Griff, may I interrupt just for a moment? I have some news." The joy on his face was obvious.

"Dick, go ahead. My words aren't nearly as exciting by comparison!" All eyes turned to Dick who took center. "Dana and I are parents! Our son, Michael Richard, showed up on Christmas morning. Everyone's doing great!" Cheers and applause erupted as cast members hugged Dick, extending well wishes.

"When can we visit?" Kathy was keen on babies, having recently become an aunt. The *Bravo Business* cast was unanimous about seeing the new arrival. "Dana can have visitors now, but only for a few minutes - hospital policy. She'll be there until Saturday when we bring Michael home." "Let's pay her a visit," suggested Mally. Pat agreed, as did Kathy and Marcy, old pals from tour. Kathy would check her partner Sonja's availability. She usually had only one class on Friday.

"Hey don't leave us out," insisted Jonas, eager to get a group of the guys together. "Remember, only brief visits, you can take turns," Dick reminded, touched by the group's enthusiasm.

"Now, if that's all, please keep the same energy, drive, and focus you had prior to Christmas," reiterated Griff. "He's right," said Owen, cutting through the group. "Let's drive this baby home. We have less than two weeks to keep our wits together and not lose the edge. Break a leg!" The group dispersed as the familiar "Places, please" was heard.

Chapter 38

New Arrivals

The wind created a swirl of white as the girls trudged into St. Vincent Hospital. Stopping at the reception desk, they were told maternity was on the 4th Floor. Eagerly they stepped into the elevator, pressing the button as they loosened coats and scarves. "I can't wait to see her," enthused Sonja. "She looked stunning at the party, pregnant and all!"

"Well, you know what they say about expectant mothers?" The girls were all ears, especially Sonja, the most curious. "What, Honey?" "Pregnant women have a special glow. It goes with the territory," said Kathy.

Pat couldn't resist and chimed in. "I'll bet that special glow disappears fast! All that nursing on already sore nipples, the baby's constant peeing, pooping and throwing up! No thanks!" Sonja frowned at Pat while the others razzed her all the way to the 4th. "Cold hearted,

Pat. You'll be cursed with triplets someday," teased Kathy. "A star on Broadway billed as *Byrne Plus Three*," Mally chuckled. "That's not remotely funny," said Pat suddenly crabby.

Dick called Dana early that morning to let her know her pals were stopping by. She quickly fixed her hair and applied light make-up. She had received a beautiful robe, sent by her mother and sisters from Atlanta. Something new and loose fitting, she was eager to put it on.

Exhilarated as Dana was with baby Michael, she craved some girl-friend time. The day nurse had just taken him back to the nursery. Moving to the bathroom, she sat down to relieve herself. The stitches from the episiotomy stung as urine made contact. Her body felt assaulted in general and she longed to be home with Dick.

A soft rapping on the door got her attention as she stood and wiped. "I'm in the bathroom. Be out in a sec," she called. Back into the room, four happy faces greeted her with enthusiasm. Arms wound around, hugging, kissing and shedding tears. Kathy held a large floral package, a bright bouquet arranged in a pretty blue vase. Handing it to Dana, she found a spot near the window to set it. "God, you are the best," she cried. "I've missed you so much!" Feeling slightly light-headed, she walked to the bed and sat.

"We're so happy for you and Dick," said Kathy taking a seat. Sonja joined Dana, sitting next to her on the edge of the bed. "When can you bring baby Michael home?" Pat pulled up an extra chair for herself and one for Mally. Questions were popping right and left.

"Was labor painful?" Pat delighted in details, the more the better. Dana smiled, noting how eager her pals were to hear a running account. "It all happened so fast! First my water breaks at the party. We grab a cab, and in minutes, we're at the hospital. I was prepped right away. We barely had time to check in!" "Were you scared?" Mally was curious. Dana shrugged, "Not really. I had nine months to get used to the idea."

"Did your doctor deliver Michael?" Kathy had recently heard details of her sister-in-law's delivery by an unfamiliar doctor. "Yes, thank God! I was already nine centimeters when they wheeled me in. I pushed two or three times and I heard wailing! Dick held my hand through it all." "Wow, that was so fast!" blurted Sonja.

"No fooling! I thought I might have the baby on the street or maybe in the cab! Dick was so calming. When Michael popped out, you should have seen him standing there in a white coat, hairnet and mask on his face. He may switch from stage management to obstetrics!" she giggled. "Well, we're absolutely thrilled for you two," said Kathy. "You girls are so wonderful to stop by! Thank you so much," said Dana, having perked up with the arrival of her gypsy pals.

Pat checked her watch, noting their approaching performance. "We'd better get a move on. I need a nap and a bite to eat before half hour. Mal, can I crash at your place?" "Sure, you won't have time to run home." "I think we should leave our new mommy," Kathy said with a smile. The others agreed. Another round of hugs and kisses and they left.

Dana lay down on the bed, completely exhausted. A flood of feelings arose. She wept quietly, trying to cope with mixed emotions. She was happy she and Dick were parents at last. She was relieved that baby Michael was a normal, healthy little boy. But she was so tired and this was only the beginning. Conflicted, she fell into a deep sleep. Sleep was needed, temporarily bringing relief from her raging hormones, her mind temporarily stilled. Reality was setting in. She and Dick were parents forever.

Owen entered the stage door during intermission. There was a note on the call-board to stop by Griff's. Working his way through the dimly lit backstage, he knocked. "Come in!" Owen stepped in. Griff was taking a short break between acts, sipping coffee and doing paperwork. Looking up, he smiled, putting down his pen.

"We had a call today from *the New York Times*. Their entertainment reporter would like an interview with you prior to the opening. She wants to run a feature on you and *Centipede* the Sunday before opening. The photo coverage is done, but they want to meet with you also. The reporter is Stephanie McNeil. She's an ace and well-followed by their readership."

"I know her by reputation. She's an excellent journalist," said Owen, lighting a smoke. "Yes, I've heard that. I think a well-placed story will do us well," said Griff. "I couldn't agree more," said Owen, smoke easing out of his nostrils. "Would you like me to schedule for you? She's available and willing to do the interview at your place." Owen thought for a second. "I'd like operating in my own space, so yeah, please set it up. How about next Monday, 5:00? I'd prefer late afternoon." "Done." They shook hands.

Owen finished shaving and wiped his chin, as the door buzzer rang. He grabbed the wall phone.

"Mr. Matthews, Stephanie McNeil, here."

"Yes, of course, I'm in 8C, I'll buzz you in." There was a click. While waiting, as twilight set in, he turned on lamps and plumped pillows. The bell rang.

At the door, he looked through the peephole. Delighted with the view, the woman in the hall was quite attractive, not reporter-like at all. "Miss McNeil, please come in." He stepped aside to let her pass. "Please have a seat. May I offer you a cocktail or glass of wine?" She turned and frowned.

"Not really, perhaps later," she said, abruptly. 'This broad's to the point,' mused Owen, pointing to a leather settee. Stephanie sat and pulled a pad from her briefcase, a pen from her handbag.

"May I take your coat?" She nodded, slipping it off. Owen placed it on the sofa, took a chair opposite. "Mr. Matthews, let's get started," she said, flipping the cover of her notebook. "Owen, please. We theatre folk aren't used to such formality," he said somewhat facetiously.

"Oh? Well after all, this is an interview, not an informal lunch," she said, volleying back. "I have a limited amount of time. May we begin?" "Yes, by all means, Miss McNeil," replied Owen, lobbing back. She eyed him carefully.

"You're a rather controversial fellow. How did you find your artistic direction?" "It's more like a direction found me. I was a hoofer coming up in the ranks. I always had an edge. I'm risky, Miss McNeil." Stephanie's eyes never left the page as she wrote. "I see. How did you find a concept for your new show? I believe it's titled, *Centipede*." "That's correct."

"It's an odd name," she intoned, crinkling her nose. "That metaphor might be a put-off!" "Miss McNeil, you have to use your imagination, note the symbolism. A centipede has a lot of legs. We have an ensemble of dancers with legs that are constantly moving! So now do you get it?" His tone took on an edge. The lobbing continued.

"It's a stretch, but yes, I get it now," she said. Stopping for a moment, she crossed her legs, legs that were shapely, noticeably long. "You have great legs, Miss McNeil. Ever danced?" She looked up, surprised by his candor. "No, Mr. Matthews. I'm a journalist. May we get on with this?" He smiled, the corners of his mouth turning up slightly. 'That one's for me,' he thought smugly.

"Now then, tell me about your concept. Why an all-dance review? You've always done book shows, I'm told." "You've been told? Have you ever seen one of my shows?" "I can't say I have. Musicals are of no interest to me. I find them shallow and tedious," she proclaimed, her expression never changing. 'That's one for her,' he thought drily.

"This show might change your mind. I've put together a two-hour collection of my best work to date, with the finest dancers on Broadway. I've taken unused material giving them a fresh twist." Stephanie looked up, curiosity growing. "What sort of a twist, Mr. Matthews?"

"My choreography is erotic, sensual and very stylish. I insist on subtext underlying all my work. Ever hear of subtext?" "Not really, Mr. Matthews. I'm a journalist, not a theatre buff." Determined to win the match, he was keen to set this broad straight.

"There must be underlying emotional motivation in my people. This impetus comes from within, manifesting in movement that clearly conveys the sexual intention of my work." "But will people accept such a blatantly suggestive show?"

Owen smiled smartly. "I have a track record, Miss McNeil. I find that people like to experience what they don't have in their lives. That's why theatre is so popular. It's escapism, fantasy, idealism! If it were not so, Broadway wouldn't exist. My shows attract and draw, making it possible for people to live out their desires."

"I see your point," said Stephanie, taking off her glasses. "I'm not one of your public minions, nor care to be, but I do understand the public's desire for titillation. The more sensational, outrageous and drastic a news story, the more papers sold. That's why rags like *The National Inquirer* do well." 'One for her,' mused Owen.

He liked her mind, her formality. In the lamplight, he observed her features. She was pretty in a small-town way, fresh complexion, big brown eyes and blonde hair pulled back in a tidy bun. Her body was okay but, those legs! What attracted him most was her veneer, a new challenge.

"Is there anything else, Miss McNeil?" He winked and she blushed. "No, I have a direction for my article. Thanks." "May I offer you a cocktail? It's after 5:00," he suggested. "Well, if you insist, yes. It's been a long day. Do you have white wine?" Owen went to the bar and checked the fridge. "Looks like I have a Pouilly Fuisse. Will that do?" He noticed she had removed her shoes.

"What is Pouilly Fuisse? I imagine it's not available in Casper, Wyoming," she said with a chuckle. "It's made from a unique grape, something just for you, Miss McNeil," his voice now soft, sexy. Her blush was obvious. 'Well, this is promising,' he thought. Uncorking the bottle, he filled a glass. Reaching for Glenfiddich, he poured his own. Returning to the settee, he set the drinks down and settled back.

"Tell me, Miss McNeil. How did you become a reporter?" "Oh, my background is fairly mundane. I grew up in Casper, Wyoming, my dad a rancher, my mom, a housewife. I'm the youngest of seven sibs."

"I thought you might be an only child," he said, casually. "Why would you think that?" She slipped her wine slowly, watching him with curiosity. "Well, you appear independent, a maverick of sorts. It was just a guess."

"Mr. Matthews, where I come from, you have to be independent or die on the vine. Not one of my sibs left Wyoming. They all grew up, got married and had big families." "How did you get to New York and *The Times*? Pretty prestigious, I'd say."

"Well, thanks. I love to write. I never went to college. When I turned eighteen, I got on a bus and came to New York. My family was outraged and practically disowned me. I made rounds and finally got hired by *The Village Voice* as a cub reporter. I was there for five years."

"Then the *Times* offered you a job, right?" "Not exactly, it was through a connection. I had a friend in sales at the paper. A feature writer there was expecting her first baby. They needed someone to fill in while she took maternity leave. She liked having babies, so she never came back. They kept me on. That was four years ago." "That was good timing for you!" "Yes, I'm pretty lucky. I love my job." The wine was taking hold and she had dropped her guard. "Would you like another?"

Stephanie took a last sip. "I'm afraid I can't. I have a deadline to meet in the morning," she replied, business tact suddenly returning. "Thank you for your time," she added, slipping on her shoes. She stood and reached for her coat. "Here, let me help," said Owen.

As he held her coat, his fingers brushed her neck. Stephanie shivered and faced Owen. Leaning in to kiss her, she pulled away. "Here's my card. I can be reached at this number." Picking up her briefcase, she turned to go. "I'd like to see you again sometime," he soothed. "Thanks again," she said, exiting.

Owen felt tightness in his pants. 'Miss McNeil, this isn't over, not by a long shot!' Pouring another scotch, he put on some soft jazz, settled back in his favorite chair and closed his eyes. Stephanie McNeil was stuck in his mind.

Chapter 39

A Smash

The New Year arrived. Previews were ending soon; *Centipede* would face the final step, a Broadway opening!

There had been extraordinary hype regarding Owen's newest. The *New York Times,* Sunday, January 10th, was about to hit the newsstands. The show was frozen and ready for the New York critics. An unprecedented response to previews created a sellout of seats for the first two months. The Royal box office was flooded with phone requests. Hopeful patrons stood in lines down the block.

Kaplan-Maggli handled the plum 'house' section. Clients, colleagues and celebrities clamored for seats, some looking for favors. Some, lucky enough to receive them, were considered prestigious.

Sunday, January 10th started with a phone call, Owen picking up on the third ring. It was an excited Joe Kaplan, whom he expected at noon. "Owen, have you seen the Sunday *Times*? Incredible! We're almost there my friend!"

"Joe, calm down. I haven't seen it yet. I just got up. Give me a minute, all right?" Putting down the phone, Owen moved quickly to the door, retrieving the paper. With the receiver under his chin, he found the variety section. The bold headline read, "A New Kind Of Bug, Dancing Centipede—The Arthropod Take-Over of Broadway."

"Have you found it?" Owen quickly glanced over the entire page. Kaplan held on, breathless. "It's catchy, no?" "Yes, it's catchy, Joe. Give me a chance to read it, I'll see you soon." He went to the kitchen, java and a smoke would jump start the day. Last night's coffee would do for now; a half full pot was still on the burner, he turned it on.

Feeling the need, he peed and flushed. A splash of water on his face woke him a bit more. A look in the mirror reminded him to shave. Back in the kitchen, he turned off the burner and rinsed out a nearby mug. The dark brew looked inviting as he poured and picked up the paper. Lighting his morning cigarette, he began perusing the article. The by-line caught his eye immediately, "By Stephanie McNeil."

The article took up most of a full page. At the top, a dated photo of him, probably furnished by Kaplan's PR department, stood out. There was a group shot and a particularly good photo of Pat and Jonas, his two aces.

"Once in a generation, a new concept arrives on the Great White Way, one that produces anticipation, excitement and speculation. This coming theatre season promises such an arrival. Director-Choreographer Owen Matthews has conceived and staged a never-before, all-dance review to open Broadway's new season. To make it happen he's aligned himself with Joseph Kaplan and Leonard Maggli producers. Selecting a troupe of the finest dancers of the day, an eclectic score of musical numbers by several composers minus a libretto, Matthews created a brave new work, using original and some under-utilized choreography to wow his fans. Titled simply Centipede, *the wriggling arthropod known for its many legs and quick action, Mr. Matthews leans on his dancers to meet his standards of agility, sensuality and timing to bring his concept to fruition. Centipedes are known to startle when scurrying in and out*

of dark places. Here, Matthews glorifies the creature, celebrating through dance its existence. Broadway has long awaited a new twist, a change of pace, a fresh achievement. It looks like this season the New York Theater is welcoming exactly that. Put the bug spray away. Get down to the Royal Theater to experience the return of truly exciting entertainment.

Owen sat back and smiled. Short and sweet. That's what it was. Pleased by Stephanie's words, he shook out another cigarette and returned to the kitchen for a second cup of coffee. 'I'll have to reward that broad,' he thought.

At 11:15, the phone rang. Owen picked up, impatiently. "This is Matthews," he said, abruptly. He heard a lengthy pause, an exhale of breath, a catch in the throat. "Hello. It's Vera." Owen's breath slowed, as he cautiously waited. Hers was the last voice he expected or wanted to hear. He was barely civil. "Vera. What do you want?" Another pause, then a less-than-pleasant come back.

"Why are you such an asshole? I'm calling for Joe. He's running a bit late and asked me to let you know." "I see. Well, when should I expect Mr. Kaplan?" Owen reached for a lighter; ironically, it was the gold lighter she'd given him commemorating their first hit.

"I would say closer to 1:00. He had to swing by the office first," she said, her voice dry. "Very well, I'll expect him then." He waited for a zinger that didn't come. "Well, that's it. Oh, by the way, I hear the show is sensational. Congratulations." "Thanks." A gap of silence held between them. "See you around." There was a click. For a few moments, Owen stood holding the receiver. Any contact at all with his ex was unsettling. He wanted her to stay out of his life—no contact, no information, or reminders.

Reheating the second cup of coffee, he paused to take another drag. As he glanced at the rest of the Variety Section, Pat's photo caught his eye. She was exquisite, her body perfection, leaving him weak with longing. Silently he admonished himself for any attraction to the McNeil broad. She was hardly as desirable as Pat. But then, variety had always been the spice of his life. Putting out his smoke, he headed to the bathroom and a quick shower.

The rush of water felt terrific on his tired bones. Once he was soaking wet, he lathered with a bar of Irish Spring, a new soap Pat had brought. Rinsing with a cooler spray was preferred, the contrast in temperature regenerating his senses. He had a lot to consider with the show less than a week from opening. He never doubted his concept or the cast he chose to carry it out. It was the public who would either love or loathe it.

Stepping from the shower, he dried and slipped into fresh briefs. His electric razor took longer than usual to remove stubble from the past two days. 'The mustache could use a little trim,' he thought as he carefully snipped the edges. He'd always preferred slight facial hair and had worn his hair cropped short. A stop at the barber shop was needed before the opening. At 12:40, the buzzer sounded. Owen picked up the phone.

"Yes?" "Owen, it's me," said Joe Kaplan. "One sec, I'll have you in," Owen pressed the admitting button. Glancing at a wall mirror, he looked as tidy as he cared to on a Sunday. Walking to the door, he waited for Joe's ring. A minute or two passed and, there was a knock instead. Opening the door, he saw the frown on Kaplan. "Joe, what is it?" "We need to talk, Owen." His manner was edgy, less friendly than other times.

"Come in. Care for a drink?" Owen pointed to the main sitting room as Joe brushed past him, silent and brooding. "I'll have a Bloody Mary," he said without a trace of warmth. Owen opened the Smirnoff's, adding tomato juice, a bit of Lee & Perrins, Tabasco and ice to a tumbler. He poured himself a Glenfiddich on the rocks and sat.

"What's going on, is it the show?" Joe scowled and shook his head, taking a large swallow. He eyed Owen carefully. "It's about your ex-wife, Matthews." Owen didn't move, keeping a steady gaze on Kaplan, who stood and paced. Covering his eyes he started to weep, startling Owen, who quickly joined him.

"Hey Joe, come on. You can talk to me," he said, reassuringly. Joe reached out to steady himself as he sunk in a nearby chair. It was odd that this highly successful Broadway entrepreneur was falling apart. He waited patiently for Kaplan to calm down.

"What's going on with you and Vera?" Joe pulled a large hanky out and blew his nose. A fog horn sounded, almost comical. Owen held his composure. "I'm in love with her like a dumb ass school boy!" Owen, quiet, remembered his distant past. "Vera is still a beautiful woman, but she's a lot to handle."

"I want to marry her, Owen. I've repeatedly asked her. We get so far and she puts on the brakes," his hurt evident. "I give her everything and try to make her happy. There's always some Goddamn excuse."

"Are you satisfying her sexually?" "Fuck, what kind of a question is that? I'm insatiable, she's insatiable! The sex is good and plenty," he said defensively.

"Well hell, is there someone else?" Joe stopped, looking hard at Owen. "I asked her once if she was still hung up on you, but she said no!" "How's her drinking?"

"She likes her booze. It calms her. I can handle that," he said, the bravura obvious. "Joe, I don't know what to say. Vera is a complex person, but so am I. Neither of us could sustain a marriage. I have no designs on my ex, its over." Joe smiled weakly. "I guess I just needed some feedback. Thanks for listening!" "You're welcome, Joe. Can I refill your drink?" "Yeah, hit me again. Let's get back on track with *Centipede!*" Taking his glass, he added more ice and poured another.

"How are the numbers?" Owen leaned on the bar with a fresh drink. "Opening night thru February is already sold out. We've never had that happen before." "Once the show is a hit there won't be a seat to be had for six months or longer. You mark my words, it's incredible!" Owen was pleased. "Where's the party?"

"We've booked Sardi's. We're taking over the whole joint. For starters, we've invited Jackie Kennedy, Truman Capote, Oleg Cassini and that new kid on the block, Vidal Sassoon. There will be a lot of Hollywood celebs plus a bunch of big wig New York politicians. It should be quite a bash!"

The two talked further into the afternoon about everything and anything, but Vera wasn't mentioned again. Owen hoped it would stay that way; Joe left for home and everything was okay, for now.

Chapter 40

At Long Last

January 15, 1965, began like any other, with one exception. *Centipede* was about to be birthed. Months of preparation had created challenging, sensual choreography performed by brilliant dancers. The ensemble, one of the best ever cast by Owen, was perfection. Success in Philly, acceptance in Detroit and feature article in *The New York Times* defined this critical night. The only guarantee for Kaplan and Maggli was a potential mega hit. Succeeding as an artistic and commercial venture was the goal and toward that end, *Centipede* was on the track.

At Sardi's, preparations were being made for the big night. Vincent Sardi Jr. having recently taken over the operation from his father would see to their needs. It was rumored that Andy Warhol had accepted. Jackie Kennedy had a conflict and declined. Her sister, Lee Radziwill, would attend, accompanied by famed designer Oleg Cassini. Truman Capote and Vidal Sassoon had yet to respond. New York's Mayor, Robert F. Wagner, was expected, along with Police Commissioner, Michael J. Murphy. The invited press would be vying for the most prestigious interviews. Coverage included all major news sources—papers, magazines and networks.

The Royal staff was in full swing, preparing the theater for an onslaught of guests. Backstage, Griff's crew was checking all technical elements. The dressers arrived early, getting the change areas in order with costumes and shoes marked and placed. Housekeeping busily vacuumed and dusted everywhere. Sandy's orchestra had a cue-to-cue run through.

Flower arrangements, telegrams and cards began arriving. Staff members placed all items in the green room. They were busy running back and forth as gift deliveries continued. Kaplan and Maggli ordered thank-you notes to accompany mini-bouquets for each performer.

The cast was called for 1:00. Griff, Owen, and Jonas arrived, conferred and waited for the gypsies. The air was electric as hours ticked closer to curtain time. With everyone present, Griff began.

"Ladies and Gentleman, you are about to open on Broadway! In just a few hours, this stage will be alive with your work. This production is wildly anticipated and expectations are higher for this show than any I've managed. Tonight, be here an hour before curtain. Owen?" He stood admiring his cast. Together, they would drive *Centipede* home!

"Gang, we've traveled a long way together. This idea in my head started over three years ago. It was time to show the theatre public something astounding, even outrageous. I never doubted it would work. But it took you all to bring it. You never gave up. Tough as my demands and my probing insistence were, you hung in. You've given your 150 percent. For that, I am truly grateful. So, this is your night to shine! Be bold, have fun and above all, watch your numbers!"

At 2:00 pm, the cast was excused. Most of the gypsies left the theatre to do last minute shopping and chores. Rest and relaxation was a must before the big push. Pat was invited to stay at Griff and Mally's before the show. Jonas and Phillipe headed home to nap and a light supper. Owen, Griff and the producers met to discuss last minute details. Jeff and Nora retreated to his apartment until the call to check in. The producers had arranged standing room for them during the performance.

Tim went to his apartment. A loner, he wasn't at all interested in the hoopla that preceded the opening, but he would most likely attend the party. The food and drink was always top notch. Plus, there was a wide assortment of hangers-on, women eager to play. Fantasies were ongoing about show folk. His M.O. was simple—move in, compliment, tantalize and bam! He made it his business to act quickly, take a woman, be pleasured and make sure there were no returns.

Joe and Jim had slipped over to a friend's apartment for a three-way quickie. Nothing like sexual release to get the performing fire stoked. They were often engaged in multi-partner trysts. Today was no exception. Other cast members took time to shop for gifts, plan party attire, call home to share pre-opening excitement with family and friends and wait out the few remaining hours before curtain.

Vera hated openings. She loathed having to attend. The fact that her ex's show was predicted to be a hit was galling. She'd have to stay on her toes which meant little booze. Worst of all, she despised having to hold court, surrounded by people she had little interest in or tolerance for. She was Vera Daniels, a former star; unfortunately, now, a has-been.

In a hotel room near Shubert Alley, Jordan Hendrix called Manhattan information requesting a listing for Joseph Pinto. Jordan had run into Joe in a hotel bar during the Philly tryout. He followed *Centipede's* progress, determined to catch up with Joe once again when the show returned to Broadway. His company had bought a block of seats and he hoped to see Joe that night. The phone rang and rang at Joe's. Jordan, discouraged for the moment, decided he would just show up after the show and find him. He had to see him one way or other.

Dana's mother, Dorothy Beaufort, was visiting her new grandson. Dick asked Dorothy to babysit so Dana could attend the opening. Granny was only too happy to have baby Michael all to herself. Dana was psyched to see *Centipede* and all her old pals.

Kathy bought Sonja a mezzanine seat. She was excited to see the final product after weeks of separation. Sonja's decision to return to college had taken her from theatre. At times she missed her former life. Still, it was an adjustment and one she was still growing into. She would welcome a night away from academia and a chance to see her lover perform.

The local weather report was forecasting snow. No one paid much attention to predictions because New York City rarely experienced extreme winter weather. It started at 5:00. Flakes of light fluffy snow began over Manhattan. By 7:00, it was coming down heavily, starting to slow traffic and pedestrians alike. Regardless, the show would go on.

Chapter 41

Ovations and Interactions

Showtime approaching, traffic in Times Square was crawling along. Enthusiastic ticket holders were slowly making their way toward the Royal. Large searchlights sent columns of shimmering snow waving across the Manhattan night.

Limos and taxis arrived with a blare of horns, discharging the rich and famous into the crowd working their way into the clogged lobby. Cameras flashed. Reporters pushed aggressively in search of any tidbits they could nail for their columns. It was open season on celebrities tonight! An exclusive on tomorrow's front page could mean a reporter's raise. All through the roiling activity, there was little doubt that *Centipede's* big night was here.

Royal employees with snow shovels and floor brooms maintained a safe path for playgoers; the falling snow forcing traffic to a snail's pace. As the well-heeled stepped from vehicles, it was difficult to navigate the soggy carpet runners. The hoi polloi gaped and shoved for a glimpse as limos brought the rich and famous. On the other hand, the noted moved as quickly as possible to the dry lobby, gaining distance from gawkers.

Coats and furs were checked, tickets shown to ushers and invitees directed to the bars for complimentary drinks. Special edition programs were offered to guests. A roar of conversation, greetings and introductions filled the cavernous lobby as the crowd gathered.

Joe made his way with Vera on his arm. Maggli and his domestic partner, Sam Wolfe, followed. Gary and Steve took up the rear of the producers' entourage. Steve had never been to a Broadway opening and was predictably star-struck.

"Gary, look! It's Andy Warhol! Oh my God, he looks just like his photos. And isn't that Mayor Wagner?" Gary smiled, enjoying Steve's exuberance. Giving him a playful nudge, he pointed to a small man wearing glasses and a large fedora, swooshing through the throng in a long cape. "Recognize him?" Steve stared, recognition finally hitting. "It's Truman Capote!"

Through the crowd, Jordan Hendrix found his way to one of the bars, requesting champagne to steady his nerves. Earlier efforts to contact Joe had failed and he decided to show up. He couldn't imagine how Joe would react, but he wanted to see him.

A stretch limo pulled up, Blaine Courtman got out. Every eye from the street to the lobby was fixated on the stunning gentleman. Just who might he be? Was he a prince, a count, an international playboy? Both men and women were drawn to him. He was a standout even in that illustrious crowd.

Joe spotted Blaine and waved. Blaine returned the gesture and walked toward the producer, extending his hand. "It's good to see you, Blaine. It's grand of you to come!" Blaine noticed Vera right away and smiled. His stature and good looks were not missed. Joe made introductions. "Blaine, I'd like you to meet my fiancée, Vera Daniels. Vera, this is Blaine Courtman, one of our chief investors. Maggli stopped talking and shot Blaine a look of approval. 'He's gorgeous.'

"I'm delighted to meet you," said Vera. "Joe mentioned you were one of our strongest backers. It's lovely to put a face and a handsome one at that, to a name," she purred. Blaine bent down and kissed her hand. "You're lovely, Miss Daniels. Joe never stops talking about you!" Vera blushed and requested another glass of champagne, her third, which she downed immediately.

"Blaine, this is my producing partner, Leonard Maggli. I believe you two have spoken on the phone." "Yes indeed. How are you Leonard?" Maggli returned a firm handshake. "It's good to meet you, Blaine. I have to thank our mutual friend Gregory Morgan out of Houston, who is key in our connection. How is he?"

"Greg is doing well. His oil business keeps thriving down in Texas, but his recent interest in furthering his investments brought him to theatre. He's a big fan of musicals, hosting shows that come through Houston. We've been friends for years. My brother, Eugene, is his chief legal advisor." Maggli listened with interest. "Well, I think you'll be pleased with the production. Your investment was well made!" He turned to Sam in an effort to include him, "And this is Sam Wolfe." Blaine shook his hand. Gary noticed and joined the group with Steve close behind. "Leonard, would you introduce us?" Gary had found his confidence working for the producer and was an indispensable asset.

"Blaine, I'd like you to meet my chief assistant, Gary Hanson and his friend Steve Jackson. Gary is a former dancer, now working for us." "Might I have seen you in a show? I do travel extensively and enjoy theatre immensely."

"My last job was in the national tour of *Bravo Business* last year until I was injured and forced to retire from performing," explained Gary. Blaine brightened. "What a coincidence! I saw that production last year; the first time was in Jacksonville, then Houston, and finally in Vancouver. I knew one of the young ladies in the show," he said, as Vera suddenly stopped sipping and listened. Blaine continued.

"Did you work with Patricia Byrne? What a fabulous woman and amazing dancer!" "She was one of my best friends in the company," said Gary, with a smile. "We spent a lot of time together until I got hurt. I had to stay behind as the tour moved on. I lost track of her until this show." "Patricia Byrne is our leading dancer," said Leonard, proudly. "She and Jonas Martin put a shine on Owen's work. I think you'll be impressed!"

"Well, if it's the same Patricia Byrne, it won't be a stretch," Blaine remarked, knowingly. Vera stopped drinking and glared at Maggli. "She's not that good, Lenny. I've worked with better," she said with an edge. Blaine heard the remark and turned to Vera.

"Are you in the theatre, Miss Daniels?" Hearing Blaine's question, Gary snickered quietly. Maggli interceded at once. "Miss Daniels, former Broadway star, is now retired," he said.

Joe took Vera's hand, a conciliatory gesture, adding, "Taking care of me is a full time job for this lady and no one does it better." Vera ignored the remark and pulled away.

"You need a lot of care, Joseph," she said, acidly. Reaching for her fourth glass of champagne, she grabbed on to Blaine, who suddenly felt cornered. "What are you doing later, Mr. Courtman?" Joe was becoming annoyed as he took her glass and set it on the bar. "Perhaps we should go in," he said as the curtain warning bell sounded. Taking Vera's elbow, he brusquely led her away, followed by Maggli and the others.

Feeling slightly put off by his encounter with Vera, Blaine waited until the Kaplan group had entered the theatre. Reaching in his pocket, he walked to an usher, handed him a ticket and was directed to a VIP box, house right.

Meanwhile, backstage was alive with preparation as Griff and crew went over the tech check list one last time, readying the pre-show. The wardrobe people were positioned and ready in the quick change areas. The orchestra tuned as they waited for Sandy to enter the pit.

At 7:55, Griff called the gypsies to the green room. Collectively, the company, powerful as a tsunami, was about to engulf the audience. Bright faces brushed with color, striking hair arrangements, form-fitting suits of Lycra left little to the imagination as they clung to perfectly sculptured bodies. The women were stunning, their bodies fit and sensual; the men - strong, ultra masculine and suggestively bold. Griff was the first to speak.

"Company, I want to thank you all for the months of hard work, dedication and fortitude. You are directly responsible for *Centipede's* success. Without you, this production would not be where it is tonight. Break a leg!"

Owen was next. "It's hard to believe we have come this far together. You are a brilliant group, whatever goes down, thank you. *Merde!*"

The company dispersed at "Places!" Taking opening positions, their resolve was palpable. There was no turning back. Yes, they had come a long way together and keen to perform the gift of Owen's choreography.

Lights lowered, the audience hushed. Sandy Irvin stepped to the podium, a single light noting his perch. The audience welcomed him with deafening applause as he turned and bowed with a snap. Raising his baton, the moment was now. With a downward thrust of his arm, the first glorious chords of brass rang out. The show was off and running!

When the overture ended, the giant curtain slowly rose. And there, center stage, *Centipede* stood, frozen in a stop frame. An explosion of applause greeted a dancer moving languidly at first. Another, then another joined the sequence until the stage was fully alive, a colorful, amoebic presence. The men, virile and strong, lifted their partners, their contact expressly sexual. Each took a turn sliding his counterpart down. Gasps were heard throughout. Owen's first piece offered an orgiastic display of sexual fantasy. The dancers were in high gear, reaching as far as their bodies would allow movements full and rich.

From his seat, Blaine found Pat stage center, her phenomenal body hard to miss. Clad in the skimpiest fabric, his breath nearly stopped as she undulated through the choreography, her movement reminiscent of past intimacy. How he ached for her! He had fallen hard and proposed a year ago. She had turned him down, making it clear that her first love was the theatre and would always be.

As the evening progressed, something special had taken hold of the Great White Way. The Arthropod was now king! Number after number brought unanimous and fierce applause.

During the finale, the audience didn't wait, scrambling to their feet. They had seen something unprecedented. As house lights rose, animated conversations continued, patrons making their way to the lobby and more complimentary champagne.

Still on stage, the cast whooped and hollered, hugged, kissed and celebrated. Owen worked his way through the bodacious clump of gypsies and was immediately lifted and carried around stage. They chanted praises as he tottered overhead, a broad smile radiating. Griff joined them and called for attention. "Three cheers for Owen!" A trio of hip-hoorays ensued followed by rousing applause. Owen was the heart of *Centipede.* As he was set down, Griff made an announcement. "Owen, we got together to give you this," handing him a gift wrapped box. The gypsies quieted.

"You have inspired us, believed in us, your confidence never wavering." Owen was clearly moved. "I don't know what to say. Your talent is gift enough," he said softly, as he opened the box. Lifting the lid, he parted the tissue and found a stunning marble ashtray noting:

"To Owen Matthews, our inspiration and mentor,
With our gratitude and love,
The Centipede.
January 15, 1965."

Collecting himself, he turned to look at his beautiful dancers, their shining faces and wide smiles evidence of their devotion. "Thank you all! I will keep this nearby, always!" Another round of applause ensued. "Now it's time to celebrate! See you at Sardi's", he shouted as he walked away. Griff took over. "Cast, there is a fierce snowstorm, but the party isn't far. Please change and join us at Sardi's. It's time to wallow in your success," he chuckled. This will be a night to remember.

Chapter 42

The Sardi's Blowout

Sardi's upper floor was alive with conviviality as *Centipede* arrived. Applause broke out as guests recognized the cast. Kudos abounding, flashbulbs popped and ticket holders pushed to get a glimpse of the gypsies, who had just turned Broadway on its ear.

Griff and Mally visited with several guests, including the mayor and his entourage. Pat arrived with Jonas and Phillipe and immediately got swept up by the barrage of praise. Nora and Jeff found a table off to the side where they could view the action. There was a large crowd where producers Kaplan and Maggli held court.

Vera, already tipsy, was nowhere to be seen. Weaving down the hall to the "Ladies," she entered and passed a woman sucking a cigarette. Paying little attention, she entered the stall, pulled up her gown and squatted, relieved to be alone. She was woozy as she opened the door. At the sink, she rinsed, an attendant handing a towel. "Thanks honey," she slurred.

Glancing in the mirror she shuddered, "Lord, you're completely lit, Verna." Verna, her given name, was a fact shared with no one. Brushing hair out of her eyes, she attempted to smooth the loose strands back into her chignon. "There, no more straggle!" A touch of lipstick helped. Feeling more put together, she started for the door. Suddenly, the stranger stood.

"You're Vera Daniels, aren't you?" Vera tossed a smile. "I am indeed!" The woman followed her out the door, falling in step. "You were married to Owen Matthews, right?" Vera stopped in her tracks, eyeing the woman suspiciously. "How do you know that?"

"Everybody knows that. He threw you over for some chorus piece last year." A flash emanated from Vera's eyes, her booze-fueled stupor clearing. "And who might you be? "Jackie Eldridge to you." She suddenly realized. "Wait a minute, just a minute. I recognize you! You were a dancer in my husband's shows, right?" "Ex-husband's and yes, guilty as charged!"

"You have some nerve! This conversation is over!" Vera was dying for a drink. "I know who your ex is fucking," Jackie hissed. "Stop it," shouted Vera, clearly distressed. "Miss Daniels, we have a lot in common. We both have a sordid history with Mr. Matthews." Vera had heard enough. "Get the hell out of here, or I'll have you thrown out!" "By whom? Your sugar daddy, Kaplan, doesn't have the balls!"

Vera made a sudden lunge for Jackie, shoving her to the floor. Jackie screamed and kicked as Vera repeatedly slapped her. During the scuffle, a waiter happened by, saw the fight and hurried off. Before long, he was back with two security men, who grabbed the two brawling women, pulling them apart.

"Get this piece of trash out of here," blurted Vera, sobbing. "Get Joe Kaplan now!" Jackie was brought to a storage room and was forced to sit. Vera was escorted to Vincent Sardi's private office to wait for Joe. In minutes, the door opened and Kaplan was at her side. "Baby Doll, what happened? Are you all right?" Vera grabbed Joe, buried her face in his chest, and sobbed.

"Some bitch ex-dancer cornered me and said vile things. I was cold sober when it started, Joe. She came out of nowhere and was horrible! I want her ass out!" "Okay, okay, Baby Doll. I'll take care of it. I'll talk to her; do you want to press charges?" "No, just throw the bitch out in the fucking snow," cried Vera. A security man entered.

"Please escort Miss Daniels to my car and see that she gets home," Joe ordered. For Vera, the evening was ruined and she wanted out. Too many reporters around! Helping Vera to her feet, Joe walked her to the rear of the restaurant, his driver was waiting. It would be a slow ride home.

Joe was angry. Entering the room where Jackie sat waiting, he approached. Jackie didn't move.

"Whoever you are, you have a hell of a nerve busting up my night and terrorizing my lady." Jackie rolled her eyes. She was calm, remorse nonexistent. "Oh please. Your lady is a washed up whore! And as for your night, it belongs to the gypsies, not to your fat ass!"

Joe snapped, grabbing Jackie by the shoulders and back-handing her with such force she fell from the chair. "Get this piece of trash out of here," he ordered. Jackie was pulled to her feet. As she was escorted from the room, Joe pointed a finger.

"If I ever see you around Miss Daniels again, you'll regret it. Now, get the hell out of here!" Jackie was shown the door. The snow was heavy, her shoes disappearing in large drifts. Snow shrouded the entire city. Turning onto 45th St., she trudged to Broadway looking for a cab. She had lost again. Nothing was fair in love, war and, especially, show business.

Back at the party, a jazz trio played. A young black singer warbled, her sound filling the cocktail lounge, reminiscent of the incomparable Sarah Vaughn. Some party-goers were on a makeshift dance floor, enjoying the post show celebration.

Joe Pinto grabbed a seat at the bar. Gazing about the room, he checked out the action. There were plenty of good looking men and he hoped for a late night tryst. He wasn't interested in any cast member. Phillipe was taken, Chad didn't qualify and Jim, old news. As he looked over the smoke-filled room, a handsome man approached. 'Jeez, he looks familiar,' he mused.

"Hi Joe, long time no see!" "Jordan, what the fuck? How is it you're here?" Jordan moved closer, giving Joe a squeeze.

"I'm living in Boston now but here on business for a month," he said, adding a wink. I noticed, in the *Boston Herald*, that your show was coming to Broadway, so I thought I'd check it out. I got my seat weeks ago."

"Did you try to contact me? I'm listed," said Joe. "I tried but there was never an answer." Joe took a long, hungry look at Jordan. "Good to see you, can I buy you a drink?" "Yes, thanks. I'll have a Manhattan.

Seems appropriate," he chuckled. He felt a warm flush as Joe's hand touched his knee. Reciprocating, his fingers grazed Joe's thigh.

"The show is amazing. You dancers are so impressive. I envy your commitment." "Glad you enjoyed it," said Joe, suddenly aware Jim was walking toward them. "Who's the honey?" Joe wasn't interested in sharing, but Jim was.

"Jordan, this is Jim, also in the company," he said, irritated. Jim moved closer, looking him over, hoping for action. Jordan smiled, turning his attention to Joe. Jim realized he was not part of the equation, tonight. 'Damn, a three-way would have been heaven,' he thought. Excusing himself, he left, determined to make a night of it anyway.

Joe whispered, "Where are you staying?" "I'm at the Warwick on 6th Avenue. Care to check it out?" "Let's go. One-on-one is much better," he agreed. Retrieving their coats, they stepped into a winter wonderland. The snow was dense, still coming down hard. It was difficult to see across the street.

"Come on, let's walk to Broadway. We might find a cab," said Joe, eager to get to a warm bed. Grabbing Jordan's scarf, he playfully pulled him along through swirling white and persistent wind. With each step, he grew hornier, determined not to waste a minute of flesh time. He was fixated on Jordan, which surprised him, given his penchant for casual sex.

So often in the past, he'd forgotten the name of a trick before the action was over. But Jordan Hendrix was an exception. He'd never forgotten their interlude the previous year in Des Moines. This guy was his sexual fantasy—insatiable, malleable and unbridled! Their previous passion for each other was about to be made fresh. He relished the thought, 'What could be better?'

The party began to thin at Sardi's. Pat, returning from the restroom, felt a tap on her shoulder. Blaine Courtman! "Hello Patricia! How are you?" "My God, Blaine! What in the world brings you here? I never expected to run into you," she said, slightly embarrassed. "It must be my fate and happily so. Actually, I'm one of the principal investors in the show." "You're kidding! How did that happen?"

"Do you remember Gregory Morgan, the wealthy philanthropist you met in Houston last year?"

"Yes of course. I attended his fabulous party with you. Is he the connection to Kaplan-Maggli?"

"He is indeed. Greg invests in many things, but he has a particular fondness for show business. Leonard Maggli is an old college pal. When *Centipede* was offered, I came along. I must say it is a winning choice, for a number of reasons."

"Did you know I was in the show?" Blaine smiled. "My dear Patricia, I'm not psychic. Frankly, I never expected to see you again." The memory of Pat's rejection still stung. Pat changed the subject, resorting to small talk. "How long will you be here?"

"I'm here for three months. I'm working a deal for Courtman Enterprises and if it goes through, we'll be building on Long Island." "I'm happy for you Blaine. Take care and much success," she said formally, extending her hand.

Blaine sensed she was looking for an out. "Here's my card, Patricia. If you'd care to join me for dinner some evening, you can reach me at the Plaza." Pat put the card in her bag.

"Thank you." She left in search of Owen. Blaine reluctantly watched her go. He was still mad about her. Spotting Leonard Maggli and party, he joined for a nightcap.

Pat looked around. Owen was at the bar with an attractive young woman, someone unknown. Approaching, she could see they were deep in conversation, her pulse, pulsing faster. As Pat drew closer, the woman smiled, "Hello." Pat felt a wave of jealousy. "Owen?"

He brightened when he saw her. "Baby, I've been looking for you the last half hour! Come join us," he said, patting the seat at his right. "I'd like you to meet Stephanie McNeil. Miss McNeil wrote the feature article on *Centipede*, appearing in last Sunday's *Times*. Pat had little interest in Miss McNeil and stepped between them, her displeasure obvious. Stephanie tried to gracefully pick up the conversation.

"Miss Byrne, what a fabulous performance! You do Owen's work proud." "Thank you. Owen, could I speak to you in private?" Owen shifted, slightly puzzled by Pat's slightly rude edge. "Will you excuse us, Miss McNeil? It's great to see you again. Enjoy the rest of your evening." Owen took Pat by the hand and led her away.

When at a discreet distance, he stopped and turned to her, "What the hell was that all about, Baby?" "You seemed a little too cozy with that woman. What's going on?" The question baffled Owen. "I was having a conversation with a member of the press, someone who favors the production and wanted to congratulate me personally," he said, annoyance building.

"Is that all? You weren't interested in something more?" "Pat, knock it off. You can't be serious. Why would I be interested in something more? I'm obligated to speak to the press. *Centipede* is a major hit and requires certain etiquette. I've told you before, you're the only woman I want, so don't start that shit again!"

Tears sprang to Pat's eyes as she realized she'd overreacted. "I'm so sorry, Owen. I misunderstood, but you did seem a little too interested in her." "I'm interested in what she can do for the show, nothing more. Drop it, okay?" Noticing Maggli, he waved. Pat was ready to get out of there.

"Are you going to stick around for a while? I'm beat and with two shows tomorrow, I need to leave." Owen agreed. "I agree. Why don't you stay at Griff's? You can head to the theatre tomorrow with Mally. Come stay with me Saturday? How does that sound, Baby?" Pat felt a wave of relief. "Yes, that's great."

Across the room, Owen spotted Griff and waved. Griff noticed and came over. "Say Griff, I was wondering if Pat could stay with you two tonight. The weather is lousy, it's late and the girls have two shows tomorrow." "Good idea. We can share a cab, if there's one to share. It's bad out there," remarked Griff.

"Thanks, I'll stick around awhile. It should be easier to find a cab later. The smart people have already left. Do you think there'll be a delay in our start time tomorrow?" "I seriously doubt it, Owen. City plows will be out as soon as the snow has passed. We should be clear by noon."

Owen pulled Pat close, kissed her gently, his warm breath soothing. "I leave you in reliable hands, Baby, until tomorrow. We have serious catching up to do." Her relief was obvious. Before leaving, he stopped, his tone serious, "Pat, no more assumptions, understand?" His tone was compelling. She hurried away with Griff and Mally to retrieve coats.

Opening the door was difficult, the wind pushing him back. Griff peered into the snowy night, the street deserted and no cabs in sight. "Ladies, I'm going down the block to look for a ride. If I'm lucky, we'll soon be on our way. Sit tight and stay warm!" He disappeared, pulling his collar up high against the swirling snow. 'And I thought winters in Chicago were tough.' The cold eroded his cheeks.

Inside, Mally and Pat occasionally glanced out the door. It was late and they were exhausted. With two shows later today, the time for sleep was short. Pat stifled a yawn and closed her eyes. She appeared distracted. "Pat, what's going on? Owen seemed upset."

"I saw him talking to that reporter who did the *Centipede* feature. They were sitting at the bar together. She seemed too friendly and he wasn't exactly fighting it." "Oh Pat, come on. I can't believe you'd feel threatened by her. That's Stephanie McNeil, who is just doing her job. By the way, she wrote a great article about us."

"I don't give a shit if she wins a Pulitzer Prize for literature. I didn't like seeing her with Owen," she said, her voice rising. "Pat, you're tired and paranoid. You know Owen draws lots of attention wherever he is. This is his big night." Pat frowned. "I want him to enjoy his big night, but I don't want him humping the first woman who strokes his ego!" Mally sighed, 'It's the same old stuff.'

The door opened with a whoosh. "Okay ladies, we have a cab, let's step on it!" The girls hurried to join him. They could barely stand upright as the wind bore down. With a few steps to the curb, their shoes and nylons were soaked. Gingerly, they made their way to the cab with Griff guiding them. Once they were piled in, the cab slowly pulled out onto 45th and headed toward 9th Avenue. It was a slow ride to Chelsea.

Centipede had an auspicious birth. The public approved; the weather challenged; and the media, captivated. Kaplan and Maggli had a monumental hit on their hands! Ah, the sweet smell of success!

Chapter 43

Unexpected Emergency

Two shows passed on Saturday, with enthusiastic and sold-out houses. The cast survived a demanding week, a triumphant weekend and over-the-moon reviews.

The *New York Times* proclaimed: *Owen Matthews, the celebrated director-choreographer, has outdone himself this season. With a tasty offering titled* Centipede, *Matthews has fashioned a work so outlandishly controversial, so brilliantly executed, so unusually conceptualized, Broadway will never be the same!*

The *Post* added: Centipede, *Owen Matthews' latest contribution to the Broadway stage, offers up a core of the most exciting, erotic, technically brilliant dancer-performers in recent memory. Hurry down to the Royal Theater for this tasty treat of outlandish, outspoken and controversial work. This show has Tony Award written all over it!*

The *Herald Tribune* was more conservative but nonetheless appreciative stating: *The many offerings from Owen Matthews have been topped this season with his latest production known simply as* Centipede, *an all-dance review. It's a brilliant concoction of suggestive and downright erotic choreography executed by the best dancers in town. If pure sensationalism and outrageous innovation is your style of entertainment, then this two-hour journey is a guarantee of titillation. A must for visual voyeurs!*

Variety had its say with a different take: *Run, don't walk to an exciting happening, currently at the newly renovated Royal Theater. Owen Matthews, the director-choreographic genius, has brought about a new theatre form. His all-dance review,* Centipede, *is so sensuous, so suggestive you'll squirm in your seat! The work, not at all for the faint-of-heart, will carry you on a two-hour orgiastic ride of pure pleasure. Not to be missed!*

Following the Saturday evening performance, Owen looked forward to sharing his success with Pat with a private party. And of course, he would show his appreciation in his usual way. Bedding Pat was always a dive into carnal oblivion, lovemaking at his best, as their history would attest. He hurried home to prepare his turf for the night to come.

For his newest Broadway star, three dozen long-stem roses from his favorite greenhouse were arranged in an exquisite Tiffany vase. In addition, for a bit extra ambiance, candles were lit in the den, dining room, bedroom and gardenias floated in decorative bowls. His final touch was a selection of soft jazz.

Pat, as usual, would be starved, after the show. Bottles of Moet's best bubbly, Russian caviar, for starters and a tray from the corner deli with cheese and sandwich makings would be just right. Romantic as they may appear, late night meals had a way of spoiling the romance. They would have desert in the bedroom; the finest Belgian chocolates, more Moet and, each other. At 10:30 sharp, the buzzer sounded. One push of the button and Pat would be there. Checking over the scene a final time, he was pleased with the surroundings.

A knock brought excitement. There she stood, voluptuous, long auburn tresses cascading over her shoulders, coat partially open and a dress that might have been X-rated elsewhere. His breath shortened as he admired Pat from head to foot. He had never been with a more exquisite lover. Owen's jeans suddenly got snug.

"Oh Baby, you look incredible! Come in. Let me take your coat." His lips found hers, the kiss deep and promising. Pat sighed and stayed put, as his tongue took over. "Baby, make yourself comfortable," he motioned to the candlelit living room. Pat noticed the roses. "Oh God, Owen, are these for me?" He smiled and indicated a card, which she opened excitedly: '*To my inspiration, my life and muse. I love you! Owen.*' Emotions swallowed her up as she kissed him repeatedly. "I love you Owen! Thank you for everything!" Owen allowed himself to pull away gently and walked to the bar.

"Baby, let's have a toast!" Taking the chilled bottle of champagne, he uncorked and poured. "To our success, Baby!" They clinked, kissed and downed the bubbly. A refill later, Pat was feeling tipsy. "Care for some caviar?" "Yes, I haven't eaten since lunch." "Come on, let's sit in here," he suggested, picking up the bottle. "Bring the caviar and crackers, will you Baby?" Pat followed, feeling mellow, anticipating a special night of love.

They settled on the sofa and sampled the caviar as he repeatedly poured. "Are you enjoying this, Baby?" By now, the champagne had gone to her head; she was feeling amorous and playful. "I'd enjoy this more," she said, reaching his fly. Owen set his glass down. He'd never seen her this aggressive and was letting her take over, enjoying it fully. Opening his pants, she noticed he was without briefs. 'Heaven,' she thought as she reached for his shaft, hard and ready. Delighted with her treasure, she pushed him down on his back and proceeded to take him. Owen moaned with pleasure, cooperating fully as he felt her warm breath and tongue sliding up and down. "God, Pat, this is good. This is really good," he mumbled coarsely, as she applied pressure. She felt mad with power as he begged for more. Again and again, she slid up and down, a toy to her liking, as she licked and sucked. Then, she stopped!

"Baby, don't stop! What the hell? Come on, play fair!" Pat smiled, her plan taking hold. Reaching for her glass, she took a mouthful, allowing the liquid to run over his shaft, she sucked him dry. "Oh God Baby, you're amazing," he shouted, the tingle of the liquid adding to his pleasure. He couldn't hold back and came, while she fondled and licked.

When he calmed down, he took her in his arms. "Baby, you're the best, the absolute best," he held her snuggly. Pat pulled away playfully, lifting the bottle and pouring him another. "Want to go another round?" Taken aback, he nodded, slipping off his jeans. Pat stood still while he unzipped her dress. "Come here, Baby." Lifting her in his arms, he carried her down the hall to his bedroom, placing her gently on the bed.

Gazing down, he admired the lean, long torso and beautifully rounded breasts. Her long legs rose to heaven, her neatly shaved mound beckoned. Long auburn hair over her shoulders in waves that tangled and twisted. He wanted to be lost in that voluminous mane, to be totally consumed by her sex, skin, smell, drawing him to carnal excess. And so it began.

From a bottle of baby oil, he poured a small amount in his hands. Slowly, deliberately, he started with her feet, kneading, massaging and rubbing. Pat let out a satisfied sigh as he inched his way up her legs. He intensified over her calves, knees, and her thighs. When he reached her mound he stopped. Pat arched her back, begging for more. Inserting his fingers, he slid them in and out as she moaned her want. "Oh Owen, give me all of you," she cried. Without hesitation, he entered and pulled himself tightly against her. The two became one as they pulsated, their intense heat erupting in mutual explosion.

For a few minutes, they lay locked together, their breathing slowly returning to normal. Owen slowly pulled out, caressing her where he had just been. Pat sighed as she felt him release. Rolling to her side, she watched him, stand, stretch and turn; his legs and tight buns a model for Adonis. In need of the usual after sex smoke, he lit cigarettes for both. Although an infrequent smoker, she took a puff, let it out slowly, savoring the afterglow. She was spent, but felt delicious.

"Baby, how do you feel?" He sat on the bed and kissed her gently. "You're incredible. You never cease to amaze me!" Pat smiled, feeling powerful. After all, she was Owen's lover, the only one. Wrapping her legs around him from behind, she rubbed his neck and shoulders. "Oh, Baby, that feels good!" He sighed under her touch and put out the cigarette. Pat continued, enjoying his response. Reaching around his torso, she worked her way down to his penis and playfully tickled.

"Oh no, don't start that again, or I'm a goner. Besides, it's late. Let's get some sleep, Baby. I'll be right back." Surveying the room, he blew out the remaining candles and turned off the lights. Pat was quickly under the covers, waiting. A short trip to the bathroom and he was ready to snuggle.

"Oh Owen, I love you," she murmured, feeling him move in close, spoon fashion. Good night, Baby. I love you too." In minutes, they were asleep.

Sunlight invaded the bedroom, as a ringing phone cut the stillness. Owen stirred, groaned and rolled over. The phone stopped. A moment later, it began again, a relentless intrusion annoying him to the core. Lifting the sheet, he sat up and reached the receiver.

"Matthews," he said irritably. "Owen, Griff. I'm sorry to disturb, but I just received an urgent phone call from Sean Byrne. Apparently, Pat's dad has suffered a heart attack." "That's the worst kind of news, Griff. I'll try to break it to her gently, if that's even possible."

"I have few details at this time, but if you could get Pat over to our place, one of the Byrne brothers will pick her up, probably in an hour." Owen glanced at his clock. "That's not a lot of time, but better she should be at your place. Who's coming?"

"I believe Mickey, the oldest. Apparently, Mrs. Byrne is with her husband now. They took him to New York Presbyterian Hospital in Manhattan."

"I'll tell Pat and get her there by cab as soon as possible," said Owen, the sudden news weighing on him. "She'll see you soon, Griff. Thanks for being so quick on this." Putting down the phone, he had to get a move on and nudged her gently.

"Baby, wake up!" Pat rolled over, muttering, "Just thirty more, please!" Owen nudged again, harder this time. She shifted, slowly sitting up. "What time is it, Owen?" Rubbing her eyes, she was disoriented from the deep sleep and too much champagne. Owen gently enfolded her in his arms. "It's early, Baby. I need to talk to you." Noting his serious face, Pat's eyes widened. "What is it? Tell me!"

"Baby, I just heard your father has been taken to the hospital. He had a heart attack. Your brother called Griff. He'll be there in less than an hour to pick you up and take you home."

Pat let out a low cry as she pulled back from Owen. "Are you sure?" Trembling, she began to sob, her body shaking, Owen held her closer.

"I'm afraid so, Baby. Your mother is with him at New York Presbyterian. You should get there as soon as possible." "Oh my God, I have to get out of here!" Owen got dressed, slipping into jeans, a pullover, and his desert boots.

"Let's find your clothes and get you to Griff's as fast as we can. It's better if Mickey finds you there. "I'll have Ralph call a cab." Pat found her underwear, dress and heels. Owen zipped her in, fetched her coat and dance bag. "Come on, Baby, there's no time to lose." Opening the door and letting her go ahead, he grabbed his key and hurried Pat to the elevator. Clinging to him as they descended, her sobs muffled in his chest.

At the lobby, they hurried through the entrance and found Ralph holding a cab. Owen opened the door and turned to Pat. "Call me, Baby. I'll be waiting for an update." He kissed her gently and helped her into the back seat. "Please send my best wishes to your family. I love you, Baby. Everything will be all right! Please take the lady to 319 West 22nd Street in Chelsea. This should cover it," he said, handing the driver $20. The cab pulled away. Feeling a sudden chill, he hurried into the building and back on the elevator. When he got to his apartment, he dialed Griff. "She's on her way, Griff. Keep me posted, okay?" "I sure will, Owen. Talk to you later."

How would this play out? Owen contemplated his next move. No doubt, he would have to replace Pat during her absence. He'd have Mally cover Pat's show. She was the only one he would trust with the lead spot and Nora would swing Mally's until Pat returned. Thoughts gelling, Owen recalled the night with Pat. How she moved him! He could still smell her fragrance, her taste on his lips. He could only hope she would not be away too long. Waiting would be a bitch!

Chapter 44

Making Do

Mickey Byrne wasted no time getting to Griff's. He found Pat being comforted by Mally, as Griff opened the door. "Oh, Mick, tell me. Is Dad all right?" Mickey held her firm, calming her. "Dad's right where he should be. The staff at Presbyterian is the best. We'll just have to sit tight. Mom wants you there right away. Let's go!"

"Please update us when you can," said Griff opening the door. "We'll cover for you as long as it takes. Not to worry, Pat, you're on leave right now." Pat hugged them. "Thanks! I love you both so much."

When they were gone, Mally sank on the sofa, Griff joining. He took her hand kissed it gently, her look said it all.

"This is going to be rough for Pat, Griff. She's so close to her father." "It sounds like they got him to the hospital in short order. I'm sure he'll be fine, but you never know." The situation brought a flash of his father's fatal heart attack years before. "They know so much more now, I'm sure he's in good hands." Mally was aware of Griff's family history. "I'm sorry you lost your father, Griff. I can't imagine what you went through." He was silent for a moment. "I lost my best friend back then, but I've been blessed with you." Holding her, all was right with the world.

Mickey wasted no time getting to the hospital. Pulling into the visitor's lot, they hurried to the emergency entrance. At 'Information,' a hefty woman behind the desk gruffly asked, "What can I do for you?"

"Our dad had a heart attack and was brought here early today. His name is Alan Byrne. Could you direct us to him?" The woman referred to a list and picked up the phone. "Who shall I say?" Pat jumped in. "We're Mr. Byrne's son and daughter! What room is he in?" The woman blinked, threw a frown in Pat's direction and continued her call.

"Yes, this is the front desk. We have relatives of Alan Byrne down here. What? I see, very well, I will tell them." Her officious manner intact, she announced, "Mr. Byrne is in critical care at the moment. Take the elevator to the 3rd Floor, a charge nurse will direct you. Look for the nursing station straight ahead when you exit." "Thank you. We appreciate it." Mickey took Pat's hand to the elevator, pushed the third floor button. She was trembling when the doors opened; a nurse with a kind face looked up. "May I help you folks?"

"Yes, we're Mickey and Patricia Byrne. Our father, Alan Byrne, was brought in earlier today. May we have an update on his condition?" "Of course," replied the woman, pointing toward a room across the hall. I believe Mrs. Byrne is waiting for the doctor as well. He should be here any minute." Pat rushed toward the family lounge, Mickey close behind.

"Oh my God, what's going on, Ma?" Maureen rose, extending her arms and cradling her only daughter. She spoke softly, gently rubbing

Pat's back. Calming her down from simple trauma was near impossible, but this? Catastrophic! Noticing Mickey, she gave a little wave.

"Dad is going to be okay, but he did suffer a heart attack. Luckily, we were all with him at the time. We were cleaning up when he cried out. Before he hit the floor, Sean caught him. It all happened so fast!" Mickey intervened. "What now?"

"The doctors are saying he is weak but will survive," said Maureen. "Oh, Ma, I'm so sorry," said Pat, barely able to hold back. Mickey hugged them both. "I'll be here for you, Ma," said Pat reassuringly. "I've been given a leave-of-absence while things are sorted out." "Who will cover you? You're the star!" Pat replied, "We have covers who do our spots, Ma. Mally will sub for me, she's the best in the company."

"I beg to differ dear, she's number two!" Mickey chuckled. It was typical of Maureen to think Pat the best. "This is not your concern, Ma. The show will go on." As they conversed, the doctor walked in and introduced himself. "Mrs. Byrne, I'm Dr. Luca Marini, resident cardiologist here at Presbyterian. I've been seeing your husband."

"How is my husband?" Dr. Marini observed three anxious faces, waiting for word. "Mr. Byrne is lucky to be alive, but we can help. We are running intravenous lines to thin his blood. Once he's past danger, your husband will need from three to six weeks bed rest to regain his strength. Do you have any questions?" Pat jumped in.

"Dr. Marini, how does something like this happen? My dad's diet is reasonable, he doesn't smoke or drink to excess. He's always been fit and vigorous!" "Much of what we know is from observing family history. Have there been any heart problems in the family before?" Maureen replied, "My husband's father and two of his uncles died from heart attacks, all were hard working men." Dr. Marini continued.

"Heart problems repeat, such as your husband's event. I promise we'll do all we can. My associate, Dr. Warren Abernathy, did his residency here at Presbyterian under Dr. Thomas Killip, one of the best in the field of cardiac medicine." Somewhat relieved, the Byrnes relaxed a bit.

"Thank you so much, Dr. Marini. We appreciate everything you're doing for Alan." As he started to leave, Pat touched his arm.

"Can I see my dad?" Marini looked into Pat's eyes, noting fear and sadness. "We have your dad in ICU. He's resting comfortably, most likely asleep. You may look in, but only for a moment." A nurse appeared, they conferred briefly. Pat waited until he left. The nurse approached. "Dr. Marini has asked me to escort you to ICU. Please follow me." Pat took Maureen's hand. "Walk with me, Ma?" Mickey followed.

The lights were low. The few beds in ICU cordoned off by curtains. The nurse stopped, pulling one back. Pat gasped seeing her dad lying there, inert and silent with tubes stretched here and there, an oxygen mask over his nose and mouth. A monitor beeped softly, indicating his heart rate and pressure. It was all too much!

Pat reached his hand, lifting and kissing it gently. Maureen leaned on Mickey, tears falling. Mickey tried to be strong for her, fighting back his own tears. "Dad, I love you," murmured Pat. Maureen touched his face briefly and turned away. They were shown out. Returning to the elevators, Mickey pushed the lobby button. "Come on Ma, there's nothing we can do right now." "Okay, let's go home. We can all use a bite and some rest." They headed to Mickey's truck. Today had been ghastly.

At the Royal, it was business as usual. Monday night arrived and with it, another eight-show week.

Mally was ready. Jonas had rehearsed and placed her that afternoon. Running through Pat's show had been painstaking, a lot of material to absorb in one rehearsal. Nora had been called to work with Chad, Mally's partner. It was a scramble, but gypsies were adept at making adjustments. The adrenalin rush was palpable as they prepared and warmed up.

"Ladies and gentleman, please report to the green room at 7:50 on the dot. Thank you!" The dancers made final touches on make-up and hair, change areas to dress. In moments the ensemble was ready to go.

"Company, some of you are already aware Pat Byrne's father was taken ill this past weekend. She will be out of the show at least a week, maybe longer. In her absence, Mally will fill in and Nora will cover Mally. All have been rehearsed, so please be patient and make any adjustments necessary. Chad will be with Nora, Jonas with Mally. Are there any questions? If not, then places, please!" The gypsies took their opening positions. Sandy's downbeat brought the show to life. The show crackled with renewed vitality. Change always energized a cast, the challenge, a booster of sorts. This was the first full week for Broadway's latest hit.

During the second act, Owen slipped in to watch the show. Pat's absence was difficult for him, she had been his inspiration. However, Mally was in great form that night, hardly a neophyte to his work. He would eventually find a lead spot for her in a future show. For now, he was grateful she filled in so well.

He had called Pat earlier that evening. The sound of her voice warmed him. He missed her more than he could have imagined. The fact that he couldn't be with her was frustrating. She sounded calm in the knowledge that her dad would survive.

Following the show, Owen stopped at the Taft Hotel Bar. He was in need of scotch, the weather having turned raw. He took a seat loosening his scarf and coat. Shaking out a cigarette, he lit and filled his lungs. Smoking was his pleasure at all times, especially after heavy sex. He imagined Pat, what a night they had! A wave of frustration rose as he recalled her smell, taste, and body. Lost in thought, he failed to notice her. "Say, don't I know you?" Startled, Owen looked up. "I'll be damned! Miss McNeil," he said, his mood brightening. Stephanie's warm smile spilled over him.

"We're destined to meet again," she enthused. "How is the masterful Owen Matthews, the toast of Broadway?" Owen smiled, his dimples deepening. "I'm very well, thanks! And you, Miss McNeil?" She giggled and gave him a playful nudge.

"I'm slightly intoxicated, thank you! A group of my *Times* colleagues are helping me celebrate my birthday!" "Well, happy birthday! May I buy you a drink?" "I'd love it if you bought me a drink. It's not every day a girl gets an offer like that," she purred. "You flatter me, Miss McNeil. I bet plenty of guys offer to buy you drinks," he nudged.

"I'll have a gin martini, straight up with a twist." Owen signaled Andy, his favorite barman, who was working the late shift. "Hey Andy, may we have a gin martini, straight up with a twist? I'll have my usual scotch, neat." "Sure thing, Owen," said Andy, giving a wink. Owen's friend was attractive and slightly high, an easy mark for some naughty play.

"How's the show? I imagine it was good for your dancers to have a night off," she said, making small talk. "It was. They've been working pretty hard for the last 14 weeks. I'm not easy to work for," he confessed. Andy arrived with their drinks. Owen took his and handed hers. Lifting his glass, he smiled. "To more chance meetings," he murmured, clinking. She joined him and took a big swallow. Owen detected a lovely scent.

"Let's get back to why you're not easy to work for," she said with curiosity. "Because, Miss McNeil, I'm a real bastard, hard as nails!" Stephanie couldn't resist the reference. "I'll bet you get hard in other ways, too," she whispered.

"Wow, Miss McNeil. What's this, a come-on?" She winked and continued her drink. Owen's pants fought the urge. He could imagine taking that hair down, stripping off her clothes and fucking her within an inch of her life. He changed gears quickly.

"How's your drink?" He was losing the fight, his need for serious flesh growing, his pants having more trouble with each glance at Stephanie. When they first met, she appeared too business-like, snippy, over confident. He had little interest in the unattainable vibes she was handing out. But tonight, he was more than interested. He wanted to tear down that veneer of self-righteous professionalism and fuck her into submission. He'd have to move fast before she was too wasted to feel what he was capable of.

She put down her empty glass. "Boy, I think I'm a bit tipsy." "Anything I can do?" "How sweet, Mr. Matthews. You could see me home. I think I'm too drunk to go alone." Owen signaled Andy and paid the tab. "Where is your coat, Miss McNeil?" She giggled and pointed to a group across the room. "It's the green cloth one on the end." Owen walked over to fetch it. One young man noticed and looked around for Stephanie. "It's okay, pal. I'll see her home, I'm a friend," said Owen. The fellow nodded and returned to his drink. Owen slipped on Stephanie's coat and closed his. Together they walked to the door.

Stepping out into the cold, Owen put his arm around Stephanie, as he waved a cab over. Helping her in, he sat next to her. "Where am I taking you, Miss McNeil?" She giggled and leaned toward the driver. "Take us to 350 East 79th Street, please." Owen sat back, glancing at Stephanie, whose coat was open, skirt high on her thighs. They were shapely, compelling, the nearest route to his favorite place. 'Time to get laid,' he thought.

Chapter 45

Better Times

Alan Byrne was improving. His family history of heart issues had not escaped him. The week following his episode was touch and go. Although weakened by trauma to his body, by the second week, he was feeling better, able to talk and eat more but still bed-ridden, much to his displeasure. Oxygen was no longer needed during the day, but he still had to wear the mask at night as a precaution.

Just before the attack Alan had been looking over the Blarney's event bookings noting up-coming parties. His specialty was planning birthdays for special patrons and his immediate family. The Irish were a clannish lot and he took pride in being the self-appointed leader in the neighborhood.

Thomas O'Brian, Alan's long-time friend, with ties to the old sod, would turn 65 next month. His party had to be grand, he was retiring from 23 years working the docks and being the local union agent. The event would be a big one, the Blarney closed to outsiders. After three weeks he was feeling much better and allowed to walk the halls with aid. It was time to get back to business, O'Brian's party was close. He was forced to delegate his plans to others, much to his chagrin. 'Thank God for my boys, they will fill the gap,' he thought, relieved.

Pat visited her dad daily, helped at the Blarney and kept her mother distracted. She spoke with Griff every few days, keeping him updated and sending love to Mally, Jonas and Phillipe.

Owen was another matter. Though she tried several times a day, he was impossible to reach; the best she could do was leave messages with his secretary, Gina. She missed him terribly, always wondering where he was. Mally noted worry in Pat's voice whenever Owen came into their conversation. Mally's usual tactic of reassurance was to no avail. After two weeks, Pat was eager to return to work. The boys had the bar well in hand, dividing the chores in addition to their regular jobs. Ma kept close watch over Dad, his health continuing to improve.

Alan was grateful to be alive. He'd always been a humble man; hard-working, in love with his family. The thought of suddenly leaving them shocked him, as he reflected over the past weeks. He was determined to be a good patient, follow his doctor's instructions and get back to work.

Pat discussed her departure with Maureen and the boys. They were unanimous, she should return to work and enjoy her first Broadway experience. She dialed Griff at home, a familiar voice answered. "Griff Edwards." "Griff, it's Pat. Can I come back next Monday?" "Pat, it's good to hear from you. How's your dad doing?" "Dad is doing amazingly well. Ma is happily playing head nurse, the boys have the Blarney under control and they've decided to throw me out," she said chuckling.

"That's great news; I'm sure next Monday will work. We'll be looking forward to your return. Everyone misses you," he said with enthusiasm. Pat paused for a moment. "How is Owen?"

"He hasn't been around. When all is well, the boss usually doesn't stop in." "I see. Well, I haven't been able to reach him. I hope he's okay." "Oh, I'm sure he's fine. I'll leave him a message you're returning Monday." "Thanks, Griff. Hug that lady of yours for me!" "I will do that, Pat. Best wishes to your family and thanks for the call."

She put down the phone and stood thinking. 'What is going on? I have to find out!' In the background, she heard Mickey and Sean chatting; Patrick was out shoveling the walk. There had been an unusual amount of snow since Christmas. She put on her coat, hat, and scarf, opened the door and caught Patrick's eye. Putting down the shovel, he looked at her quizzically. "Where are you headed, Sis?" "I need to go into the city. I'm going back in the show next Monday and need some stage make-up." Patrick shrugged and continued shoveling. "It's kind of late, you know. Ma doesn't like you on trains at night. Why don't you go in early before you have to report Monday and take care of it then?" The suggestion made sense, Patrick was right. She'd wait. Monday was only three days away.

Owen was a busy man, busy with Stephanie McNeil. After all, she was filling the gap during Pat's absence. That night at the Taft had cinched it. While Pat was tending to family, Owen was tending to business, flesh business. He'd repeatedly tried to quell his rampant libido. He lost the fight.

It had been a hell of a night following that cab ride. Stephanie was more than ready for a roll. After all, it was her birthday! Her wild attraction to Owen, alcoholic consumption and his offer to take her home broke all barriers or resistance she'd had. No more playing hard-to-get. She wanted him, pure and simple. Who was she to resist the celebrated director? When they arrived at her building, she insisted he come up. How could she not?

Opening her door, she wobbled in and flipped on the lights. Owen, close behind, followed her lead. Slipping out of her coat, she kicked off her pumps and Owen went to work. He had already removed his coat and scarf. Taking her wrists, he pulled her close. He located hairpins tidily holding her upsweep. As the pins came loose, her hair cascaded to her shoulders. It was thick, wavy and fragrant. He kissed her hard, his tongue penetrating to the back of her throat. Stephanie kissed back, her tongue joining his. As they continued, he reached around, sliding the zipper down. Touching her back, the rest was easy. One quick move, the dress was off.

She had more curves than his usual, not typical of a dancer. Her rounded hips and soft belly were enticing as were her breasts, full and perky. Nipples peeked through her bra. He liked her see-through lace panties, her mound thick with curly hair. He did little to resist as she reached for his fly. She seemed less experienced than others he had messed with.

Stephanie tugged the zipper finally sliding it down. Gasping at the size of his erection, she gingerly pulled it out. He sighed at her touch. Guiding her, he encouraged her discovery.

"Sweetie, that's right! Come on," he urged. Taking his direction, she kneeled to take him. His eyes closed, sighs punctuating her action, he writhed with pleasure. He stopped her. "Where's the bed?" His voice was coarse as he pulled her up. Taking his hand, she led him to the bedroom, stopping for a moment. "I need to use the bathroom. Make yourself at home."

Owen slipped out of his clothes and stood at the foot of the bed in hardened glory, his eyes on the bathroom. The door opened, she was nude. He could see she was ready and wasted no time. Pulling her wrists to her sides, he pushed her down on the coverlet. Stephanie moaned then flinched, as his hands tightened, she was to be his. Then, what she craved most, his warm breath between her legs! He was masterful, inventive, not at all like the dullards she dated. Squirming at first, she began to relax. Owen's tongue probed, owning her. Moaning, she felt an orgasm building and, suddenly, eruption, vivid, intense beyond compare, the first time ever by tongue. Screaming for more, he held close as her tremors calmed, surprising her with a wet kiss. Another first!

Releasing her wrists, he climbed aboard for round two, his hardened shaft ready to plunge. Entering, he felt her warmth surround him pulling him deeper. Savoring the moment, they began to pulse in unison, she raising her hips to match his thrusts. Her legs wrapped around as the rhythm of their moves continued to blend. 'Sex was never like this before,' she thought. Owen was magic! Slowing for a few moments, sensations lingering, another round of pulsing motion, faster and faster and then, wild release encompassing both. Even Owen was impressed!

They were silent for a few minutes. When their breathing calmed, he slipped out and rolled to the side. Locating his jeans on the floor, he found his cigarettes and drew one out. Lighting the much-needed smoke, he sat down and gazed at Stephanie, still prone, caught up in a post-coital fog. Her moist skin was beguiling, the look on her face, satisfying.

"No one ever fucked me like that," she whispered. "You sure know what you're doing, Mr. Director." She sat up and reached for the cigarette, inhaling deeply. "Your reputation holds true." Owen glanced over and took the cigarette back. "My reputation?" Stephanie grinned. "They say when a woman is done by Owen Matthews, she stays done," she giggled.

"Oh? Why don't you come here and explain that a little more," he said slyly. Stephanie slipped over to his lap and playfully fondled his mustache. "It means you'll need to fuck me a lot," she said confidently. "Oh yeah, that's true. You've got what it takes, Miss McNeil," he said, playing with her nipples. She sighed. "Want a second go?" He stopped. "Hey, I'd love to, but I have an early meeting today."

"Want to stop by later? I have to work at the *Times* until 7:00, unless they throw a deadline at me," she added. "That sounds great, Miss McNeil. Give me a call when you're home." He rose and dressed as Stephanie watched. There Owen stood like a confident Peacock, grinning at her. They kissed again; hard-to-get was over. Miss McNeil and Mr. Matthews had formed a club for two only!

The conference room at the Kaplan-Maggli office was set up for 10:00. Joe, Lenny, and assistants, Bebe and Gary arrived. Bebe served coffee. A box of donuts was on the side table. Griff and Dick were next followed by Owen, who had a noticeable lightness in his stride. Jonas hurried in last, having had difficulty getting a cab. When all were seated, Joe began.

"Gentleman, thanks for coming. We wanted to give you an update on *Centipede*. The weekly grosses are outrageous. Never before in our history has one show taken the town like this one. And this is just the beginning. We're already sold out for three months with potential of a half year. The only available seats are house seats and, as you know, we keep those for VIPs only.

"This is great news," said Owen. I knew we'd cause a stir, but I didn't know how much!" Joe continued, "There's more! A Japanese producer, Mr. Hiro Watanabe approached me at Sardi's opening night. He wants to discuss a possible engagement of *Centipede* for the fall of '65 at the Nissei Gekijo, in Tokyo, Japan's newest performing arts center. According to him, American musical theatre artists are revered. An opportunity like this could fill our coffers and guarantee international attention. I'll update you as this develops.

Griff stopped taking notes. "Gentlemen, I have good news. Patricia Byrne will be rejoining us next week. Her father is doing well and the family has encouraged her return. Apparently they have all family matters covered." Owen had just taken a sip of coffee; news of Pat's return went down wrong, gagging him. All eyes turned as Joe asked, "Matthews, you okay?' A second sip cleared his throat and he reached for another cigarette. The first drag a welcome ally.

Lenny chimed in, "We should show support for the family. Mr. Hanson, please call our florist midtown and order one their finest arrangements to be sent to the Byrnes. Their address is on file." Joe agreed, adding, "Write a note wishing Mr. Byrne a continued recovery." Owen was only half listening.

'God, Pat will be back on Monday and I've been a bad boy,' he thought. He felt slightly off as his mind turned over. 'I'm dead meat if she finds out.' The meeting ended at noon.

It was Friday night, and Owen was in the kitchen looking for a snack, but the cupboards were lean and peanut butter wouldn't do. Taking a drag off his smoke, the phone rang. 'Ah, maybe it's Miss McNeil." He picked up. "It's me, I just finished up. Care to meet in midtown for a bite? There are a couple of nice places near Rockefeller Center. We could meet at the info desk, Time-Life, say about 7:30?" Owen let out a long breath. "Great, see you then."

It was already 7:00. The shower would wait, they'd do it later. Picking up his smokes, lighter, money clip, and keys, he was off. Ralph, at the door, always ready, "Can I get you a cab, Mr. Matthews?" "Thanks, Ralph, appreciate it," he said, handing a tip. A yellow pulled up, Owen got in. "Time-Life, 50th and 6th, please," as the meter flag dropped.

Stephanie was impatient. Pacing back and forth she glanced at pedestrians of all description as they bustled by. It was Friday night and rush hour was far from over. Owen pushed through the lobby crowd, looking. Spotting her, he approached. "Good evening Miss McNeil." "You're late, Mr. Director. Come on, I'm really hungry." "Where to?"

"Not far, it's a cute little bistro. Ever eaten at Petit Saint Germain?" "Not that I recall. I'll take your word for it." He leaned down and whispered, "Ever been told you're sexy?" "Why Mr. Matthews, I'll cream my panties!" "That's the idea, Miss McNeil. That's the idea."

Arriving, they stepped to a lower level café. It was cozy, a one-room affair with a quaint bar up front. Eight tables were set, linens, candles and flowers on each. "Good evening, Mademoiselle et Monsieur. Welcome to Petit Saint Germain. I'm Roland, come with me." They followed and were seated at a corner table with a view of the charming room. It was quiet and intimate, with few customers.

"Let me order, Owen. What kind of wine would you prefer?" "Any wine I can pour over your gorgeous parts and suck dry." She blushed. "I don't think they allow that here," she giggled. "No, seriously, what would you like to drink?" "Let's get the house white," he suggested. "Okay with me," she said, waving to Roland. "Yes, what can I do for you?" "Roland, we'd like a carafe of your house white, *s'il vous plait.*" "Certainly, Mademoiselle, here are our specials for today," offering a one-sheet menu.

"I can't wait to fuck your brains out," whispered Owen. Stephanie smiled. "So you like me, yes?" "Hell yes," he murmured, his hand moving up her thigh. Stephanie sighed, his fingers playfully brushing her mound. "Do you like this?" "Yes," she whispered. "You're moist, Miss McNeil," he said, taking pleasure in her arousal. He stopped, noticing Roland with the wine.

Have you decided?" "I see your special is fois gras appetizer and grilled Sole Almandine. May we each have an order?" Roland smiled, "Very good." Owen added, "Do you have oysters tonight?" "Mais Oui, Monsieur." "I'll take a dozen." "Excellent, Monsieur!"

They drank with pleasure, the wine settling them. Owen studied Stephanie; her country girl looks and beguiling curiosity. She was malleable, loose, willing to submit to his dominance. Yes, Miss McNeil was a real turn-on.

Dinner arrived and they ate with pleasure. The wine enhanced the flavor of the sole, each mouthful a tantalizing morsel, a mixture of flavors and textures. When they finished, Owen asked for the check. "No no, my treat tonight. Do you want a demitasse? French coffee is strong but delightful," she enthused. Owen motioned to the door. "Let's get on with the business at hand." She paid the check; they slipped on their coats and left. "Excuse us," a couple said as they passed.

Owen signaled a nearby cab, they got in. Stephanie was eager. "Your place or mine?" "Let's go to yours, Miss O'Neill. My cleaning lady is coming in the morning." The truth was he didn't want her on his turf. It was risky. As they sped off, Owen hadn't noticed two men turn and stare.

"Hey, that was Owen Matthews," said Gary Hanson to his partner, Steve. "I'm certain of it, but I didn't recognize his squeeze. Gosh, I wonder if he and Pat broke up." Steve was curious. "Were they heavily involved?" "Well, they were hot and heavy last year, at least while I was in the company, added Gary." "Looks like he moves fast," observed Steve. Gary sighed, "You have no idea!" The two continued walking arm and arm.

Chapter 46

Reunion of Sorts

Pat counted the days until she was back at the Royal. Trying and failing, she hadn't reached Owen. Hopefully, he would be there Monday. It was an unsettled feeling, as though something had shifted. What was it that troubled her? Something was off. She called Jonas. A cheery, upbeat voice picked up. "Hello, Jonas here." "Jonas, this is Pat. I'm coming back tomorrow night!" "I heard, Irish, can't wait!" There was a pause. "How did you hear?" "We had a production meeting yesterday at Kaplan-Maggli. Griff told us. We're all relieved to hear your dad's improving."

There was a long pause. "Are you all right, honey?" "I'm fine. Was Owen at the meeting?" "Of course he was and in great spirits, too! Irish, we're sold out for the next three months. The money is rolling in! There's talk of an international engagement. Joe and Lenny couldn't be happier." "That's wonderful! Say, do you need me in early to run anything? It's been almost three weeks."

"It's up to you. Do you need it? I figured the show was wired in your bones after all this time." Pat giggled. "You think so? Jeez, I don't know, four months of doing the same choreography!" Jonas laughed. "Why don't you come in a little early and just do a long warm-up, okay?" "Okay." "See you tomorrow at half hour. Come lay your lips on mine, okay?"

Monday arrived soon enough. Pat decided to go to the city early; to shop, grab lunch and stop by Mally and Griff's before heading to the Royal. Kissing her dad goodbye, she cautioned him to be careful. He promised he would. She hugged her mom and brothers. How she loved them! She took the noon express, got off at 42nd Street and, up the stairs. At a nearby Rexall she picked up Max Factor #2 pan stick, a double set of eyelashes and lipstick. Lunch at Howard Johnson's was an excellent idea, their clam rolls were tops.

Times Square was bustling as she made her way to the H-J at Broadway and 46th. The place was packed. Sitting at the counter she fished for her wallet in her dance bag and found enough cash for a clam roll, fries and shake. As the noon rush continued, a familiar person walked by. "My God, Gary Hanson!" "Pat! Pat Byrne! It's great to see you!" They hugged. "Sit here, next to me." Gary shrugged off his jacket and scarf, hanging them on the back of his seat. "How is it you're here? This is such a sweet coincidence!" Gary smiled.

"Well, Kaplan-Maggli is just down the block and I was starved! Lenny was magnanimous today and said to take my time. We lackeys usually order in!" "I forgot the office is nearby. It's been a while since I was in there." "Joe and Lenny are floating on cloud 9 these days. We have a big hit show on our hands!"

"So I've heard," said Pat, changing the subject. "Did you know my dad had taken ill?" "Yes, we heard. How is he now?" A busy young waiter approached. "What are you folks having today?" He was pleasant in spite of the rush, his pad and pen poised.

"I'll have the clam roll special with fries and a small Vanilla shake," said Pat. "And you sir?"

"Make mine the Howard Double Cheeseburger with fried onions and a large order of fries. I'd like a large Coke, no ice," he added. "Be right up." Gary gave him the once-over as he hurried away. Pat caught the stare and gave him a nudge.

"My, do you fancy him, Mr. Hanson?" "I've finally gotten into cruising. Must be arrested development," he giggled. Pat decided to back-track the conversation where Gary had left off. "My dad has improved so well, the doctors are surprised. However, he still requires complete bed rest for another three weeks. It's driving him bonkers and everyone else, too." Pat changed the subject, moving on to the show.

"So how is life treating you, Gary?" "I love my job, *Centipede* especially, has been a revelation. I never realized how much work was involved away from the stage." "This is Owen's best work by far," said Pat. "Yes, he's topped himself. House seats are in hot demand."

"How do you like working for Leonard Maggli? Do you ever miss dancing?" "The accident in Atlanta was a life changing. At first it hurt, but now my life is settled. I have a fabulous partner in Steve. I believe you met him at Jonas' Christmas soiree. He's the best thing that's happened to me." "I'm so happy for you."

The waiter returned with their orders. Placing plates down, he slapped down their checks. "Can I get you anything else?" "Ketchup and mustard," said Gary. "And more water please," said Pat. As they ate, Gary glanced at Pat. "May I ask you a personal question?" "Sure. What is it?" "Well, I haven't seen you since Christmas and Owen didn't come to the party, so I wondered if you two have split?"

The question caught her by surprise. She coughed, as a swallow went down wrong. Reaching water, she took a large sip. "Pat, are you all right?" Pat frowned. "Why would you think that?" "I don't know. It's just that I haven't seen you for a while, or Owen at the party. I thought maybe you had broken up."

"Well, you thought wrong, Gary. We're just fine," she said, her voice tinged with hurt. "I meant no offense, Pat. It was just a question," said Gary, suddenly uncomfortable. "And I just gave you an answer. Drop it!" They continued lunch in silence. When they had finished, Gary took his check. "Good seeing you, Pat. Break a leg tonight!" He gave her a furtive hug, picked up his things and left. Pat sat for a moment processing Gary's question. 'Where would he get an idea like that?'

Lunch finished, she paid the cashier and was on her way. Feeling a slight chill, she wound her muffler around her neck and closed her coat. Now, feeling more uneasy, she looked for a pay phone. 'I need to talk to Owen.' A booth on the corner would do. Dime in hand, she dialed. An operator said, "Deposit ten cents, please." It rang and rang. At the fifth ring, she was about to hang up when she heard the voice she wanted. "Matthews."

"Owen, it's me. I'm back!" There was silence. "Baby, I'll be damned. Where are you? God, it's good to hear your voice!" "Oh Owen, I've missed you so much. I have been calling and calling. Where have you been?" Navigating carefully, he paused. "I've been tied up in meetings, Baby." "Will you be stopping by tonight?" There was longing in her voice, Owen could tell. "Of course, Baby. I wouldn't miss your home-coming. I'll see you then. Bye for now!"

He hung up, leaving Pat with a dial tone in her ear. Outside, traffic was moving rapidly, horns blaring, voices in every octave, the constant bustle of people passing by on New York's most famous thoroughfare, Broadway.

Chapter 47

Back at the Game

It was an hour before half hour. Pat checked in and made her way to Griff's office. She found him going over paperwork, his back to the door. She knocked. "May I come in?" Griff turned and smiled when he saw her. His glasses perched precariously on his nose, giving him a professorial look. "Welcome back, Pat! It's good to see you."

"Thanks, Griff. It's great to be back. I came early to do a long warm-up." "Good idea. Feel free to work on stage. I'll bring the work lights up for you." "Thanks, Griff. No wonder Mally's crazy in love with you." With a pat on his arm, she was off. While changing, she con-templated her future. Working with Owen had paved the way to her current status. He must have seen something special in her to give her the lead. About their personal life, she wasn't as sure, but being back on stage felt right.

Beginning a warm-up with slow stretches, her muscles were rigid, her body sore. Each move brought a groan. 'Ugh, too much time off,' she thought. Relentlessly, she pushed herself until; at last, she was mov-ing effortlessly. Muscle memory came back as she executed turns and glided across the stage. At moments, she was floating. At others, earthbound, it was magically there. Each move was pure Owen. 'Damn, this feels incredible,' she thought executing several turns in a row. As she finished one routine, she worked another. There were no mistakes, not one misstep to show she'd been out. Sudden hand-clapping got her attention. Pat stopped abruptly and gazed into the dark house. A lone figured walked down the aisle straight toward her. Owen! In moments, he was on the stage holding her. "Baby, you are exquisite," he soothed, running his hands through her hair. Before she could respond, his lips met hers. His heat overpowering, Pat gave in to the moment, forgetting his neglect. They were together now.

"Oh Owen, I've missed you," she murmured. His hands explored, leaving her breathless. "Come back to my place tonight." "Yes, I will." "Will you be watching the show?" "I can't tonight, Baby," he said, kissing her fingers. "I've agreed to have a drink with a potential backer. I'll see you after the show. Grab a cab and come up." He disappeared, walking into the backstage shadows. Pat felt a wave of relief as she finished her stretches. 'He has missed me and does care,' she thought, a smile growing.

The night began with: "Company, please report to the green room at 7:50. Thank you." The dressing rooms were a bustle with activity, as the cast began the fourth week.

The girls welcomed Pat, each giving a hug, expressing concern for her dad. Nora walked over.

"Pat, it's good to have you back. We've all missed you." she said. 'Maybe Nora's not so bad after all. She's a terrific swing and a very hard worker,' she reasoned. Mally was happy to return to her spot. As much as she loved dancing the lead, she was more comfortable partnered by Chad. They had been friends since *Bravo Business,* buddies from the beginning of tour rehearsals.

At 7:50, the troupe gathered in the green room. "Pat's back tonight, so let's give her a hearty welcome," Griff said graciously. The gypsies exploded in unison, some whistling, others clapping. "Keep in mind that Mally will do her regular spot, Nora will sit out. The rest of you make adjustments as needed. Thank you and break a leg!" Sandy began the overture, another week of *Centipede* now off and running.

Later, Pat hurried through her post show routine, Mally noticing her haste to leave. "Are you staying at Owen's tonight?" She nodded, brushed her mane and pulled it back to a pony tail. A bit of lip color and she would be out the stage door. On the way to 8th Avenue she got lucky, an empty cab was midblock; she knocked on the window, the driver waved her in. "Driver, 67th between the Park and Columbus, please." The cab headed north.

Back at the theatre, Jonas and Phillipe prepared to leave. "Hon, do you feel like a drink?" Yes Cheri, how about Barrymore's?" "Sounds good," said Jonas, winding his muffler. They stepped into a chilly mist hand in hand, crossing the street.

Barrymore's was busy, the after-theatre crowd having taken most of the tables. They decided to sit at the bar. Jonas ordered a tap beer and Phillipe a cognac. Waiting for their drinks and chatting quietly, Jonas spotted Gary and Steve entering and waved them over.

"Hey guys, good to see you. Out slumming tonight?" Gary chuckled. "Hey, I'm the producer's assistant, not the producer," he said with a wide grin. "Join us, friends," said Phillipe. "Sure." Gary took a moment to order. "Bourbon on the rocks and a Manhattan for my friend." "You bet. Say, there's a table clearing in the back, take a seat, I'll bring your drinks."

Drinks arrived. "Let's toast the future," said Gary, raising his glass. The boys raised their glasses, chanting, "To the smash hit, *Centipede*!" "So what's new, Gary? How do you like having Maggli's ear?" "It has its advantages. My body isn't sore, no more lines and questions at the unemployment office and a nice expense account." "Sounds terrific, but do you ever miss dancing?" "Not in the least. I love working 9:00 to 5:00 and, this guy," giving Steve a squeeze. "You guys still going strong?" "Stronger than ever," said Jonas, looking at Phillipe. We'd be married if the law allowed it, but you know how that is." "Well, maybe someday, huh?" They ordered another round.

Gary changed the subject. "How did you make out without the fabulous Miss Byrne?" Phillipe was quick to respond. "Mally went on for Pat and she did an amazing job. I doubt the audience knew the difference." "I noticed the difference, my friends," added Jonas. Mally is terrific, but Pat has an edge. I've never known another who can top her!" Gary smiled. "You're not turning straight are you, Jonas?" Jonas grimaced playfully.

"Gary my friend, she's got charisma to burn and she's gorgeous. No wonder Owen has stuck around!" Gary put down his drink, turning serious. "While we're on the subject, are they still together? I mean are they still hot and heavy?" Jonas looked shocked. "Of course, they're madly in love." "Well, if they're madly in love, somebody goofed," said Gary, with a knowing air. "Do you know something?" "Please keep this quiet, but I have reason to believe otherwise."

"Come on Gary. What do you know that I don't?" Gary's eyes met Steve's.

"The other night, we saw Owen come out of a little French bistro with a woman on his arm, a very attractive woman I might add. They were kissing and fondling before they grabbed a cab and took off. At first, I thought I was mistaken, but when I took another look, it was unmistakably him. He looked pretty smitten, right, Steve?" "From my view, they looked like two people about to have sex!" Jonas grew pale.

"This is absurd, Gary. Are you sure?" "I thought I might have been mistaken, until I ran into Pat at lunch today. I asked her if she and Owen had split and I practically got my head handed back to me. I thought I was diplomatic, not mentioning that I saw him. I'm certain she's unaware. At least it seems that way." "I can't believe it! This is the worst," Jonas said, growing agitated.

Phillipe tried to calm him. "Cheri, we need to be sure about this. We don't know the circumstances. For now it's best to drop it," he said calmly. Gary spoke up, regret in his voice.

"I'm sorry if I opened a can of worms, but I know what I saw. Right, Steve?" "Gary's right. Those two were absolutely all over each other," said Steve. "Let's hope Owen comes to his senses. Pat's delicate and this would destroy her," said Jonas, deeply concerned. They all agreed to keep quiet. Finishing the second round, they paid their checks and said their good-nights.

Up on 67th Street, the mood was hot and heavy as Owen and Pat indulged in a night of randy sex. Her hunger was intense, insatiable and he was only too happy to cooperate.

Chapter 48

Wedding Plans

With *Centipede* well underway, Mally and Griff proceeded with wedding plans. Valentine's Day Sunday, February 14th, seemed perfect! They began to work out details, eager to be married at last.

It would be a simple wedding. Guests would include cronies from *Bravo Business* and *Centipede* casts; Kaplan and Maggli; Mally's folks and of course, Owen Matthews. Griff had no family to speak of. Both his parents had passed away years before. Dick would serve as best man and Pat, Mally's maid of honor. Jonas and Phillipe would usher. Sardi's was their first choice for the ceremony and reception. Griff phoned Vincent Sardi to make arrangements.

The upstairs room had ample space for the ceremony, with an adjacent area ideal for the reception. Griff asked an old friend, Dr. Andrew Mason, to preside. They decided to exchange traditional vows. Dana was asked to sing "One Hand, One Heart," Mally's all-time favorite from *West Side Story*. Sandy offered to play the ceremony. Enthusiastic about participating, he put a trio together for the reception.

Mally and Pat went dress shopping at Best and Company on 51st and 5th Avenue. Since it was a winter wedding, she looked for a heavier satin fabric in ecru, tea-length. She selected one with a small train, high fitted neck and long sleeves of Chantilly lace. French heel shoes would match the dress. On her head, a pill box cap with a small veil would be just right with her hair set in a French twist.

Trying the dress on for Pat, it was a perfect fit. "Oh Mal, you're so beautiful! I can't believe the wedding's almost here." Together they hugged and cried. Mally took the dress off and slipped back into her street clothes. Carrying her choice to the clerk, she paid cash out of her wedding stash she'd saved. The clerk carefully wrapped the dress and put it into a box, including hat and veil. "While we're here, maybe you could find your dress."

Pat looked through the department. She wanted to look beautiful for Owen. Spotting a forest green silk suit with a bolero-style jacket, ideal! She tried it on, the color and style smashing on her. Satisfied with their choices, the girls set out for lunch at Schrafft's.

With the coming wedding, the gypsies took action. Kathy and Sonja planned Mally's bridal shower and invited the women's ensemble including Dana. It would be Sunday, the 7th, the weekend before the wedding.

The guys planned a surprise bachelor party for Griff that same Sunday. They chose the Hotel Astor Bar, a show-biz-friendly establishment. Jonas talked to the manager and arranged a side room for the group. The boys pooled a few bucks for a stripper. Joe suggested a friend, a show girl at the Copa, who also worked private parties. The fun would begin around 8:00. Dick would to invite Griff for a drink and the boys spring the surprise.

Pat and Owen were together matinee days between shows and Saturday nights. On Sundays she'd return home to the family. Alan had greatly improved and now able to work part-time. Whenever he appeared tired, Maureen would insist he rest. Pat spent extra time with her dad; they loved to play cards, especially poker, but just for pennies. Alan delighted in his youngest beating him and having to cough up coins from a Mason jar stash.

Owen continued to see Stephanie. She was coltish, intense and sexual, qualities which reminded him of a young Vera Daniels. In spite of loving Pat, for Owen, sex was oxygen. He simply had to have it and, frequently. He called the shots, she cooperated. His kind of gal!

As the weeks passed, Jeff and Nora had moved to a new level. After the show opened, they moved in together. Jeff had proven a friend during a trying time. Nora was grateful for his kindness. Other men might have considered her damaged goods, but not Jeff. He was her protector, confidant and now, boyfriend. They looked forward to a long, healthy run, personally and professionally.

Joe and Jordan were together continually. It was ironic for Joe to be exclusive with anyone. However, with Jordan, he had found sexual satisfaction and continued interest. They would meet at the Warwick Hotel, Jordan's business base during the week, or at Joe's flat in the Village on weekends.

Tim Bartel remained a loner, not allowing his personal business to be known by anyone connected with *Centipede,* particularly Griff and Jonas. There were plenty women around to satisfy. He was in a mega hit show, at the top of his game and one of the best dancers in New York. He would bide his time, collect his pay and give notice when a better opportunity came along.

Dana and Dick had settled nicely into parenthood. Baby Michael Richard was a strapping, healthy infant, who brought them unimaginable joy. They christened him following *Centipede's* triumphant opening. Dana's family flew in from Atlanta, as well as Dick's mother from Philadelphia. Dick's brother and sister-in-law traveled from their home in Syracuse. It was a delightful family affair; baby Michael the center of their world.

Vera had stayed under wraps since the Sardi's incident, badly shaken by Jackie Eldridge's verbal ambush. Jackie's vitriol opened old wounds, shaking her to the core. Joe tried to sooth her with a week-long vacation in Bermuda. There was nothing he wouldn't do for his lady. Their villa overlooked the ocean and included a private pool; maid and room service 24 hours a day and a complete salon nearby. Vera took full advantage; Joe was mad for her and saw to all her needs and desires.

She was set as she wanted to be, yet unable to let go of her feelings for Owen. Hiding the truth maintained Kaplan's adoration and perks. In exchange, she offered her body, continuing the charade. The deception was working, but she was drinking more and, as needed, she added pharmaceutical support. Vera Daniels was starting to slip into the background and dangerously close to self-destruction. It was only a matter of time.

Chapter 49

Pre-Nuptial Festivities

Today was Mally's bridal shower. Kathy and Sonja had cleaned and decorated their apartment, shopped for food and a bridal gift. The festivities would begin at 1:00. The wedding theme atmosphere was done in various shades of pink, Mally's favorite color, with white accents here and there. Everything matched, crepe paper flounces, balloons and table accessories. Kathy was excited to use her good china and cutlery, given by her mother years before. It was the perfect addition to a special occasion!

Kathy took a survey amongst the women and it was unanimous. They would buy gifts creating a lingerie trousseau. How perfect! Griff had been a bachelor for many years and adding household items to his established set-up was redundant and hardly romantic! Mally wearing sexy underwear, lovely lounging clothes and other intimate items was a perfect way to include him.

At 1:00 sharp, the doorbell sounded. "Honey, the guests are arriving," chirped Kathy, caught up in the spirit of the moment. Sonja pushed the button unlatching the door. In moments, Pat and Mally walked in. Hugs were the first order of business as Sonja took their coats. "Oh Mal, you're glowing!" exclaimed Kathy. "Come on in. Make yourselves comfortable!"

Pat carried a beautifully wrapped package. "Where should I put this, Kath?" "Set it over on the coffee table. There's plenty of room!" The bell rang again. After buzzing in the next arrival, Kathy offered beverages. "We have coffee, tea and punch made with ginger ale and strawberry sorbet!" There was a knock at the partially open door. Dana stood with baby Michael in her arms.

"Oh my God, it's Dana and the baby!" The girls rushed over to greet her and to fuss over Michael. Pat took Dana's gift and put it with the others. "Oh, he's beautiful! He looks just like Dick," remarked Kathy. "I disagree. I think he looks like Dana," countered Sonja. "He's a definite cross between you two," suggested Mally. "Well, he's definitely not the milkman's," joked Pat.

"I fed him an hour ago, so he'll probably sleep for a while," said Dana. May I put him in the bedroom for now?" "Of course! There's plenty of room on the bed. Please, make him comfortable!" Dana handed her coat to Kathy and disappeared down the hall. "Dana looks sensational. Motherhood agrees with her and her figure is still fabulous," noted Sonja.

The girls settled in the living room to chat. Sonja disappeared in the kitchen and continued food preparation. Kathy answered the door on the next ring. In moments, Cynthia, Fran, and Liz appeared. Greetings were exchanged, as the girls hung coats. As they brought gifts into the room, Kathy offered drinks and went to check on Sonja. The bell sounded again. "Business is definitely picking up," tossed Pat.

Dana returned and was immediately introduced to the group. From the kitchen, Kathy heard the bell once more. She pressed the button again allowing the downstairs door to open. Looking down a flight, she spotted Marcy and Nora climbing the stairs. "Ah, we're all here now," said Kathy. Coats were taken, drinks offered and Marcy introduced Nora to Dana.

Enthusiasm was in high gear as the girls chatted, ate and shared their excitement over the coming wedding. Sonja had prepared her mother's tasty curry chicken salad on a bed of greens. Kathy's contribution was a variety of homemade breads, from Olson family recipes and a delightful relish tray. A mixed fruit bowl was appealing. Petit fours and Jordan Almonds added a touch of dessert.

"Okay, ladies, time for the goodies," announced Kathy, making her way to the gifts. Kneeling by the table, she handed each present to Pat, who sat next to Mally. Kathy continued. "Sonja honey, will you take care of the gift list? Who wants to make a ribbon bouquet?" Marcy eagerly raised her hand and was given a paper plate with a hole cut in the middle. "I made one of these for my sister's shower five years ago. She still has it," she enthused. "We all took a vote and decided on lingerie which, of course, includes Griff as recipient," Kathy said, with a chuckle.

There was wild applause when Mally was offered the first package. Reading the card, she began tearing. Opening the gift she gasped. Pat had found an exquisite nightgown in soft pink rayon, trimmed in lace with spaghetti straps. "It has a matching jacket in the same fabric," said Pat, lifting off an extra layer of tissue. "Oh Pat, it's beautiful," she sighed, hugging her. "It's for your wedding night at the Waldorf," whispered Pat.

"Oh, tell us about that," said Nora, eagerly. Pat threw her a look but softened, as she realized Nora was unaware of the *Bravo Business* cast gift. "We pooled our resources last summer and gave Mally and Griff a one-night stay at the Waldorf. Actually it was Jonas' idea." "Oh, how special," Nora remarked. "What a thoughtful gift!" Cynthia, Fran, and Liz agreed as it was news to them as well.

As each gift was opened, more applause. Bras and panties, baby doll pajamas with matching scuffs, a satin robe in hot pink and bikinis, a pair for each day of the week added to the fun. Kathy and Sonja selected bath products knowing how much Mally enjoyed long soaks. After checking with Pat, Marcy and Nora pooled their resources and bought Mally's favorite perfume, Replique, by Raphael.

As afternoon turned to evening, the girls departed. Dana bundled baby Michael for the trip home. He was content after his bottle. She was pleased about the fuss made over him. Mally and Pat offered to clean up, but Kathy and Sonja refused. They had the rest of the evening to put their flat back in order. Pat would help Mally get her gifts home. Kathy offered three shopping bags to make the trip easier.

"Kath and Sonja, this has been such a special day. I'll never be able to thank you enough," said Mally. "Griff's a lucky man," she said giving her a bear hug. Sonja found their coats and helped slip them on. It was a cold day and their outfits no match for the weather outside. The shower had been a success and just the beginning of new lives for two special people.

The men of *Centipede* were at the Astor Hotel Bar. The management had set aside an area for them to hide. Dick's invitation worked. The two strolled in a little before 8:00.

Griff ordered his favorite, a Tanqueray martini up with a twist. Dick ordered a Rob Roy. Settled at the bar, Dick raised his glass. "Griff, I wish you and Mally a wonderful life, like ours!" They touched glasses and each took generous sips. Dick checked his watch. "Let's go sit in a little quieter area. What do you think?" Griff was game as the two rose and walked to the other end of the bar. A few steps later, the men sprang.

"Surprise!" they all shouted. Griff, startled at first, caught on. "Oh my God, you guys! This is great!" The group included Jonas, Phillipe, Chad, Joe, Jim, Jeff, and Gary, who was happy to be included. Jerry Thompson was invited but would be a bit late. Tim hadn't bothered to attend. He had no interest in fraternizing. Owen was elsewhere, whereabouts unknown. Sandy declined, it was his 20th wedding anniversary and he was in Atlantic City.

"Drinks! We need more drinks!" shouted Jonas, motioning to a waiter. "It's an open bar on us, so drink away, Griff!" Phillipe and Chad led Griff to a large table and insisted he sit at the head. Pockets of conversation, more toasts, and fun spilled over the room. "Joe, grab the gifts, okay?"

"Who's got the cigars?" Jim located them on a table nearby. Jonas took the box and passed them out. Each took one, as a lighter was passed. Griff was given the first light. Taking a drag, he grimaced and coughed. The group broke into laughter. Joe placed a pile of gifts on the table.

"Griff, let's get started! Come on, you have to open this first," declared Chad. Griff loosened tissue around the first package and grinned. "Look, these should last one night," Joe said pointing. The men laughed uproariously as Griff pulled out several packages of Ramses Condoms. "Thanks, Joe. I imagine this was your idea," he said chuckling. Joe responded, "Who else?" Chad reached for the next gift, a handsome square box wrapped in plaid paper. "Read the card, Griff!" He opened the envelope and read the contents aloud,

'For Griff and Mally.
May all your years together be wrapped in love!
Congratulations,
Jonas and Phillipe.'

Griff removed the wrapping paper and lifted back the tissue. A beautiful cashmere blanket appeared in Griff's favorite color, royal blue. Lifting it out of the box, he smiled his voice catching. "This is beautiful!

Thank you so much, guys." "It's rumored you two spend a lot of time cuddling," cracked Jonas, creating another group cheer. More drinks were ordered. Gifts included a bottle of Moet, massage oil and a gift certificate for two at Mama Leone's Italian Restaurant. A waiter approached.

"Another round of drinks, please and also the hors d'oeuvres for the Martin party," said Jonas. As the gathering continued, an attractive woman entered the bar, dressed in a trench coat, fedora over one eye. Joe pointed her toward Griff, who was deep in conversation with Dick. Slowly, she sidled over to the guest of honor and tapped him on the shoulder. Griff turned.

There she was, all six feet of her, in stilettos. She put a small tape recorder on the table. Jim and Chad, taking the cue, led Griff to a chair front and center. A button was pushed, a raunchy blues number began; the stacked babe went into action. Moving toward Griff, she removed her fedora, her long hair flowing down. Whistles and shouts began. Stopping in front of him, she posed.

Slowly opening each button at the front of the coat, she taunted and teased as each closure was released, the last revealing the briefest of bikinis, one that barely hid her assets. Moving to the beat, her breasts beckoned as she shimmied and swayed. Moving closer, she rolled her pelvis, undulating suggestively.

Lifting a leg over one of his, she sat spread eagle on Griff's lap, the group cheered. Twining her fingers in his hair she feigned a licking motion toward his mouth. As the cheers got louder she grew more aggressive, her lap dance clearly sexual. Griff tried to be a sport, going along as best he could.

Slowly she rose from his lap and began to remove her bra. Gasps encouraged her. Reaching behind her back, she unsnapped, it fell. Bright, sparkling pasties popped into view as she moved closer to his face. Playfully wiggling her breasts at close range, Griff was clearly uncomfortable.

Stepping back, she turned, moving her hips back and forth while untying the bikini bottom. In a flash, she whipped it away, clothed in only a G-string. The group went wild, applauding as she turned again, leaving little to the imagination. Winding up her routine, she reached for Griff, kissed him on the lips, leaving him shaken. Bowing, she whispered, "What a handsome groom-to-be! Some lucky girl has all the luck!" The guys applauded enthusiastically, Griff chivalrously reached down and handed her the bra and bottoms. "Thanks," he said softly. Joe's stripper friend took her belongings, tape recorder and left.

"What's a bachelor party without a stripper?" The group agreed. "This calls for a smart toast, guys," shouted Jonas. They all raised their glasses at once as Jonas did the honors. "Griff, we can't think of another gentleman who has your class, your character and is the perfect man for our Mal! Best wishes for a fabulous marriage," he said, his voice turning emotional.

"Speech, Speech," Joe shouted. Griff stood, raising his glass and began, his voice faltering.

"Thank you all for this! Having your support means more to us than words can ever convey. I can't speak for Mally, but if she were here, she'd share my gratitude." Taking a sip, the men followed suit.

It was late as they dispersed. Jonas needed a restroom stop before heading home. Excusing himself, he walked from the bar to the men's room. Suddenly, he saw a familiar figure a few feet away, an attractive blonde keeping step. 'Holy shit, that's Owen,' he thought, ducking behind a potted palm. The two were walking arm in arm, totally engrossed in each other as they passed by. Jonas remained hidden and continued to watch. They stopped at the front desk, spoke with the concierge briefly and headed to the elevators.

From his view, Jonas stood frozen. 'How could this be? Who was the woman?' Many thoughts flooded his mind as he went into the men's room. Stepping to the nearest urinal, he unzipped and peed. He was feeling slightly tipsy, a bit difficult to remain upright. He felt as though someone had punched him in the stomach.

He couldn't put his mind around it. Finishing, he repaired himself and started toward the sink. As he looked up, he saw Gary, who had just come in. "Gary, could you come over here for a minute, please?" "Damn, I think you're right! Owen's messing around! I just saw him in the lobby with some blonde babe. He didn't show up for Griff's big event, but he has time to cheat on Pat!"

"I hate to say I told you so, but all evidence confirms it," said Gary, knowingly. Jonas sat down in the lounge and put his head in his hands. "I don't fucking believe this! How could he do this to Pat?" Just then, Phillipe walked in. "Cheri, what's wrong? Are you all right?"

"I just saw Owen in the lobby with a blonde I've never seen before. They were acting cozy, if you get my drift," he said softly. "Cheri, are you sure?" Gary jumped in. "This confirms what I tried to tell you earlier. I saw them together that night over by Rockefeller Center. I wasn't imagining it!"

"What are we going to do? If we tell Pat, she'll go cuckoo. You know how she feels about Owen, how insecure she is." "I think we should keep this to ourselves for the time being, Cheri." Gary agreed. "What she doesn't know won't hurt her."

"This is making me sick. Maybe you're right, though. Let it go for now, at least until after the wedding this coming weekend." They all agreed and returned to the bar. Jonas had sobered up fast. 'How will I keep this from Pat?' Sadly, a happy occasion was left with a taint.

Chapter 50

Soul Mates

Early Monday, wedding week, the Herman phone rang several times. Paula, at the back of the house, hurried to pick up. The young voice was ebullient and direct. "Mom, it's me! When can we expect you?" Paula chuckled at her daughter's enthusiasm. Mally had been that way since birth!

"Muffin, we'll be in on Thursday evening. Frank wants to get settled and do some sightseeing on Friday. What time is the rehearsal on Saturday?" "We'll do it at 11:00. Between shows would be too rushed." "Oh, that's right. You have two shows on Saturday." "We made a reservation for you and Frank at the Abbey Hotel, 51st Street and 7th Avenue. It's centrally located and very pleasant. How will Toots manage without you?"

"Oh, Frank couldn't see boarding him, so the neighbors are going to take him in. They love critters, especially bulldogs. Toots has it made," she said, chuckling. "How are you and Griff managing?" "We're good! Everything is working out beautifully. The girls in the show gave me the most wonderful shower, Mom. And the guys held a bachelor party for Griff, totally a surprise! He was so pleased."

"Wonderful! We can't wait to see you both. Will Frank require a tux? He has one, you know, through his Masonic work." "No, a dark blue suit will be fine. He'll look so snazzy!" "Well, we're looking forward to being with you, Muffin. Only three sleeps to go! Oh, take this down. We're flying Northwest Airlines, Flight 410, due at Kennedy International about 7:30 pm. We'll take an airport bus to downtown and cab to the hotel."

"Have a safe trip, Mom. Can't wait to see you both! Love you!" "Love you back!"

On Thursday, Mally was eager to hear from her folks. She and Griff left the theatre quickly and headed home. They weren't in the door ten minutes when the phone rang. "Paula! How good to hear your voice. How was the trip?" "Griff, it was perfect, so smooth all the way! As we were approaching, the plane flew over the ocean! Frank was thrilled to pieces!" Griff smiled as Paula's excitement spilled over. "Well, welcome to New York! It's wonderful that you could come. Here's Mally." Griff took out a beer and poured two glasses.

"Mom, so glad you're in! How's the hotel? Is the room okay?" Paula chuckled. "Muffin, it's just fine. We love the location, so close to everything. Frank is in seventh heaven. He loves New York! Can we meet for lunch tomorrow? I can't wait to see you!" "Sounds good, Mom. I think Griff might be able to get away as well. We'll call in the morning, okay?"

"Yes, of course! Oh, before I forget, is there any way we can see the show tomorrow night? I've heard you're sold out and it's impossible to get tickets!" "They've put aside house seats for you. Griff requested them. After all, you're my VIPs," she giggled. "Wait until you see *Centipede*! You'll recognize some of the dancers you met last year in Minneapolis. You'll love it!"

"I'd hate to have come all this way and miss it! We'll talk in the morning. Frank's already snoozing!" "Good night, Mom. I love you!" Mally put the phone down and looked at Griff, smiling from ear to ear. "What?" "I love your relationship with your folks." "They're the best! I'm so lucky to have them, Griff." "And I'm so lucky to have you!"

Gently he kissed her. Soft kissing led to touching, causing them to turn on. As their passion grew, he took her hand and led her to bed. The clock ticked as they made love, euphoric, knowing that they would soon be married.

Pat was frustrated. She had seen less and less of Owen in the past week. His phone rang and rang, but he didn't pick up. He had been scarce at the theatre, causing concern. 'What was going on?' He'd been scarce since her return. It felt like he was losing interest. Needing reassurance, she phoned Jonas. Phillipe picked up right away.

"It's Pat. Is Jonas there?" Her voice was tight and on the verge of tears. "Cheri, he's right here." In moments, Jonas took the phone. "Irish, what's doing?" He could tell she was distraught. "Hey, what's wrong?" "Oh Jonas, I need to talk. I'm worried," said Pat, her voice breaking. "It's about Owen, something's wrong. He's been distant." Jonas looked at Phillipe, carefully navigating.

"He's been pretty busy negotiating. There's talk of a run in Tokyo, at the end of the year." "No, this is different. Something's wrong, I can feel it!" "Irish, are you sure you're not imagining crap?" "This isn't crap. When we're together, he's distracted." Jonas tried a new approach.

"You have enough to think about as Mal's maid of honor, this Sunday. Forget this Owen stuff, it's probably nothing." "You're right, of course. Owen will be at the wedding, I'll see him then." "So, Irish are we good for now?" "Yes Jonas, I love you!" "I love you, too! See you tonight!" Pat put down the phone and closed her eyes. 'Why am I so afraid, so uncertain?' These and other questions riddled her until, feeling the need to nap, she lay down.

Meanwhile, Owen wrapped up a meeting with Joe Kaplan and was ready to leave, when Joe stopped him. He looked deeply troubled. "Owen, have you got a minute?" "Sure Joe, where to?" "My office, down the hall, follow me."

"Have a seat, Owen. May I offer you a drink?" Owen looked at his watch; it was after 5:00. "Scotch on the rocks, no water. Thanks." Joe stepped to the bar, poured two drinks; his was bourbon, straight up. They sat opposite each other. Moments passed, weighing heavily on Kaplan. He took a large swallow.

"I need to talk and I hope you'll understand. This must be confidential, or, there'll be repercussions." "What is it, Joe?" "It's Vera. She's going downhill. Her drinking is out of hand and she's now taking prescription drugs for the blues. I'm about at the end of my rope these days." Listening impassively, the situation was all too familiar to Owen. Joe continued, attempting to choke back tears. "What do you suggest? I'm in love with her. I'd do anything for her. I'm afraid if she continues, she won't survive!"

"Have you thought about getting her help?" "Hell, no! When I broach the subject, Vera goes ape shit! You know, throws punches and curses me until I have to physically restrain her! I tell you, I can't take much more of this crap!" "Joe, for your sake, you need to send her away. Bring in the experts. You have the dough to handle it. The fees will get you up the ass, but if Vera is willing, it may help."

Joe calmed down. "The thing is, Owen, she has to be willing. She doesn't think she has a problem. Vera drinks all day while I'm at the office. When I get home, she's tanked and abusive. Our sex life is in the toilet! It never used to be like this. When we first got together, we fucked like rabbits, now, zilch." "Joe, that's personal. You need to know why the drinking has accelerated."

"Bottom line, Owen, she's still hung up on you! It's like she's obsessed. She doesn't say it in so many words, but when I mention your show she cries and leaves the room." Owen took a deep breath and continued listening.

"I caught her masturbating one night. She was whispering your name as she was doing herself. When she came, she sobbed. She thought I was asleep, but I heard the whole thing." "I'm sorry, Joe. I really am. I've had little to no contact with her since the divorce. I'll admit I've run into her on occasion, but I've rebuffed her."

Joe was now on a roll. "The topper was opening night at Sardi's. She was verbally abused by some broad, Jackie Eldridge, I believe. That bitch threw Vera into a tailspin, taunting her, telling her she was used goods. It got pretty personal, down to a cat fight. I had the Eldridge bitch thrown out and sent Vera home. She's been pretty withdrawn ever since. What's with that bitch anyway? How does she know so much?"

"It's ancient history, Joe. Jackie and I met when I first started choreographing. She was exceptional, beautiful, a hell of a dancer.

Admittedly, we got involved. She fell in love. I fucked around. Then it was over. She's made it her mission to get back at me ever since. Why she came after Vera is anyone's guess. Personally, I think she's off. She's out of the business now as far as I know."

"Christ, no wonder Vera was distraught. This explains a lot." Owen looked at his watch. "I really have to get going, Joe. I'm sorry for your trouble. It appears we have a lot in common." Pulling out a cigarette, he reached for a light, took a deep drag and gave Kaplan a hard look. "I hope Vera gets some professional help, for her sake and yours." Excusing himself, he walked to the door, Joe following.

"Thanks for listening, Owen. It helps to get it out, you know?" Owen gave Kaplan a pat on the arm and left, closing the door behind him. Joe poured another drink and eased into a chair. The amber liquid soothed. 'What next? I can't live without her.' Slowly he dozed. Going home tonight could wait.

Owen grabbed a cab to Stephanie's. They had a date at 5:30; it was now close to 6:00. He needed sex, the need growing in recent weeks. Miss McNeil was hard to beat!

Chapter 51

Wed At Last!

The next days were a blur! The Hermans ran around Manhattan all day Friday, thrilled to explore New York. They met Mally and Griff for lunch at Tavern on The Green. At afternoon's end, they took a ride to and from Staten Island on the ferry. The Manhattan skyline was impressive, how different from Minneapolis!

Griff was able to score two house seats, fifth row center, orchestra. *Centipede* was beyond their expectations. The incredible choreography and dancers! Their daughter on Broadway! How she'd grown since she danced at the Orpheum last year! Following the performance, they renewed acquaintance with some of the *Bravo Business* gypsies. Jonas suggested the Taft Bar for nightcaps, being right across the street from the Abbey, it was convenient for Mally's folks.

Griff bought the first round. They chatted until he reminded them of tomorrow's two shows.

Pat was nowhere to be found. She ducked out of the theater after the performance, taking a train home. Weary over Owen's lack of contact, she needed time to step back. It was hard to know what to do or how to feel. Owen had vowed she was the only one, but was she really? Hopefully, they'd spend time together at the wedding.

The bridal group met for rehearsal on Saturday at 11:00. Jonas and Phillipe were told of the seating set-up. Frank and Mally did a practice run walking down a makeshift aisle. Dick escorted Pat to the front of the room. They would stand next to the bride and groom during the ceremony. Andy Mason, the pastor, did a brief run of the service and Sandy marked through music. Dana ran her solo, while Paula held baby Michael. Satisfied with the rehearsal, everyone dispersed at noon.

Sunday began with a pre-ceremony breakfast at the Abby, the Herman's treat. It was time to fuel up and then leave for Sardi's. Griff had his usual, a short stack, sausage and coffee. Mally was too excited to eat. Paula reminded her that protein was essential and ordered her an omelet. They left the hotel at 11:00.

The Sardi's staff was busy prepping the rooms. Chairs were placed in rows with an aisle in-between. Jonas and Phillipe had offered to decorate, renting a white lattice arch, six floor-standing candelabras and pink bows for each. They also provided all the bridal party flowers from a stash they'd saved for months. The color scheme of pink and white was perfect.

Sandy had a baby grand brought in, tuned and ready. Sardi's PA system was set up for the wedding and reception needs. Prior to dinner, champagne and hors d'oeuvres would be offered. Vincent Sardi had suggested a menu that included a choice of Filet Mignon or Chicken Kiev, Caesar Salad, twice-baked potatoes, asparagus with Hollandaise and a variety of rolls. The final touch, a three-layer carrot wedding cake, the couple's favorite. Vincent added extra staff to assist that evening.

Griff and Mally offered their place to Pat so that she could get ready for the wedding. Since transporting her formal clothes on the train would be cumbersome, her brother, Mickey, insisted on driving her. Everyone involved was to be at Sardi's by 4:30.

Owen had pulled an overnight at Stephanie's. By now, they were seeing each other several times a week. He had to accept Griff's invitation knowing full well that a no-show would be rude and unacceptable. At 2:00, he returned to his place on the West Side. The phone was ringing when he walked in. Shaking out a cigarette, he grabbed his lighter with one hand and the receiver with the other. "Matthews."

"Owen, it's Pat." "Baby, I'll be damned! This is unexpected. What's new?" There was a moment of silence. "I might ask you the same," said Pat, her voice tight. "What do you mean? I've been in meetings. It's difficult to get away, Baby. You know how it goes." "Yes I do, but why the long silence?"

"Pat, for God's sake, stop it! I can't always be at your beck and call!" "I think you've made that clear," she said facetiously. "Are you coming to the wedding at least?" "Of course I am, Baby, wouldn't miss it for the world. I'll see you then, all right?" There was a click.

Pat stood trembling. 'This is crazy. What's wrong?' As she rehashed their conversation, Mickey walked in. "You ready, Sis? I want to get you there on time." Pat picked up her belongings and they left. Her mood was morose, not appropriate for a day like today.

Joe asked Vera to come to the wedding. She flatly refused adding, "What the fuck for? I don't need to see happy idiots celebrating! Forget it, buster. I'd sooner have pins stuck in my eyes," she snarled. Getting up from the bed, she wobbled her way to the bar and poured another Jack Daniels. "Why can't you stay home and fuck me instead?" Vera had been on a 24-hour bender and was slowly medicating.

"Baby Doll, I can't be with you when you're like this," he said, reining in his anger. "Stay home, if you want. I'm obligated to go. I'll see you later." He reached for her, but she turned away. "You damn well better have it up when you come back." Pushing past him, she returned to bed, sank back into the pillows and continued drinking. Joe watched Vera for a moment, heartsick.

It was 4:45. The wedding party assembled. Jonas and Phillipe were in their finest suits, pink boutonnieres jauntily attached to their lapels. Frank stood waiting, admiring the décor. In the men's room, Dick was assisting Griff. Dana had a sitter for baby Michael and extra bottles of formula. Giving the first bottle before the ceremony, she placed a towel over her clothes to stay free of burps and drool. Sandy tested the piano.

Meanwhile, Pat helped Mally into her dress; cap and veil followed. Slipping into her French heels, she was ready! "Oh Mal, you are the most beautiful bride ever!" Gently they hugged. There was a knock on the door. "May I come in?" It was Paula.

"Oh Mom, it's finally here!" Paula's eyes welled. "You look exquisite, Muffin!" Pat was fighting envy. "Imagine marrying your soul mate," she said as she wiped away tears. Paula reached for Pat's hand. "Your time will come, sweetheart." The two hugged. The last minutes crept along.

Wedding guests began arriving. Embraces and exuberant voices mingled with the air of anticipation. Phillipe and Jonas escorted attendees to their seats. The women of *Centipede* looked fabulous, beautifully dressed and coiffed. Cynthia, Fran, and Liz were radiant as they came in. Kathy, Sonja, and Marcy followed. They sat together.

The men looked handsome in a variety of suits and sports jackets. Jordan was Joe's date, while Gary insisted his partner, Steve, accompany him. Kaplan and Maggli arrived without dates. Murmurs filled the room. Jeff and Nora walked in holding hands. Owen Matthews suddenly arrived, causing a stir. Rarely seen in a suit, he looked like a model for Hart Schaffner & Marx.

Sandy went to the piano, resplendent in a black silk suit. He began, a selection of love songs filling the air. Stunning in lavender, Dana sat next to Sandy. Paula, on Jonas' arm was seated in the front row. The ceremony began. All eyes turned to Pat and Dick as they moved down the aisle. As they peeled off at the front of the room, Griff joined his best man. Dr. Mason took his position.

The moment arrived! *Here Comes the Bride* was heard as Frank gave Mally his arm. Pulling the veil down over her face, she took a deep breath. The crowd rose in waves as they passed. At the front of the room, they paused. Frank lifted her veil, kissed her cheek, placing her hand in Griff's. Returning a smile, she squeezed his hand and whispered, "This is it!"

Dr. Mason introduced himself and shared a childhood story of his friend, Griff. He described Mally, the joy she had brought Griff, the meaningful way they had come together. The homily was personal and touching, bringing tears to many. During the ceremony, Owen studied Pat, exquisitely beautiful and breathtaking. 'I'm a fucking fraud!'

Following vows and exchange of rings, Dana rose. Singing "One Hand, One Heart," her magnificent soprano filled the room. When the song ended, Andy took over. "And now, by the power invested in me by the State of New York, I now pronounce you man and wife. Griffen, you may kiss your bride." They kissed and kissed, bringing the group to their feet, cheering!

"Ladies and Gentleman, it is my honor and pleasure to introduce to you Mr. and Mrs. Griffen Edwards!" The applause was deafening as Mally took her bouquet from Pat. They walked together, beaming at the crowd, followed by Pat and Dick. Jonas and Phillipe escorted the Hermans. Dana was next, as Sandy continued to play. Vincent Sardi announced, "Drinks and hors d'oeuvres are now being served. Please join the bride and groom at 7:30 for dinner and dancing. Thank you!"

All around spirited conversations underscored handshakes, hugs, kisses and some tears. Champagne was uncorked and offered by servers moving through the crowd. Trays of delicious hors d'oeuvres were passed. The mood throughout was heady, infectious. One who was not as enthused, but tried to be cordial, was Joe Kaplan. His preoccupation with Vera hung over him like a thick blanket. Working his way through the crowd, he extended his hand.

"Congratulations, Griff. I'm pleased for you and this beautiful young lady." Kissing Mally's cheek, he forced a smile, adding, "I'm sending you two on a week-long honeymoon, all expenses paid, to Bermuda. When you're ready, give me a call." "Thank you so much, Joe! We'll see when we can get away once the show is further along."

"Sounds like a plan," he said, excusing himself, leaving them speechless.

Owen approached, hugged Griff and kissed Mally. "Congratulations, you two make love possible!" "Thank you for coming, Owen. It means a lot to us," said Griff. Owen raised his glass. "Here's to your great run!" They chuckled, returning the gesture. As he took a sip, he spotted Pat across the room. "If you'll excuse me, I have a beautiful lady to see." Griff and Mally watched as Owen moved. "Maybe Pat will be next," whispered Mally.

Pat was chatting with Jonas and Phillipe as Owen approached. "Good evening! Baby, you are breathtaking! Excuse us," he said, winking at the boys, as he led her away. Jonas watched them disappear through the crowd. "Better not mess up, boss. It won't be pleasant!" "They'll be fine, Cheri. Leave them be."

Owen walked Pat toward a back hall, out-of- the-way. Nudging her against the wall, he covered her mouth with his. He was forceful, his warm breath impossible to resist. Aggressively, his hands traced her breasts, the silk smooth to the touch. His lips found her ear. "Baby, I want to fuck you right here!" Looking furtively around, she unzipped his fly and began what Owen loved most. "I have to be here until after dinner," whispered Pat. "Please, will you stay? There will be more of this," she teased.

Owen wanted to let go, the urge to climax building. Reluctantly, he made her stop. He zipped his fly and let out a deep breath. "Baby, you have me half crazed. Meet me back at my place later, all right? Take a cab as soon as you can." "Why not stay for dinner? It would mean a lot to Mal and Griff." "I can't, Baby. I'm better one-on-one," he whispered. Lifting her chin, he kissed her deeply. "So, I'll see you later, Baby. Don't keep me waiting." "I'll be there as fast as I can."

In seconds, he was gone. She felt the tug once more, the tug of uncertainty and the desperation of pure want. Preoccupied, she reluctantly returned to the party.

Vincent announced dinner, guests filled the tables. Mally and Griff sat at the head table with Pat and Dick at their side. Next to Pat were Jonas and Phillipe. Dana sat next to Dick with Sandy next to her. Completing the group, Paula and Frank seated on the end. Andy Mason had another commitment that evening. With the cast and other guests seated, the toasts began.

Tinkling of glass was heard as Frank rose. Addressing the couple, he smiled and blew a kiss to Mally. "Griff, my friend, welcome to our family! You couldn't have picked a better woman than our Mally and she, a better man. May your lives be blessed every day and may you know the joy that Paula and I have shared. Cheers!" Everyone drank and glasses were refilled.

Jonas rose next. Turning to Mally, he choked back tears as he spoke. "I met this gem of a girl last year on tour. I loved her right away. To see her so happy, with this great man, gives me faith in the human race! So Griff and Mal, may happiness be yours always from us!" Cheers and whistles broke out around the room as the group drank another.

It was Dick's turn to honor his friend and mentor. As he was unaccustomed to public speaking, his voice faltered as he tried. "If there's any truth to the phrase, "a match made in heaven," then heaven is present in this couple. Griff, I value you as a friend and mentor. Mally, I admire your talent and integrity. What a pleasure to see you together. Best wishes and love always from Dana and me!" As applause rang out, glasses were refilled, again.

Pat followed, already slightly tipsy, but eager to share. Standing, she wavered slightly but caught herself as she raised her glass. "I met Miss Minnesota last year when we auditioned for *Bravo Business*. It was friendship from the get-go. Mal, you're a true friend. I love you like the sister I never had. I couldn't be happier for you and Griff!" As Pat took a swig, she accidentally spilled on her blouse. Giggling, she added, "I guess that's enough for me," causing laughter.

When the toasts concluded, waiters served. The cuisine was excellent, Sardi's hallmark. The guests dined and chatted as the evening progressed, the mood ebullient, the atmosphere joyous. At the end of dinner, Griff and Mally rose and were led by Vincent to a tiered cake in the center of the room. They sliced together and fed each other first bites, as was tradition. Servers cut the remainder for guests. Coffee and cognac followed.

Sandy set up his trio in the corner, in minutes, music filled the room. Frank led Mally to the dance floor. Griff offered Paula his arm and joined them. Applause greeted the couples as they danced. At the end of the first number, they switched. Griff held Mally near as they moved to Gershwin's "Someone To Watch Over Me." Bending close, he whispered, "My darling Mally, this is the best moment of my life! I love you more than anything."

Looking up at Griff, her eyes conveyed it all. Was she dreaming? Had she really married the man who stole her heart at first sight? Yes, it was true! Griff was her forever soul mate, proving that life couldn't get any better.

Dana and Dick followed suit, enjoying one dance before they took their sitter and Michael home. He had been an angel all day. Vincent had provided his private office for the Landry's sitter and they were grateful. Having someone to take care of the baby had made attending the event possible.

Jonas asked Pat to dance. Whether on stage or off, they danced as one. Phillipe cut in at the earliest opportunity, enjoying Pat's ability to follow; female dancers were likely to lead when dancing socially. Jeff and Nora joined the others. There was a stir of interest amongst the gypsies, speculation over the couple's involvement. As the evening wound down, guests excused themselves, expressing congratulations once again. Saying their goodbyes, Paula and Frank returned to the hotel. They would leave for Minnesota in the morning.

Jonas, Phillipe, Gary, and Steve decided on a nightcap and went downstairs to the bar. Joe and Jordan took off to spend some private time before the work week. The girls dispersed, each to her apartment to relax in the remaining hours of their day off. Pat was about to leave for Owen's when Mally stopped her.

"Pat, it's very late. Do you want to stay at our place? We'll be heading to the Waldorf just as soon as we wrap up here." "Not to worry. I'm staying with Owen tonight. I told my folks I'd be at your place, so I'm covered!" "Well, if that's the plan," said Mally, always hoping for the best when it involved Pat and Owen. They were hugging just as Griff walked over. "Thanks so much for asking me to be part of this. You two are very lucky. I love you both," she said, choking up.

"Can I find you a cab, Pat? I don't like the idea of you out there alone at this hour," cautioned Griff. "No thanks. I'll find my way." Gathering her things, she walked to the door. Griff watched her exit. "Is Pat all right, Darling?" "She's fine. She'll be at Owen's tonight. The Byrnes were told she's camping at our place."

Sandy approached. "What a great night, you two! Thanks for the opportunity. The boys and I had a great time." "Do you have everything, Sandy? Do you need help loading up?" Sandy chuckled. "No stage managing tonight, my friend. It's time to start the honeymoon," he said winking.

In a few minutes, the room was cleared. As they were the last to leave, Griff found Sardi.

"Please send me a bill for the evening, Vincent. The food and service were impeccable. Mally and I appreciate your attention to every detail." "It's been my pleasure to host you and your group. You are truly Broadway's finest. Thank you for your business." The two shook hands.

Griff came downstairs carrying a hanging bag with their street clothes and small overnight bag.

"Mrs. Edwards, let's head to the Waldorf!" "I love the sound of that," she said, holding tightly to his hand. Flagging down a cab, he helped Mally in and settled next to her. "I remember a similar scene like this a while back," said Griff reminiscing. "Our first cab ride together back in Norfolk. Remember?" The two kissed, eagerly awaiting their first night of marriage in one of New York's finest hotels.

Pat hurried from the cab into the building. Greeting Ralph, she pushed the elevator call, counting seconds until the door opened. Inside, she pushed for Owen's floor, running her hands through her hair. 'He loves it loose and flowing.'

Ringing his bell, she waited. Moments passed. The door opened, revealing Owen in a pair of tight jeans, his package tantalizing. A cigarette hung precariously from his lips, a bottle of champagne in his hand. He drew her into the warmth of his body, a place of mystery and promise. Pat was ready for whatever Owen had in store.

Chapter 52

Honeymoon, Honeymoon

The Waldorf Astoria Hotel, revered as New York's finest, stood impressively at 301 Park Avenue, magnificent against the night sky. The Edwards' cab pulled up to two uniformed doormen in morning coats—one to assist passengers, the other, their luggage.

Mally stared at the grandeur of the portico; a large ornate entrance over a carpeted walkway. How different it was from the modest hotels she encountered on tour! At the reception desk, an immaculate gentleman stood ready, his charm and precision apparent.

"Welcome to the Waldorf Astoria. How may I help you, sir?" As Griff talked to the clerk, Mally looked at the grand lobby details, observing everything from carpeting, drapes and furnishings to beautifully cultivated plants placed throughout. Ornate chandeliers provided mood lighting, soft music in the background. "We have a reservation for tonight. The name is Edwards, Mrs. and Mrs. Griffen Edwards," he said with delight. The concierge pulled a file and began to check names.

"Yes, here it is. I have a reservation for one night in the name of Edwards for our honeymoon suite. It is ready for you now, Mr. Edwards, please sign here. The clerk rang, a bellhop appeared. "Charles, please see Mr. and Mrs. Edwards to Suite A on the 40th Floor. And may I offer my congratulations to you both?" "Thank you so much," said Mally, clearly thrilled.

"Is there anything else I can advise you of?" Griff had a question. "What service and amenities are included?" "Yours is our finest suite which includes an arrangement of flowers, chilled champagne, fresh strawberries on ice and chocolates. Complimentary room service for a late dinner and breakfast are also provided and checkout time is 3 pm. They are aware of your arrival, just dial number 10 on your phone." Griff was impressed. "And what is your name, sir?" "My name is Graydon. If there is anything we can do to make your stay with us more enjoyable, dial number 4."

Charles waited patiently. "May I assist you with your belongings, sir?" Griff chuckled handing him the hanging bag and small case. "Please follow me," he said, indicating the row of elevators. "We will be taking the VIP elevator." As they walked away, Mally turned and waved at Graydon, who returned a smile. "Mrs. Edwards, your smile would beguile anyone," said Griff, hugging her close. "What fun," said Mally, enjoying every nuance of their adventure.

Arriving on the 40th Floor, Charles opened the double doors and stepped aside for them to enter. Placing their belongings on a stand, he asked, "Will there be anything else, Mr. Edwards?" "No Charles, thank you very much," said Griff, giving him a ten.

"Mrs. Edwards, we forgot something, come here." Mally stepped back into the hall. With a whoosh, he swept her into his arms and carried her across the threshold. Before he put her down, he kissed her softly, relishing the moment.

"Oh Griff, I still feel I'm dreaming. You'd better pinch me," she said, giggling. "I'm going to do more than that my sweet. Are you hungry?" "Yes, I'm famished. I was much too excited to eat at Sardi's. What sounds good?" Griff found a menu and quickly looked it over. "We definitely need protein, how about a couple of steak sandwiches, fries, and a salad?"

"Sounds heavenly, let's order." "Are you sure you don't want something more posh, Darling? After all, this is the Waldorf." "Nope, a steak sandwich sounds yummy! Please order mine well. I don't want it to moo!" Griff laughed as he dialed. The kitchen answered, he identified himself and ordered. "It'll be about a half hour." "Gee, what do you want to do while we wait?" "Oh, I can think of many things, but let's wait for fuel. In the meantime, let's look this place over."

The bedroom was lavish beyond compare. Heavy brocade fabrics gave a rich, traditional look to the bedclothes, drapes and pillows in shades of mauve and deep purple. The bed was elevated, plush and inviting, a fireplace crackling warmly. A large silver bucket with champagne chilling, plump strawberries on ice and Belgian Chocolates nearby were ready and waiting. Two vases of red roses added splendor.

Let's get out of these things," suggested Griff. "Do you need some help, Mrs. Edwards?" "I'd like to do that," he whispered, pulling the zipper down. Mally wore a brief chemise and panties. Her garter belt was fetching, her beautiful legs in silk. Griff's shorts were becoming snug, they had to go, soon.

"Come here, Darling." Mally shivered, as his fingertips lightly brushed her skin. He removed her remaining underwear and took her in his arms. Lost in the moment, a sudden knock startled. He quickly found two hotel robes. "I'll get the door, Darling. You stay put."

The waiter rolled a cart into the suite. "Will this be satisfactory, Mr. Edwards?" "Yes, thank you. Hold on a minute." Reaching his money clip, another ten. "Here you are and thanks very much." "Good night, Mr. Edwards, enjoy your stay." "Thanks." Closing the door, he double locked it. "Moo, moo, moo," he chanted.

Following the meal, they enjoyed the fire and champagne. "I remember every moment of our first time making love," he whispered. "Time for bed," he said, rising. They pulled back the coverlet and slipped in. Making love, wrapped in each other's arms, sleep followed until dawn.

Across town, a different scene was playing out. Owen made up for lost time, taking Pat to bed, ravishing her without missing a beat. Wonton and eager, he was his best, more attentive than usual, fucking her out of guilt. Pat had no thought about his motive. All she knew was he was pleasing her.

In the morning, they jumped into the shower and resumed their randy play. Pat felt extraordinary pleasure as he knelt and tongued her. She held his shoulders, begging for more as orgasms repeated. Pat returned the favor with her mouth until he came. The shower cooling, they had to quit.

Owen dressed and went into the kitchen. Pat slipped on her clothes, her jeans and long sleeved comfy after yesterday's formal wear. Towel drying her hair and pulling it into a ponytail her sneakers felt great. The smell of coffee drew her to the kitchen. Owen was making breakfast, a rare treat.

Setting places, he scooped a fluffy mixture of eggs, cheese, and bacon crumbles out of the pan onto each plate. Toast popped and quickly buttered, jam was optional. Pat enjoyed this burst of domesticity. Pouring coffee, he brought the steamy brew, cutlery and napkins. Gesturing to Pat, she joined him and enjoyed the moment.

"Baby, did you enjoy last night?" Pat took a bite of egg and swallowed. She was always starved after sex. "It was incredible, Owen. I've missed being with you, depressed actually." "Baby, I've been preoccupied. *Centipede's* a major hit and you're a big part of its success." Pat put down her fork. "Maybe I just need to hear we're a success. Are we Owen?" Owen stopped midway through a bite. "What kind of fucking question is that?" "I think it's a fair one," said Pat, not letting up.

"Where is this coming from, Baby? I made you a star! I've touted you from day one! What more do you need, for Christ's sake?" "I'm not just a body on stage. This is about us; I want to know where I stand!" "Listen to me, I've told you from the beginning how it is. No expectations, no commitment, no fucking piece of paper. You're here because I want you to be. Don't you get that?" "I get that nothing ever changes, does it? I can have you if I play by your rules, right?"

Owen reached for cigarette support. Taking a drag, he searched for a response. The phone suddenly rang, breaking his train of thought. "Matthews." The distortion of sound from the other end couldn't hide the female voice. Pat's pulse quickened as Owen turned his back and spoke quietly. "No, I'm not alone. No, it's not a good idea today. I'll phone you later. Ciao." Pat sat stone-faced, tears running down her cheeks.

"Okay, who the fuck was that, Owen?" He looked away, trying to think, as he sucked his cigarette. "It's no one, no one important." "You're a liar! It's a fucking woman," she screamed. "It's nothing, honestly nothing. The *Times* wants an interview. That's all!"

"Do you expect me to buy that bullshit? It was that McNeil babe, right?" Owen sat silent, refusing to answer. "Does she want you to fuck her, does she? Or have you been? Answer me!" Owen suddenly exploded, squashing out his cigarette, grabbing her wrists. Glowering he held tight, his face tight and darkening. "Now you listen to me, Pat.

What I do and who I do is none of your fucking business. I've told you from the beginning, I won't make promises, a commitment, not to you, not to anyone!"

Pat wrenched free and slapped him hard across the face. Falling against the sofa, he recoiled and rose, taking a threatening step toward her. "Back off, you bastard! You couldn't keep it in your pants, could you?" Sobbing hysterically, she grabbed her clothes and headed to the door. He tried to stop her, but she pushed him aside. "Please Pat, wait a minute," he insisted. "Go to hell," she screamed, running down the hall. Owen watched her disappear into the elevator. The moments ticked by. Slowly closing the door, he took a deep breath, calming down and walked to the bar. 'What the use? I've fucked up, again,' he thought, reaching for a scotch.

At the lobby, Pat hurried to the door, her manner alarming the doorman. "Are you all right Miss? Do you need help?" Pat ignored him as she continued to the street. Her first thought was to find a cab. But, where would she go? Her mind raced, consumed by Owen's betrayal. 'How could he do this? I thought he loved me!'

Reality hit! It was over. Her stomach lurched as she felt the first wave of nausea. Hurrying to the curb, tasting bile, she threw up breakfast. 'This can't be happening, can it?' The retching stopped; she wiped her mouth and chin. She felt alone, her world had collapsed. Spotting a booth, she thought of Jonas and dialed. 'Jonas, please answer!' Several rings later he picked up. Mixed with sobs, the voice was Pat's. "Irish, what's going on?" "Oh Jonas, I need you. Can I come over now?"

Chapter 53

A Rude Awakening

Jonas hurried from the bathroom and buzzed Pat in. 'This is going to be rough, she's beyond hysterical,' he thought. Moments later, she stood at his door, eyes swollen; sad and broken.

"Oh Irish, come here," he insisted, opening his arms. Holding her tight, stroking her hair to calm her, the sobs subsided. "Jonas, it's over," she whimpered. Jonas took her things, setting them aside. Pat sunk into the sofa and hugged a pillow.

"Would you like a drink? It's a little early, but what the hell," he said, trying to elicit a smile.

"I need caffeine, not booze." "Coffee coming up, he said," heading to the kitchen. Grabbing two mugs, he poured. "Do you take cream or sugar, Irish?" "Black, and strong," she said impassively. Jonas returned and sat. "Okay, Irish, tell me what happened."

"After the wedding, Owen invited me up. We made love all night. It was incredible. This morning, he made breakfast. While we were eating the phone rang. I could hear a woman's voice. He was uncomfortable and kept the conversation brief." Jonas listened, his heart in his throat. "Shit, I knew it!" Pat's eyes widened. "What do you know?" "I had reason to believe he's having an affair. I was afraid to tell you, but now it's adding up." Pat's mouth opened, moans heartbreaking, as she tried to speak. "Tell me please. What do you know?"

"A few weeks ago, Gary and Steve were walking in midtown. He thought he saw Owen come out of a restaurant with some blonde and get into a cab. He wasn't sure, so he mentioned it to me, thinking you had broken up. I told him he was mistaken." Pat began crying again.

"Now hold on Irish, there's more. The night of Griff's bachelor party, I needed to take a whiz, and on the way to the men's room, I spotted Owen walking through the lobby with a blonde. Thank God, he didn't see me. They stopped at the front desk, talked to the concierge, then headed to the elevators."

"Oh God, then it's true. He's been fucking someone else," cried Pat. "How will I live without him? How will I work for him? What will I do?"

Jonas listened patiently. "Irish, you're still the star of *Centipede*. Give it time. He's been an asshole. Eventually he'll come to his senses, believe me," he said. "Are you kidding me? I'm supposed wait and forgive him?" Jonas tried a different approach. "Irish, you knew about Owen's reputation, as far back as Norfolk. Did you think he'd magically change?" "I thought he would," said Pat, sadly.

"Fuck me, the oldest rationale! So what happens now, Irish?" "It's noon already. I can't go home like this. Besides, we have a show tonight," she reasoned. A sound at the door drew their attention, as Phillipe walked in. "Cheri, how are you doing?" Jonas rolled his eyes. "The Irish maiden has been better. I think Pat should stay and go to the theatre from here. Tomorrow you go home, collect essentials and return. You can stay with us." Pat looked up, surprised at the offer.

"You need time to decompress, Irish. What's better than hanging out with two fags who cook, entertain and don't want in your pants? And you'll have a room of your own!" Pat smiled. "Well, all right, if you insist." "Better than all right," said Phillipe, giving her a big hug.

Jonas interrupted. "Then it's all settled. Now, how does a bite of lunch sound, or have you permanently lost your appetite?" "As a matter of fact, I'm starved," she said, her mood lifting. "You boys are the absolute best!"

Mally and Griff left the Waldorf at 2:00. It had been a phenomenal night, a perfect end to a perfect day. They grabbed a cab to Chelsea. Once again, he carried his bride across the threshold. As they settled, the phone rang; it was Joe Kaplan, apparently distraught.

"Good afternoon, Joe. What's wrong? The producer's voice was low and strained. "Griff, I thought you should know. Vera's in the hospital on life support," he said, his voice breaking. "Good lord, Joe. What happened?"

Kaplan attempted to control himself. "When I returned from the wedding last night, I found Vera unconscious. I attempted to wake her, but she didn't respond. I called the medics and they took her to St. Vincent's." "Do you have any idea what happened?"

"I'm requesting your discretion," he said, gravely. "It was just a matter of time before this would happen. Vera has been progressive in her alcoholism and, now, drug abuse. She refused to attend the wedding with me. She was completely drunk, so I left her at home."

"Joe, I'm so sorry. Is there anything I can do?" "Pray. Just pray." "Do you want me to make an announcement to the company tonight?" "You may, but please don't disclose the cause. Are we clear, Griff?" "You can rely on it." "I will update you when I can. Thank you for your time."

For a moment, Griff processed the news. Mally entered the room. "Darling, who was that?" "Joe Kaplan. Vera Daniels is in critical condition at St. Vincent's." "Oh my God, that's horrible! What happened?" "She overdosed. Joe found her after the wedding and immediately called the medics. It doesn't look good." "Oh Griff, this is so sad. Has Owen Matthews been informed?"

"I have no idea. I'll wait for an update. I have Joe's permission to inform the company with discretion. Let's keep Vera in our thoughts. In the meantime, I have to get to the theatre by 5:00 today. Why don't you get some rest? I'll wake you before I leave."

"Thanks, Mr. Edwards. Mrs. Edwards is kind of pooped." They kissed, absorbed in each other, their first full day as husband and wife.

Chapter 54

Coping

The news of Vera Daniels' condition spread through the business. A notice was released by the Kaplan-Maggli organization and sent to the New York press:

Vera Daniels, former star and toast of Broadway, has suffered a critical stroke. Miss Daniels is in grave condition at an undisclosed New York hospital. No further details are available at this time.

For the past 36 hours, Joe Kaplan's insistence to be at Vera's bed side had associates worried. The producer refused meals, sleep, or work in order to be near her. The otherwise tough impresario was fragile and terrified. He refused to acknowledge he might lose her. Vera remained in a coma, machines keeping her alive.

The news left the *Centipede* cast in shock. Griff reported her condition as a massive stroke in deference to Kaplan's request for privacy. His call to Owen wouldn't be easy, given their history. What surprised Griff was his indifference when told.

Meanwhile, Pat had concerns of her own. She was still trying to process Owen's cheating. How could he throw her over for another? Hadn't she been his inspiration, his chosen lover? Staying with Jonas and Phillipe was her refuge, a necessary buffer for the pain she carried. Dancing his show every night was like a deep cut that wouldn't heal. All her effort, devotion, and sweat perfecting Owen's vision only magnified the hurt of his betrayal. He hadn't dropped by the theatre since the previous weekend. At the end of each show, she hurried to Jonas and Phillipe's hoping to separate from the reality that Owen was with someone else.

Midweek, the call came. "Griff, I regret to tell you that Vera died earlier today." His voice broke as he continued. "Please inform the cast, crew and orchestra." "Joe, I'm so sorry. What can I do for you?" After a pause, Joe continued.

"In deference to a great star, I'm requesting all Broadway Theater marquees be dark for 10 minutes prior to curtain tonight." "I will see to it from our end at the Royal," said Griff. "Is there anything I can do for you personally?" "Perhaps you can assist me in planning a memorial service to honor her memory. We can talk later. Right now, I must make arrangements." "Mally and I send our condolences to you, Joe. Please stay in touch."

That evening, Broadway went dark preceding each performance on the Great White Way. There was a heavy sense of loss for those who recognized the name Vera Daniels. Her reputation equaled that of Ethel Merman and Mary Martin. When the lights returned, Broadway went on. *Centipede* was electric that night. The audience response was overwhelming, as the company took bow after bow.

Following the show, Chad invited Pat for a drink. He'd heard rumors about the break-up. He considered Pat a good friend and hoped to cheer her up. She agreed to join him at the Taft.

The night was chilly as the two headed down the street. Once inside the lobby, they loosened their coats and found stools at the bar.

"What are you drinking, Pat?" "I'll have a glass of red wine, maybe two," she said, a smile growing. "That a girl," said Chad encouragingly. Pat could be fun when tipsy. The drinks arrived and they toasted. "To better days, Pat!" "Thanks, Chad," she said, taking a sip.

"So how are you doing?" "I've been better, but life goes on. And Vera Daniels' death is a big wake-up call." "No kidding. What a shock, I wonder how Owen is doing?" Pat stared in disbelief. Chad suddenly realized his faux pas.

"Jeez, I'm sorry, Pat. I didn't mean to bring him up. I just meant, with their history, it must have been difficult to hear." "I know what you meant. I'm just touchy these days," she said, taking a large swallow. "Order me another, will you?" Chad signaled the barman.

"Do you have a cigarette?" "When did you start smoking? I've never seen you with a cigarette," he said, pulling out a pack. "Here, help yourself." Pat's grin was mischievous as she took one.

Accepting a light, she inhaled deeply, letting the smoke out slowly. "You don't know a lot of things about me, Mr. Chapman," she murmured, giving him a playful poke. The wine was taking hold as she accepted the second glass. Chad joined her, lighting a smoke. "So tell me about Owen," he said boldly.

Taking another drag, Pat was ready to talk. The wine was encouraging. "Owen and I were lovers. He found someone else to fuck. It's as simple as that." "Wow, Pat. You're certainly taking it well," said Chad, easing closer. "So that's been eating at you, huh?" "Yes, but I've decided to let it roll of my back. There are other fish to fry," she said with forced bravado.

Chad slipped his arm around her back and nuzzled her neck. "You can fry me," he murmured softly. "Chad, don't! You're a good pal, but that's where it ends," she said, removing his arm. "Okay, whatever you say," he snapped, disappointment all over his face. "Buy me another?" Recovering, Chad signaled the barman for another round. "I have to pee. I'll be right back," she hastened. Chad followed with his eyes as she left. 'I'd give anything to have her,' he thought.

Pat found the restroom and relieved herself. The wine was working. At the sink she loosened her hair, it fell over her shoulders. 'How could he give me up? There must be a way to get Owen back,' she thought. Reaching for lipstick, her hand found a business card instead. It read: *Blaine Courtman, President, Courtman Enterprises,"* and, handwritten on the back, the Plaza Hotel and phone number. Her heart quickened. 'Blaine's card, how perfect!' She tucked it back in her purse and returned to the bar.

She was tired and slightly tipsy as she joined Chad, who had ordered another round in her absence. "Gee, I don't know, I'm feeling a little wasted." "Oh come on, let's have one more. Don't worry, I'll see you home, okay?" They drank in silence. It was obvious to Chad she had no intention of going back to his place, though he had hoped for a different scenario. When they had finished, he paid. "Ready to go?" "All set!" They exited into a fierce wind toward 8th Avenue.

"I'm staying at Jonas and Phillipe's place at the moment." "Let me grab you a cab, I can walk from here." "Are you sure, Chad?"

"Absolutely," he responded, trying to act compliant. Feeling little pain, she kissed him fully on the mouth. He sighed as she pulled away. "You're a sweetheart, Chad. Thanks for tonight." A cab pulled up and she got in, clumsily. Waving to him, she was off. At the light, Chad waited to cross, disappointment cutting through his mind. 'No chance there, Chapman.'

Chapter 55

Hello and Goodbye

Pat was eager to phone Blaine Courtman, but it was too late that evening. Discovering his business card was a surprise. 'Time to bring out the ammunition; create an advantage, but first, a good night's sleep.'

Arriving at the boy's apartment, she let herself in. It was quiet and dark, save for a small light at the end of the hall. She was sloppy, bumping along the wall on her way to the bathroom.

The door opened, Jonas, in his bathrobe was half asleep. "Irish, is that you?" Pat paused, returning a whisper. "Well, of course, you silly Mary, who else?"

"Are you all right? You look like a train wreck." Pat giggled, moving gingerly toward him. Standing on tiptoes, she planted a big, wet kiss on his face. "I'm tanked," she said contritely.

"No shit," tossed Jonas, backing up. "My dear, your breath! Come with me! You need supervision." He walked to the kitchen pulling Pat along. "I think black coffee and a Bromo are in order, Irish!"

As he nudged her onto a stool, she reluctantly sat, letting him take over. Jonas reached for the tap and filled the pot, measuring the coffee. Pat sat with a silly grin, Jonas noticed. "You're grinning now, Irish, but wait! Unless I ply you with a remedy, you'll wake up with a humungous hangover!" She put her head on the table, resting on her arms and groaned.

"What happened? Tell me!" Lifting her head, Pat mumbled, "I needed to relax and Chad invited me for a drink." "How many drinks?" "I lost count, maybe four." "I'm surprised at you, Irish! Getting shit-faced isn't the answer. And bullshitting doesn't work. I know you're still hung up on the boss."

Pat sat up. "Well, if you must know, I drank to forget, because there's someone else I'm going to date," she slurred. "No shit?" Jonas turned off the burner and reached for mugs. Pouring two coffees, he handed Pat hers. Blowing on his, he took a careful sip, leaning in for further details. "Okay, time to spill." "Remember the rich guy with the limo, the one who showed up a lot on tour?" "I think so, vaguely. He wanted in your pants, if memory serves." "Bingo!" Pat took a tentative sip and continued.

"Well, I ran into him at Sardi's opening night. He's still hung up on me," she said smugly. "Keep drinking, Irish. You're wasted." "I'm going to call him." "You're not thinking clearly," said Jonas, patronizing her. "Well, I've made up my mind." "Irish, drink up. I'll mix you a Bromo. You've got to work tomorrow." Jonas left the kitchen just as Pat began to cry. Returning, he brought the fizzy and a box of tissues.

"Aw, Irish, come on. Drink this and blow your nose," he said, gently. A small wail erupted. "Oh Jonas, how can I live without him? I can't stand this! Please help me!" Jonas hugged her tightly. "Sweetie, this will take time. Please try to be patient. Phillipe and I are here and you have people who love you," he soothed, trying to calm her. "Now, drink! Let's get you to bed. It's already 2:00 a.m."

Pat took a tissue and blew into it, making a loud honk. "Yikes, I hope I didn't wake Phillipe," said Pat, wiping her nose, as she looked down the hall. "My Phillipe sleeps like a bear in winter," he said, smiling. "Now come on, down that fizz and go to bed. That's an order!"

She chugged the remaining Bromo and struggled to her feet. Jonas took her in hand and guided her along. Helping her undress was a challenge. Pat collapsed face down on the bed. Once her clothes were off, he tucked her in, turned off the light and headed to bed. Tomorrow was already today.

Joseph Kaplan set Vera's memorial tribute for Sunday, March 1st at 1:00. The Shubert Organization offered its theater adjacent to Shubert Alley, a venue Vera had performed in during her career. Those invited to eulogize included Vincent Lehrman, now retired. It was Lehrman who discovered Vera and made her a star, with Owen Matthews orchestrating her rise. Though invited, Owen declined as a speaker. A news release was circulated to radio, TV and press.

Vera Daniels, former Broadway musical star, passed away February 15th at age 45. Miss Daniels, revered for her breakout roles, was a true luminary of the Great White Way in the 1950s. A memorial service to honor her life and career will be held at the Shubert Theatre, Sunday, March 1st at 1:00 p.m. The public is welcome. Memorials to Actors Equity Association in her name preferred. Contact the Kaplan-Maggli Organization for details.

At Kaplan's office, phones rang off the hook as callers expressed condolences. Joe had returned to work following a week of seclusion. He took care of arrangements for Vera, having her remains cremated and placed in an ornate urn, there to be with him always.

Vera had no family to speak of—no siblings, offspring, or remaining parents. Her assets came from the sale of the co-op she and Owen owned during their marriage. She'd always spent beyond her means and what remained went to support her drinking.

She had rented a small apartment after the divorce. While there briefly, she met Joe Kaplan, who fell hopelessly in love with her, insisting she move in. The offer came with benefits, benefits beyond Vera's means. In exchange for a lavish lifestyle, she provided Kaplan companionship and sex. He doted, protected and proposed marriage frequently. Vera played the game brilliantly until drinking and drugs took hold, taking her in the end. One of the most influential stars of Broadway was gone.

The phone rang in Blaine Courtman's suite at the Plaza. He'd just finished shaving, his morning coffee and the *Wall Street Journal*.

"This is Courtman." "Hello, Blaine. Do you know who this is?" His breath stopped short as he recognized the voice. "Hello, Patricia. This is a surprise," he said, feigning nonchalance. "To what do I owe this pleasure?" "I found your business card and thought I'd give you a call," she said.

"I'm glad you did. How's the show going? "We've been sold out for weeks. A lot's been going on," she said, her voice tight. "My dad had a serious heart attack right after opening, so I was out for a while."

"I'm so sorry, Patricia. How is he doing now?" "He's doing well. Listen, Blaine, I really would like to see you," she said, cutting to the chase. There was a pause before he responded. "I've missed you since Utah, Patricia. You don't know how much," he whispered.

"Well, why don't you do something about it?" Her voice was sensual, soft, her sexual heat pulling at him. He couldn't believe it! Not again! Hadn't she rejected him? No other woman had affected him like she had. He was mad for her, enough to marry her and she'd thrown him away. Now she wanted back. He was suspicious, the pull was agony. He craved her, wanted her. Was dating her again worth the risk?

"Are you sure this is a good idea? I'm not up to being your discard again," he said, a tinge of caution in his voice. "Blaine, I was wrong and I'm sorry. Please forgive me," said Pat, her apology precise. Blaine thought for a moment, weakening.

"All right, Pat. Are you free tomorrow for lunch?" Her pulse quickened. "Yes." "Good. I'll meet you in the lobby here at the Plaza at 1:00." "I'll see you then," she enthused. "Bye for now." "Good bye, Patricia." The conversation ended. The wheels were in motion and she would have her way. Owen would be sorry. At least that was her hope.

Chapter 56

Showdown of Sorts

Pat was excited as she hurried to the Plaza. It was close to 1:00. She had taken special pains to look irresistible. Her heart beat faster as she entered the impressive lobby. Blaine was nowhere in sight. She stopped in the restroom for some last minute primping. She had purposely worn her hair down, remembering how much Blaine loved it. She added lip color and checked her outfit, a soft low-cut blouse and form-fitting skirt. Yes, she was ready to entice Mr. Courtman, resolving to win him back. Back to the lobby, she didn't have to wait long.

"Good afternoon, Patricia!" Blaine was at her side. He was Madison Avenue perfect in a three-piece suit, charcoal-grey, light blue shirt, burgundy tie, with a matching pocket hanky.

"Blaine. How wonderful to see you," she purred, her smile incandescent. He reached for her hand, kissing it gently. "I have a reservation," he said, leading her across the lobby. She caught a whiff of exotic aftershave as she accompanied him. His sophistication was alluring as ever. The host smiled as he saw them approach.

"Good afternoon, Mr. Courtman. Your table is ready sir," he announced. "If you will follow me," leading them to a beautifully appointed corner table. The host pulled a chair for Pat and waited while she sat. He did the same for Blaine and signaled a steward. "Enjoy your lunch, Mr. Courtman," he said, smiling. The steward poured water and placed cloth napkins in their laps.

"This restaurant serves one of the best lunches in Manhattan. Would you care for a cocktail?"

"I never drink on a show day," she said, winking. A waiter came.

"Good afternoon, Mr. Courtman. Would you care for a cocktail before lunch?" Blaine glanced at Pat. "I don't have a show today. I'll have a Beefeater Martini, dry with a twist, George. It is George, correct?" "Yes, Mr. Courtman. And what may I bring the lady?"

"May I have a Coca Cola with extra ice, please?" "Yes, of course." When the waiter had left, Blaine sat, studying Pat. "I never expected to see you again, Patricia. And yet, here you are," he said, with a slight edge. "What can I say? Running into you at Sardi's brought back a lot of memories and regret." "Regret? Why?" "I realize how foolish I was not giving you a fair chance. I want to make it up to you," she said.

Blaine's reserve was locked in; he continued cautiously. "Surely you've seen others since our break-up. I can't imagine you being alone after all these months." "What do you mean?"

"Oh Patricia, come on. You're stunning and talented. You exceed every other woman in the universe!"

"Oh Blaine, I was a fool. I screwed up! Are you going to hold that against me?" "I don't know. I have to think about it. You're beguiling but a heartbreaker, Patricia." The waiter arrived with beverages. "Are you ready to order, Mr. Courtman?"

"We haven't looked at menus as yet. What do you recommend?" "Our poached salmon with the chef's special dill sauce is excellent, or perhaps you'd prefer Oysters Rockefeller. And, our Tournedos Rossini, the best in the city."

"Patricia?" "The salmon sounds wonderful. I'll have it," she said, suddenly hungry. "I'll have the Oysters Rockefeller," said Blaine. "And another martini, George."

"So, where do we go with this, Patricia?" "Do you still want me? I'm offering myself to you," she said, trembling. "I don't need a business arrangement. I know of any number of attractive women a phone call away." Pat was stunned. "What do you take me for, Blaine? I'm not an arrangement," she said, starting to cry. Blaine tried to calm her. "Please, Patricia, don't do this."

"Couldn't we start fresh, take it slowly? I won't mess it up this time," she pleaded. "I don't know. I'll have to give it some thought." Pat sat frozen. She hadn't considered his reaction. The waiter returned with their orders and Blaine's second martini. They ate in silence. The wall around Blaine was high.

"Tell me about the show. The choreography is extraordinary." "It's demanding, a challenge," her voice catching. "He's a sure winner! On that point alone my investment was safe." "Blaine, I don't want to talk about the show. I want to discuss us," she said, trying to hold it together. "I'm not at all sure about this," he said firmly.

"Blaine, either you want to see me or you don't! How long will you be here?" "For a few months, but if you recall, distance was never an issue for me where you were concerned." "So I'm supposed to wait for you to call?" "Patricia, maybe we can have dinner soon. I'll have to check with my secretary." Blaine's business-like approach was distressing.

Putting down her fork she stared him squarely in the face. "I remember many things about you, Blaine, but I don't remember your being cruel!" "Oh, you think me cruel? What about leading me on until I was hopelessly in love, then dropping me like a hot rock?" Blaine's voice rose until he saw George approaching.

"Would you care for dessert, Mr. Courtman?" Blaine glanced at Pat, who shook her head. "I think not, George. Please bring the check." "Yes, Mr. Courtman. I trust lunch was satisfactory?" Blaine nodded approvingly. George walked away. Pat waited until he left. Turning to Blaine, she was livid.

"Well, Mr. Courtman, you certainly have everyone under control! Thanks for lunch," she said rising. Blaine rose, taking her hand. "Patricia, it would be so easy to fall under your spell, but I won't be hurt again. I hope you understand."

Pat readied her come back. "I'll have to give it some thought," she snapped, pulling her hand away. "Ciao!" Without another word, she left. Blaine felt a wash of pain engulf him. 'God, I love that woman.'

Sunday, March 1st brought legions of colleagues, fans and friends to the Shubert. As the theater began to fill, the old guard and new arrived to pay tribute to one of the brightest stars Broadway had ever known.

The stage was bare save for two enormous floral sprays, one on each side of the speaker's podium. The arrangements were Vera's favorite blooms—gladiolas, mums, peonies, and sunflowers—in various shades of gold, maroon, white and yellow, her preferred colors. Overhead, an enlarged photo of her hung for all to see. Taken at the height of her success, the black and white was the size of a picture window. The image was pure Vera in one of her signature roles.

In the lobby, floral arrangements were placed along either side, from box office to house, with hand-written notes of condolence and tribute from prominent persons of every profession. Expressions of respect came from the mayor's office, film, radio, TV personalities, the press, national politicians and colleagues from all areas of show business and around the world. The one-time unknown from the plains of Nebraska had become one of the most acknowledged in New York Theatre.

A palatable reverence was felt as colleagues met. The Kaplan-Maggli organization was seated in the first few rows. Joe Kaplan was noticeably soft spoken and pale as he attempted cordiality. Key note speaker, Vincent Lehrman, sat down front. Others invited to share remembrances were Sandy Levin, Vincent Sardi and Dick and Dana Landry. Griff was asked to stage manage, lights and sound. Owen Matthews slipped quietly into the back of the house just before 1:00.

The entire cast of *Centipede* was grouped in one section of the house. Pat, Mally, Jonas, and Phillipe sat together and former gypsies from Owen and Vera's many hits throughout the years were present. Reporters were told to refrain from taking photos during the program.

At a few minutes before 1:00, a recorded medley of Vera's hits filled the house. Her three-octave range caused spontaneous applause throughout, as the music continued. At 1:00, the house lights dimmed. Lehrman rose and proceeded to the stage. A hush, then a spotlight on him. At the podium he took a moment to look at Vera's picture, her image moving; he turned to the crowd.

"About 20 years ago, I was mesmerized by a young woman, belting out song after song in a tiny bistro in Greenwich Village. The voice was extraordinary, unlike any I ever heard then or since. This young woman's charisma and physical beauty convinced me she was a star in the making. Convincing her was another story. New to New York City, this fresh upstart from the Nebraska plains was feisty, grounded and stubborn to boot! She was coltish, guarded and tough to take in hand. She desperately needed coaching, grooming, guidance and a mentor. Well, as you all know, or have guessed, I was that guy. But I couldn't do the daunting task alone. I needed someone brilliant, someone who could inspire, fine-tune and bring to Broadway a future star, one we all came to know as Vera Daniels. That someone was Owen Matthews." Wild applause and whistles burst forth from the gypsies. Seconds ticked by as the crowd slowly came back to order.

Lehrman continued. "As we all know, Mr. Matthews can put the shine on anyone or show, which he proceeded to do. He was not fully convinced that Miss Daniels could take Broadway. I practically had to strong-arm him, which I did. The rest is history. Miss Daniels and Mr. Matthews made Broadway history with no less than a half dozen major hits as collaborators. It was and always will be the Great White Way's finest of times. Now, that voice is silent and we will never look upon Vera Daniels again. So Vera honey, if you're listening, hats off to you, one of the greatest! Love you."

A resounding applause rose as attendees stood, some cheering and whistling, some stomping. Lehrman returned to his seat. Following his appearance, other guest speakers took the stage one by one as the tributes continued.

Owen listened and reminisced. Vera had been his greatest challenge, his finest accomplishment. He remembered the excitement of birthing their shows, the triumphs, the hours together working the process and their personal life. That aspect was the more challenging. They just didn't mesh domestically, never considered children and were two powerhouse egos under the same roof. Throughout their marriage, Owen and Vera fought and made love with equal intensity. Now, she was gone, a victim of her excesses and some of his.

Vincent Sardi was the last to speak. At that moment, Owen slipped quietly out of the theatre. He needed a drink and Miss McNeil. Booze would anesthetize, sex would distract. Unaccustomed to feeling regret, there it was, deep within. Knowing it was a disquieting place to be.

Chapter 57

A Change of Heart

Pat was crushed by Blaine's ambivalence. Owen threw her away; Blaine was stand offish, her hope for a new start in serious question. Adding insult to injury, she was shamed into going to Vera's Memorial by her pals, reluctantly agreeing to attend. They sat midway in the house.

Distracted, Pat glanced around looking for Owen. She assumed he'd be there. Her heart raced when she spotted him at the back of the house. Missing him was unbearable! A light tap on her shoulder brought her back, the concern on Mally's face, obvious. "Pat, you okay?" "All this praise for Vera just reminds me of Owen," she sniffed. "Stop sulking for a minute and focus on the occasion." Mally, annoyed, had grown weary of Pat's constant "poor me."

Pat was going to stay with Jonas and Phillipe, indefinitely. Discussing it first with her family, they agreed, it would be an easier and safer commute. It was working well. They appreciated help with rent and Pat could save money for a place of her own. Moving in with her two best male friends was a relief.

At the end of the memorial, the audience filed out, expressing condolences to Joe, red-eyed and rigid. When the crowd thinned, Jonas suggested a drink, their group agreed. Griff stayed back to wrap up and would join them later.

It was another blustery night as they hurried to the Taft. Shaking off coats, they claimed a corner table. It was good to be together. "Hey kids! How are you tonight?" It was Andy Klein, the bartender. "Andy, how goes it? Here on a Sunday?" "I'm covering for a pal. His wife went into labor this morning. It kind of gets me circulating. What brings you in?"

"We were at the Daniels' memorial. Didn't you dance in a couple of her shows?" "I did indeed. Vera Daniels, what a legend! She kept me working for years, until I tore up my knees! Had to quit," he said, with a shrug. Jonas continued.

"I remember when you had your accident. God, what a nightmare! It happened recently to one of our own back in Detroit. Do you remember Jerry Thompson?" "Absolutely, he was a strong performer, if memory serves." Jonas changed gears.

"Andy, these are my friends, Pat Byrne, Mally Edwards and my lover, Phillipe Danier." "Great meeting you all, what're you having?" The girls ordered wine, Jonas, beer on tap, and Phillipe, a Dubonnet. "Be right back with your drinks." Jonas' eyes followed Andy as he walked away. "Andy was one of the best. He was lead dancer in my first show for Owen. Vera already had a few hits."

"Tell us, Jonas," pushed Phillipe. "What happened to Vera to end her career?" Jonas, reluctant to mention Owen in front of Pat, eased his way. "Vera's rise was rapid and spectacular. She and Owen's love affair began with their first hit. They got married during the run of their second. Troubles started after they got hitched. Can you imagine two mega egos under the same roof? It became ugly," he said knowingly. "Owen strayed. Vera drank. Owen left. Vera drank more and refused a divorce. You get the picture?"

Andy returned with drinks. Raising his glass, Jonas made a timely toast, "To Vera, you had a fabulous run!" They clinked and sipped. Pat held back, Vera was off her radar. Mally noticed and changed the subject.

"How do you like living with these fabulous, gorgeous guys?" "I love it. They're great roomies and, I might add, Monsieur Phillipe is a fabulous chef!" "It's got to be better than commuting to the Bronx. I worried about you on those trains." Pat gave a hug. "Thanks, Ma!"

"Can anyone join?" Griff approached and caught Andy's eye. "Hey Griff, what's your pleasure, "the usual?" "I'll have a Smirnoff martini, dirty, straight up, no ice, please." "Got it!" Griff pulled up a chair next to his wife. The mood was festive in spite of the solemnity of the occasion.

"How did it go, Griff?" "From my view, great." "I was impressed, the guest speakers were spot on, especially Lehrman," Jonas added.

Griff continued. "Floral arrangements were sent to Joe's home and office. It's been a rough couple of weeks for him; he was barely able to get into the cab on his own."

"How sad," said Mally. "He seems like he's all bluster until you know him. You know, rough exterior, softy inside." "My wife is very perceptive. Joe is all business, but if you are in trouble, he's the first to help. I've known him for years. He was a terrific friend after my divorce," said Griff.

Andy returned with Griff's drink. "Would any of you like a second?" "I think we'll pass," said Jonas, tugging at Phillipe. "Are you coming, Irish?" Pat took a last swallow. "I'm ready to go, guys." "We'll take care of the tab," said Jonas. "Thanks guys," said Mally. The three left, leaving Mally and Griff to sip and reflect.

"Such a sad end to a brilliant career," said Mally. "Yes. I had the pleasure of working with Vera on two of her later productions. She was a pro through and through. Would you care for another white wine, Darling?" "Yes, I could use it tonight. Pat has been a handful lately." "What's going on?" Griff signaled Andy, pointing to Mally's empty glass.

"Pat and Owen broke up and she's not handling it well." "Really? I didn't know." "I'm worried about her." Griff took her hand, giving it a squeeze. "Darling, Pat's over 21 and responsible for her own actions. Worrying does nothing for either of you." "Yes, I know, but Pat has that Irish wiring and it short circuits a lot."

Andy returned with a second glass of wine. "Is there anything else, Griff?" "Yes, bring me another just as dirty," he laughed. "You bet. Be right up." They were silent for a moment. "I warned Pat last year about Owen, I knew she could get hurt." Griff moved in close. "Who can explain chemistry, huh?" They kissed.

During the memorial, Owen had left the Shubert and grabbed a cab for Stephanie's. Scotch and flesh were needed. He let himself in the building and at her door he rang the bell. He waited and waited. At last, she opened the door.

"Owen. What a surprise! I wasn't expecting you this afternoon." "I've never needed an invitation," he snapped. "I have company, you should have called first!" "Is that right?" A large stranger walked toward him.

"Steph, is there some kind of trouble?" The guy was good looking, over six feet, muscular, his manner like a bouncer. "Owen, this is my editor, Carl Norris. Carl, Owen Matthews." Carl extended his hand, but not Owen, who stood scrutinizing the hulk. "I've heard about you," said Carl, trying to make conversation. Owen gave him the once over. "I'll call you later, Miss McNeil," he said, miffed to the bone. He left, thirsty, horny and at full speed.

"What the fuck, Steph? Now I'm your editor?" Stephanie reached up, giving him a deep, torrid kiss. He responded by grasping her ass, pushing into her. "Oh Baby, let's get on with it!"

The week wore on, the show packing them in. Pat had lost her edge, concerning Griff. He called her in. "Pat, what's going on? You're not doing your best. That's not like you."

Pat sat stone-faced, fiddling with a sleeve. "Nothing's going on," she said unconvincingly. "I'm going through a low energy period at the moment. I haven't been feeling very well." "Pat, it's not my job to pry but when your performance is not up to par, I must inquire. Mally told me about your break-up." "It's not a secret Griff, he's moved on." "How do we remedy this? Do you need some time off? Mally covered your spot before and could do it again if necessary." Pat looked aghast. Griff continued.

"What concerns me is your mental state. Are you able to fulfill your contract?" "For heaven's sake, Griff, I'm not mentally unbalanced. I'm down-in-the-dumps!" Griff walked over and put his hands on her shoulders. "It's all right, Pat. Tell me what you want to do. It's your call." "Maybe I should take a couple of weeks off, if that's okay?"

Griff agreed, "I think some rest and stepping back from the show is a good call. I'll announce you're taking some personal time. It's not out of line. You've been with the show over six months. We'll wave your one-year and make an exception. Don't worry. I'll handle the Kaplan office and Owen, if need be."

"Thank you so much, Griff. I know I've been a drag. Even your wife thinks so," she admitted.

"What others think isn't as important as you sorting this out. Starting Monday, you're on leave." Pat rose and hugged Griff. "Griff, you're a true friend. If anyone asks where I can be reached, feel free to give them Jonas' number." "I'll do that."

Pat left Griff's office and was off to Toffenetti's to join Jonas and Phillipe. Feeling relief for time off, she resolved to keep Owen out of thoughts. Her resolve was shaky at best.

Saturday's shows were packed and audiences highly responsive. What a great way to end the eight-show week. Unknown to Pat, Blaine was in the audience for the second performance. Following the show he waited amongst the throng of fans, hoping to spot her.

"Patricia! Wait up!" "Mr. Courtman, what a surprise! What are you doing here?" She felt edgy and unforgiving until he took her hand, kissing it gently. "I came to see the show, but mostly to see you," he soothed. Pat blushed in spite of herself. "Well, thank you. Now, I really must be going," she said, turning. He caught her sleeve.

"Would you like to have dinner tomorrow night?" Pat stopped short. Surprised and totally unprepared for his invitation, she looked back. Blaine continued. "The last time I saw you, lunch didn't go so well. I'd like to make it up to you," he said, his charm drawing her in. "Did your secretary clear your calendar? I mean your sudden availability is confusing, Blaine."

"I deserve the rebuke. Please come to the Plaza tomorrow night for cocktails. We could meet at 7:00 and dine following. I'd love to take you to Club 21. Tony Bennett is performing." Pat's mind was swimming. Thrilled that Blaine had taken this turn. "I'd love to come," she said, earnestly. Blaine smiled. "Then it's settled. In the meantime, may I find you a cab?" "No, thanks, I'll walk from here. Where I'm staying isn't far."

"See you tomorrow at 7:00, Patricia. Come to Suite A on the 30th Floor, I look forward to spending time with you." They parted. All the way home, Pat was floating. How could she resist. Blaine wanted to see her. 'He's a perfect opportunity to let Owen go, he deserves it.' It was time to move in a new direction. Blaine Courtman was her compass and, perhaps, a new port.

Chapter 58

Waterloo

Owen wasn't pleased with the brush-off. McNeil was playing him; nobody was allowed to do that. He dialed her number and waited. Hearing his voice, she was contrite. "Owen, I'm sorry about the other day. Carl and I had material to go over for Sunday's edition. It's been crazy at work." "You put me off, Miss McNeil. No one does that." "You were unexpected. I didn't have a chance to call." Owen changed gears.

"Drop it. I feel like going out. Let's go to Club 21." "Oh, I'd love that, should I meet you?" "No, I'll pick you up. How about 6:00? You can fix me a drink first." "Fine, see you." Owen heard a dial tone. 'I'll show her,' he thought smugly. 'No one passes on me.'

Griff informed Jonas, Pat was taking personal time. They agreed she needed to back off to clear her head. The word was passed to Mally and Nora, their need for a brush-up, unnecessary, having recently covered her.

Pat was ebullient as she prepared for evening. Jonas and Phillipe watched with interest as she danced in her undies. Even to gay eyes, she was stunning, waltzing past them in her skimpiest black bra and bikinis.

"Anita's gonna get her kicks tonight," sang Jonas, gleefully. Pat broke into steps reminiscent of *West Side Story* shouting, "You bet your sweet ass, boys! *Ole!*" They howled as she continued to prep for what she hoped would be a romantic night. Recalling their previous affair, Blaine appreciated easy access. She fully intended to cooperate, selecting a sheath, slit above the knee, the bodice low-cut. He would be pleased.

In the past they had been daring, imaginative, insatiable. She succumbed to oral sex at a party in Houston, hidden, with guests a few feet away! Intense nights at his Vancouver condo, wantonly indulging for hours, his sudden dominance, in Salt Lake City as he aggressively took her in the backseat of his limo. The memories were delicious, her want growing. Next would be a cab to paradise, at the Plaza.

Owen showered, shaved and slipped on a sports coat. Grabbing smokes, lighter, keys and money clip, he didn't bother with a top coat. Truth be told, he preferred the comfort of rehearsal clothes.

Cabs were plentiful at Central Park West and 67th. During the ride, he imagined Stephanie nude, breasts perky, skin, soft to the touch; her sounds of pleasure as he tongued her. His briefs began to tighten with each tantalizing thought.

He pressed the button for her floor and was shortly at her place. He rang, he waited, waited, his horniness painful. Stephanie was at the door in a see-through negligee, a long silk scarf around her neck. Smiling impishly, she took his hand, leading him to the sofa. Without word, she pushed him down and undressed him. Dominant and in charge, she would give him what he craved.

"Roll over." Owen was breathless with excitement as she tied his wrists behind him with the scarf, the binding tight, just the way he liked it. She matched her need for erotic play with ingenuity. Rolling him back, she knelt, hands massaging his erection. Gloating, she enjoyed her power over him. He was panting, close to climax and, she stopped! 'Such fun, he's begging.' "Does the famous director want to come?" Owen moaned, "Fuck, yes!" She continued to goad him, a smile on her face. "I'm not sure you're ready. Want to try a little harder?" She chuckled and stroked faster. "Yes, that's it! Oh fuck, yes, Miss McNeil," his explosion consuming him. This time, she had the control, relishing every second of her plan. Going to the bar, she poured Dewar's on the rocks, lit a Camel and glanced back. Owen, prone, was still recovering. As he opened his eyes, she was there, a drink in one hand, a smoke in the other. Swinging his legs down, he managed to sit upright, wrists still bound.

Setting the glass down, she snapped, "You came for a drink, remember?" Taking a puff she put the cigarette in his mouth. An immense grin on his face, he took a deep drag, the smoke trailing from his nostrils. While removing the scarf, she whispered, "How was it?" "Best ever, Miss McNeil!" Reaching for the glass, he took a large swallow and frowned. "What's this shit?" "Scotch, what do you think?" "Tastes like swill, McNeil." "It's Dewar's, something wrong?"

Putting down his drink, he reached for her, kissing her aggressively. His hands, in overdrive, reached for her breasts. "Your turn, let me tie you," he insisted. "Owen, stop it!" "What's wrong?" "I'm hungry, Owen. You promised 21, remember?" Finishing his smoke, he gathered his clothes. "From the way you took me, I figured you were horny as hell," he muttered, slightly annoyed.

"You know, just once we could get together without sex." Owen, slipping on his pants, stopped, his look, incredulous. "I thought that's what you want! You never seem to get enough." "I'm more than a quick fuck, Owen. I have other goals and interests," she said frostily. "Well pardon me, Miss McNeil. Let's skip the rhetoric and get going," he said, clearly pissed.

Stephanie dressed. When ready, she came into the living room. Owen was on the sofa with another drink and smoke. "I'm ready. Shall we?" Owen stubbed his smoke and chugged his drink. The air tense between them as they left. A cab was nearby. "Driver, Club 21, please."

It was 7:00 sharp. Pat took the elevator to Blaine's suite. As she knocked, the door opened and Blaine was there, handsome as always, a feast for her eyes. "Come in, Patricia." He greeted her with a kiss on the cheek. "Welcome to my New York home." He helped her off with her coat. "Would you like a cocktail, wine, champagne?" "I'd love some champagne."

Blaine led her to the salon, exquisite in every detail. "You look astonishing tonight, but then, you always do," he said softly. A bottle of Veuve Clicquot was chilled and ready to enjoy. Popping the cork he poured two flutes, handing one to her and toasting, "To a new beginning." Pat took a sip, the bubbles tickling. She studied Blaine carefully. "Why did you change your mind?"

Setting his glass down, he took her chin in hand and kissed her gently. "I want to start over." Pat settled back, grateful for his change of heart. Blaine moved in closer, putting his arm around her shoulder. "I couldn't stay away, but, let's take our time." "Yes," said Pat, finishing her champagne. "May I have another?"

"Perhaps we should have dinner. I have a table reserved floor side at Club 21. Tony Bennett has been packing them in and their steaks are the best." "Oh, I love Tony Bennett and I'm ravenous!" "Good, my car is waiting. As I recall, you enjoy limos." Pat blushed at the memory of one ride in Salt Lake. The night was brisk, more snow flurries slowing traffic. Minutes later, they arrived at 21 and checked their coats at the door. Heads turned as the host showed them to their table. Blaine ordered drinks.

"I've never been here," said Pat with enthusiasm. "The entertainment is top notch, all the big names play here." "I've loved Tony Bennett for years. My folks have all his record albums," said Pat, clearly impressed with Blaine's choice. "If you enjoy a good steak, this is the place," said Blaine, with authority. "I do and I will have one, if it's all right." "My dear, Patricia, where you're concerned, the sky's the limit. What's your preference, a filet?" The maitre d' arrived.

"Mr. Courtman, how good of you to dine with us this evening." "Thank you, Arthur. This is my guest, Miss Byrne and her first visit to 21." "Wonderful, certainly something to celebrate." Snapping his fingers at a nearby waiter, he said, "Lewis, champagne for our guests." In moments, the server returned with a bottle of chilled Moet. The cork gave a healthy pop. Blaine raised his glass and intertwined arms with Pat. "To new beginnings," he whispered. Locking eyes, they each took a sip, aware only of each other.

Across the room, Owen and Stephanie made small talk, an apparent cool air between them. The evening started with promise, but had turned chilly. "Let's order dinner. I'm absolutely starved." Owen caught the eye of their waiter. "Good evening, sir, may I take your order?" Owen glanced at Stephanie. "How about steak?"

"Sounds perfect, please make mine medium." "I'll have rare," added Owen. "Your entrée comes with a choice of tossed salad, Caesar, or coleslaw, potatoes au gratin, twice baked, or French fries." Stephanie ordered Caesar and twice baked, Owen, the cole slaw and fries. There was silence between them.

"Would you care for a cigarette, while we wait?" She declined. "So how's the show going? I hear you're sold out for months," she said, feigning interest. "Great, better than expected. There's also international interest." "Oh Owen, that's sounds intriguing, where?" "Japan." "I hope it works out." Owen changed the subject.

"I'd like you this enthusiastic about us," he prompted. "I sense a distance, Miss McNeil. What the fuck is going on? First you dismiss me when I stop by unexpectedly and tonight, you weren't interested in my pleasuring you." "As I said, I was hungry, you expected sex."

Dinner arrived, much to her relief. The steaks were sizzling, the aroma beckoning. Food was on her mind, not his. She dug in, the filet, perfect! Owen reached across, taking her wrist. "I asked a question, McNeil. What's with you?" She pulled away and set down her fork. "Stop goading me, Matthews. I'm eating dinner, not in court! You invited me, remember?"

Owen sat stone-faced. He was invisible, as she ate. Glancing, she noticed he hadn't touched his dinner. "What's the matter? Aren't you hungry?" Owen reached for a cigarette. Before he could light, she took it from his lips. "You know I can't stand smoke around food, wait 'til we've finished." "Oh, so now, you're telling me when and where I can smoke?" Stephanie continued eating. "You're pissing me off. Answer my question!" His voice louder, adjacent diners stared.

She put down her fork. "All right, since you insist, there's something." He took another cigarette, lighting in spite of her, blowing in her direction. "Well?"

"I've been seeing someone, a colleague at the *Times*. I want to see him exclusively, now." "Oh, is that right?" "Yes, I don't want to sneak around." "Well, you're over 21, fuck whoever you want." "I want more than just fucking, someone with integrity, intelligence and values." Owen rose.

"We have nothing more to discuss. Buy your own fucking dinner." Pushing his chair in, he called to the waiter. "Yes, sir, is there a problem?" "The steak you brought me is tough, the lady's fine with hers. She's buying." On the way out, he noticed a stunning couple locked in conversation, oblivious to others. He recognized the woman. What the fuck? Pat? Who's she with?' His mind raced. He had to be sure. It had to be now!

Chapter 59

Further Doings

Owen turned in their direction. 'Pat with another man, unthinkable!' At their table, he stopped and stared at her. Surprised to see him, she mustered a greeting; casual on the surface, a knot in her stomach. "Owen. This is a surprise. What are you doing here?" Without invitation, Owen pulled out a chair and sat down. "I might ask you the same, Pat." His usual cool displaced, he looked the stranger over. The guy was handsome, impeccable, GQ all the way.

Pat looked from Owen to Blaine, her mind working the next step. She needn't have worried as Blaine took the reins. With his usual aplomb he turned to Pat. "Patricia, would you kindly introduce us?" "Blaine, this is Owen Matthews, director and choreographer of *Centipede*. Owen, this is Blaine Courtman, of Courtman Enterprises." "How do you do, Mr. Matthews? I am a great fan of your work," he said cordially.

"Oh? What do you know of my work? Are you a Broadway devotee?" Edgy, aloof and definitely off his game, Owen seemed loaded for bear. Pat tensed, given Owen's temper. She didn't want a scene. "As a matter of fact, I wanted to meet you for some time," said Blaine.

Trying to reel in the obvious tension, Pat continued, "Owen, Mr. Courtman is the chief investor of *Centipede*. He and his partner, Gregory Morgan of Houston provided the principal capital for the show." Owen's face was priceless, he took a different tack. "I had no idea. How did that happen?" Blaine took over.

"I've been friends with Joe and Lenny for years, but it started months ago. I caught *Bravo Business* last year in Jacksonville, Florida.

I was impressed with your work and wanted to meet your lead dancer. Patricia was kind and gracious to me and several colleagues when I brought them to the show. When I read your new show would star this lovely lady, I mentioned it to Greg, who knows a sure winner. Greg saw your show and insisted on meeting Patricia. Once I introduced them, he was hooked! Miss Byrne is special; I hope you appreciate her as much as we." Owen's off guard smile was noticeable.

"Of course I do! I know a brilliant dancer when I see one and Pat is the absolute best," he said defensively. Pat looked surprised. This heavy concentration of superlatives was rare. "You obviously have instinct for selecting the best. Patricia is the glue of *Centipede* and the ensemble is superb," Blaine said with respect.

"Thank you Mr. Courtman. Did you know we are considering an international engagement in Tokyo?" "Yes, it's a solid idea. Japanese audiences love American musical theatre. I've done trade with them for years. They are sound economically and very progressive. If you're looking for further investment, I might be interested, Mr. Matthews. May I buy you a cocktail?"

"No thanks. I have to get going. Pat, I'll call you tomorrow," he said, slightly shaken. Blaine stood, extending his hand. "It was a pleasure meeting you, Owen." "Thank you."

As he started to go, he glanced at Pat, who was fixed on Blaine. "Good night, Pat." She failed to respond. Walking out of the club, Owen felt a chill hit his face. Signaling a cab, reality hit hard. He had messed up, Pat had moved on. 'Heaven help me if she leaves the show.'

They enjoyed dinner and the show. Tony Bennett was superb; he did several encores for the appreciative crowd. At the end of the show they retrieved their coats and waited for the limo.

The doorman signaled Keith, Blaine's driver, who pulled forward. When they were on the way, Blaine kissed her gently and whispered, "Would you come back with me?" "Oh yes." "Keith, back to the Plaza. Please."

Arriving at the hotel, Blaine stopped at the front desk. "Good evening Fred, any messages?" He checked the mailbox and handed Blaine a few. "Is there anything else, sir?" "No, thank you, Fred. Goodnight."

Blaine took Pat's hand, leading her to the penthouse elevator. In minutes, they were in Suite A.

"Come in Patricia, enjoy the fire." "I love fireplaces, especially in winter." Slipping off her shoes, she rubbed her cold feet together. "It's lovely being here." "I'm happy you are, I've missed you." "Would you like a brandy or perhaps a glass of wine?" "Wine please." He poured a Courvoisier for himself and Vouvray for Pat and sat next to her.

Gently swirling the snifter, he stopped for a moment, touching her glass. "To you, Patricia," he whispered. Taking a sip, his eyes never left hers. Pat followed, tasting the chilled wine. "This is delicious, Blaine. What is it?" "It's a Vouvray from my vineyard in the Loire, a very unique region in France. I'm pleased you like it." "I envy your opportunity to travel, your exposure to the finer things." "You just need the right opportunity to do so," he said smiling.

They sat in silence for a time, enjoying the fire and each other. "You're beautiful, Patricia. I'm still in love with you." Taking her hands, he kissed each finger tenderly, never shifting his gaze. "Let's make love," he whispered. Without a word, they walked to the bedroom.

Kissing her deeply, his tongue traced her mouth. His hands roaming, her hair fell to her shoulders, pins giving way. A tug of the zipper next, the dress loosened and slipped off. Pat stepped out, her body taut with anticipation. Blaine began exploring. 'It's been too long, I mustn't hurry,' he thought, gently touching the lace. He squeezed each nipple, bringing a sigh, Pat eager for more. The gentle touch of his hand brought ecstasy. He was persuasive and tender; unhooking her bra, her breasts were now his. He removed her panties and backed her to the bed. The coverlet was soft against her skin as Blaine's passion and tongue took over. He was intense one minute, delicate the next, Pat writhing and softly moaning. Relishing each sound, he paused to undress, his erection outlined in his black briefs. "Please come inside," she begged.

The pressure was excruciating as they connected, each riding a wave of total pleasure. It was a perfect duet, an incomparable match of pure joy and wanton lust as they peaked. They lay together for a time, enjoying the warmth of their reunion. He kissed and stroked her, she responded with tears. "Patricia, what is it?" "You're so kind and forgiving," she whimpered.

Blaine gently held her, his voice soft and reassuring. "This is the way it's going to be from now on. You'll never want for anything, ever again." Somehow, from the depths of her being, she knew it was true.

Chapter 60

Moving On

Owen was informed Pat was on a leave, an added blow to his already bruised ego. He'd been replaced by a civilian, not an artist like himself. 'The guy has more money than God,' he reasoned! He was irked, jealous, but admittedly certain his wandering eye had destroyed the good he had. One question remained. "Would Pat stay with *Centipede*? After agonizing concern, he called Jonas. The phone rang several times.

"Jonas, here." "This is Owen." "Boss, this is a surprise," he said, caught off guard. "I need Pat. Do you know where to reach her? Her parents told me she moved out." Jonas glanced at Pat, her scowl said it all. "She's rooming with us now, Owen. She's out right now. Can I take a message?"

"Tell her to call me. I have something to discuss. Can you do that for me, Jonas?" "Of course, Owen, I'll let her know." Jonas hung the receiver. "Irish, what's up? This is a first. You don't want to talk to the boss?"

"I'm not ready. I've backed off. I intend to keep my distance from Owen." "Okay, whatever you say." Changing the subject, he brightened. "I trust your date with the millionaire went well." Pat stretched and smiled. "As a matter of fact, he's a slice of heaven, perfection, amazing!"

"Are you kidding me? This is the best," he said, picking her up and whirling her around. "Phillipe, come in here!" He hugged her, in his inimitable fashion and shouted, "Anita got her kicks last night!" Phillipe came bounding in. "More than kicks, Jonas, we reconciled. I have someone who genuinely cares and we've decided to try again."

"Did you hear that? Irish is on her game again!" Phillipe kissed Pat. "This is wonderful news, I'm happy for you." "Me too," said Pat, glowing. "We're going to try again, but I have to finish with Owen." "He left a message to call. Do what you will, Irish!" "Oh, I'll call all right—when I'm good and ready!" "That's our girl! I love your new tact! Enjoy your time off and get as much mattress time in as you can," he said with a wink. "Jonas!" They all broke into gales of laughter.

Pat reluctantly phoned Owen a few days later. His voice was cold, she had to be firm. "I would like to meet with you, Pat." "I'm not sure that's a good idea, unless it's business. What's this about?" There was a long pause. "Meet me at the Taft Sunday night. It won't take long." "I'd prefer during the day, say for lunch?" There was another pause.

"If you insist," he said, gruffly. "I do insist, Owen, where?" He thought for a moment. "How about Le Cheval Blanc on East 45th Street? It's quiet and good." "Very well, I'll see you on Sunday at 1:00." 'He'll no longer spin my world,' she thought.

Owen's team met at Kaplan-Maggli. As they were seated, staff associates brought refreshments and French pastry. Joe and Lenny started the meeting, Joe, first.

"I've asked you here to propose something exciting. We're currently engaged in talks with a prominent Japanese producer, Hiri Watanabe. He's interested in bringing *Centipede* to Tokyo next fall. Mr. Watanabe attended opening night and was taken with the show. I've discussed this with Lenny, our investors and associates, but we need more capital to make it happen. Morgan and Courtman have agreed to meet with us."

Lenny cut in, "Economically, it looks like a sound call. It could fill our coffers, providing funds for two national companies in the future. Mr. Watanabe has a great track record in Japan and internationally." "Lenny's right. We need to make this happen," said Joe. "We need your feedback. Griff, what are your thoughts?" "If our production is any indication of success, another company and one far reaching, could prove artistically and economically satisfying. Owen?"

"I'm interested, it sounds like a great opportunity, but to do this right, I would select those leaving the New York cast and staff to carry it through." "I agree," said Joe. "We want to send the best production stage manager in the biz. Griff, how do feel about a stint in Japan?" "I would welcome the opportunity, Joe, I have a few suggestions." Owen smiled, knowing his confidence in Griff was well-earned. "What are your thoughts?" Griff continued.

"Mally could take the dance lead, leaving Pat in New York. Dick Landry could take my spot. He's ready. Jonas is fully able to remount the production. Phillipe would make an excellent assistant and dance captain. I think Chad Chapman is an excellent choice to partner Mally. Nora Blake and Jeff Jenkins are ready to move up as well. We would need new swings."

"Your suggestions are very sound, right, Owen?" Owen, distracted, was thinking more about Pat. He might have a chance to win her back, but he would have to plan carefully. If Courtman was the main money source, he couldn't rock the boat, at least not now. "Owen, are you with us? Your thoughts, please," said Joe. Grabbing a cigarette, Owen rejoined the meeting.

"I think all of Griff's suggestions are sound. With financial commitment in place, we could set auditions for next summer, late August." "Great! For now, let's adjourn and work out the details with Watanabe and his associates. We'll contact Courtman and Morgan. In the meantime, enjoy your weekend!"

Pat had decided to walk to Le Cheval Blanc. It was a mild day, snowing lightly and she wanted the exercise. Along the way she thought about what to say to her former lover and mentor; he could be unpredictable. 'Would there be problems?' Jonas had encouraged her to stand her ground and get it over with.

At the door, pleasant aromas greeted her. Entering, she spotted Owen at a table in the back, a copy of *Variety* in hand. She was about to speak when he looked up. "Have a seat, Pat. I was just finishing up the week's totals. He folded the paper and set it aside, gazing at her intently. A waiter approached.

"*Bonjour, mademoiselle.* May I bring you a beverage? Owen had already consumed a scotch, indicating need for a second. Pat was chilled. "I'd love coffee with cream and sugar on the side, please." The waiter placed an empty cup in front of her. "I'm brewing some fresh," he said, "I'll be back shortly." Pat shrugged off her jacket and unwound her scarf.

The tension was obvious; eye contact, difficult. Owen's gaze was uncomfortable as she sat fidgeting. The waiter returned with coffee and Owen's drink. Pat found steam from the coffee soothing against her face. Owen took a swig, put down the glass and reached for her hand. She reluctantly allowed it. "Pat, I wanted to see you, because I need to clear the air. This is not easy for me." Pat took her hand away. Picking up her coffee, she took a long sip. The brew was comforting. "Clear what air, Owen?" "I have been a fool, I fucked up royally," he said softly. Pat put down the cup, her demeanor changing instantly.

"Why? Why did you do it?" "It was a game, my ego in overdrive. You were with your family. She was a challenge, nothing more," he admitted. "And yet you continued. You had an affair behind my back. How was she, Owen? Was she enough to throw me away?" Pat was trying to keep the lid on, her temper rising.

"In the end, I was wrong. I'm willing to admit that." "So you think admitting you were fucking someone else makes what you did okay? I'm not buying it! I should have seen it coming; I was warned about you from the beginning. You were a god to me, an icon! I was head-over-heels in love with you and you allowed it! You kept me on the string for your convenience." "That's not true. I loved you. I still do! I'm asking for another chance," he said, his voice cracking. "It's too late, we're done! I'm done! I'm not sure I want to continue the show."

"You can't mean that. I built the show around you! You are *Centipede*! Anyone can see why I made you the star, the standout. This is your career launcher! If you don't want me, fine. But don't be foolish enough to throw away your star opportunity because I behaved like an asshole."

"I don't know, Owen. I'm going to have to think on this. Blaine and I are together now." "What the fuck does your being with some rich guy have to do with your obligation to fulfill your contract?" "It doesn't have anything to do with it. Blaine isn't just some rich guy. He made the financing possible for your show. To tell you the truth, you'd be sunk without him."

"Oh great, throw that at me! We're talking about you're staying with the show, not about screwing this guy!" "Careful, Owen. You had best watch who you're dealing with." "Is that a threat?" Owen had lost all civility, his anger causing heads to turn. "Not a threat, just reality. I'm through with you and I need time to think about whether or not to stay with *Centipede*."

"I'm done being reasonable, Pat!" "So am I. You'll have my decision by the end of the week!" Without another word, she took her coat, scarf and left. Owen sat motionless, his pulse pounding. He had pushed away the thought of Pat leaving the show; but now, it was possible. His world seemed to be collapsing, a world he had built, now close to implosion.

Chapter 61

A Forward Move

Owen was concerned. Attempting to apologize had failed. Pat, on the other hand, felt triumphant! She held the line without regret and had moved on to Blaine. He was wonderful in every way and now she had another chance. Blaine was ammunition. After all, he and Greg Morgan were chief financial backers of *Centipede*. For the first time, her future did not depend on Owen.

Blaine invited Pat for a weekend at his upstate retreat. Among his holdings throughout the U.S., he owned property overlooking the Hudson River, two hours north of the city. The cabin, originally built by his grandfather, had been updated recently; top-of-the-line kitchen, luxury bathroom with sauna, sunken tub with whirlpool and a master bedroom with stone fireplace. A wraparound screened porch looked on a tranquil scene, woods stretching in all directions. Just a short walk away was a bluff overlooking the valley. It was perfect!

Early Friday afternoon, the limo pulled up to Blaine's get-away. Keith Noonan, Blaine's New York driver assisted them and unloaded the weekend supplies from Gristedes and D'Agostino. Keith put the perishables away and brought luggage to the bedroom. "Will there be anything else, Mr. Courtman?" "No thank you, Keith. We will expect you Sunday at 4:00 pm. Thanks for your assistance. Have a great weekend."

"Thank you, Mr. Courtman and you as well!" The long car disappeared through the trees. Blaine enfolded Pat in his arms. "I'm so glad you came, the weekend is ours! Come on, let's build a fire and take the chill off."

Opening a rear door to a woodpile, they gathered several pieces and set them on the hearth. Blaine crumpled some newsprint, stacked wood and the pile was ready. With a long wood match, he watched the tiny flame grow to an orange burst. In minutes, a roaring fire had the room toasty. Blaine and Pat snuggled on the couch. Mesmerized by crackling flames, heat and their new shared passion, their weekend began, hours that would change everything. They sat together for a while, until Pat broke the moment. "I could have sworn I saw Keith bringing in sustenance," she giggled.

Blaine took the hint and went to the fridge. Vouvray was chilling, along with a platter of shrimp, paté and cheese. He set the table with plates, napkins, cutlery and wine glasses. Food was next. Pat found gourmet crackers, olives, pickles and spicy peppers. "Oh, look at the desserts." Blaine smiled, adding, "Cream puffs, éclairs, and fresh strawberries, to satisfy cravings later."

Pouring wine, he handed Pat hers, raising his own. They sipped, eyes locked on each other. Pat opened crackers. When all was ready, the two ate with relish. Pat's appetite was in high gear, Blaine observed, chuckling. "You dancers have high metabolisms! I mean just look at you, how fit and svelte!"

Pat took another large shrimp, pulled the tail and dunked. Blaine joined her, dipping and eating. Soon they were feeding each other, laughing between bites. The flavor and taste created growing tactile sensations. They began sharing bits, kissing as they sampled each treat. Becoming aroused, they undressed between nibbles and refills.

Blaine pushed the food aside, laying Pat gently on the table. Taking a swig of wine, he held the liquid in his mouth, warming and allowing the liquid to spill to her breasts. He licked and teased, playfully exploring her nipples and curves. His hands continued down her body.

Then, a first! With another sip of wine, slowly letting the liquid flow over her, he followed with his tongue. His fingers played as his mouth brought excruciating pleasure. Unable to hold back, she let go, her orgasm exploding. He kept kissing, her body moving in waves. When she was calmed, he took her hand and helped her down. "Come, my lovely. Let's leave this mess and continue somewhere more comfortable," he whispered. Together they walked to the bedroom. 'Surely, this must be heaven,' she thought. Blaine led the way.

The weekend upstate had brought added commitment and plans for the future. After her hiatus, she was back into the show, refreshed, confident and glowing! Everyone noticed the obvious change, especially those closest to her.

Jonas and Phillipe were delighted with Pat's turnaround. Her confidence, energy and humor had returned. She stopped sleeping late, insisted on learning to cook, was tidier than usual, sang around the apartment and glowed like a woman in love. Mally was thrilled to have her pal back. Handing her a small package, her grin was infectious. Pat examined it carefully.

"What in heaven's name, Mal?" "Open it. It's kind of symbolic. You'll see." Pat tore the wrapping off and opened the box. Inside was a tiny Sterling object attached to a silver chain.

"It looks like a seed encased in a locket. What is it?" Mally turned it over and pointed to inscription. Pat squinted at the tiny engraving:

"If ye have faith, as in a grain of mustard seed,

Nothing shall be impossible unto you."

Matthew 17:20

"Oh Mal, this is precious! Tell me about it, please." "It's one of my mom's favorite quotes. It symbolizes faith in times of challenge and one's ability to overcome adversity. She gave me one like it when I first came to New York. Before *Bravo Business,* times were tough. I honestly think reflecting on it got me over some big hurdles."

"Well, who would know my big hurdles more than you, Mal? You never gave up on me when I was so lost over Owen. I'm sure I was a drag to be around, but you stuck it out. I love you!" Pat handed Mally the locket. "Help me on with it, will you?" Griff's voice cut through, "Half hour, please!"

Kaplan and Maggli secured a pro forma agreement from Hiri Watanabe, to bring *Centipede* to Tokyo. Courtman and Morgan were on board, backing the venture. A meeting to finalize a contract was set for March 31.

It was 9:45. The conference room was ready. Staff had put together a buffet breakfast, impressive to match the business at hand. They were about to seal a deal for the first major export of a Broadway show. The team arrived and promptly shown in, investors right behind. When all had gathered, Joe made introductions.

"Gentlemen, I'd like to introduce Blaine Courtman and Greg Morgan, chief investors of *Centipede*." Handshaking and pleasantries were exchanged. Owen was wary of glad-handing and social politics, but had his game face on to get through the details. Blaine was cordial as he extended his hand.

"Good to see you again, Owen. I'd like you to meet my partner, Greg Morgan." "It's a pleasure to make your acquaintance, Owen. I'm a big fan of your work. I saw *Bravo Business* in Houston last year and was tremendously impressed! My colleague here convinced me to back your new show. Splendid, absolutely splendid," he gushed.

"I appreciate your interest, Mr. Morgan," said Owen, treading lightly. The speaker phone buzzed. Kaplan picked up. "Yes, Janice?" "Mr. Watanabe has arrived, sir." Joe brightened. "By all means, have Gary show him back." In moments, Gary walked in, followed by Watanabe. "Ah, Mr. Watanabe, welcome!" Watanabe bowed and smiled. Joe continued.

"I'd like you to meet our chief investors, Mr. Courtman and Mr. Morgan. And our production team, Messrs. Matthews, Martin, Edwards, and Landry." Elaborate bowing continued until Joe called the meeting to order. "Please, Mr. Watanabe, have a seat," he said, pointing to the chair adjacent his. When all were seated, he began.

"Mr. Watanabe is the producer, our direct contact and administrator in Tokyo. He saw *Centipede* opening night and believes our production a perfect fit for Japanese audiences. Mr. Watanabe, would you like to explain your interest?"

"Yes, of course. In my country, we admire and revere your American musicals. For instance, the *West Side Story* film enjoyed a sell-out for over two years. Our public scrambled for tickets, waiting in line for hours. The popularity and impact of the film convinced us that your invention, musical theatre, is a sure winner. *Centipede* is unique enough to translate in our country. I guarantee it will be a hit! We are asking for the opportunity to make this happen," he said with enthusiasm. Lenny spoke up.

"Messrs. Courtman and Morgan are ready to invest in the project. We here at Kaplan-Maggli are prepared to supplement additional funding, as well as Mr. Matthews, who will invest a percentage. As far as monies earned, we will work out the details and percentages contractually. Are we agreed?"

"Yes, that is equitable," replied Watanabe, adding, "You will provide the investment to bring the production over. We will arrange a rehearsal location and your production staff will advise the technical aspects and guidance to our design team. Our people will build and furnish what is needed, hire the orchestra and provide wardrobe execution. Our office will take care of the PR and any contacts thereof."

"Are there any questions for Mr. Watanabe?" Griff spoke. "Where will our people be staying? Will this be arranged at local hotels before we arrive?" "We will arrange housing at the Nikkatsu Hotel near the Ginza. We will get you the best group rate during your engagement. There are a few apartments to rent near the theatre as well. All accommodations will be within walking distance to the Nissei Gekijo."

"What airline will provide transportation to and from the U.S.?" Joe interceded, "There are no direct flights from New York to Tokyo. We will rely on a domestic carrier and connect with Japan Air on the West Coast." "What are the exact dates for all this?" Jonas was keen on the whole idea, but wanted assurance of the timing.

"Your company would depart New York the 1st of October and rehearse in Tokyo for three weeks, plus a week of previews. Your official opening at the Nissei Theatre is scheduled for the first week in

November and will run to the end of December, just before the start of our Kabuki season, January 1, 1966."

"It sounds pretty cut and dried," said Owen, lighting a cigarette. "Let me understand this. The New York show will continue its run and an entirely new *Centipede* will be remounted with a new cast and production team." "That is correct, Owen," reiterated Kaplan, who was eager to settle the contract. "We've asked your team here today to clarify who will remain in New York and who will go to Japan."

"*Centipede* is my vision, so I will choose the staff. An audition call in late August will allow me to select members of the new company and replace a few in the New York production. Agreed?"

"Certainly, it would be as if we were remounting a national tour, only this production will be performing internationally with a limited run," said Maggli.

"There is no one more qualified to take my work abroad than Griff Edwards. He has agreed to take the production over with my approval." "Consider it done. There's no better in our business," reiterated Kaplan. "What are some of your other choices, Owen?" "I would insist on my assistant, Mr. Martin, to restage *Centipede*. I'm willing to loan him to this project with the understanding that he would return to New York when the production opens."

"I would like to have Phillipe assist me on the project, Owen," said Jonas, clearly resolute. "I agree. Phillipe is a perfect choice to assist, provided he returns as well." "With Griff tending to the Japanese run, who would you suggest to take over the stage management in New York?" Griff spoke up immediately. "I have been training Dick Landry for over a year. He's ready to take the reins in my absence. He will have to leave the ensemble, which he is willing to do."

Blaine spoke next. "Owen, are you planning to replace Patricia Byrne? Or will she remain in the New York cast?" It was a fair question, but one that irked Owen to the core. "The show was conceived for Miss Byrne. It would be impossible to replace the finest female dancer in town. No, I will assign another lead. Griff, didn't you make a suggestion that fits?"

"Yes. My wife, Mally Edwards, has been Miss Byrne's standby. We would be working together. I think it makes perfect sense." "Agreed," said Owen. "There are dancers in the New York cast, who would also be great representatives. Chad Chapman has partnered Mally for months and is capable of replacing Jonas in the remount. Nora Blake and Jeff Jenkins, our swings, are excellent and deserve the opportunity to go as well. The rest of the ensemble will come from Equity and open calls late summer."

"Excellent! Are there any other questions, or may we work out the details with these gentlemen, Owen?" "No, it's clear enough, you handle the details. Now, if you'll excuse me." The others stood as Owen shook hands with Watanabe. "Thanks for your time, sir." Watanabe bowed and smiled. "*Domo Arigato*, Mr. Matthews-san." Owen left the room, ready for a scotch. Business meetings were not his forte. 'Let the suits work it out.'

"Gentleman, let's get on with the contract details. Griff, Jonas, and Dick, thank you for your time and input. We will get back to you as soon as the project is finalized."

Following the Wednesday evening show, Blaine sent Keith for Pat at the stage door. They would have a late supper. Approaching the limo, she felt a hand on her shoulder.

"Owen! This is unexpected," she said, trying to be cordial. Owen checked out the limo. "So I guess the rich guy has you all tied up now?" She caught Keith's eye. "Keith, would you give us a minute, please?" He waited.

"Are you planning to honor your contract?" "For now, I'll stay with the show. We haven't made any far reaching plans as yet." His expression was dark. "What do you mean, we? Are you referring to the rich guy?" "He has a name, Owen. It's Blaine, Blaine Courtman to you."

"Be careful, Pat. You aren't the only brilliant dancer in town." "Oh really? Well, you're not the only director in New York." "Don't think I can't replace your ass," he snarled. Dismissing the comment, Pat opened the limo door and went off to dinner.

Owen stood alone, rebuffed again. The chill of the night prompted him to close his jacket and head to the Taft, his favorite watering hole. 'Man, do I need a drink.' Settling at the bar, Andy Klein, his favorite barman, approached. "Greetings, Owen. What brings you out tonight?" "I need scotch and conversation. Do you have both?" Andy reached for the Glenfiddich.

Owen lit another cigarette.

Andy poured a scotch on the rocks. Taking a long swig, Owen leaned on the counter, lost in thought. Andy noticed. "Is something bugging you?" Owen looked up. "Nothing this drink can't cure." "What's new with you, Andy?" "Not a heck of a lot, except her," he said, gesturing toward a stunning redhead seated alone.

"Who's the dish, Andy? Anyone you know?" Andy gave him a playful poke. "Her name is Catherine. She's new in town and, coincidentally, a dancer from what she's said." Owen perked up. He picked up his drink and walked over. "Hi." She looked over, a look of recognition obvious. "Hi. I'm Catherine. Aren't you Owen Matthews?" "I am indeed. You look like a dancer. You certainly have the body," he soothed.

Catherine blushed, as he offered a cigarette. Declining, she sat quietly. Taking a deliberately slow drag, he studied her from head to toe. "Am I making you uncomfortable, Catherine? You're so beautiful," he murmured. "May I buy you drink?" "Thanks, I'd love a Bacardi." "Andy, please bring this lovely lady a Bacardi and I'll have another scotch." Owen felt confident, in charge, ready to make his play as he continued his best approach. "How old are you, Catherine?" She moved closer, mesmerized by his interest toward her. "I'm 20."

Owen stopped short. 'Holy shit, she's a baby,' he thought. Andy brought the drinks, handing Owen the bill. "Can I get you anything else, Owen?" He winked, knowing full well what he was about to do. "No thanks, Andy. I think I have what I need," he murmured, smiling at his latest catch.

Chapter 62

Looking Ahead

Pat lay tucked in Blaine's arms. She felt safe, secure, and unconditionally loved. Blaine provided her with constancy, security and a lovely lifestyle. So much had occurred recently.

Owen's infidelity had rocked her world to the core. He'd strayed after all they had been to each other. Apparently, she wasn't enough and that cut deeply. Another major change had occurred moving away from home. To leave family, her constant security blanket, was a big adjustment. However, rooming with her dear pals, Jonas and Phillipe had proven an opportunity to grow and be independent.

Blaine was back to stay. How she looked forward to a new future. As she lay gazing at him, he stirred. Slowly opening his eyes, he smiled and pulled her close. "My God, you're lovely, I'm so in love with you" he murmured. Pat sighed and stayed put, enjoying the pleasure of his body against hers. Glancing at the clock, Blaine realized the morning had slipped by.

"Are you hungry, Patricia?" "I'm starved," she declared, reaching for a piece of hotel chocolate.

"What would you like?" He was slightly erect. Pat playfully pointed to his penis. "Do we have time for some of that?" Blaine chuckled, planting a kiss on her nose. "Later, my lovely, I have calls to make." He gave her the room service menu. "Order whatever you like. I'll have black coffee, a white egg omelet and dry toast, please!" Pat ordered for both and jumped into the shower. Blaine fetched the *Times,* poking under the door.

After breakfast, she felt the need to talk. Pouring herself another coffee, she waited for him to finish the investment page. "Blaine, I have a concern. Would your investment in *Centipede* be jeopardized if I left the show at the end of my contract?" He put down the paper and studied her for a moment. "That's an interesting question, Patricia. The show is a hit, a guaranteed winner. I think it will run for years. Are you growing tired of it?"

"I appreciate the opportunity to be given the lead. It's been an incredible experience, but I'd also like to work for other director-choreographers. There's a tendency for producers to pigeon-hole you with one director, if you continually work for that person. I want to grow as an artist and at times, I question how long I will be able to dance. It's a short career, Blaine. Even if you're exceptional, your body wears out. I'm just thinking ahead to the future." "Your future includes me, right?" "Of course, I want to be with you always!"

"I'm glad you brought this up. I will always encourage you to follow your heart, Patricia. If by the end of your contract you wish to quit, I will support your decision. I love you and want us to be together." Pat began to cry. "Hush, my beautiful girl. Don't cry. I'm here for you. From now, it's only carte blanche!"

Kaplan and Maggli did it! The deal was sealed with Hiri Watanabe and *Centipede* International was to be. Thanks to principal investors, Courtman and Morgan, plans were underway for the fall of 1965. The news spread quickly through the biz.

After conferring with Owen, Griff arranged appointments for those involved. Jonas and Phillipe were first. "Well guys, it's official! You're going to Japan. I can't think of a better team to remount *Centipede*. When the show opens, your spots will be waiting for you in New York."

"Thank you so much for this opportunity!" Jonas beamed. "This is an amazing project," added Phillipe. "I never dreamed it could happen." "Your contracts will be ready in September. We will hold Equity and open calls for the Japanese production and replacements for the New York cast. You guys better start learning Japanese," he chuckled. "How do you say, thanks?" "*Domo Arigato Gozimasu!*" "Wow Griff, that's impressive," said Jonas, a grin on his face. "Get used to it, Jonas. Get used to it." They all laughed as the meeting concluded.

A day later, Chad, Nora and Jeff were told they were selected for the Japanese cast and could return to the Broadway cast. This assurance made acceptance of the Japanese project easy. Mally would take Pat's spot in Tokyo. She was excited for the opportunity to travel and be with Griff. Chad was delighted to be given Jonas' spot, to partner Mally, whom he adored.

Dick eagerly told Dana he was taking over during Griff's absence. The opportunity allowed him a break from his tiring dance career. He was ready for the challenge and additional income would allow them to buy a home in Jersey.

Pat wanted her business with Owen settled. She decided to stay on until the end of her contract. Choosing not to talk to him directly, she informed Griff of her decision. He agreed to be her intermediary, understanding her need for distance. Having made her decision, Pat was free to plan her future.

As Owen considered the remount, his involvement included casting the Japanese company and replacements in New York. When complete, he would seek other projects. Sipping a scotch and enjoying a smoke, the phone rang. "This is Owen Matthews."

"Mr. Matthews, this is Karen Eliot, secretary to Shel Friedman, Vice President of Project Development at Universal Pictures." "Yes?"

"Mr. Friedman has an upcoming film project he would like to discuss with you. May I arrange a conference call tomorrow, at 1:00 Pacific? Are you available?" Owen stubbed out his smoke and lit a fresh one. "I certainly am. That's 4:00 Eastern, correct?" "Yes. I will inform Mr. Friedman. Thank you, Mr. Matthews."

Owen's mind began to whirl as he digested the call. He had always wanted to direct a film. The call had potential, possibly a golden opportunity. Whistling, he topped off his scotch. The buzzer sounded, he picked up. "Yes?"

"This is Catherine." Owen pressed the button and looked in the mirror. Self-satisfaction smiled back. He'd snagged another Canary.

There was a soft knock at the door. Slowly, he opened it and gazed at the beauty in the hall. "Baby, come in. I've been waiting for you."

Centipede was firmly established as one of Broadway's top shows, a mega hit from the start. The show sold out for over six months. Rumors began of a national tour in spring, 1966.

Those involved with the production from the beginning knew instinctively it was a winner. The commitment, faith and hard work of all involved shared that success. *Centipede* would run for years as the brightest star in the Great White Way's firmament, continuing as the most unique show of all time.

Glossary of Show Business Terms

Audition: the process by which the production team of a show decides who will be cast in the project. The call can be for dancers, singers, or actors. Performers must execute a dance combination, sing their best 16-32 bars of a song, or read cold from a script.

Backer: investors who provide the money necessary for a production to be mounted.

Callback: the second audition call after a performer has made it through the first audition cut.

Call-Board: the communications center for notices and cast sign-ins.

Dark: the day off in professional theatre.

Dry Tech: the tech staff running the show from cue to cue without the cast, also known as a dry run.

Green Room: the actor's lounge.

Grip: a tech working backstage to shift scenery, secure rigging and fly equipment before, during and post-production.

Hazard Pay: a stipend paid a performer for executing dangerous procedures or stunts.

House: where the audience sits.

Jobber: crew members added to the base tech staff.

Libretto: the book/script of a musical.

Out-of-Town Tryout: performance cities where changes may occur prior to Broadway.

Pre-production: planning of a show before it goes into rehearsal, also a pre-check by tech team before the performance run.

Process: development and rehearsal of a show.

Producer: oversees the production financially and all decisions regarding all aspects of show's operation.

Production Stage Manager/PSM: person in charge of calling the show, delegating tech assignments, handling details pertaining to company, crew and staff.

Reviews: critiques, evaluations, or notices by the press whether print, radio, or TV.

Run-through: running through the entire show, usually without an audience.

Swing Girl/Boy: understudy, stand-in covering in event of illness, injury, or vacation time of the regular ensemble performers.

Travel Day: day the production travels from one city and venue to another.

The Gypsies' story continues in:

Gypsy World—Beyond Broadway

Here's a sneak preview:

Chapter 1

A Foreign Affair

"Oh my God, look at that line! It's humungous," shouted Catherine, pointing up 45th Street as they made way through the gridlock, Her sidekick, Julie, followed close behind trying to keep pace. Dozens of women were waiting at the Royal Theater where *Centipede,* the biggest hit on Broadway, was playing. "Let's cross here," she said, jaywalking between cars and trucks, Julie in tow. They joined the line-up to audition.

The previous week, the trades announced a remount of director-choreographer Owen Matthews' greatest hit, to go international for a two-month engagement in Tokyo. The project was rumored for weeks but, today, was the day for both union and open calls for dancers. Hundreds of hopeful women would be put to the test for places in the new production and replacements in New York.

Catherine and Julie waited in line, discouragement rearing its ugly head with each passing minute; oppressive heat, nerves and competition, made passing muster seem impossible.

Catherine Andrews, from Milwaukee, was new to New York. With solid technique, great look, young and determined, she hoped to convince Mr. Matthews she was ready. Julie Jansen, a Detroit native, was quite pretty, a different physical type from Catherine. She, too, was new to the city, hoping to land her first big job. Her technique was strong and she had an affable presence.

The line moved slowly, the wait seemed endless. "I don't know why I'm such a wreck," said Julie, re-combing her hair. "Have you ever auditioned for Owen Matthews?" Catherine smiled. Secretly, there was more on her mind than the audition. She met the famous director one night at the Taft Hotel Bar. Owen, always the canny seducer, had taken her to bed, now insisting she audition. Proving herself worthy as a dancer was a bonus. What better way to be with him?

Twenty-five minutes passed before the girls were given audition cards to complete. Dick Landry was at the stage door, replacing Griff Edwards, who was now organizing the Japanese remount. Having been trained by Griff for months, he was ready to take the reins.

"Please fill this out and return it to me. You'll dance in order of the number on the card. You may change downstairs, just follow the signs. Thanks."

The girls felt instant relief as they entered the air-cooled theater. Descending in dim light, they passed others hurrying upstairs, nods of encouragement from some and cool stares from others. It would be a rumble of sorts—only the most attractive and technically best would survive the cuts.

"God, I'm nervous! I didn't eat breakfast and now my stomach is protesting," declared Julie, undressing. Her jeans and blouse stuck like glue, as she pulled with great effort. Bringing a small hand towel was an asset.

Catherine wore a light sundress, which allowed air to move under her skirt. She unbuttoned and slipped out. Peeling off her panties, she put on flesh-toned tights, followed by high cut trunks. Normally bra-less, she added one for comfort and support. A tight t-shirt followed, held in place by a wide belt. Slipping into socks and jazz shoes, she tied the laces with a double knot. A long or loose shoe lace could prove a disaster! The last step was to fix her long hair in a ponytail. When ready, they returned to the stage, quickly filled out their cards and returned them to Dick.

Jonas Martin, Owen's assistant and male dance lead, was conducting the audition. Owen observed from the house, taking notes. He was reputed for clarifying his style nuances once the group was taught the combination.

"Good morning, ladies! Welcome to *Centipede*! You are auditioning for the international company. There are a few spots open in the New York show as well. We are looking for those with solid dance technique who can act. We will be learning in groups of twelve and dancing in groups of three. Let's begin." The women took staggered positions, spaced so they could observe Jonas.

"Starting on the right foot, four single turns to stage right, step on right foot, *relevé*, left leg extended in *arabesque*, arms developed and extended up at angles to the sides. The counts are 1 and 2, 3 and 4, step 5, *relevé* 6, hold 7, *développé* of arms on 7 and 8. Repeat to the left. Third set of eight begins with right leg down on 1, joining left to *relevé* and turning on 2, step out on 3, *pas de bourrée* on 4, step on right, cross with left on 5, *battement* on 6, with right leg, double *pirouette* inside on left leg 7 and 8. Hold. Last set begins on 1 with scoop leg forward from inside out with parallel leg landing in *plié* in jazz second on the right, repeating with left on 2, right on 3, and left on 4. Impulse up on 5 with a shrug, impulse on six with a shrug, step 7 and 8 are step right, step left ending in a parallel *plié*. Arms are relaxed at your side during the jazz portion with a shrug of shoulders on after beat of 8. Then repeat the whole combination of 4 counts of 8. Let's run through it again. Ready, 5, 6, 7, 8!" The group, clearly overwhelmed, followed him, as he danced under tempo for their benefit.

"What's this bullshit?" A tall brunette in the front line was frustrated and vocal. Jonas noticed and stopped. "Is there something I can clarify?"

Caught, she stammered, "It's a weird combination with so many ridiculous switches." Jonas glanced out, aware of Owen, who suddenly rose. There were murmurs, eyes glued on him, as he moved down the aisle and up the stairs. "What is your name?" "Carol Cramer, Mr. Matthews."

"Why are you here?" The air was thick as he waited. "I need a job, Mr. Matthews. Why does anyone put themselves through this crap?"

"Please don't put yourself through this crap another second, Miss Cramer. Thanks for stopping by." He gestured to Griff. "Mr. Edwards, please show Miss Cramer out. We have many other dancers to see this morning. Jonas, let's continue."

Carol Cramer was shocked, rigid, as Griff approached. "Thank you for your time. Please remember to take your personal items and follow me. I'll show you the way out." But she had just begun. With fists raised, she rushed toward Owen. "You fucker, I know about you! Everyone knows," she yelled. Jonas watched horrified.

"Owen, look out!" Owen tried to duck as she took a swipe. Caught on the chin, his cigarette was airborne. Griff grabbed her, assisted by Phillipe, Jonas' assistant. Carol let out a piercing scream in the scuffle. "You degrade and disregard women, you asshole!" "Get this harridan out of here," yelled Owen.

"Let me go, you God damned bullies!" Miss Cramer was strong, trying to break Griff and Phillipe's hold. Forcing her off stage, she was totally out of control as they carried her up the aisle. The screams continued. Security was called. Those on stage were shaken. Owen quickly regained his composure. "Ladies, please excuse the interruption. Jonas, keep going." Jonas picked up where he left off. For the rest of the morning, scores of dancers passed through, Owen's scrutiny in high gear. By noon, most dancers had been cut with the exception of Catherine, Julie and four others. The Equity call for female dancers was at 2:00.

The girls hugged with enthusiasm. "Oh my God, we made it through the first cut," said Julie with relief. "Wait until the final callback. You haven't seen anything yet, my friend," declared Catherine. "Personally, I'd rather have all my wisdom teeth pulled at once." Julie shrugged, happy to have passed the first elimination. "When do the men audition? Do you know?"

"Same deal. The open men's call is at 10:00 tomorrow with the Equity call at 2:00. Then everyone is called the next day; women in the morning, men in the afternoon." They changed and left the theatre. The heat hit them with a jolt as they walked to 8th Avenue. Julie suggested lunch, her blood sugar seriously plummeting. "Where do you want to eat? How about trying Mulfetta's? I hear they have the best Greek food in town."

"Sure, why not?" The girls headed north looking for the restaurant. Spotting a sign, they crossed at the light and headed inside. The contrast of air-conditioning to the sultry air outside was encouraging. A host seated them by a window, handing menus and filling water glasses.

"Wow, does this cool air feel good," sighed Julie. "I hate heat and humidity. It was never this bad in Detroit during the summer." "It could get bad in Milwaukee, near Lake Michigan and all. Downtown Chicago was worse, though. No escaping those skyscrapers holding the heat," said Catherine, swallowing half a glass of water. "God, I'm thirsty!" They looked the menus over for specials. An attractive waiter approached.

"Good afternoon, ladies. Our lunch special is Mousaka. It comes with oven-roasted potatoes and a small Greek salad for $4.95. We also offer a choice of beef, chicken, or lamb gyros, with a side of fries for $3.95."

"I'd like a glass of Retsina to start," said Julie. "And for you, Miss?" "I'll take a large Coke with extra ice, please." "Certainly, would you care to order now or later?" "I'd like a small Greek salad," said Catherine, never overly hungry right after dancing. "And you?" "I'll take the chicken gyros special with the fries, please." "Thank you, ladies." As he left, he turned and smiled at Julie. "God, he's adorable! Did you notice those beautiful brown eyes and all that dark, wavy hair?" Catherine played with her fork, thinking only of Owen.

"I wonder if he's available. He's really sexy," whispered Julie. "Shouldn't you be thinking about nailing the callback and not getting laid?" Julie shrugged. "I guess so, but I'm kind of horny. Say, what was that harangue about at the audition? It was pretty upsetting." "I have no idea," said Catherine, tossing it off. "Yes, but those accusations," insisted Julie. Catherine was uncomfortable, defensive.

"Look, Mr. Matthews is the most important director-choreographer on Broadway and extremely attractive. Women will fight for his favors. She was an exception, a total bitch and obviously twisted!" "Well, I hope he hires us. We need jobs and doing *Centipede* would be a tremendous credit."

"We'll know in a couple of days, so be prepared. It's going to be the toughest audition ever. Imagine going to Japan! I hear the Japanese revere American artists. What an honor it would be," said Catherine.

The waiter returned with their orders. "Will there be anything else?" Julie smiled and winked, "We're fine for now, I think. We just need the check, please." The waiter tore the bill from his pad and placed it on the table. "Come again, ladies. It's been my pleasure serving you." Julie couldn't resist. "What is your name?" Catherine gave her a kick under the table.

"I'm Nicholas. Stop in any time Monday-Thursday between 11:00 and 6:00. I hope to see you again." "God, Julie, how obvious can you get?" Julie giggled as she took a large bite of her Gyros.

'Obvious when I care to be,' she thought, chewing happily. Catherine shrugged and picked up her fork, suddenly hungry. "Well, let's eat and take the next 24 hours to recover, okay?" "I agree. Whatever happens from now on is anyone's guess." Lunch continued.

During the break, Owen and his team huddled, sorting through dance cards. Pulling Carol Cramer's information, Jonas shuddered. "Where did that piece of work come from?"

"She looked familiar," remarked Dick, who had worked with many gypsies over the years.

"Boy, she is trouble on the hoof for sure," added Jonas. "Relax, gentleman. On occasion, we stumble across a crazy," said Owen unruffled. Sorting through the cards, he spotted Catherine's name. Smiling, he pulled hers.

"I think we should strongly consider Catherine Andrews. She's an obvious replacement for Mally, while she's in Japan." "Which one is she?" Jonas had looked at so many dancers that morning, he was numb.

"The striking redhead with amazing extension, long legs, crisp technique. She's perfect for us," said Owen, obviously pleased and secretly prejudiced. "The others were good, but she's exceptional."

"We still have the union women this afternoon. I imagine we'll get some veterans to check out," said Jonas. Griff continued sorting, pulling those kept for callbacks. "We'll need seven women and seven men, plus two swings to cover for Japan. Most of our original cast is staying put. We'll have to temporarily replace Mally, Chad, Nora, and Jeff."

"Keep in mind that Kaplan and Maggli are strongly considering the first national company of *Centipede* some time next spring. If that happens, we will need dancers for that production also, so we should be on the lookout for potentials from this audition."

"What is the status with Miss Byrne?" "She has decided to stay on until the end of her contract, January 15th," said Griff.

"Well, it's a perfect opportunity to observe Miss Andrews during the fall. She might likely replace Miss Byrne if she proves herself," said Owen, charting his course. Catherine would soon be his, 24/7.

Following lunch, the group returned to the stage for the Equity call. Dick was again at his stage door post, admitting only those dancers showing union cards. Owen and Griff conferred in the house while Jonas and Phillipe warmed up. It would be a long afternoon as the line of women at the door and down the block waited eagerly to take a crack at the demanding work awaiting them.

Chapter 2

Decisions

The following day, open call for male dancers began at 10:00. As with female dancers the day before, at least 100 non-union men stood in the heat and humidity, waiting to dance and be seen by Owen Matthews. It was not unheard of for an unknown to be hired on the spot, but with this crowd, individuals had to be exceptional technicians, attractive and have endurance to survive Owen and his razor-sharp scrutiny.

Jonas placed the men in groups of 12. Phillipe took his position downstage for them to follow. In the past year, he had refined his technique, emulating Owen's style perfectly. Jonas taught a combination suitable for male dynamics, including leaps, turns, and slides—heavy on jazz and ballet adagio. Owen looked for and selected dancers who could handle contrasting styles, the more versatile the better.

Through both calls, there were several standouts. The level of exceptional talent had improved in just a year with growing numbers of dancers coming to New York to try their luck. He kept at least two dozen men for callbacks and let the rest go. It was a long day but encouraging to have such quality performers try out.

Following the audition, Owen invited his team to the Taft for drinks and conversation. It was still hot and sticky, with no change in the forecast. Ducking into the air-conditioned lobby, they entered the lounge. Happy hour was in full swing, but they managed to find a corner with a large enough table to confer. Griff brought the audition cards, accompanied by Dick. Like shadows, Jonas and Phillipe stuck close to Owen, who immediately ordered his usual, Glenfiddich.

Dick chose beer on tap, Phillipe, a Dubonnet chilled and Griff his usual, a martini straight up with a twist.

"I need a beer, preferably a Heineken," Jonas mumbled, easing his way into a chair. His hamstrings protested with the slightest move and his mouth was dry as cotton. "After this day, camels have nothing on me!"

One look at Jonas, and Dick could relate. "A little dry and weary, are we?" He, too, felt the effects of aging in a youthful dance culture. "Our bodies start protesting at 30 and are relentless at reminding us we're getting older."

"You're telling me." Jonas removed his shoes and began rubbing his toes gingerly. "I've hired an old man," said Owen, needling his assistant. The director was still fresh, even after the long day. He was eager to cast both productions.

"Boss, you never cease to amaze me. You must have a secret elixir somewhere. You're holding out on us!" Owen shrugged, lit a cigarette and took a deep drag. Work and sex always created a need for nicotine, his true allies.

"You were great these past two days. Dick, you handled those long lines like someone who's been stage managing for years. Jonas, your execution is nothing short of a miracle and Phillipe, you're a model dancer. Christ, we must have seen every out-of-work dancer in the five boroughs." "I couldn't get over the numbers! They must have doubled in a year," remarked Jonas knowingly.

Owen continued. "The callback will tell the tale. We have to hire the finest of the bunch.

"I believe we've called back at least 60 men and women, nothing short of amazing," said Griff, reaching into his briefcase. He handed over audition cards. "Here are the callbacks," he said. "Do you want to take a look?"

Owen began perusing each card, with his comment code written on the upper right hand corner of each. Dick looked over his shoulder, puzzled by the abbreviations. It was impossible to guess what each meant. Jonas clarified.

"The boss uses a code to evaluate each dancer. It saves time and keeps our assessment confidential. It's a great system." Dick was still curious. "Please explain, would you?" "Go ahead, Jonas" said Owen.

"Well, LOT means Long of Tooth. LITL means Light in the Loafers. WT means Weak Technique. DU, Definitely Unattractive; NFTS, Not for This Show; and my personal favorite, NOMS, Not On My Stage. Laughter ensued as the group sipped their drinks. "Short and sweet," remarked Dick, settling back. Griff chuckled, "If it lightens the load, it works for me."

Owen insisted on another round as he reviewed the candidates, gathering opinions from his team. It had been a demanding two days for all. The final callback would bring decisions affecting the fate of newcomers and experienced dancers alike.

Next morning, the stage filled rapidly with those waiting to catch Owen's eye and approval, approval that would lead to employment. First to be tested were the combined women, selected from open and Equity calls, now on a level playing field. Promptly at 10:00, a group of dancers, each technically able and hoping to be cast, lined up, ready for Jonas' counts. The air was electric with anticipation and dread.

As Jonas led each group, muscles tensed, sweat flew, bodies stretched and twisted into impossible positions, making breathing loud and labored. A cacophony of curses, gasps, sighs and whispers underscored the effort as Jonas continued, his voice breaking through the activity.

The combination at the preliminary audition was now doubled in counts and technically more difficult; the detail and nuances, pure

Owen. Bodies stretched, balance and control precisely noted. Double and triple *pirouettes* had to be perfect, as many as possible. Each gypsy was expected to perform with technical brilliance, including subtext, the underlying emotion let loose with abandon as they jumped, twirled and drove themselves through count after count.

As each group danced, some were cut immediately, while others were asked to wait and repeat the combination. It was agony to stand and watch the competition, waiting with dread, but hoping to remain.

That afternoon, it was the men's turn. Around the perimeter of the stage and in the wings, male dancers gathered to wait. They were there with one purpose, to make it into Owen's world.

Dancers of every description ran the gamut. A definite asset was to possess a built-in sensuality beyond looks and technique. Owen's reputation was controversial, sexual and uncompromising. Never had there been a director-choreographer on Broadway more sought after. To be cast by Matthews was to 'make it.'

With auditions finally over, the team gathered. Who would they choose? Attempting to put together the best ensemble was first and foremost in their minds.